ObitUCrime

A Cape Cod Mystery/Thriller

By: F Edward Jersey

A CreateSpace Book

BOOKS BY F. EDWARD JERSEY

(non-fiction)

Softwhere

(fiction)

Paines Creek Mystery

Copyright © 2009 by F. Edward Jersey
Edited by Wendy H. Jersey

ISBN: 1448605709
EAN-13: 9781448605705

PRINTED BY CREATESPACE
www.createspace.com
Scotts Valley, California

This book is dedicated to my family and friends who encouraged me to keep writing.

Chapter 1

The obituary read:

> Dennis, MA – Samuel Sterns, 41 of Dennis, passed away unexpectedly on Wednesday in a tragic ice fishing accident. He was born in Hyannis on March 21, 1964, and lived in West Dennis for the past twenty years. He was formerly managing partner at Sterns and Dunn, LLC. an accounting firm, 51 Commerce Place, Hyannis, MA 02601. His wife, Katherine, of West Dennis, survives him. His father, Michael Sterns and his mother, Helen Sterns, predeceased him. Funeral services will be held Friday 11 a.m. at Hallett Funeral Home, 273 Station Avenue, South Yarmouth. Burial will be at Woodside Cemetery, Yarmouth. Calling hours are Thursday 7-9 p.m. at Hallett Funeral Home. To leave online condolences or for directions please visit: www.hallettfuneralhome.com.

Charles Chamberlin read the obituary carefully. "Here was a fairly young professional", he thought to himself. He was a part owner in an accounting firm. He probably had a good insurance policy on his life and maybe his business had been successful. He left a wife and she seemed to fit the profile he had established for himself. He cut the obituary out of the paper and made plans to go to the wake Thursday night to check out the potential target.

Charles Chamberlin had a plan to get rich and disappear. He thought he had figured out a way to amass a fortune by deceiving new, young widows. Mr. Chamberlin, or CC as he preferred to be known, had devised a scheme to obtain information from widows who had come into money and to then take, or rather steal, some of that wealth from them. His basic tact was to regularly scan the local obituaries looking for mid-life widows between thirty and fifty years old who appeared to have had successful spouses. He would attend the wake to garner information about the dead person and about the widow. He then would attend the funeral and burial, and hope to get invited to an after burial gathering in order to get to know the widow better. His goal would be to gain access to the widows' home at some time and to then look for a home computer. If things worked out, he would install a computer software program on the widow's computer that would capture any keystrokes entered using the computer and to then transmit information back to himself for his benefit.

Besides the woman who injured him in his car accident, Mrs. Katherine Sterns, widow of Sam Sterns, was his first real target. CC had decided it was time to see if his plan could work again.

CC's first task was to gather as much information as possible about Sam Sterns; he would request a Google Search on Samuel Sterns. The search revealed that Sterns was the majority owner in an accounting firm. There were references to articles about the firm indicating it had been growing in recent years and had numerous local businesses as clients. The search also identified a few newspaper articles regarding the disappearance and death of Sterns. CC gathered all the materials and studied them in detail.

Next, CC requested the phone book information on Sam Sterns. That search revealed a Sam and Katherine Sterns lived on Pond Circle in West Dennis, MA and listed their phone number. He wrote all of the information down in his notebook. He was starting to keep track of targets identified, research done, problems encountered, and especially, successes realized.

CC liked how his plan was coming together. He knew a few things about his target. That information would all become valuable to him in the near future. He read the information in his notebook over and over numerous times until he thought he had enough memorized to make a favorable impression with anyone he might speak with at the wake.

On Thursday night, he dressed in his best suit and headed out for the Hallett Funeral Home on Station Avenue in Yarmouth. The number of cars in the parking lot eased CC's apprehension since blending into the crowd would be much easier with a larger group. Upon arriving, he stood at the back of the room surveying the crowd. Next to him was another man standing alone, so CC introduced himself.

"Hi, my name is Charles Chamberlin."
"I'm Tom Bowman."
CC recalled some of the information he obtained via his research and quickly said, "Oh, you're the person who was ice fishing with Sam when he died."
"Yes, it was terrible."
"How did you and Sam end up out on the Atlantic Ocean on an ice-flow?"
"I had talked to a few guys at the Bridge Bar who had gone ice fishing on Cape Cod Bay. They had a compelling story about having gone ice fishing on the Bay and said they caught quite a few cod through the ice. After hearing their story, I spoke with Sam, my fishing partner..." Tom paused, and CC could see he was swallowing hard to maintain his composure. "And we decided to give it a try."
"That was real risky."
"It sure was and I wish we had just gone ice fishing at our usual place in Nickerson Park instead of Cape Cod Bay."
CC looked at him and said, "You went ice fishing on Cape Cod Bay based on information you got from a few guys at a bar?"

Tom didn't look up but said, "Yeah, that was one of the worst things I have ever done in my life. And now, my best friend is dead because of it."

As they were speaking, a woman approached Tom from the other side and took his arm. He didn't say anything else to Mr. Chamberlin. He turned as if to say something as they were walking away but just waved instead. CC looked at her and guessed she was Tom's wife.

CC thought it really couldn't be this easy. He had gathered enough information about Sam Sterns to be able to bluff his way through the wake. He thought the fishing and bar angles would work just fine. He decided it was time for introductions.

CC approached the widow to offer his condolences. He took note of the fact that his potential target was a very beautiful woman. She was dressed in a three quarter length black dress. She had diamond earrings and a gold necklace around her neck CC guessed cost a bundle. Her blond hair was shoulder length with a slight wave to it. Initially he thought maybe he should try to get to know her more than his plan called for but he quickly brought his mind back to the task at hand. He had gathered the basic information he needed to begin his quest to prove, or disprove, his theory.

As Katherine was receiving condolences from the many mourners who had come to pay their last respects to Sam, she noticed Tom standing in the back of the room speaking to a man she didn't know. When the man approached Katherine and offered her his condolences, he introduced himself as Charles Chamberlin. He said he knew Sam from the Bridge Bar. Many of the people attending the wake had known Sam from the Bar, so Katherine assumed that's how Tom must have known Charles. Katherine thought Mr. Chamberlin was a rather polished gentleman. He was neatly dressed in a dark pin-stripped business suit, a blue shirt with a white collar, and a green and blue print tie. He was well groomed, and smelled good, too. Katherine guessed he was in his mid-forties. Mr. Chamberlin said he had helped Sam out a few times and he was sorry for her loss.

At the time, Katherine didn't think much about the introduction. Mr. Chamberlin was just another one of the people who knew Sam. As he walked away from her, her eyes followed him to the back of the room. When he stopped to talk to a few other people, she turned her attention to the next person in line.

After mingling with some of the other mourners for a few minutes, CC went outside the funeral home having completed his first tasks. He met the widow, gathered basic information and felt he had enough to go on. His initial assessment was positive. Katherine Sterns was becoming a qualified target. Tomorrow CC would continue to carry out his plan. He returned home to record the information he had gathered in his journal. CC felt careful preparation, attention to detail, and the ability to keep his cool were the skills necessary to carry out his plan.

On Friday morning, CC dressed in a double-breasted, somber grey suit, nothing flashy, but appropriate for a funeral. The shirt was very pale gold; the tie was black, grey and yellow. He grabbed the directions to the Sterns house, got in his car and traveled to the Hallett Funeral Home for the service. The morning was overcast with a heavy fog that had rolled in off Nantucket Sound during the night. While attending the funeral, he was provided with directions to the Woodside cemetery in Yarmouth for the burial that followed immediately after the service.

During the funeral, CC observed Katherine staying very close to the man seated next to her. He could see she held his arm and the two spoke a few times during the service. From time to time, the man would hand her a new Kleenex to wipe away tears. When the service concluded, Katherine, still holding onto the man, followed the casket out of the funeral home. A long procession of cars lined up to follow the hearse to the cemetery.

As CC turned south off Route 28, he could see a number of cars lined up next to the cemetery. The cemetery is a very old cemetery. Many of the headstones in it indicated the residents had been there for a very long time. There were at least fifty people gathered there to hear the last words and final prayers for Sam Sterns. At conclusion of the burial, the Pastor announced that Katherine had invited everyone to the Sterns residence.

When the man Katherine had been holding on to so tightly left her side to speak with some of the other mourners, CC took the opportunity to speak again to the widow. After all, he wanted to appear as familiar as possible.

CC approached Katherine at the gravesite and said, "Again, Mrs. Sterns, I'm very sorry for your loss."

"Thank you. You are Mr. Chamberlin, right?"

"That's right, but please call me Charles."

"Ok, Charles, thank you for coming."

"Please let me know if there is anything I can do for you."

"That's kind of you, but I think I'm alright for now."

"I understand, but please don't hesitate to call on me for anything at all."

He gave her a business card. It read Mr. Charles Chamberlin, Consultant, Chamberlin Financial Services, 111 Financial Place, 297 North Street, Hyannis, MA 02601.

Katherine said, "Thank you for your offer."

CC added, "Possibly we could talk more this afternoon at your place."

"Possibly."

As the man who had been with Katherine returned, CC said, "I'll look forward to that."

He turned and walked away. Katherine's eyes again followed CC for a few moments. Leaving Katherine, CC could hear her speaking with the man she had been with and saying something about not wanting to speak with the other mourner CC had met at the wake, Mr. Tom Bowman. Then after a minute or two later, he could see most everyone had returned to their cars. There was some kind of commotion between Katherine, the man she had been with, Mr. Bowman and the lady CC saw Mr. Bowman with at the wake.

About the only thing he could hear was the woman with Mr. Bowman saying to him, "What were you thinking?" Then they all turned and went to their respective vehicles.

CC joined the rest of the mourners exiting the cemetery. He got in his car and pulled out the directions to Katherine's house. He looked at the directions making it look like this was the first time he had learned the Sterns address. Step two was complete. He was ready to move forward.

It only took fifteen minutes to get to the Sterns' residence from the cemetery. CC parked on the street and walked up to the house with a few of the other people he recognized who were at the cemetery. He went inside along with the others and stood just inside the front door. Katherine arrived soon after the others and began to mingle with the crowd.

Katherine saw Mr. Chamberlin standing by the door.

She approached him and said, "Thank you for coming. Where was it again you knew Sam from?"

"I met Sam a few years back when I was fishing on one of the park ponds and got to know him more from seeing him at the Bar."

"Oh."

"Sam had recently asked me to look into a few items relative to his business. I had helped him with a few business things in the past."

"What kind of business help was it you were doing?"

"Business consulting, finance things. He had wanted my assistance with a couple of corporate accounts."

"Well, I wasn't really involved in Sam's business. But I guess I'll have to be in the future."

"Well then, if there is anything I may help you with as you get involved with the business, please feel free to call on me."

"I might just do that. I think I might be able to use a coach as I'm getting involved. You see, Sam's business had been growing quite a bit lately and I'm sure it's worth a considerable sum. I had planned on seeking professional advice now that I am going to have to become familiar with the financial matters."

"That would be wise. If you like, I could just point out a few things for you and act as a sounding board if you needed one."

"Would you mind if I called on you during evening hours?"

Shaking his head, he said, "No, no, I do quite a bit of my consulting over dinner and during evening hours. Consultants have to be flexible."

"I like flexibility."

"Call on me whenever you like. I'll make time."

Katherine looked towards the other room and said, "And here comes my partner now."

As they were standing there, Andrew Dunn brought her a drink and Katherine introduced Andrew to Mr. Charles Chamberlin. She said Mr. Chamberlin was a business and fishing acquaintance of Sam's.

Andrew looked at Mr. Chamberlin, offered him his hand and said, "Nice to meet you. How did you know Sam again?"

"I met Sam when I was out fishing a few years back and we struck up a conversation. After that, I spoke with him again a few times at the Bar. One thing led to another and we ended up speaking business.

"He never mentioned it to me, but that doesn't mean anything. Sam had his accounts and I had mine and we didn't always check with the other about everything."

"Yes, he had said to me once at the Bar he had a very capable partner."

Andrew looked at CC and said, "At the Bar huh?"

8

CC smiling said, "Well, now I can put a face to the name, but it could have been under better circumstances."

"That's for sure" said Andrew.

"That commotion at the end of the service at the cemetery was pretty poorly timed. What was it all about?" CC said to Andrew.

"That was Sam's fishing partner, Tom Bowman." Katherine said. "I had an..." Katherine paused. "An indiscretion with him some time ago and somehow he got the impression there was more to it than that. His wife just found out about it when he spoke to me at the cemetery. Let's just say she wasn't very happy with Tom at that particular moment."

"I'd say not." CC said.

"That's history now and I'm trying to move on."

Sensing Katherine's agitation, Andrew whispered "Katherine, you're emotionally drained right now. Let's not bring up the Tom incident again today."

"Andrew, I know you're right. I'm sorry Mr. Chamberlin for bringing up my past."

"Don't be. I understand."

Andrew turned to Katherine and said, "I had sent Sam files from work last week. Might I have a few minutes with his home office computer to send them back to the office?"

Katherine said, "Can't it wait?"

"I have been putting it off since the news broke about Sam, but the client keeps calling and is getting concerned."

"Well ok, but there is something wrong with the computer because it doesn't want to work."

"Let me take a look at it" Chamberlin said. "I know a little about computers. Possibly I could be of assistance."

Andrew had been in Sam's home office many times. He told Katherine he would be quick about it and turned to go to the office. He invited Mr. Chamberlin to follow him.

Sam's home office was a room about twelve by fifteen feet in dimension. One wall was all glass overlooking a garden with the bay off in the distance. The far wall was lined with file cabinets and the back wall behind the desk had many

9

shelves with books of all kinds from business to pleasure reading. To the right of the door was a table that contained a printer, fax machine and copier. Sam's desk was large and made of oak with a computer sitting off to one side opposite a phone. It was neat with only a few papers in the basket. The calendar stood on Friday of two weeks ago, the last day Sam had sat there.

When Andrew turned the computer on, the first thing he saw was a screen that said the computer had been infected with a virus and action needed to be taken. Andrew said, "I don't know what has to be done with this but it looks like Katherine will have to get the computer serviced."

Mr. Chamberlin said, "I don't think that will be necessary, I think I know what is wrong."

"What do *you* think it is?" Andrew asked.

"The infected files just need to be dealt with and then the computer will return to normal."

"How is that done?"

"The virus protection program will quarantine the infected file or files and then the computer will be fine. It should only take me a few minutes to remedy the situation."

"While you're doing that, can I get you a drink?"

"Sure, I'd like a beer."

"I'll get a couple and be right back."

"Thanks."

As Andrew left the room, CC took a CD out of his pocket and put it in the CD ROM drive. He typed in a command and the computer began to load a program called "PCTrackR". As soon as the CD had been loaded onto the computer, CC ejected the CD and returned it to his pocket. Before Andrew could return, CC had fixed the virus problem and loaded his program on the computer. He quickly clicked on the PCTrackR program and selected the settings he desired. He instructed the program to capture all keystrokes and to e-mail him with the results bi-weekly. He also instructed PCTrackR to put the words "Sterns Strokes Included" in the subject field of the e-mails to be sent to him. The last thing he did was to select the ghost feature of PCTrackR so it would run undetected in the background on the computer. He closed the PCTrackR setup feature. PCTrackR was now running in the background unknown to Andrew or Katherine.

PCTrackR is a computer software program available at most computer stores and via the Internet. There are a number of these programs available that can be installed on a PC that will monitor all of the activities being performed by the person using the PC. Probably the most common use allows parents to keep tabs on the activities of their children using a home PC. Some of the nice features allow the program to run undetected to the person using the PC and to then periodically make the captured information, or keystrokes, available for viewing. Some of these software packages even allow for the captured information to be forwarded to a specified e-mail address periodically allowing parents to keep track of what their children are doing when using their computer away from the home. Charles Chamberlin was tracking keystrokes, but it certainly wasn't to protect anyone from harm. In fact, he was using PCTrackR to harm.

When Andrew returned, CC declared the computer ready for use and allowed Andrew to continue with his business tasks. CC rejoined the other mourners in the living room exiting as though nothing had happened. Katherine was completely unaware something had been installed on Sam's home business computer, which was now her home computer. Andrew used the computer to retrieve the files he had sent to Sam a week earlier. When done, he turned the computer off and returned to join the others. He told Katherine Charles had fixed the computer and it would be ok for her to use it if she needed to.

CC decided he had met his objectives and said his goodbyes. He left the Sterns residence and hoped his efforts would produce the desired results in the very near future. This was not the kind of relationship he thought would be long lived.

CC's plans included retrieving e-mails from his target's computer periodically and then breaking down the e-mail into meaningful components. He knew if the unsuspecting target did what he thought she would do, she would utilize the computer to monitor her assets and provide him with the information he needed to gain access in the future to the accounts holding those assets; Information like account numbers, passwords, expiration dates, and the likes.

When the timing was right, CC intended to raid the accounts holding those assets and to have a significant portion sent to an untraceable offshore account only he knew about. Getting into his car, he took out his journal and promptly wrote down all of the information he had gathered at the funeral. He even made a note of the confrontation he had observed at the end of the service. By the time he had finished writing everything down, he had over four pages of information about Katherine and Sam Sterns, rest his soul.

CC arrived home feeling good about his plan. All he had to do was sit back and monitor any e-mails coming from the PCTrackR software package. He went to his desk, took out his journal, turned his computer on, and began to enter his notes into his computer. When he had finished, he saved the collected information under a file labeled Sterns.

Target identified and qualified, and its name is Katherine.

Chapter 2

Mr. Charles Chamberlin, or CC, was forty-six years old, not married and had no children. Last spring, he was in a serious head-on collision with a car driven by Sharon Kelly, who as it turned out, had recently been left a widow.

CC had been heading home from his work as a business consultant in Hyannis, Massachusetts on Route 28 when Kelly ran a red light, crossed the centerline and hit his BMW head-on. CC, who was ejected from his vehicle, suffered head trauma, lacerations all over his body, broken ribs, a broken leg and some internal injuries. He ended up spending four months in the hospital healing and another three months in physical therapy. While the physical injuries were healing, CC had a lot of time to think and developed an irrational prejudice against widows. To make matters worse, his insurance didn't cover all of the medical expenses and he was faced with a lengthy battle in court to get the widow Kelly's insurance carrier to pay for the balance of his medical bills. While fighting for reimbursement, he was forced to file for bankruptcy; an absolute humiliation for someone who worked since fifteen years old building a reputation of competency. Born Charles Connors, he decided to change his name after the accident and filing. His rationale was that he could operate more freely under a new identity and if necessary, revert to his birth name when the time was right. He was intent on revenge.

As CC worked through his therapy session one day, he recapped his misery. "There was a widow who ran into me;

she probably got a huge life insurance payment when her husband died; I should be able to get some of her money to pay for my medical bills." He thought long and hard about his predicament. If only he could get access to her accounts, he could probably just take what he needed from them.

For the heck of it, he decided to use his computer skills to find out about the widow. The Web is a wonderful tool, and he was able to gather information about the widow's former spouse, Henry Kelly, and discovered he had been an attorney in Dennis. CC discovered Attorney Kelly had an active practice for twenty years so he assumed the guy must have had some money tucked away. Digging further into the search results, he found the obituary for the deceased. It had some basic information listing the wife, the place of the funeral, and he had lived in South Dennis. He saw an entry from the online phone book, and he took note of the address.

After his next therapy session, he decided to drive by the address he got from the Web. The home turned out to be in an upscale neighborhood. From the outside, the house seemed quite big and he estimated it was around 6,000 square feet. On Cape Cod, this kind of house could easily be in the seven figures range. Plus, the house was right on the edge of Cape Cod Bay so CC knew this family had money.

"How could he get access to her assets?" he thought to himself that evening. He could sue her, but that would take more money and if he had any money left, it would be going towards paying his medical bills. No, there had to be an easier way.

Before the accident, CC had provided consulting services to companies and wealthy individuals. His specialty focused on computer security. He would help companies install safeguards on their computer networks to ensure the company information remained secure, and company employees could not access risky web sites. For individuals, he would set up home computer systems and networks that would carry extra security measures ensuring protection and privacy for his clients.

One of the most frequent requests he had from individuals would be to install software on the home computers to allow the parents to monitor what the children were viewing when the children used the computer. CC would install a software package called "PCTrackR" that would run in background mode on a computer keeping track of all of the keystrokes entered into a computer. Then, the parents could view the captured information at their leisure to evaluate which websites the children had been viewing when on the computer. It was a kind of 'big brother is watching' service.

Some parents went as far as to have CC set up an "automatic notify feature" that would send an e-mail to the parents at a specified frequency alerting the parents to the children's use of the computer.

CC thought that he might be able to utilize the software package to obtain financial information about someone. If somehow he could gain access to the home computer of widow Kelly, he might be able to find out what assets she had, where she had them and if he got very lucky, he might even be able to obtain the access information to her accounts. All he had to do was configure PCTrackR to suit his purposes and to then install it on his target's home computer.

To test his theory, CC installed PCTrackR on his own computer. He familiarized himself with all of the options the package offered and set his computer to send an e-mail back to him in one week. He entered "Strokes Test" into the subject line and entered 'CC@ChamberlinFinancial.com' into the recipient field. Then he selected an option that instructed the program to run continuously in the background.

Having set up the program, he exited the setup feature and then began to enter different web site addresses taking notes on each entry. At a few sites such as his bank account, he paid particular attention to the account information he entered. He went to a mutual fund web site and again noted the site name, account and password entries in his written notes. After twenty minutes of data entry, CC wrapped up his test session. He had written down three pages of notes he would use to compare to the file PCTrackR would send to him the next week.

Right on schedule a week later, he opened his e-mail account and saw an incoming e-mail with "Strokes Test" in the subject line. PCTrackR had come through. CC downloaded the attached file and selected the file open option. Comparing the data in the file to his written notes, CC was able to quickly distinguish the website entries, account numbers and passwords had been entered. Everything checked out, and everything was working out, too.

Feeling good that PCTrackR would do the job and knowing Mrs. Kelly was a recent widow with no children (CC loved how informative those obituaries were), all he had to do was to break into her home and install PCTrackR on her computer. The whole thing shouldn't take more than ten minutes. For the next few days, he parked near her house and just watched. On one occasion, he saw Mrs. Kelly remove something from under a flowerpot just to the right of the front door. He realized it must have been a key because she then went to the door and let herself into the house and returned to put something back under the flowerpot as the door swung open.

CC made note that every other evening at around six thirty, she would leave the house dressed in a workout suit and carrying a gym bag. She was gone for about two hours. One night, CC followed her. She went a few miles from home to a local gym. CC thought maybe she was participating in a class or some kind of program because she did the same thing every other night at the same time. He decided he would use the key she kept under the flowerpot to let himself into the home and see if she had a home computer.

On the next exercise night, CC was watching at six o'clock. At six thirty, Mrs. Kelly left her house right on schedule. CC felt confident he had at least an hour and a half to do the job, although it wouldn't take that long. He waited ten minutes and then got out of his car and went to the side of the house. It was dark on the side of the house, illuminated only dimly by the streetlight from in front of the house. CC found the flowerpot and looking under it, found the house key. He used it to open the front door. He returned the key to its home, and closed the door behind him. The room to the right of the door was a study and it had a computer on a desk. It was easy to find because the blue glow from the screen could be seen through a house window from where he was sitting in his car.

The computer had been left on and was in screen saver mode displaying randomly selected pictures. CC clicked the mouse and the computer returned to the ready mode. He took a CD out of his pocket and inserted it into the CD drive. The CD automatically loaded on-to the computer and when done, prompted CC to have him select options for operation. CC instructed the program to capture all keystrokes in a file and to then e-mail the file monthly to him. The last thing he did was to select the option allowing PCTrackR to run in ghost mode making it undetectable to an untrained person using the computer.

Having finished his task, CC checked to make sure everything was as he found it when he had entered the study. He removed his CD from the drive. When he got up from the desk, he stood there for a few minutes until the computer returned itself to the screensaver mode displaying random pictures on the monitor. CC thought everything had gone as he had hoped. He then retraced his path going back out the front door. Exiting the house, he looked around to make sure no one had seen him and quickly went back to his car. All he had to do now was wait and see what information PCTrackR would capture and send to him. Now he almost wished he had set the program to report back daily, or weekly, just to be sure it was working. Oh well, patience was a virtue, and he had none.

CC was not always like this. Before the accident, he was a hard working individual who liked the good things in life. He would travel whenever he could and liked to spend time in the outdoors. He was well built and actively worked at staying in shape. CC had never married but had romances from time to time with a number of women. As a teenager, he became involved in computer programming and quickly became addicted to it. He belonged to a few computer clubs and would show interest in anything computer related.

Graduating from high school with B+ credentials, CC went to Georgia Tech on a scholarship for students with computer potential. At college, CC excelled, expanding his horizons from programming to networks and security. CC's degree program required him to take some business courses as well, and it didn't hurt. He found the challenges of business intriguing. One professor had suggested to CC he combine his computer talents and business interests into a career of computer business consulting. The professor pointed out that with all the innovations taking place with computer technology, security and business was in its infancy and should provide a challenging and rewarding career for individuals who had the aptitude and talents necessary to succeed. CC had decided he would make his career choice in that area.

After graduating from college, he returned to the Cape Cod area and set himself up in business. His first business was called Connors Consulting, LLC. He rented an office in Hyannis, purchased office furniture, designed and ordered business cards and stationary. Then he built a website for his business and began making cold calls to companies in the area, soliciting work. To his amazement, a number of the companies he initially contacted asked him to come in and consult with them. He quickly found himself established with a consulting practice that had enough business to sustain itself. Most of the business consulting focused on security related issues. In a short period of time, CC found himself providing consulting services not only to his business clients, but had also found a market niche doing computer security consulting for individuals. Most of the individuals started as corporate clients, but wanted to protect themselves at home, too. This was how he came to learn about the PCTrackR software package.

After the accident and his subsequent recovery, CC set up a parallel business, Chamberlin Financial Consulting. He used the same address as that of the original business but added a new phone line and website for the new business. He had new stationary and business cards made up for this business to complete its image.

One morning, about a month after CC had broken into the widow Kelly's house and installed PCTrackR on her computer; CC got an e-mail from SKELLY or more specifically, PCTrackR. He downloaded the file and selected the open option. The file revealed Mrs. Kelly used the computer for many things. PCTrackR had recorded all of her e-mail entries along with various online shopping sessions Mrs. Kelly initiated. One of the e-mail entries CC read caught his interest. The e-mail was from Mrs. Kelly to a William Stoner at Prudential Securities. Mrs. Kelly had been requesting investment advice from Mr. Stoner regarding her account. She had indicated in the e-mail she was looking to invest the proceeds of an insurance benefit she recently received and had indicated the amount in question exceeded two million dollars. She asked Mr. Stoner to get back to her as soon as possible.

The next entry in the file sent from PCTrackR showed access to a Rockland Trust bank account. CC wrote down the apparent account number and password Mrs. Kelly had entered. He wrote down the URL Mrs. Kelly had used. The rest of the data in the file didn't produce any more leads into Mrs. Kelly's assets. CC had a start though, and next he entered the URL into his computer and went to the Rockland Bank web site. From the Sign On screen, he entered the account and password information. The next screen was like music to his ears! 'Welcome, Mrs. Kelly. What can Rockland do for you today?' Listed was a single account number, a checking account he assumed. She had over two million dollars sitting there. He thought about it for a minute and then decided not to take any action. It was possible this was only the tip of the iceberg. Maybe she had more assets somewhere else. And if that were the case, all he had to do was be patient and wait and see what other information PCTrackR returned in subsequent disclosures. It would be better to take a little from a lot of accounts, than a lot from one. It would be less noticeable.

The success with PCTrackR got CC thinking about just how he would go about looting the widow's accounts. If he had an offshore or Swiss account, he could tap into her accounts and wire transfer some of her funds directly into his offshore accounts: nice, untraceable. He remembered hearing about accounts in the Cayman Islands offering this kind of feature the same as Swiss accounts. Since both could be done online, he decided to look into setting up an account in the Cayman Islands.

While he was searching for Cayman Island Bank account information, an advertisement popped up on his computer telling him how he could get a secure e-mail account in the Cayman Islands as well. CC saw that as a sign to him, so he decided to get an offshore account for e-mail and banking. While setting these up, he learned he was able to redirect the e-mails from the Cayman Islands account back to his US based e-mail account. He was assured any e-mail sent through his Cayman Islands account would be untraceable to him in the US. This was too perfect, and easy. For a practice test, he wire transferred three hundred dollars to his new Cayman Island Bank Account, account number 79215322463. A few days later, he wire transferred half of it back to his regular account.

Satisfied the process worked, CC turned his focus back to the widow Kelly who caused the accident. To his dismay, the next file of captured information intimated she was moving to Florida in the near future. There were e-mails being sent and received from a real estate company in Florida and based on her responses, it looked to CC like the widow Kelly had closed on new living quarters. From the e-mails, he also determined her relocation date would occur within the next month. What he wasn't sure of, however, was whether it was a full-time relocation, or if the widow was becoming a snowbird. Snowbird was the name given to northerners who spent winters in Florida and summers in the north.

CC called his attorney and mentioned to him he thought there was a chance the widow Kelly would be moving in the near future. His attorney promptly followed up with the tip and discovered it was true, the widow Kelly was planning on moving to Florida in the near future. It might be more difficult following through on his legal plans if the widow Kelly were in another state and his attorney agreed it would most certainly make it more difficult and more expensive. CC was also concerned he might lose contact with her computer and the account information he had already gathered might be replaced with either a new computer or new accounts or both once the widow Kelly relocated. But if she kept the same accounts, and the same computer, he had what he needed to be able to access them. It was a big if, and he was not happy about the odds. "What a bitch", he thought to himself.

He had information about Mrs. Kelly's checking account. He would continue to monitor the information coming in from PCTrackR and see what else showed up. Even if she took her computer with her when she moved, the physical address didn't really mean anything to him from this point on. Anything he had to do with Mrs. Kelly from here on could be done electronically. He was trying to be positive, and how many people got new computers just because they moved? Not many, he thought.

Since she was going to be in Florida, CC figured it would not be practical for him to try to gain access to her computer again not that he thought he would have to have access again, but he thought the plan he had was workable as long as she didn't replace the computer. Even if she set up new accounts in Florida, as long as PCTrackR was running, CC was getting accurate access information.

CC knew the offshore account process worked. He was satisfied he could get untraceable information from Mrs. Kelly, his target. And when the time was right, he felt confident he would make her pay for what she had done to him.

The next morning while reading the newspaper, he read a story about a middle-aged man who died in an auto accident, leaving behind a grieving widow. "Another widow gets wealthy and another poor slob gets killed. Somebody has to get these people." He decided his plan might work in other situations besides his own. The seed was planted.

Reading the obituary of the guy killed by another errant driver, CC thought why not try his ingenious scheme on that widow as well. She might not have been to blame, but he was sure she had done stupid stuff in her past had never been dealt with. That was his job. He chuckled to himself, "in for a penny, in for a pound. Why not? If I'm going to steal money, why not steal as much as I can get my hands on." While he felt it would take a month more to complete the fleecing of Mrs. Kelly, CC thought he could identify another couple of promising widows and make them targets as well. Nothing wrong with multitasking. Nothing at all.

Chapter 3

Katherine Sterns possesses the physical characteristics commonly considered for a model: Tall, five foot ten, with long blond hair, sparkling blue eyes and a figure any woman would be proud to show off. Katherine carried herself confidently, and at the age of forty, she could easily pass for thirty.

Katherine didn't have any children. She worked at the local Silver Gym. There, she managed the memberships, oversaw the front desk and the administration needs of the Gym. When things were slow she would take the opportunity to work out.

Katherine had an obsession for sex. Before her husband died she had affairs with numerous male partners including her dead husband's best friend, Tom Bowman, and a few men she had met at the gym. In fact, when her husband had been struggling for his life, stranded on an ice-flow, Katherine was having her husband's business partner Andrew over for consolation on more than one night.

Sam Sterns' death had been well documented in the news for the past few months. Sam Sterns and his friend Tom Bowman became stranded on the ice that had formed on Cape Cod Bay. When the occupied ice-flow broke out of Cape Cod Bay and traveled into the Atlantic Ocean during a winter storm, the two ended up trapped on the ice for five days. Sam died on the fourth day.

Mr. Bowman's version of the tragedy was also well documented. He and Mr. Sterns went out on the ice on Cape Cod Bay at Paines Creek one Saturday morning for a day of ice fishing. At sometime during the day, undetected by the fishermen, the ice separated from the land and went adrift. During the first night, the ice-flow traveled out into the Atlantic Ocean. The two spent a few days and nights struggling to survive with what they had, but because it was meant to be a day trip during seasonable temperatures, that wasn't much. Mr. Bowman said Mr. Sterns died as a result of hypothermia after having fallen through the ice.

Mr. Sterns had been drilling a hole in the ice with a power auger when the ice gave way. He and his auger went into the water, and the safety line he had tied to Mr. Bowman was the only thing that saved Mr. Bowman from losing Mr. Sterns when he broke through the ice. Mr. Bowman successfully pulled Mr. Sterns back onto the ice. Mr. Bowman gave up his snowmobile suit to Mr. Sterns to keep him warm, however, the damage had already been done.

Mr. Sterns succumbed during the night to exposure and hypothermia. Eventually, a trawler saw Mr. Bowman stranded on the ice-flow and about the same time, a passenger on a flight going into Boston's Logan Airport also saw a help message Mr. Bowman had written on the ice-flow. Local police, the Coast Guard and the parties who had information about the stranded men coordinated a rescue. The Coast Guard rescued Mr. Bowman just as the ice-flow broke apart. Mr. Stern's body was also recovered during the rescue operation.

The wake held for Mr. Sterns was a somber event. The casket was closed. A picture of Sam was sitting on the coffin. Many colorful flower arrangements surrounded the casket and the area behind it. Many people showed up to pay their last respects to Sam. That was where Katherine Sterns met Charles Chamberlin.

Sam's Last Will and Testament left everything after burial expenses to Katherine. Sam also had a personal life insurance policy for three million dollars and Sam had a Key Man life insurance policy through his company worth another three million dollars. While she wouldn't benefit directly from the Key Man policy proceeds, Katherine would become the new majority partner at Sterns and Dunn.

After Sam's death, Katherine spent many nights at home. Some nights were spent alone and some were spent with Andrew. From time to time, Katherine would use the home office computer for e-mails and to check on her financial matters. On one occasion, she sent an e-mail to her friend Dotty Masters. In the e-mail, she talked about some of the liaisons she had with Andrew. She also mentioned that she met what she described as 'a rather distinguished, good-looking gentleman' at the wake and funeral: Charles Chamberlin. She would like to get to know Mr. Chamberlin better, once she was done mourning, of course.

While at the computer, Katherine typed in the web site www.ingdirect.com. When she got to that site, she logged in as KSTERNS and entered KS812 as her password. She viewed her account balances. To her dismay, her money market account was only paying two and a half percent interest. She looked at the balance and thought there must be some way she could earn more on the one and a half million dollars she had in that account. Next, she logged into her mutual fund account at www.vanguard.com again using the same id and password. That was where she had invested the other half of the inheritance in three different mutual funds and the three were just starting to show modest gains.

As she sat there, she noticed the business card for Charles Chamberlin on the desk. She picked it up, "Maybe he can help me." She decided she would give him a call in the near future.

Katherine then went to the business's website, www.sternsanddunn.com. Once there, she selected the

Employees' button. She had earlier located Sam's login information from Sam's file cabinet and used it to get into the Sterns and Dunn site. Once granted access, Katherine selected the Management Information tab and then selected the Financial Accounts tab. To get into this section of the web site, a second id and password were required. Katherine looked up the correct login information in Sam's files and entered SADFIN and a password of ASST4US. Katherine didn't know if there was any significance to the name or password as she was granted access. The computer returned a display summarized the financial picture of Sterns and Dunn. She could see Sterns and Dunn had just over two million seven hundred thousand dollars in the various accounts displayed. She selected the Benefits tab and then the 401k tab. She entered Sterns in the name field and was able to see Sam had a balance of just over five million dollars in his retirement account. After viewing the information, Katherine selected the log out button and exited the site. She wasn't sure why she did this, as not much was changing anymore on a daily basis, but it made her feel good to see what would be available to her as she moved forward in her life.

She had no more interest in computer information for that day, so she went to the living room. There, she turned on the television and decided to watch the evening news. The business outlook looked good, and the pundit called for aggressive investing for those with the funds to invest. She decided she would call Charles Chamberlin the next day.

Just after lunch the next day, Katherine called the number on Charles' business card. After three rings, Charles answered the phone, "Chamberlin Financial Services, how may I help you?"

"Mr. Chamberlin, this is Katherine Sterns. Do you remember me?"

CC quickly looked at his calendar. What a coincidence she is calling me just days before I'd know everything I want to know anyway. He was still awaiting his first PCTrackR e-mail from her computer. "Ms. Sterns, how nice to hear from you. Of course I remember you. What can I do for you?"

"As you know, my husband Sam died in a tragic accident. As a result, I have come into a significant sum of money and I think I could use some advice regarding investments."

"Yes, I think of Sam often. It was a tragic accident. As you know, I am a Consultant providing financial advice to my clients. While you are not a client of mine yet, I would feel privileged to explore investment opportunities with you." Charles didn't know why, but just saying those words made him feel a little dirty. What kinds of thoughts should he be having about the widow of a "friend"?

"I have your business card here in front of me and that's what I thought. When could we get together to get things started?"

Charles thought about it for a few seconds. He couldn't be too available and anxious. That wouldn't look right. He needed to act like a financial consultant doing other things, normal. "Right now, I'm pretty busy helping my clients prepare Income Tax Returns. In another few weeks the tax return deadline will have passed and I should be able to step out of the office for some fresh air."

"Oh, I was hoping to meet with you this week."

"About how much are you sitting on that you want to get invested?"

"I have a little over a million and a half dollars sitting in a money market account earning a minimal rate."

"That much money should be earning much more."

"If you don't have any time during your day schedule might we be able to get together during the evening? You did say evenings were an option, right?"

"Why don't we get together for a dinner meeting the day after tomorrow."

"That would be fine. Do you have a place in mind Mr. Chamberlin?"

"How about we meet at Captain Parkers Restaurant on Route 28 in Yarmouth the day after tomorrow at say seven. And please, call me Charles."

"Great, I'll see you there then. Charles."

The next day, Charles did some homework regarding investments are easily liquidated and also provide for a decent rate of return. After all, he already felt like what was her's was his. He printed information from his computer and put together a file folder he would give to Katherine for her consideration. He also put his standard consulting agreement in the folder that specified his business terms. The document specified Chamberlin Financial Services would provide ongoing consulting services in return for a fee of 10% of the increased value of the account. The account value could be increased due to gains, dividends, interest or distributions. Chamberlin Financial Services would calculate its fees quarterly and expected to be paid within thirty days of each quarter end. The fees could of course be deducted directly from the client's accounts.

Dressed in dark slacks and a button down blue shirt, Charles arrived at Captain Parkers a little before seven. During the off-season, getting a table at Captain Parkers was not a problem. The hostess seated him in the far corner of the building overlooking the Parker River. From his seat, he could see down the row of tables towards the bar. The entrance to the restaurant was to the right of the bar. Promptly at seven, Katherine came in and quickly scanned the restaurant for Charles. The hostess indicated a single fellow had already been seated, and she escorted Katherine to that table.

Charles rose and took Katherine's hand. Shaking it, he said, "Hello Ms. Sterns. I'm glad you could come."

"Please call me Katherine."

"Ok, Katherine it is. Can I order a drink for you?"

"Yes, I'd like a dry martini, dirty."

Charles turned to the hostess and said, "Can you have our waitress bring us two extra dry martinis, one dirty?"

The hostess said, "Absolutely. She'll be right with you."

Charles turned his attention to Katherine and said, "I'm glad you called on me. I'd love to help you reach your maximum investment potential. I have prepared some materials for your consideration, and I have included my consulting agreement should you wish to engage my services."

"Why don't you summarize for me what's in there?"

"I can if you would like."

"Please."

"I did some research regarding limited risk investments that also are fairly liquid. This means you can get at the funds pretty much on a day or two notice. The investments provide for returns more than double what your money market is currently paying you."

"Well, that would be nice."

"These investments are Money Market Accounts with some of the Internet banking companies. They pay about double what conventional banks pay."

"You said limited risk. What risks are there?"

"They are FDIC insured up to two hundred fifty thousand dollars per account. The risk is about the same as what you are used to with your existing accounts."

"Well, is there any downside?"

"Not much. Some withdrawal transactions you would normally do the same day with your current accounts might take a day or two. The Internet companies like to do transactions with signatures. Even faxing is OK, but they do like the hard copy. You can however set up your new account to accept deposits from any other accounts you might have."

"I think I can work with that."

Charles continued, "In time, we can work on getting you into other investments that should provide much greater returns. But for the time being, you might as well make as much of a return as you can in a low-risk account."

"That sounds good to me. What does your consulting agreement specify?"

"I base my fee on your asset's performance. If you make money, I make money. If you don't, I don't."

"That sounds fair enough. Why doesn't everyone do that?"

"Most consultants, brokers and personal asset managers try to get an annual percentage of your assets. They take a percentage-based fee whether they make money for you or not. I charge 10% on all increases in asset values in accounts I am providing advice."

"So, let me see. You get ten percent of the profits and I get ninety percent of the profits and keep all of my principal?"

"That's one way of looking at it. You will also be subject to fluctuations up or down and be responsible for all tax implications, the same as you are now."

"I don't see how I could go wrong?"

"If I don't give you good advice, you won't make any money and I won't get paid. I have incentive to see you make the most of what you can."

"I'm in, how do we start?"

"Just sign the last page of the agreement and you'll have me as a personal consultant."

Katherine turned to the last page and signed. Charles gave her a copy of the agreement for her records and put the original signed copy in his briefcase.

Charles gave Katherine the information he had printed from the web site for the Internet Bank. He told her she would have to use her computer to open the account and she could link it to her checking account for ease of access. Charles indicated once she finished the account setup, the Internet bank would provide her with an account and password in a few days and the bank would automatically get funds from her existing account once she entered her existing account information on her computer.

Katherine raised her eyebrow, "This sounds kind of easy."

"It is. It should only take you an hour or so to get everything set up. Then, in a few days, you will be up and running earning double what you are earning now. Remember during the set up process to select the option to deposit your earnings into your checking account monthly. It will give you a little extra, unexpected spending cash."

"I like the sound of that."

With that, she finished her martini and said, "Let's order another drink."

Charles motioned to the waitress and asked for two more. Katherine said, "Let's toast to a new relationship."

"Here, Here."

The two ordered dinner and a few more drinks. When finished, they had a nightcap at the bar. Katherine was feeling pretty good about the evening and when they had finished their drinks, she said, "I only live a few miles from here. Maybe you could follow me to my house and help me get started with setting up the new account."

"I know where you live. Remember, I came to your house after the burial?"

"Oh, that's right and you helped Andrew fix my computer."

"I did."

Charles didn't know where the evening was headed, but he didn't want to end up in a situation for which he was unprepared. He told Katherine he had to make a quick stop on the way and he would be there in a few minutes.

Katherine rose from the bar and put on her coat. As they walked to the door, she said, "I'll see you at my house in a few minutes."

"Got it."

Leaving Captain Parkers, Charles went east on Route 28 and stopped at the CVS store. There he bought a pack of condoms so he would be prepared should things head in that direction. Nothing fancy of course, no colors, or ribs, or ticklers; just the basic glove. Having made his purchase, he headed in the direction of Katherine's house. When he arrived, he saw Katherine was already in the house with her car in the driveway. He got out of his car and noticed the next-door neighbor was in the window of the house next door looking at him. The neighbor pulled down her shade when she saw Charles look in her direction.

When Charles knocked on the door, Katherine answered and invited him in. Charles noticed Katherine had changed in the few minutes since he saw her last. She now had on a pair of loose fitting sweat pants and a sheer low cut top that barely skimmed the top of the pants. Quickly he took note of a belly ring, and two very noticeable nipples.

Katherine asked Charles if he would like a cocktail. He asked if she had the makings for martinis. She said she did and went to the kitchen to make the drinks. She told Charles to make himself comfortable in the living room and she would be right back. Charles looked around the room. It was nicely decorated with floral design furniture. There were a few pictures on the wall of different settings around Cape Cod. The lights in the room were set at a dim setting giving the room a warmer feeling. An oversized chair sat in one corner next to an entertainment center. Charles took a seat in the oversized chair. It was really comfortable, and Charles could imagine reading a good book in it. The end tables had fresh flower arrangements on them and the mantle over the fireplace had a few mood candles already lit. By scent he guessed they were a vanilla or cookie. The entertainment center was turned on and playing an acoustic John Mayer song.

"I hope these are on par with the drinks at Captain Parker's" Katherine said as she entered the living room.
"I'm sure they will be."
Katherine took up a seat on the ottoman next to the oversized chair and made a toast. "To a new relationship."
Charles wasn't exactly sure what she was referring to and added, "May all your assets grow beyond your expectations."
"And yours also."
Charles looked at her and didn't know how to respond.

32

Katherine set her drink down and took the drink from Charles and placed it on the table. Then she came back to him and put her arms around his shoulders, leaned in and kissed him.

Charles didn't resist. He opened his mouth and accepted her tongue. They kissed for what seemed like a half hour. Charles slowly moved his hand under her top and caressed her. She was very firm and sighed. Katherine continued to kiss Charles and with her hand she undid his pants. She reached inside and felt him. "Very nice." Charles slid his hands down to her sweat pants and slowly slid them down her sleek body. Katherine had nothing on under them. She unbuttoned his shirt and began to kiss his chest. As she stood, he continued to drop her sweat pants until she was standing bottomless in front of him. Before he knew it, she bent down and slid his pants down. She held him in her hands and rubbed his sensitive tip in the palm of her left hand. This action drove him absolutely crazy. Finally, he said, "Lets move to some place more comfortable."

On the way to the bedroom, Charles retrieved one of the condoms from his pants pocket. Katherine said, "You won't need that."
"I just want to be safe."
"I'm safe. And I love that feeling of warmth inside of me."
"Ok, if you say so." And he discarded the condom.

The bedroom had the same feel as the rest of the house, a woman's home. There was a long bureau that had a jewelry chest on it. A sitting chair in front of a make-up table sat off to one side. There room was decorated in soft colors of light green with white trim. The windows had sheer drapes with delicate floral patterns throughout. A king size bed was the centerpiece of the room. A fluffy comforter covered the bed. At the head of the bed, there had to be eight soft feather pillows. Two doors other than the one they entered through went off the bedroom from the other side. One went to an oversized walk-in closet. The other led to a large bathroom.

Katherine took his hand and led him to the bed. She threw back the comforter and pulled back the sheet. She lay down on the bed and reached for Charles to join her. Before she would allow him to enter her, she took his hands and led them on a journey of her body. He felt both captive, and in charge. His hands were exploring the parts of her she would eventually let him have access to. Then he was led to her breasts; and using just his fingertips, she let him massage her nipples until they were hard, and she was moaning softly. Just as he thought he would need to bite something, hard, to control himself, she pulled him down on her, at her left breast. He reached down with his left hand and massaged her softly. Charles wasn't sure where the relationship was headed or even what he was doing, but he wasn't complaining, and was along for the ride.

They had rough, fast, savage sex. At first, Charles was in command, on top and driving hard. Then, Katherine rolled Charles on his back and took charge. She moved slowly at first. Then, increasing the pace, they climaxed together. It was slow motion, and lasted at least one minute. At the end, Katherine shuddered in one final gasp of pleasure. After five or ten minutes of soft breathing, she asked him if he thought he could do it again.

"I don't think so. It will take me a little while to regain my composure."

Katherine said, "Let me see if that's true or not."

She utilized her oral skills and in a few minutes, Charles was ready to go again. This was not something Charles had ever done before, but he was sure he would have to do it again.

When they came a second time, Charles picked up the unopened condom and put it in his pants pocket. "Charles, you didn't need to use a condom because I'm already pregnant."

Charles was a little taken back and said, "You are?"

"Yes. I am a few months along."

"Did you get pregnant just before your husband passed away?"

"It looks that way."

"I didn't know."

"There was nothing to know. I wanted you."

Charles thought Katherine must be in a depressed state or something or she was just an evil woman. He said, "Do you think it's alright to be having sex with a new acquaintance while pregnant?"

"Let's not be old fashioned Charles. I have my needs and desires just like the next person. My desire for sex didn't die with my husband."

Charles didn't know how to respond. He let the conversation die out.

After getting dressed Charles said, "Did you want me to help you with your account setup?"

"That can wait till tomorrow. Will you stay the night?"

"I can't. I have an appointment first thing in the morning so I have to go."

"If you have to. But I would like some more consulting soon."

"What have I gotten myself into?" Charles thought.

He knew what his plan *had* been, but where was it headed now?

Chapter 4

CC felt good about his plan but he wasn't sure about his newfound relationship with Katherine. He had put the pieces in place. His plan was to seek out targets over the next few months and then when the time was right, he planned on looting the accounts of his targets. Katherine Sterns was his first real qualified target. He would monitor his incoming e-mail for a message from PCTrackR originating on her computer. When they arrived, he would have to spend time analyzing the data to determine if what he was looking for was present. In the meantime, he would let the relationship with Katherine take its course. For now, Katherine Sterns was safe.

Every day, CC read the local Cape Cod Times. Most of the time, the obituaries were about people he didn't feel met his criteria. After a week, he started to think it might take longer than he anticipated finding six targets. CC had arbitrarily set six as the number of targets he intended to pursue based mostly on how much data he guessed he would have to analyze. It wouldn't make sense to bite off more than he could chew. Plus, most of the obituaries were for people over sixty years old.

The next morning was like most of the rest. He made his coffee and toast. He retrieved his morning newspaper from the front door. He read the paper from front to back. When he got to the obituary section, he took care to scan the initial line of each entry. On this particular day, the fourth obituary down was for a fifty-eight year old Peter Lee. It read as follows:

Peter Lee, 58 of Brewster, husband of Theresa (King) Lee, died Tuesday at Cape Cod Hospital resulting from complications suffered in an automobile accident. Born in Boston, he had lived in Brewster having moved from Rockland three years ago and had been employed by Duval Real Estate, in Yarmouth. Besides his wife, he leaves one brother Kenneth Lee of Orleans, MA and one sister, Mary Hamilton of Springfield, MA. His family invites friends Friday from 10 a.m. until 2 p.m. and from 7 p.m. until 9 p.m. at the Kelsy Funeral Home, 29 Main Street, Brewster, MA followed by burial services at Overlook Cemetery, Brewster, MA. For condolences please visit www.kelsyfuneralhome.com.

At first, CC thought the widow Theresa Lee might be a little older than he would like. But, he hadn't been getting many hits given his criteria in the past week so he decided he would go to Kelsy Funeral Home on Friday and take a look.

CC continued to read the obituaries and didn't find any other prospects that day. When he was finished reading the paper, he turned his computer on and did a search on Peter Lee of Brewster, MA. The search returned a reference to a recent newspaper article that reported on the accident that caused his death. Retrieving the article, CC could see Mr. Peter Lee had been in an automobile accident with a tractor-trailer truck where the truck driver had been cited for traveling erratically and at excessive speed leading up to the accident. A national trucking company owned the truck, so CC figured this widow would probably be in for a large settlement. "Looking more promising all the time. Who says age matters?"

On Friday morning, CC put on black slacks, a v-neck light blue cashmere sweater over a striped blue oxford, and a sport jacket. He traveled to Kelsy Funeral Home and sat in his car in the parking lot. As people begin to arrive, he could see most were driving nicer automobiles. A few of the mourners had decided to remain outside to have a cigarette so CC thought he would start there.

CC approached the smokers and took out a cigarette for himself. As he was standing there, one of the other smokers came over to him and said, "Hi, I'm Jason Prescott."

CC responded with, "Charles Chamberlin. Nice to meet you."

Prescott said, "Did you know Peter well?"

"Not that well. I knew him through the real estate business."

"Oh, are you in that business as well?"

"No, I was looking at some real estate."

"Peter was my neighbor."

"Oh so you two must have been close?"

"Sort of. I knew him from the neighborhood. We had cookouts and other neighborhood outings he and Theresa attended with the other neighbors."

CC added, "It must be tough on his wife, Theresa, then."

"Yeah, she's a wreck."

"From what I gather, Peter had been pretty successful in the real estate business. He knew as much as anyone else about business transactions when I had talked with him recently."

"Yes he was very successful. Last year, Peter sold all those condominiums at the place that used to be Snows Landing. I think he made nearly a million in commissions on that deal alone. He was very good at what he did."

"The nice thing about him, though, was he didn't flaunt it."

"Not really, but Peter put on the biggest neighborhood party we had ever seen right after he closed that deal. He had lobster, filet mignon, champagne, and fireworks. It sure was the event of the year in our neighborhood."

"That must have been something."

Prescott looking up said, "It sure was."

Then Prescott said he was going inside to pay his respects.

CC said, "Nice to meet you."

Prescott said the same and went inside.

38

Another one of the smokers, Lucy Carmichael, approached CC and said, "I overheard some of your conversation with Prescott. I'm from the neighborhood also."

CC said, "Yes?"

"Yeah. Prescott doesn't like me very much."

"And why's that?"

"I'm thought of as the loose woman in the neighborhood."

CC looking at her with eyebrow raised said, "Interesting."

Lucy looking around said, "I live a few houses down the street from the Lee's. Theresa and I belong to the same gym and we work out together from time to time."

"Oh, I go to the gym also. Which one do you belong to?"

"The Bond Gym on Route 28."

"I know the place. I have been there a time or two. I usually go to the Center Gym in Hyannis."

"I have never been there. Do they have a big facility?"

"The usual stuff, not really that big."

"Maybe I'll try your gym and see you again?"

"Maybe." CC thought there was an awkward pause, but wasn't sure what else she wanted him to say.

Lucy Carmichael then waved and said, "Bye." Then she kissed CC on the cheek. "Hmmm. Maybe the rumors were true." She then turned and went into the funeral home.

"Did she just come on to me?" CC thought to himself. He thought she must know herself pretty well, the loose woman of the neighborhood. He had made note of all that had been told to him so far. He decided he would take a shot at the widow and see what materialized. But the ancillary benefits might prove fruitful as well.

As he entered the funeral home, he saw a few people seated to the right of the casket. The last person in the row was a very attractive blond woman. She looked to be in her mid-forties. She was dressed in a three-quarter length black dress. Her eyes were red and swollen. From time to time, she would bring her handkerchief to her face to cover her grief. She was talking with Lucy Carmichael when he got at the back of the receiving line. Before speaking with Ms. Lee, Lucy said a prayer at the casket and then walked to the woman CC presumed to be the widow. After a quick conversation, and an obligatory hug, Lucy walked to the back of the room. As she passed CC, she said to him, "Hope to see you again Mr. Chamberlin." CC nodded.

Prescott was standing just off to the side of the receiving line and overheard her comment to CC. After she had passed, he leaned over to CC and said, "That one is trouble."

CC said, "Interesting."

CC then moved on to the casket and stood for a minute appearing to say a prayer or something for the late Peter Lee. In actuality, CC was thinking to himself he was about to meet another very attractive widow who just might qualify as another target. When he went home, he would make notes documenting all of the information he had gathered. He didn't know how much information he would need in gaining access to the widow, so he would write down all he could remember.

As CC reached the front of the line, he leaned over to Theresa Lee and said, "I'm sorry for your loss Mrs. Lee. I am a business acquaintance of Peter's."

Theresa Lee said, "Thank you for coming."

CC said, "I think I have seen you before over at the Bond gym?"

"I do work out there from time to time."

"I have been there a few times. But I usually go to the Center Gym in Hyannis."

"I have never been there."

"Well, if I do see you at the gym, I'll certainly stop and say hello."

"Thank you again for coming."

"Your welcome. I know this is a trying time for you."

"It is. Peter's death, the accident, lawyers, it's all overwhelming."

"As I indicated, I was a business acquaintance of Peter's. If I can be of any assistance, please call on me."

With that he handed her his business card.

Theresa said, "That's very kind of you."

The funeral for Peter Lee was held the next morning. CC dressed in a suit and went to the Kelsy funeral home at 10 a.m. The service was all of twenty minutes long. At the conclusion, a representative of the funeral home indicated Peter would be buried at the Overlook Cemetery at a future time in a private family service. He then indicated everyone was invited to join the family at Riverside Restaurant for a gathering. CC thought that meant Peter was being cremated, as a delay between funeral and burial usually meant that.

CC was disappointed he would not be getting a chance to check out the Lee household. He thought if Theresa Lee were to be a target, then he would have to work a different angle and put in a little more time with her. At the restaurant, he spoke with Theresa for a few minutes.

Charles said, "Mrs. Lee, when I had originally met Peter, he spoke about possibly pursuing a few investments. Do you know if he was able to follow through on them before the accident?"

"I didn't get very involved in Peter's financial investment matters. Maybe I should have paid more attention."

"Well, I provide consulting services in that area and I had talked with Peter about a few possibilities. I had originally met him as a result of a real estate interest but as Peter and I talked we got to know each other better. He had an interest in what I do for a living and that led us to talk about investments."

"I'm just starting to go through Peter's computer and his files. I really don't know what is involved at this point."

"Well, if you need any professional help trying to sort it out, don't hesitate to give me a call."

41

"I have the card you gave me. I might just give you a call once I have some idea of what I'm doing."

"Any time."

Theresa Lee reasoned that since Peter had been having investment and finance conversations with Charles Chamberlin, then Mr. Chamberlin would probably be a safe route to take in seeking financial advice. After all, if Peter had been working with Mr. Chamberlin, then it had to be a good thing and she didn't have much expertise in that area.

CC went home and updated his notes. He was starting to build a file on Theresa Lee.

A few days later, Charles got a call from Theresa.

"Mr. Chamberlin, this is Theresa Lee."

"Hello Ms. Lee. It's nice to hear from you again."

"Mr. Chamberlin."

"Please call me Charles."

"Ok, Charles. I have been trying to go through Peter's files and his computer and I'm not making much progress. You had told me you provide professional consulting on financial matters, don't you?"

"I do. Can I be of assistance to you?"

"I hope so. Peter has a lot of things on his computer I'm not sure what they all mean. Do you think you could help me out understanding what he had?"

"I think I probably can help you out. When would you like to meet?"

"I thought I would come to your office, say tomorrow afternoon at four."

"Ok, and bring the laptop computer with you."

"Oh, it's not a lap top. It's a desk top model."

"Then why don't I come to your house and we can meet there?"

"That will be fine. I'll see you at four."

"See you at four tomorrow."

That night, Charles reviewed all of his notes regarding the Lee target. He made sure he had his PCTrackR CD in his briefcase and made sure he had some paperwork that looked like he had investment information to gather from the Lee computer. He figured a simple checklist would make Ms. Lee think he was gathering information in order to be able to professionally consult with her.

The next day promptly at four o'clock, Charles arrived at the Lee household. The home of Peter and Theresa Lee was situated in a nicely manicured neighborhood. Most of the homes in this area of town had been built in the past ten years. As a result, the landscapes were neat and clean. The Lee house was an oversized cape with an attached three-car garage. The front of the house had numerous flowering plants, trees and shrubs. A walkway with solar lights lined a slate walkway that led to the main door. A nameplate hanging on the front lamppost indicated "The Lees" lived at that residence.

Theresa greeted him at the door and asked him to come in. Theresa Lee had on a pair of nicely fitting designer jeans and a tight sweater. It just skimmed the top of her jeans where a leather belt was cinched. She had let her hair down since he last saw her at the funeral home and Charles thought she had a rather attractive look about her. He had not been able to take in her beauty at the funeral home but in the home setting, she showed she was an attractive woman who took care of herself.

As Charles came in, Theresa indicated she had all of the files laid out in Peter's home office and would be a good place for them to meet. Upon entering the office, Charles observed everything was very neat. All the files were neatly stacked in piles on the desk. The computer was turned on with a series of icons displayed on the screen.

Charles said, "Where would you like to begin?"
Theresa said, "I don't have a lot of experience in these matters so I'm not sure where we should begin."
"That's all right. I have a checklist here we could use to get us started."

He retrieved two copies of the checklist from his briefcase and gave one copy to Theresa.

Theresa looked at the list and thought it covered a lot of things. As she scanned it, she said, "There are a lot of things here I don't know much about."

"We'll take it one at a time and see what we end up with."

"Ok."

"The first thing to do is to see what files Peter had and then to see what he had on his computer."

Theresa let Charles sit at the computer and she pulled up a chair to sit next to him. As she sat close to Charles to be able to see the computer along with him, Charles got a scent of a very nice perfume. She leaned across the keyboard and picked up a few folders were sitting on the other side of the computer on the desk. As she did, she was only inches away from Charles. For some reason, and he didn't know why, the hairs on his arms stood up as she brushed by.

"I went through Peter's file cabinet and pulled out anything I thought might have something to do with investments or financial matters." Resting back in her chair, she said, "These files are what I came up with."

Charles scanned a few of the files and said, "This is a good start. If you don't mind, I'll take a few minutes to review what's here."

"While you're doing that, can I get you a coffee or something?"

"That would be fine."

"How do you take it?"

"Black, one sugar."

"I'll be right back."

When she left the room, Charles removed the CD from his briefcase and placed it in the computer. He typed the commands to begin loading his programs. It only took a minute for the program to load. When loaded, he ejected the CD and put it back into his briefcase. He renamed PCTrackR to UTIL0802 so it would look like a utility on the computer.

He opened the program and was entering in his criteria when Theresa came back into the room with two cups of coffee.

"Have you found anything on the computer yet?"

"I just started to look and I see he had a few icons set up for investment companies and his broker."

"I haven't been able to get anything to work in those sites. Maybe you will have better luck Charles."

"Did Peter have a logon name and password he used frequently you know of?"

"I'm not sure."

She produced a little black book Peter had kept in his desk drawer and opened it. On the inside cover, the letters PLEE were handwritten followed by a slash and the entry PL020450. She said, "Do you think this means anything?"

Charles said, "I don't know. Let's see."

He clicked on the icon for TRowePrice. The screen changed and a new screen for TRowePrice came up with a LOGIN button in the upper left corner. He clicked on the button. A screen came up that asked for a social security number. CC turned to Theresa and said, "Do you know what his social security number was?"

"Yes, it's right here under his personal information in the address book." She read it to Charles and he entered it into the field.

Next, he entered the PL020450 into the password field and was granted access into Peter Lee's TRowePrice account.

"We're in."

"Great. That's more progress than I was able to make."

"I see here Peter had an IRA with TRowePrice that has a current balance of $878,550."

"I didn't even know he had that investment."

"I'll bet these other icons are for other accounts as well."

For the next hour, he and Theresa went through all of the icons and accessed most of the accounts. Charles didn't write any of the details down. He felt confident PCTrackR would handle the details for him. At around five thirty, he said, "It looks like there is quite a bit here to digest. I'd suggest we wait for the reports we requested to come in over the next few weeks and then sit down again to assess what you have and where you would like to go from here. To recover the funds as part of the beneficiary process will require some forms I'm sure."

Theresa was looking kind of bleary eyed, "There sure is quite a bit to cover. How should I proceed?"

Charles picked up a piece of paper he had been making notes on, "Contact all of these companies to notify them of Peter's death. You'll have to provide them with copies of the death certificate and then they'll change the accounts over to your name. Once you have taken stock in all you have from the computer and from the files, we can begin to put together your plans in going forward. As a widow, your financial needs will in all likelihood be different from Peter's. He'd be pleased you were taken care of, but let's make sure it takes care of you for a long time."

"This is all kind of overwhelming."

"It might look like it at first, but eventually it will all come together. Just don't try to do it all in at once. One account at a time will make it easier to digest."

"Ok. I'll start on the files and computer accounts tomorrow."

"Don't worry, I'll be with you all the way."

As Theresa was walking Charles to the door she said, "On top of all of this work, I am going to have to spend some time with the attorney who is filing the suit on my behalf."

"What is the suit about?"

"I'm suing the guy who killed my husband. I'm asking for $10 million."

"That's quite a bit of money."

"Well, with your help, I'll put it into good investments."

"I hope to be able to do just that. Help you with your assets. I'll call in a few days to see how things are going."

46

"I really appreciate it."

Driving home from Theresa Lee's house, CC smiled and said out loud, "Wow, this widow is going to have millions."

He had qualified another target.

Chapter 5

Every day for the next week CC checked his e-mail account. He logged in as CC4ME. At first, there were no incoming e-mails with a subject line of "strokes included" listed in his incoming mail. CC realized he just had to be patient and to keep checking from time to time. Then one day when he logged in, he saw an e-mail from SKELLY with the subject line of "strokes included". This was the first real response CC had received from the planted PCTrackR sites since the initial e-mail he had received but hadn't saved. He saved this file on his computer in the Sharon Kelly folder in a file labeled SK Strokes One.

CC downloaded the attached file and opened it. Most of the initial entries were of e-mails being sent from Sharon Kelly to various people telling them of her re-location to Florida. On the third page of information, CC saw a website address of www.seminolebank.com. He saw her name, new address, cell phone number and other information had been entered. He concluded she was opening a new account at that bank.

Following the new bank entry came an entry to www.rocklandtrustbank.com. It was followed by what appeared to be an account number and what was probably a password of HKSK0921. CC wrote the information on a piece of paper. The password was followed by a few keystrokes that didn't mean anything at the time but CC wrote them down anyway.

48

After the keystrokes, CC could see where Sharon Kelly had selected the bank e-mail option. She had written an e-mail to a Mr. Coltnor indicating she was in the process of establishing a new bank account with Seminole Bank in Florida and she intended to be transferring her funds to that account in the near future. CC thought the e-mail was rather timely. He had a hook into the Ms. Kelly at her re-located address. CC took down notes and when finished with the attachment, he updated his files and spreadsheet of information he had been building about his targets.

Having completed his research for the morning, he turned his computer off and went about his business for the rest of the day. The next morning, was no different than the day before. He got his morning paper and went through his daily routine. When he got to the obituary page, he carefully read the first few lines of each obituary. Again, he didn't find a single suitable target listed.

After showering and dressing for the day, CC decided he would continue to work on the Theresa Lee target. He retrieved his computer file labeled Theresa Lee. He scanned the information he had collected since he first uncovered her husband's obituary. The file was starting to accumulate what could turn out to be valuable information. He had her name, address, bank information, brokerage information, mutual fund accounts identified and a note in the file indicated Ms. Lee was planning a law suit against the person who had killed her husband and the company he worked for. CC recalled Ms. Lee had indicated she was suing for ten million. That would make a nice addition to the funds he had already identified.

CC brought up the Google search engine screen and entered the Lee name. The first three items in the list were references to news articles of the accident that took Peter's life. The fourth item was a reference to a lawsuit being filed on behalf of Ms. Theresa Lee against the driver and the company that employed him. The suit was asking for ten million dollars. As CC read further, he surmised the suit would probably take many months before being concluded. There were witnesses to be interviewed; police reports to dissect and an actual trial could go on for weeks. Even after the verdict is issued, the appeals and actually getting the money from a judgment would take much longer. It would probably take longer than CC wanted to wait.

He decided he would focus on the assets Ms. Lee already had in her possession. She had told him there was a nice insurance policy on Peter that paid over one and a half million dollars and he knew from looking at her accounts with her she had another one point three million dollars in mutual funds alone. He was sure once PCTrackR reported in, he would find even more money to target.

Early the next week, while going through his daily routine, he logged in to his e-mail account. In his in-box he had two incoming e-mails with the subject line of "strokes included". CC quickly opened up the first e-mail. It was from Katherine Sterns' computer. He clicked on the attachment and downloaded the file. He selected the save button and put the file in the Katherine Sterns folder on his desktop, saving it as KS Strokes One file.

Next, he opened up the second e-mail. It was from Theresa Lee's computer. He promptly downloaded the file and saved it in his Theresa Lee folder as TL Strokes One file.

The first order of business was to open each file and analyze the information. Opening the KS Strokes One file, he could see the file spanned many pages. All of the data keyed into Katherine's computer was legible. All he had to do was to make sense out of it and extract what he needed.

The first entry in the file opened up an excel file on Katherine's computer. The file name she entered was Assets.xls. There next entry was a close file command for the xls file. It was followed by an e-mail address for www.ingdirect.com. Next, the ID and password CC was already familiar with appeared. KSTERNS and KS812. The next entry indicated a fund transfer was being requested in the amount of fifty thousand dollars. It was being sent from the ING Direct account to an account at www.franklintempleton.com. The entry contained a date, the amount and a fund designation. Katherine was starting to invest the funds being held in the money market account into mutual funds. Having completed the entry, the send command was indicated in the file. Katherine also accessed a Vanguard site, but it appeared to be just an inquiry transaction.

The last entry in the KS Strokes One file was an e-mail from Katherine to her friend, Dotty Masters. The keystrokes from Katherine indicated small talk initially about her pregnancy and her not seeing much of Andrew in the last few weeks. She told Dotty Andrew had become elusive indicating he had to spend more time at the business now that Sam was no longer around. The next sentence in the e-mail caught CC's attention. Katherine brought up CC. She had typed, "As I had previously told you, I met a rather distinguished gentleman at Sam's funeral. His name is Charles Chamberlin. He is rather handsome and is now providing me with financial investment advice. But you know me Dotty, when I get interested in a man, I'm in all the way."

CC thought, "What could she mean by that?"
He would have to be careful proceeding.

Katherine went on to talk about her role with the Sterns and Dunn business. She wrote to Dotty she wasn't really interested in the business and she had really only been interested in Andrew. She was going to pursue the sale if things didn't change. She concluded her e-mail by telling Dotty she hoped to be able to come down to Washington to see her in a few weeks.

CC took notes regarding the accounts. When he looked at the information in his file, he didn't see any assets under a Franklin Templeton institution. He figured she must have set this account up using paper instead of the internet since she didn't tell him about it when he did the initial consulting for her.   When done, he updated his file for Katherine Sterns and then turned his attention to the Theresa Lee file.

Opening the TL Strokes One file, CC identified the first entry as an e-mail between Theresa and a Mr. Ken Lombard. The e-mail discussed her lawsuit against the person who was in the accident with her husband. She had indicated in the e-mail she would be able to meet with Mr. Lombard and the other attorneys at the Lombard offices the following week and suggested an appointment time of 2:00 pm on Monday.

The next entry on the file was to www.troweprice.com. It was followed by the strokes PLEE and then by PL020450. A series of keystrokes followed but they didn't mean anything to CC at the time. He assumed she was checking on her investments.

Following the TRowePrice inquiry came another mutual fund designation at www.dreyfus.com. Again Theresa logged in using PLEE and PL020450. The next keystrokes indicated Theresa was making a fund transfer from one fund to another in the amount of ninety thousand dollars. Then the keystrokes indicated she logged out of the account. CC knew she had some money in mutual funds and the keystrokes file identified some of the activity between them. He would have to log into the accounts himself to see what other money she held in them.

The keystrokes file next identified another financial institution, www.sovereignbank.com.   The file indicated Theresa selected a checking account option. It appeared she was reviewing her checking account, as there were no further entries for this account other than the Log Out command.

The last entry in the file was for www.google.com. CC could see Theresa was doing research on the company that owned the vehicle that had killed her husband. He couldn't determine what she was doing but it looked like she was looking for evidence of other accidents involving the company or other information regarding suits in which the company or the driver had been involved. The string of characters went on for a while but didn't reveal anything he could make sense of.

Some of the entries were speculative such as the lawsuit Theresa Lee had filed, but CC could see his targets had significant funds he might be able to get. He considered going after the funds right then and there but decided to wait and see what the outcome of the Lee lawsuit would be before acting.

He logged into a few of the websites he had listed in his files. He tried the Rockland Trust site for Sharon Kelly. When the site came up, he used the information he had for her ID and password and was able to see the balances in that account. Next he tried the Vanguard site for Katherine Sterns and using the information in his file was able to gain access to that account as well. He checked the balances in the account against those in his spreadsheet and confirmed his files were up to date. Lastly, he went to the TRowePrice website and logged in as Theresa Lee. Again, he used the information in his file and gained access to that account. He verified the balances with his records and logged out.

CC was very pleased with his accomplishments. His program was working nicely. He verified the information he had on each of his targets and felt comfortable he had full access to their money.

He reflected on his plan to take only a portion of the assets from each target widow. As he thought about the information in his Targets spreadsheet, he realized collectively, the potential was there for him to take over five million dollars from them and if he took all they had, the potential was there for more than ten million dollars especially if the Lee suit settled successfully. CC found it hard to control himself but he thought he would just have to wait out the suit conclusion and all his problems would be solved.

Finishing up with the files, CC closed it and then using his notes, he updated his Theresa Lee file and his Targets spreadsheet.

Under Kelly he noted the following:

Prudential	$2,000,000
Rockland Trust	$2,000,000
Seminole Bank	new

Under Sterns he noted:

Vanguard	$1,500,000
ING Direct	$1,450,000
Franklin Templeton	$50,000
Sterns & Dunn	$2,700,000 est.
401(k)	$5,100,000

Under Lee he noted:

TRowePrice	$878,500
Sovereign Bank	$12,000
Dreyfus	$420,000
Insurance	$1,500,000
Lawsuit	$10,000,000?

He decided to watch the targets he already had and to look for additional targets for the next month or two.

Chapter 6

For the next week, CC read the newspapers looking for new targets. There had been plenty of obituaries but most were for people over age sixty. Every now and then, he would see an obituary for someone in his target range but for numerous reasons, he decided not to pursue the lead.

In one case the services were being held out of state and he didn't think it would be prudent to pursue a target so far away. In another case the dead person had been a truck driver and lived in an apartment. He didn't think this person would have sufficient assets worth pursuing. In another case a family of three young children were left with the widow and CC didn't want to have to include small children and their future in his plans. He was only interested in childless widows of middle or upper class stature. So far, the couple of candidates he had targeted had all met with these criteria.

As he read the morning paper he saw an obituary for a Joel Finch that caught his eye. It read:

Joel Finch, 36

Joel Finch, 36, of Plymouth, MA
Passed away unexpectedly at Plymouth General hospital yesterday resulting from injuries incurred in an accident a month ago. He is survived by his wife, Amy (Wheeler) Finch, of Sandwich MA.

Joel was employed by Cape Cod Electric Company in Falmouth, MA. He enjoyed golf, baseball and many other outdoor activities. In addition to his wife, he is survived by a brother, Ken of Barnstable, MA and a sister, Helen (Cummings) Joiner, of Hyannis, MA. Both his parents predeceased him.

Visiting hours will be held at the Chapman Cole & Gleason Funeral home, 475 Main Street, Falmouth, MA on Thursday from 7 to 9 p.m. Joel will be cremated in a private ceremony, and burial will be for the family only at a future date.

As CC read the obituary he thought the deceased might be another possible target were it not for the private ceremony part. He usually used the calling hours at the wake to gather info, and to get noticed. Then he attended the funeral service as a familiar face. This process made his next step much easier. His thinking was it might be difficult if not impossible to get close enough to the widow in just one meeting to carry out his plan, so he decided to pass.

CC knew the targets he had already identified had the potential for millions. It had been two weeks since he saw even the most basic possible potential new targets. He wondered if he had enough targets with what he had. He decided to get on to his computer and see if anything new showed up there.

After logging into his e-mail account, he saw he had five incoming e-mails. He scanned the list. Two had to do with his consulting business and the other three were from his targets. As he read down the list he saw one from KSTERNS, one from SKELLY and one from PLEE. All had "Strokes Included" in the subject line. He wondered when Theresa Lee would get around to setting up her own e-mail account instead of using her dead husband Peter's. It really didn't matter because PCTrackR captured everything entered into a computer running the software.

The first target he selected was KSTERNS. He opened his notebook to the Katherine Sterns folder and opened the spreadsheet containing her information. Next he downloaded the PCTrackR file and saved it in the same folder but named it KS Strokes two. CC started to analyze the keystrokes file. The first entry showed Katherine retrieving her e-mails. At one point, she had selected the reply tab.

"Andrew, why are you avoiding me? You know I told you I have needs and that's all this is about. Come over tonight. I'll make dinner and you can spend the night. I really have missed you. I'll plan on dinner for seven."

The next entry was to the website www.franklintempleton.com. It looked to CC like Katherine was checking on something as she had entered her KSTERNS and password KS812 and nothing else followed after that. In the next entry, Katherine had selected the Yahoo Finance site and entered what looked like a fund name. CC thought she might be inquiring about a particular fund for possible investment.

Katherine had followed up the financial sites with a visit to www.victoriassecret.com. At that site she had selected the tab for bras and proceeded to order two new pushup bras. The number two was followed by a 38 D in the string of characters. She apparently had an account because CC saw her user name and password entered followed by what looked like a credit card number. A string of separated characters followed and CC thought these were the options and instructions being captured by PCTrackR completing the transaction.

There were no more entries in the KS Strokes Two file. CC toggled back and forth between the Strokes Two file and his Katherine Sterns spreadsheet updating the information he had gathered, including her bra size. As he thought more about his last contact with Katherine and the information he had just received, he thought he might give her a call in case

Andrew didn't show. He decided he would call her at seven thirty and see how she was doing.

Following the KSTERNS e-mail he selected the SKELLY e-mail. He clicked on the attachment and downloaded the file and stored it in the Sharon Kelly folder under SK Strokes Two file. Opening the file he started to breakdown the e-mail.

The Sharon Kelly file from PCTrackR didn't reveal any new information. All of the entries in the file were e-mails between her and people she knew in her old neighborhood. Kids, husbands, PTA stuff. CC didn't detect any alarm from what he could see. If Sharon was doing anything with her assets, then it was by means other than online.

One e-mail he did take note of was to her attorney. At least that was what CC thought it was about because the e-mail went as follows:

"Mr. Benson, while I sympathize with Mr. Chamberlin's injuries resulting from the accident, I don't understand why the insurance company didn't take care of his issues. Even though I did get an inheritance from my former husband, I don't think I should have to settle with Mr. Chamberlin out of my pocket. See if you can get an agreement with Mr. Chamberlin for the two hundred thousand dollar settlement proposed by the insurance company. Please proceed with defending my interests unless I inform you otherwise. Sharon."

"So, the attorney wanted Sharon Kelly to consider a settlement and the bitch won't hear of it. Ok, if that's how it has to be. I'll get my pound of flesh." CC thought.

When CC closed the file, he looked at the spreadsheet he had set up for Sharon Kelly. He went to the websites he had stored in the file and updated the figures. Her Prudential account was still worth over two million dollars. The

58

Seminole Bank account now had a balance of $4,533.29. The Rockland Trust Bank account was worth $1,967,000.

While still logged into the Rockland Trust site at Sharon Kelly's account, he clicked on the Transfer Tab. He entered one million five hundred thousand dollars into the amount field. In the "To" field, he entered the ABA and Transit number of his offshore account in the Cayman Islands. Then he pressed the enter key. The computer responded with a confirmation of the transaction for one million five hundred thousand dollars. CC said, "Take that, bitch."

Next, he opened the PLEE e-mail and downloaded the file. He saved it as TL Strokes Two in the Theresa Lee folder.

As he started to scan the data in the file from PCTrackR, he saw Theresa had transferred funds to her attorney twice during the month. The first transfer had been for one hundred thousand dollars. It was accompanied by an e-mail in which Theresa had told her attorney she thought the suit was getting expensive but she knew the legal firm had expenses that needed to be covered. She had indicated had she known it would be this expensive she would have opted for the contingency option instead of paying as you go option. The second transfer to the attorney firm was for another two hundred thousand dollars. It too was accompanied by an e-mail in which Theresa indicated she didn't think she could go much further expense wise.

In between the transfers and e-mails, CC could see where Theresa went to her accounts and checked on her funds. CC opened up another browser window and entered the TRowePrice URL. Then he entered Theresa's ID, PLEE, and password, PL020450. He looked at her account balance that was then at $569,220. Theresa had drawn over three hundred thousand dollars from the account since last month. CC wondered if there would be any money left when it came time for him to execute his plan. Next he checked on her Dreyfus account. It had a balance of just over four hundred twenty thousand dollars in it so it had not changed. He checked her

Sovereign Bank account and it had a balance of $9921.43. CC's spreadsheet file had a note in it. Theresa was due an insurance settlement but he didn't see it anywhere. Either she didn't get the check yet or she was investing it somewhere outside of the range of PCTrackR.

CC thought he might be forced to go after whatever he could get from Theresa right then and there. But the lure of a settlement and Theresa getting her hands on the insurance money gave him what he needed. He decided he would wait and see where things went over the next month.

Wrapping up with the e-mail files, CC brought up the Google Search engine and began to inquire into the Lee lawsuit. He found a site that summarized the transcripts of trials. He opened up the latest transcript regarding the Lee suit and was able to determine in reading the summary the insurance company representing the company who employed the person involved in the accident with Peter Lee had proposed a settlement with the Lee's attorney and requested a continuance with the court. A two-week continuance had been granted.

Seeing that information, CC felt good about his decision to wait. In two weeks, he would have a better idea about how to proceed with the Theresa Lee target.

CC felt good. Things were looking up. He would look tomorrow and see if the Kelly money turned up in his account. He looked forward to the remainder of his day. Having a million dollar payday can do that for a guy.

At seven thirty, as planned, CC called the Sterns residence. Katherine answered the phone in kind of a testy tone, "Ok, what's the excuse?"
CC said, "Katherine, how are you doing?"
Katherine had to compose herself as she thought the call was Andrew, "Oh, Charles, I'm sorry, I thought it was someone else."
"Did I catch you at a bad time?"

"No, not really. I had made dinner for a friend and I have apparently been stood up."

"That would be very rude of your friend. I was reviewing my files today and thought I would give you a call and see how things were going."

Katherine's voice turned upbeat and replied, "I have been doing my homework per our meeting and I have started to do some things with the funds."

"Well, I know Franklin Templeton is a good company and I'm sure any investment you make with them will be well managed."

Katherine responded, "Yes, I have opened an account with them. I plan on taking it slow at first to get used to doing business with them."

"I'm glad to hear you are making progress."

"Charles, are you doing anything for dinner tonight?"

Charles thought, "I guess she's making alternative arrangements. He said, "I hadn't made any plans."

She said, "Why don't you come over. I already have dinner underway for two and it doesn't look like my friend is going to show."

"I can be there in about twenty minutes. Will that work?"

"Sure will. See you soon."

When she hung up, Katherine called Andrew on his cell phone.

Andrew answered, "Andrew Dunn."

Katherine said, "Andrew, I thought you were coming for dinner."

"I never committed Katherine. I thought I indicated I had a lot of work to get done. I'm still at the office and I don't think I'll be able to make it tonight."

"Oh alright. I'll do something else for the evening."

"I'll try to call you next week and we can set something up."

Katherine thought she was getting the brush off and responded, "How about I'll come see you at the office next week and see how things are going?"

Andrew thought he really didn't need her at the company. He had enough to do with running the business by himself now that Sam was gone.

"I'll call you and we can take it from there."

"Fine."

Katherine left things the way they were at her place and prepared for Charles. A few minutes after the Andrew call the doorbell rang. Charles was there. Katherine answered it and greeted Charles with a big kiss. Charles had brought a bottle of wine with him and he enthusiastically returned her embrace. Katherine dressed in workout pants and a silk top closed the door behind them. She asked Charles to open the wine and said dinner would be served shortly. The two ate Chicken Marsala, green beans, rice and a salad while talking about Katherine's research. After cleaning up the table, she asked CC to join her in the living room.

CC sat at one end of the couch looking at the crackling fire in the gas fireplace sipping his wine when Katherine joined him. She took his glass and put it on the table and said, "I'm all yours."

CC said, "Why don't we adjourn to your bedroom?"

"I was hoping you would say that."

In the bedroom, CC helped her with her top. As he was undoing her bra he couldn't help notice she was bulging out of it on all sides. He said, "Katherine, you are definitely growing out of this one. You'll need to get into those new ones right away."

"How did you know I ordered new bras from Victoria's Secret?"

"I didn't say you ordered one from Victoria's Secret. But just looking at you I can see you need to get a bigger bra."

"This is one of the benefits of pregnancy. Do you like them?"

"I liked them before."

"Well, take advantage of it now, they don't last forever. And I have already ordered a new bra, thank you."

"And isn't Victoria's Secret where you get them?"

"It is."

CC added, "I just figured that was where you get them. That seems to be the most popular place these days selling those kinds of things."

Katherine accepted his explanation without any further questioning. After all, she had other things on her mind.

As CC looked at Katherine's body, he thought he was starting to see other signs of her pregnancy. He thought better about saying anything to her about it but thought he was going to have to curtail these kinds of visits in the near future.

They made passionate love for the next hour. Katherine had her desires fulfilled and CC got a little extra from a target. He was starting to like the way things were working out. When finished, CC got dressed and told Katherine he enjoyed his evening. Katherine smiled and said, "I'm glad you were able to come on short notice."

"I could get used to this kind of consulting."

"Well, I do have needs."

"There will be no bill for my services tonight."

"That's awful sweet of you Charles."

Turning to a serious note she said, "Charles, I'm getting a new computer next week and I have made an appointment with the local computer store to transfer all of my data to the new computer from the old one. When I get the new machine home, will you come over and help me with a few things?"

Charles thought about it for a minute and then responded, "Sure. Let me know when you are ready and I'll come over."

"I'll call."

After he had left, she wondered how he knew of her Victoria's Secret purchase and how he knew about the Franklin Templeton investment. She was sure she had not told him about that either.

On his way home, CC thought about the new computer. Then his enthusiasm waned when he thought the computer technicians might discover PCTrackR and ask Katherine about it. He let it go and figured he would deal with that problem if it arose. Most of those computer techies are hacks and just do blind copies from one hard drive to the other. In any event, he would bring his PCTrackR CD with him on his next visit to Katherine's house and install it on her new computer so his plan would not be disrupted.

Chapter 7

The next morning, CC went through his regular routine. The only thing he did for the first time, however, was log in to his Cayman Islands bank account. When the screen returned he clicked on the account balance tab. The balance displayed one hundred fifty dollars. The actions he had initiated the day before against Sharon Kelly had not been completely processed yet.

CC then opened his summary spreadsheet and looked at the entries under the 'Kelly' column, making updates where necessary:

Prudential	$2,000,000
Rockland Trust	$2,000,000 - $1,500,00
Seminole Bank	new $4,500.00

The transfer he had initiated from the Rockland Trust account totaled one million five hundred thousand dollars.

CC didn't have any remorse for Sharon Kelly. After all, she was the person who had injured him and she had no interest in making him whole. Her whole attitude was her insurance company should take care of the matter. He wondered if he shouldn't just take all of her money.

He took a deep breath, composed himself and reminded himself his plan would work if he just stuck to it. The fact Sharon Kelly was setting up new bank accounts in a new location should work right into his plan as far as raising suspicion. He decided to inquire into Sharon Kelly's

Rockland Trust account and see if that side of the transaction had taken place or not.

CC brought up the website www.rocklandtrust.com. He selected the login tab and entered SKELLY and a password of HGSK0921. The screen returned indicated the current account balance was just over five hundred thousand dollars. CC next selected the history tab. He entered a date range for the past week and pressed the enter key. The screen displayed a pending entry showing a fund transfer of one and a half million dollars the day before. The transfer to field had been masked out with asterisks except for the last four digits. They showed the numbers 2463. CC knew these numbers by heart. They were the last four numbers of his Cayman Islands Bank account. He'd check again tomorrow to see if the transaction completed.

CC continued to look at his files. He checked Google for anything new about the Peter Lee lawsuit. Nothing new. He went to the county court website and checked the status of the lawsuit. The site indicated the suit was currently scheduled on the trial docket for the next day. CC thought, "If she wins this suit, he could go after millions very soon. What if she settles?"

Little did CC know Theresa Lee's attorney had been holding settlement discussions with the insurance company of the person involved in the accident that had killed her husband. The insurance company had proposed a settlement of five million dollars. Mr. Lombard, Theresa's attorney, had countered with nine million. The two sides had negotiated for hours and finally settled on nine million dollars.

Not finding any new news about the Peter Lee suit, CC turned his attention to the Sterns file. He sat back and reflected on all that had happened with Katherine. He had not intended on getting so involved with a target. He pictured Katherine in a few different settings. First, it was the funeral home the day of Sam's funeral. Then he recalled her at his wake. Then he thought about his first time in her house, how

Andrew had enabled him to activate his plan. Then he thought about the couple of times he had been intimate with Katherine. She was a beautiful woman who had wonderful talents in bed. He wondered if he could go through with his plan to steal from her. For a moment, he thought he might even have a future with her.

While he sat there at his desk, his arm had started to hurt where it had been broken in the auto accident. The pain brought him back to reality and he refocused on his initial plan. He would have no long-term future with Katherine Sterns.

The next day, he checked his Cayman Islands bank account. His account showed a balance of $1,500,150. The funds showed up. CC let out an enthusiastic whoop.

He logged into the Internet e-mail site as Sharon Kelly. He entered a command that would activate as soon as the e-mail was opened. The activation command worked similar to "Adware" that has plagued the Internet in recent years. It was kind of like a one time virus. He modified the sender field to look like it was coming from Customer Support at the Seminole Bank. That way, Sharon Kelly would probably not be very concerned with the e-mail. Under the subject field, he entered the words New Account Setup. In the text section of the e-mail, he entered the following: "Your new account is in the process of being updated. It may take up to three business days to fully activate the account features. If you have any questions, please contact your customer service representative at your local bank branch."

CC thought the e-mail would do two things. First, it would activate the command to erase PCTrackR from the Kelly computer. Second, it would buy time for the transaction to clear before Sharon Kelly might get concerned. CC was very happy with himself. His plan had worked. He had netted one and a half million dollars from Sharon Kelly. Out loud he said, "Ms. Kelly, I accept your settlement."

Now he would have enough money to pay his bills and feel compensated for Ms. Kelly's actions.

CC picked up the telephone and called his attorney representing him in the Kelly matter. He instructed his attorney to take the settlement offered by Sharon Kelly's insurance company if it was still on the table. His attorney said he was convinced he could get him quite a bit more if CC would just be patient. But CC knew a third would have to go to the attorney and it would take a long time. He didn't want things involving Sharon Kelly to go on any longer.

He said, "No, I need the money now. I have medical bills that exceed two hundred thousand dollars and they need to be paid. I'll take what I can get and move on."

The attorney said, "Ok, I'll get back to you."

Next he went to the county court website and entered Peter Lee into the search tab. A new entry was returned in the response indicated the sides had reached settlement but the terms were not being disclosed to the public. CC thought, "That's all right, I'll find out soon enough."

When CC got around to reading the newspaper for the day, one of the obituaries on page six caught his attention. It read:

William L. Denton, 48

Decorated Navy Pilot, Owner of Local Business Dies

Dennis, MA – William L. Denton, 48, of Dennis, died unexpectedly on Wednesday morning.

Bill was the owner of the Denton Computer Systems, formerly Cape Computer Systems, on Route 132, in Hyannis. Bill and his family have owned the business since 1990 and recently began providing computer services for a number of large Boston Companies as part of business expansion.

Bill and his wife, Mary (Winters) Denton, were happily married for more than 21 years. He was also survived by his mother, Miriam (Stiles) Denton of Dennis, and his sister, Helen Kroll of Athol as well as many loving nieces, nephews and cousins.

Bill and his family moved to Dennis in 1970 and Bill attended Dennis-Yarmouth Regional High School, graduating with the class of 1978. From high school, Bill went directly into the Navy, serving his country from 1979 until 1983. During that time, he was stationed on the battleship USS New Jersey in the Mediterranean. He received the national Defense Service Medal and a Navy Unit Commendation Ribbon.

Following his service in the Navy, Bill worked in the construction industry utilizing new technologies until 1986 where Cape Computer Systems employed him. In 1990, Bill along with other family members purchased the company and renamed it Denton Computer Systems.

During Bill's leisure time, he enjoyed playing golf, the beach and traveling. His lasting legacy will be all the help and counsel he offered to his family and his legion of friends. He will always be remembered for his unique stories, his jokes and his fabulous laugh.

Friends and relatives are invited to call at the Hallett Funeral Home, 273 Station Ave. South Yarmouth, on Sunday from 2 to 6 p.m. A funeral Mass will be held on Monday at 10 a.m. in St. Pius X Church, Station Avenue, South Yarmouth. Burial will be in Oak Ridge Cemetery, South Dennis.

In lieu of flowers, donations in Bill's memory may be made to the Dennis Rescue Squad, 883 Main St., West Dennis, MA 02670, or visit the Hennessey Funeral Home website at www.Hennesseyfuneralhome.com.

CC thought the obituary looked like it might be worth pursuing: a young man, probably a young wife, and no kids. He would go to the funeral home on Sunday and check things out.

Later that day, Sharon Kelly turned her PC on and logged into her e-mail account. When she opened the e-mail from Seminole Bank, she didn't think much about it. To her, it looked like everything was in order. The e-mail said it was confirming her new account setup and indicated everything should be set in a few days. When she selected the delete key, it took a bit longer for the e-mail to be deleted than usual. Sharon Kelly didn't pay much attention to the fact the activity lights on her computer were flashing intensely. Her PC was just carrying out the commands CC had preprogrammed in erasing all traces of the PCTrackR program. After about ten seconds, she was prompted to the next e-mail. Sharon Kelly selected the next e-mail and continued on with her maintenance totally unaware of what had taken place.

On Sunday, CC dressed in a dark gray suit (his "wake" suit), with his white oxford and pale blue tie, and went to the Hallett Funeral home just before two in the afternoon. When he got there, the parking lot was about half full. CC estimated there were about fifty people already in line to pay their last respects to William Denton. Using the routine he had already employed, CC stood at the back of the room for a few minutes. An elder gentleman approached him and said, "I'm Henry Denton, Bill's uncle."

CC said, "My name is Charles Chamberlin."

Henry looking at the open casket at the front of the room said, "That was such a surprise Bill dying so suddenly."

"Yes it was. I was only talking with Bill last week about some computer stuff. I can't believe he is gone."

"So you are in the computer business also?"

"Yes, my company does business consulting. Most of my clients are business owners."

Henry then said, "Did you do any work with Bill's wife Mary?"

"No, Bill was my only contact."

70

"That's funny, Mary had said Bill was only interested in the technical side of the business. She handled all of the Marketing and Administrative needs of the company."

"That's true. Bill focused on the technology stuff. I do technical consulting to businesses. Internet stuff." Henry nodded.

At that, CC started to move in the direction of the receiving line. He didn't want to talk to this Henry Denton any further.

Henry said as CC was turning away, "Well, nice to meet you Mr. Chamberlin."

CC didn't say anything.

CC went into the hallway towards the receiving line but kept walking right to the main door. He opened it and left. Something just didn't fit with the conversation CC had with Uncle Henry. He decided not to pursue Mary Denton as a target.

As CC walked away, he thought about the conversation he had just had with Uncle Henry. He wasn't sure why he had deviated from his already practiced script of being a financial consultant. Recanting the maneuvering he did on his feet with Uncle Henry, he realized he could probably have talked his way around the information Uncle Henry presented and thought he might have been able to convince Uncle Henry Bill Denton had intended on introducing him to his wife in the near future. He considered he might have been trapping himself by trying to adapt to the situation. In the future, he decided he would stick to his planned script about his role with the deceased, and perhaps a little more research into the company the deceased worked for would help.

CC got into his car and left. Even though Mary Denton might have represented a viable target, CC thought he had fumbled the situation sufficiently that he was uncomfortable pursuing it any further. There would be other targets.

Chapter 8

After the last experience CC had at the Hallett Funeral Home, he decided he would need to be more careful about learning more about his targets. The fact a relative of a deceased almost tripped up his approach had made him nervous. He had been fortunate enough to think quickly about a plausible response to Uncle Henry that got him out without being discovered. He vowed to be more careful with his questions and responses, and more prepared going in, in the future.

Over the next week, he went through his regular routine each morning looking for new target prospects. But as had happened in past days, most of the people dying were over age sixty and didn't meet his criteria. Too bad for him, but not for them, he guessed. He had one success under his belt with Sharon Kelly and had two more in the works with Katherine Sterns and Theresa Lee. Both had been successfully "pre-qualified" and had sufficient assets to make the pursuit worthwhile. CC had gathered ample data on each target where he felt comfortable his odds for success were high. The Katherine Sterns opportunity could be exercised at any time but CC had the extra benefit of sex made it worth dragging out for another month or two. He reasoned Katherine's pregnancy would become an issue after her fourth month, and that was fast approaching. If Katherine weren't pregnant, he might put things off indefinitely. She was just so darn good, and easy.

The Theresa Lee situation required more patience, however. He figured he would wait until the lawsuit disposition was better known before making a move on that target. There was just too much potential on the table to do anything hastily or prematurely. Moving too quickly, he could get a million, but the figures being tossed around in the lawsuit would be five or ten times what she currently had. He would wait. Why not?

A few days later he came across another potential target while reading the papers. Joseph C. Davis had passed away. From a Google search CC had done, Mr. Davis had been a doctor and his practice seemed to be thriving at the time of his death.

The obituary read:

Dr. Joseph C. Davis, 50

Dr. Joseph C. Davis, 50, of Mashpee, MA died Wednesday at the Hospice Care Center in Braintree, MA. Dr. Davis was a well-respected senior doctor at the facility.

He was born March 7, 1958 in Ancon, Canal Zone, Panama, the son of the late Gene and Mary (Cathert) Davis.

He is survived by his wife Angela (Somers) Davis, of Mashpee, MA, daughter Kimberly (Davis) Kohl and Michael Kohl of Rockland, MA; sisters, Mary (Davis) McKinney of New Bedford, MA and Joan (Davis) Little of Somerset, MA.

As was his nature, Dr. Davis donated his body to the Life Legacy Foundation so others may learn.

Memorial services will be held 11 a.m. Saturday at Chapman Cole & Gleason Funeral Home, 74 Algonquin Ave, Mashpee, MA.

In lieu of flowers, memorials may be made to your local hospice or to Dr. Davis's Hospice Care Center.

"This MD must have assets" CC thought. Even though there wasn't going to be a traditional funeral, he thought a trip to the funeral home just might prove valuable. And since the service was going to be held on a Saturday, he could, as always, make the trip to Mashpee and still do what he normally would on a Saturday.

On Saturday morning, CC dressed in a dark colored suit acceptable for such a service: charcoal gray with white shirt and pink/gray plaid tie. It would take him about thirty-five minutes to reach his destination so he decided to leave his place at around ten fifteen in the morning. The trip down Route 6 was un-eventful, unusual for a Saturday, but he arrived at the funeral home just before eleven. Perfectly acceptable for someone who wasn't a family member; actually, it was perfect for someone who wasn't anyone.

There were about thirty people milling around outside the funeral home talking as he approached. Heading to the main door, he could see the main service room was already full. CC decided to go back outside and start from there for his fact-finding mission. As he exited the building, a well-dressed, middle-aged woman approached him. She was about 5' tall and 50 years old, tops. But with the four-inch stilettos and bright yellow belt, she looked every inch a cougar. She said to him, "Kind of crowded in there isn't it?"

CC said, "Sure is. I didn't think it would be this crowded."

The lady extending her hand said, "I'm Kimberly Kohl. Joe was my brother."
Grasping her hand, CC said, "Charles Chamberlin. I'm very sorry for your loss. Joe was a great guy."
"Did you know my brother well?"
"I knew him through my business."
"What is it you do Mr. Chamberlin?"

"I'm a financial consultant. It sounds cold, but for me, my clients were my friends first, my clients second."

"You must be one of those guys Joe always talked about. He told everyone in the family he was making tons of money thanks to the good advice he had been getting."

"Well, I don't know about that. I did the best I could for my friends."

"That's ok. I understand. Are you here to speak with Angela?"

CC thought to himself, "Who the hec is Angela? Wife? Sister? Mother? No time to think. Just answer". "No, I'm just here to pay my respects to a friend."

"That's probably just as well. Because I don't think Joe left her anything, and as his financial advisor, she probably wouldn't be happy to see you."

"What do you mean?"

Kimberly moved closer to CC and said in a hushed tone, "Joe told me just last week he had changed his will, leaving everything to the place he worked. He said he knew about Angela's previous indiscretions and she would be left out in the cold if anything ever happened to him. And who would have known, this week he died."

"I don't know anything about that stuff but if he was still married, the widow could probably take court action to have the changes to the will thrown out. A lot of times, when someone dies within even one year of a change, the widow can claim competency in voiding the changes. "

"Well, if the Bitch was cheating on him, then she doesn't deserve a thing."

"You know for a fact she was?"

"Joe was a doctor. He was proud of his profession, he was proud of his family, and of his family name. He wouldn't make an accusation unless he thought there was something behind it."

"You may be right. But just the same, my experience has told me recent changes to a will can be difficult to uphold."

"Well, well, well. Mr. Chamberlin, here she comes now. You be the judge."

Angela Davis came out of the building with a cigarette in hand. She was a good-looking woman, at first glance. CC estimated she was in her mid-forties, highlighted blond shoulder length hair over a very nice figure. They do say forty is the new thirty, and CC couldn't argue that point. She wore a very classic black pencil skirt, with a lavender cashmere sweater set. The one-carat diamond studs were the perfect match. Angela came right up to CC and Kimberly "Do either of you have a match?"

"Not for you, Bitch." Kimberly nastily said. She turned and walked away, leaving CC alone with Angela.

CC reached into his jacket pocket and produced a pack of matches. He took one out and hit the strike pad. Angela leaned in and lit her cigarette. She said, "Thank you. I'm Angela, the grieving widow."

CC extended his hand and said, "Charles Chamberlin."

"So, how did you know my husband?"

"Through my business."

"And what business is that?"

"I'm a consultant. I provide financial advice and planning to my clients."

"Joe talked a lot about you guys. He said you and the likes of you are why I am where I am today."

CC responded with, "On the contrary, you are where you are today because your husband was successful."

"Oh, he was that. That place made him a lot of money and he made a lot more money by investing it."

"Well, isn't that what financial consultants are supposed to do?"

Angela said, "I guess so."

"Do you have a financial consultant?"

"You don't waste any time, do you?"

"I don't mean it like that. I was just inquiring if you are going it alone or if you have someone you are already working with."

"I left all that stuff to Joe but now that he is gone I guess I'll have to learn about it."

"That would be a wise move."

Angela started to walk a few paces down the walk away from CC when she turned and said to him, "Walk with me for a few minutes if you would."

CC said, "Sure."

As they walked, Angela told him she really didn't have a clue about where to start. She knew they had money but didn't know where it was, how much was there or even how to get at it. She told CC she had her charge cards and checking account. Once a month she would sit with Joe and give him a breakdown of her spending for the month. Then Joe would reconcile the accounts with his accountant.

CC said, "You will have to get involved with all of your accounts and start doing the reconciliation yourself."

Angela said, "Why can't I just deal with the accountant and let him take care of it."

"You could do that, but don't you want to know where things stand?"

"I'll ask the accountant that right up front."

"It sounds like Dr. Davis liked to do the investing himself. If that's true, the accountant probably only deals with the reconciliation end of things. You'll have to take over what Dr. Davis was doing yourself."

"Isn't that the kind of thing you do?"

"I provide financial consultation. I am not a broker."

Angela said, "But can't you take care of those kinds of things."

CC said, "Well, yes. But do you really want someone else handling all of the details?"

Angela said, "My skills are not on Wall street or in the Board Room. I do my best work in the Bed Room."

They had reached the corner of the walk and kept walking around the bend out of sight of the rest of the people. Angela said, "You are an attractive man Mr. Chamberlin. Maybe we could work something out where you handle my assets and I handle yours."

CC was kind of taken by surprise with the comments. He stopped walking and turned towards her. She put her hand just below his belt buckle and said, "Know what I mean?"

CC said, "I think I do."

"Come to my house after the service and we can discuss my proposition. Do you know where I live?"

CC had done his homework and responded with, "That's down on Shore Drive isn't it?"

She started walking back to the entrance and turned and said, "See you there say around four o'clock."

"See you then."

CC followed Angela back into the Funeral Home. She went to the front of the room and sat next to the picture of Dr. Davis. After a few minutes, a minister came to the front of the room and began the service. CC was amazed Angela Davis didn't even shed a tear during the service. When the minister was done, a procession line proceeded by Angela Davis and the other family members expressing their sorrow. CC was near the end of the line. When he approached Angela Davis, she merely shook his hand and said thanks for coming.

CC exited the funeral home, got into his car and left. He stopped at a restaurant and got a sandwich to eat. While eating he thought about how the day had gone so far and about Angela Davis. She was very attractive and she had given him the in that he needed to get inside her home. He decided he would finish his lunch and then go to Shore Drive.

Arriving at the Davis residence, CC couldn't help but be impressed with the size and quality of homes in the neighborhood. Shore Drive homes had to be valued in the millions. When he reached the Davis residence, he stopped at the driveway entrance and marveled at the size of the property. The driveway entrance had huge pillars with lanterns on top. Wrought Iron fencing surrounded the property. CC guessed the house must have twenty rooms in it based on its size. As he pulled in to the circle driveway at the front door, he thought it odd the only other car there was a new Mercedes SL 500. Where was everyone?

CC rang the bell. Angela came to the door. She had changed into comfort clothing. She had on tight pants and a loose sheer top that revealed quite a bit of cleavage. She greeted CC with, "So nice of you to come here Mr. Chamberlin."

"Please, call me Charles."

"Charles it is."

As they entered a foyer, Angela said, "Please join me in the study. It used to be Joe's home office. But I am now calling it the study. Can I get you a drink?"

"What are you having?"

"Martini, very dry."

"That would be fine with me."

"Then make yourself comfortable and I'll get the drinks."

As CC entered the office, he took note there was a computer on the credenza behind the desk and it was turned on. There were filing cabinets along one wall with a couch angled so as to be able to look out the windows and the desk at the same time. The desk was centered in the room and looked out on Nantucket Sound through large glass sliding windows that opened on to a large deck. The wall to his left was decorated with many certificates and awards along with pictures of the Doctor with notable celebrities. He walked over to the desk and sat down. He looked at the computer and clicked the mouse. The screen changed from screen-saver mode to active mode displaying a host of icons many of which meant nothing to CC. He did recognize a few, one for a bank and two for investment houses.

When Angela came into the room she asked CC to sit with her on the couch. Sipping their drinks, Angela said, "Charles, I don't know much about finance issues and the like. I assume you are one of the advisors Joe had been working with so you already know more about my situation than I do. I'd like to work something out with you whereby you help me with my assets and I promise to share some of my assets with you."

"Well, what would you like me to look at first?"

Angela pulled her blouse over her head revealing full striking firm breasts. She said, "This will be a good start."

"I don't think that's what I had in mind."

"As I said, you take care of my assets and I'll share some of my assets with you."

She rose and removed her pants leaving her totally naked. CC just looked in astonishment at this beautiful body. Angela took the drink out of CC's hands and put it on the table. Before he could say anything, she had him. Her tongue was electric. Within minutes she brought him right where she wanted him.

CC quickly looked out the window to see if anyone could see in from the outside. He didn't see anything that would cause him alarm so he looked back at her.

Angela said, "Just sit back and enjoy the moment."

At that, CC sat back as far as he could on the couch. Angela came up and straddled him. She moved back and forth for a few minutes then let out a loud "Yes."

At that moment, CC reached orgasm. Angela kept going and reached orgasm a second and third time. Finally, CC was spent.

When done, Angela said, "Now that was the beginning of a promising future."

"This isn't how I usually start new clients off."

Angela came back with, "I'm sure it isn't. But I just wanted to get my point across to you right up front."

"You did that.

As CC was getting dressed, he said, "On the serious side, Kimberly was telling me at the funeral home Dr. Davis recently had his will changed."

"Is that so. I know nothing about it."

"Well, I'd advise you to find out about it because I understand he left everything he had to the institution."

"I'll look into it. Did she say anything else?"

"Nothing worth repeating."

"Joe's siblings didn't like me. They think I am a gold digger."

"Did you and Dr. Davis have a pre-nuptial agreement?"

"I don't think so. But what would I know. Joe had me signing papers all the time. I guess anything is possible."

"I'd get it checked out right away if I were you. You might end up losing everything."

CC had put on his shirt and buttoned it. Angela still naked reached down and picked up his underwear. She handed them to CC. As he put them on, she took a hold of him and said, "I'll be seeing you again."

Then CC put on his pants and said, "You should do research through an attorney just to be on the safe side. I'm sure you wouldn't like ending up broke."

"Could that actually happen?"

"Sure could. Especially if papers exist."

"Now you are making me nervous."

"Why don't you look into it and give me a call in a few days. Then I'll come by and see where we go from there."

"Ok. I'll see what I can find out. How about next Wednesday?"

"Wednesday it is unless I hear otherwise."

Angela walked him to the door and said goodbye.

She stood there in the open doorway totally naked and waved goodbye to him.

As CC was driving away in his car he thought, "What am I getting myself into?"

Chapter 9

Every day, CC would log on to his computer to see if there were any incoming mails from any of his targets. On this particular day, he had e-mails from KSTERNS, PLEE and a few junk mails. To his satisfaction, there was no mail from SKELLY. He felt confident the destruct command had done its job and erased all traces of the software he had installed on Sharon Kelly's computer.

CC clicked on the KSTERNS e-mail. The subject field indicated Strokes Included. CC selected the attachments tab and double-clicked on the file. When prompted, he selected the save tab and indicated the file should be saved with the name KS Strokes Three. When the file was downloaded, he selected the open tab.

The first entry was to Dotty Masters. CC surmised Dotty was an old childhood friend of Katherine's based on previous e-mail content. In this e-mail, Katherine was telling her friend Dotty about comparisons between Andrew and Charles. She described both Andrew and Charles to Dotty. She said Andrew was younger and more athletic than Charles but Charles was the more polished of the two. She talked about their lovemaking and stamina. She had indicated Andrew was bigger, in fact the biggest she had ever had but Charles was the better lover. She said Charles seemed to be able to hold her spellbound during their lovemaking. He had the knack for knowing what to do, where to touch her and what to say at exactly the right time. She indicated in the e-mail she was having second thoughts about Andrew with the business involvement but she would go all out for Charles.

Then, Charles saw something in the keystrokes file that caught him by surprise. Katherine revealed to Dotty the child she was carrying was not by her deceased husband and it wasn't Andrew's either. Charles was afraid his name would come up next but the next sentence in the e-mail identified Tom Bowman as the father. Charles knew Tom Bowman was the other man that was with her husband when he died on the ice-flow. Charles wondered if the death had been an accident or not. He thought, "Did Tom Bowman know she was carrying his child? And if so, did he kill Sam Sterns?"

CC wasn't sure if he would do anything with the information. For the time being, he decided to just put it in the back of his mind and deal with it at a later point in time.

As the e-mail went on, Katherine told her friend Dotty she enjoyed making love to Charles and she would have more to say in a few weeks. The next entry in the keystrokes file CC could see where Katherine had gone to the web site www.ingdirect.com. Again, she logged in as KSTERNS and entered KS812 as her password. CC could see where she had selected the transfer funds function and she specified one million dollars to be transferred to her Vanguard account. He didn't know in what mutual funds the money was going to be invested in but that didn't bother him as he had already obtained the account information for her Vanguard account.

CC opened up his spreadsheet file containing the detail information regarding his targets and updated the Sterns balances. In doing so, he looked at the balances and thought again about the Sterns and Dunn accounts. CC thought going after the business accounts when the time came to implement his plan might present more problems than he wanted to tackle. First, he figured business accounts were probably being monitored daily by the finance department at a company plus a business would probably be very aggressive in investigating a theft. Individuals might become aggressive as well, but CC thought some of the individuals might feel some amount of embarrassment at first or they might drag their feet in pursuing the matter.

Curiosity got the best of him and he went to the Sterns and Dunn website and logged in. He entered SADFIN and a password of ASST4US. When he got there, he selected the finance tab and viewed the information. At this time, the account had just over one point eight million dollars on hand. He thought about it and recalled a few weeks ago the amount on hand was two point seven million dollars. Going after the business account would present too much of a risk so he decided to leave Sterns and Dunn alone for the time being. He decided he would focus on two million from the Sterns' Vanguard account. He couldn't see where the nine hundred thousand dollars had gone from the business account since the last time he had checked. He thought if the funds were being put aside in a rainy day fund, then that he might go after.

There were no more entries in the attachment that were of any interest to CC so he closed the file, got out of the e-mail and deleted it from his in-basket.

Next, he selected the e-mail from PLEE. It too had Strokes Included in the subject line. CC went through the process again of downloading the attachment and saving it. He gave the attachment file the name TL Strokes Three file. Once downloaded, he selected the open tab and started to peruse the file.

He could see where Theresa had gone to the TRowePrice website. It looked like she had been reviewing the account balances as only a few keystrokes appeared. Her next entry had been to her Dreyfus account. Again, it looked like she was checking balances. The next entry was directed at Sovereign Bank and it too only had a few keystrokes captured. It looked to CC like Theresa was reviewing her account balances for some reason.

The next entry was to her attorney. It was an e-mail indicating she would accept the nine million dollar settlement in the lawsuit of which she would get six million plus a return for the advances she had paid the legal firm. The quasi-contingency agreement required her to front the expenses of the legal firm with a provision of getting the advances back should the case be settled in her favor. In the e-mail, she indicated she would like to have the proceeds sent electronically to her Sovereign Bank account. The e-mail identified a bank account where the funds should be deposited. Theresa also indicated she would send a final payment for services to the law firm once she received the final invoice.

The last keystrokes in the file were to the insurance company that had insured Peter's life. In the e-mail, Theresa was requesting details regarding when and how the one million five hundred thousand dollar insurance proceeds would be paid. She had asked them to get back to her by the end of the week with answers to her questions.

There was no other information in the file that meant anything to CC so he closed the file and then deleted the e-mail on his way out.

When CC returned to his browser, he decided to see what the balances were in Theresa's accounts. First, he went to the www.troweprice.com website. He selected the LOGIN tab. When prompted, he entered Theresa's login information. He wrote down the balance. CC went to the other sites Theresa had visited and wrote down the balances of each as they appeared on his screen.

Finished with the Lee Target, CC sat back and thought about what the target could yield. CC didn't think of himself as a greedy person and had already decided he would leave each of the widows with something. The Peter Lee Suit settled for nine million, a little over six to her, and a little under three million to the attorney. CC will take five million of the lawsuit money. CC opened up his target spreadsheet and updated the PLEE information. Looking at the tally, the insurance money of a million and a half was still in consideration. He decided to make that decision at a later point in time.

Closing the spreadsheet, CC thought about the Denton target. The situation bothered him. He needed to be more cautious. Maybe he was getting a little sloppy. Maybe he was getting a little cocky. He never installed anything there so there was no reason to worry. But he did promise himself to be more cautious in the future.

As CC was wrapping up his e-mail session, his phone rang. It was Angela Davis.

"Charles, this is Angela Davis. Are you free for lunch today?"

"Why yes I am. Did you resolve the pre-nuptial situation?"

Angela in a quiet tone said, "Kind of. That's one of the things I would like to speak with you about?"

"Where would you like to meet?"

"Why don't you come by my place at eleven thirty and we can go from there."

"I'll see you then."

CC wrapped up his computer work and turned the computer off. He went into his bedroom and took out casual clothing for the day. He decided on a pair of Chino slacks and a light blue-striped polo. He selected a pair of brown loafers and dark brown socks. Then he went into the bathroom, turned on the shower and got ready for the day.

At eleven thirty, CC pulled into the driveway on Shore Drive at the Davis residence. He rang the bell and was greeted by Angela. She was dressed in slacks and a plain white tight blouse. CC could see the silhouette of her breasts through the blouse.

"Charles, nice of you to come, please come in."

"So Angela, what have you found out?"

Angela said, "I'm having a cocktail. Will you join me?"

CC responded, "It's kind of early in the day but certainly I'll join you."

Angela made and poured the cocktails. As the two took a sip, Angela said, "I have a copy of a pre-nuptial agreement here on the table. I didn't even know I had signed this thing. But it has both my signature and my former husbands signature on it and it had been witnessed."

"Do you remember signing it and if it was witnessed in your presence?"

"The date indicated it was signed over a year ago. And to tell you the truth, I don't remember signing it. But that's my signature."

CC then said, "Well, I don't know what it stipulates but if you don't like what it contains, then you will have to go to court to challenge it."

"I have read it and there are conditional things in the agreement that would leave his entire estate to the institute."

"What kind of provisional things?"

"Well, it looks like my husband was suspicious of me and he had a clause in the agreement stating if infidelity on my part could be proven while we were married, then all of his estate was to go to the institute. If it could not be proven, then half of his estate would go to me and half to the institute."

"And just how do you think this so called infidelity might be proven?"

"I really don't know."

"Well, do you think there is anything to his concerns?"

"Possibly, but I don't think anyone knows about it."

"What about the person or persons you were involved with?"

"I don't think he or should I say they know about the agreement."

"With the kind of money you are talking about, it wouldn't surprise me if the institute went public trying to uncover proof of your husband's concerns."

"Is there anything I could do about that?"

"Sure, if you think the institute is about to go public with anything that might be in that direction, have your attorney threaten them with a slander suit. Most businesses would rather settle quietly than get involved in that kind of action."

"I hope you are right."

"What else did you glean from reading the document?"

"I get to live in this house for one year. The institute would have that year to pursue the infidelity clause. At the end of one year, if nothing can be proven, then title to the house stays with me and I get to keep half of the estate. But if infidelity can be proven according to the terms of the agreement, then everything goes to the institute."

"You mean the house was in his name only?"

"Yes. He had already owned it when I married him."

"This doesn't look good for you."

"I guess not. I asked you to come over here to help me take my mind off of this whole situation."

At that, she put her hand on his pants and said, "Can you stay for a while?"

Charles thought about it and said, "I have other appointments this afternoon so I can only stay for an hour or two."

Angela took off her blouse and said, "That will have to do."

She didn't have a bra on and Charles could see she meant business. Angela undid his belt, unhooked his pants and zipped his fly down. His pants fell to the floor. Angela slid his underwear down. Standing in front of Charles, she reached for him. Charles was already growing.

"Let me help you."

He undid her pants and they dropped to the floor. He slowly slid her thong underwear down her slender legs. Angela stepped out of them. As he rose, she unbuttoned his shirt and removed it. Within a minute, they were both naked standing in the living room.

"Let's go into the bedroom."

Charles followed her. They entered the master bedroom that had a king size canopy bed against the far wall. The room was large and Charles estimated it was twenty-five by thirty feet in size. Off to one side was a sitting room containing a make-up table and shoe closet. Off the other side were two walk-in closets. One contained her clothes and the other was empty. A door on the far side of the room led to an oversize bathroom with a Jacuzzi in it in addition to a walk-in shower was completely glass enclosed.

Angela lay back on the bed and signaled Charles to join her.

They began to make passionate love in the oversized canopy bed. The setting was a first for Charles. As he looked down at Angela, he thought she was very attractive. She didn't hold back. She slid down on him until he was in a sitting position on her mid-section. She took him with both hands and gently stroked him. As he grew harder, he thought she might cause him to climax pre-maturely, especially if she took him orally. But he was able to endure. Charles maneuvered into position and Angela eagerly received him. Charles kissed her passionately and then touched her nipples with his tongue. At the same time, he craftily moved in and out growing even larger. Angela began to breath heavily. Her body became a little clammy. Then all at once, she stiffened and climaxed. Charles increased his pace and penetration and she climaxed again. Then he joined her. After a half-minute or so, Charles lay back spent. Angela mounted him and looked down at him.

"Charles, you are such a good lover. Will I be able to see you again even if I lose all of this?"

CC didn't know what to say next. Out of his mouth came "I'm not here for your money."

"That's good. In the coming months I might not have any."

"With your talents, I'm sure you will end up on top."

Angela looking down at CC said, "Yes, I guess I will."

While they were getting dressed, CC said, "Angela, you will have to pursue the legal route if you don't want to end up broke and starting over."

Angela came back with, "Well, as long as I have you to coach me and console me while I'm going through that process I'll be alright."

CC said, "I think you will always have assets that will interest me. Get with your attorney and see what you can work out. Let me know if and when I can help you."

Angela said, "Thanks. I will."

CC had been thinking to himself the whole thing might be difficult for Angela. On the surface things didn't look good. Especially since she kind of intimated there were other men. Plus, Angela's in-laws didn't like her. If they know about the pre-nuptial agreement Angela will be in for a fight. After sex, Angela had prepared a salad lunch for the two. They sat in her kitchen and ate lunch making small talk. A little after one, CC said, "I'm going to have to be going. I have another appointment at two."

"Well, if it's anything like your eleven thirty, you will be exhausted."

"I don't think I could do that again today. My two o'clock is a regular financial review with a client so I don't think I'll have to out-perform."

"Is that what you call this?"

"Well, this is more than my usual lunch meeting would entail."

"I look forward to our next meeting."

CC heading to the door said, "Call me once you have some information."

"I'll do that."

CC was glad he didn't install anything on her computer. If the situation improves, there will be plenty of time to get PCTrackR installed. For now, he just needed to get out of there.

Getting back to his office, he updated his target spreadsheet file.

CC contemplated his plan. He had already achieved one and a half million dollars and identified a few million more plus two attractive women that are screwing his brains out. His plan seemed to be working just fine. There would be more to come. He had a pretty good take so far and the sex with the beautiful women was something he hadn't counted on. Things were looking very promising.

Chapter 10

CC read the paper obituaries for the next few days. Most were the same as those of the past, older people usually over sixty years old. Then on Thursday, one obituary caught his attention.

William P. Tindle, 32

Welder, resident of Hyannis, leaves family on Cape

Hyannis – William P Tindle, of Hyannis, formerly of Watertown, died on Wednesday, at the Cape Cod Hospital in Hyannis at the age of 32 as a result of an industrial accident.

Mr. Tindle was born in Waltham, and grew up in Watertown. He attended the Minuteman Regional Vocational Tech in Lexington. He was employed as a welder for TrueWeld Industries in Hyannis. He had been a Hyannis resident for the past 8 years.

William was an avid Boston sports fan, especially the Bruins, Patriots and Red Sox. He was a former member of the Ancient Order of Hibernians, Division No. 14 in Watertown.

He was survived by his wife, Carol (Lighter) Tindle, his parents, Michael L. and Patricia (Mann) Tindle of Osterville; his two sisters, Maureen E. Tindle of Watertown and Pamela A. Hamilton and his brother-in-law Steven Hamilton, and his nephew, Kevin Hamilton, all of Watertown. Many aunts, uncles, cousins and friends also loved him.

Funeral from the Doane Beal & Ames Funeral Home at 729 Route 134, South Dennis on Tuesday at 9:30 a.m., followed by a funeral Mass at 10:30 a.m. in the Church of St. Patrick, 212 Main Street, Dennis. Relatives and friends are kindly invited. Visiting hours are Monday from 3 to 7 p.m.

CC could smell it. An industrial accident for a blue-collar worker could be lucrative. That could only mean money and maybe lots of it. CC decided he would check it out on Monday. First, he went to Google and entered William P. Tindle. The first entry that appeared was an article about an industrial accident that happened at the new addition to the Cape Cod Mall on Route 132 in Hyannis. In reading the article he learned William Tindle and his work crew were welding support trusses in an area of the new mall addition when a crane in the outside lot accidentally hit a newly constructed wall collapsing it on three workers who had been welding within the new structure. One man, Mr. Tindle, had died and the other two were in the hospital with severe injuries. The article went on to say the accident was under investigation and there seemed to be an issue with the qualifications of the crane operator.

From CC's perspective, the situation held promise. The only question in his mind was how long it would take for the widow Carol Tindle to collect a handsome payout. CC entered "construction lawsuit settlements" into the search window and took the time to browse the numerous results that were returned. In most cases, payouts due to settlement or successfully winning a lawsuit in similar situations had returned anywhere from nine hundred thousand dollars to over seven million dollars. CC knew lawyers usually take a third so that meant Carol Tindle as a target might be worth six hundred thousand dollars to five million dollars. The upper end would make it worth his time if he could qualify Carol Tindle as a target. On Monday he would take a shot at her.

On Monday morning, CC dressed in a business suit and went to the Funeral Home. Walking up to the door, he was greeted by a gentleman who introduced himself as Mr. Carl Pruit. Carl opened the door for CC and he stepped in. Just inside the door, Carl told CC the wake was rather busy and the receiving line was straight down the hall.

"Looks like quite a few people are here to pay Bill their respects."

"Yes. Bill was in a local union and I think the whole union is in there."

"Dying like that was just such a terrible way to go."

"From what I understand it was instant."

"Thank God for that."

"Did you know him well?"

"Not very well, but he was a client of mine. I'm Charles Chamberlin. It's nice to meet you."

"What is it you do Mr. Chamberlin?"

"I am a financial consultant."

"Bill was a welder. What did he need with a financial consultant?"

"Bill had come into some money along the way and I helped him with it."

"Well, I hope there is enough here for his wife to pursue legal action against all those responsible for Bill's death."

"Most attorneys take cases like that on a contingency basis. I don't think she will have any problems from what I have read."

"Negligence usually pays off real big and from what I gather, there are a number of negligent parties involved in this situation."

"Time will tell."

Carl opened the door again as another person approached and said, "Welcome to Doane Beal & Ames Funeral Home. Are you here for Mr. Tindle?"

The person at the door indicated yes and Carl began to talk to that person. CC turned and proceeded down the hall to the back of the line.

When CC reached the front of the line, he expressed his condolences to Carol Tindle.

He said, "Mrs. Tindle, I'm Charles Chamberlin. I was an acquaintance of your husband. I am so sorry for your loss."

Carol had tears in her eyes and in a shaky voice said, "Thank you for coming."

CC shook her hand and continued on.

CC took a seat near the back of the room. A nice looking lady who looked to be in her twenties took the seat next to him. She was dressed smartly in a dark blue pantsuit with a pink blouse under the jacket. After a few minutes, she introduced herself.

She said, "My name is Susan Tindle. Bill was my uncle."

CC said, "Charles Chamberlin. I was a friend of your uncle."

"That accident was such a tragedy. Uncle Bill was only thirty two years old."

"Were you close to your uncle?"

"Even though he was my uncle, he and I were close in age. Bill's father and my father are brothers but they are almost twenty years apart in age."

"Then that explains why you and your uncle were close in age."

"We were close. We did a lot together. I'll really miss him."

"How is Carol taking all of this?"

"Carol and I are like sisters. I didn't have any brothers and sisters growing up other than Bill and when he married Carol, I got my sister."

"This must be very hard on both of you?"

"It is. I just can't believe he is gone. What will Carol do now?"

"Hopefully someone will provide for Carol for this terrible accident."

Susan said, "Someone will. I know Carol is going to hire a lawyer if she hasn't already and she is very angry about this whole thing."

"Maybe I'll speak with her for a few minutes. I have had some experience with these kinds of things."

"Oh, if you would, that would be very much appreciated."

Susan got up and went to the front of the room. She said something to Carol and came back to the chair next to CC. Sitting down she said, "I mentioned to Carol she should take a few minutes to come and speak with you when she needs to take a break."

"Oh, I don't want to bother her here."

"It would be no bother. Carol is really ticked about what happened."

After about fifteen minutes, Carol came down the aisle and took the seat next to Susan. Susan said, "Carol, do you know Charles?"

Carol said, "No, I'm afraid I don't."

CC extended his hand and said, "Charles Chamberlin."

Susan said, "Charles was a friend of Bill's. He and I have been talking about what happened and Charles said he has had some experience with these kind of things."

Carol looked at Charles and said, "Are you an attorney?"

"No, I'm a financial consultant."

Carol said, "Oh, are you one of the people who helped Bill with his investments?"

It was now or never for CC and he responded, "I provided Bill with some advice."

Carol said, "I know Bill felt very secure with the advice he had been getting. I'm sure he shared that with you."

CC said, "He did."

Carol then said, "What do you think I should do about this accident Mr. Chamberlin?"

"Please call me Charles. And I think you should hire an attorney if you havn't already and pursue action against everyone your counsel thinks is culpable.

96

"I plan on doing just that. In fact, the union has provided me with the names of a few attorneys that specialize in just such matters."

"Then you are already getting sound advice."

"Well, if legal action is resolved in my favor, may I call on you in the future for financial advice?"

"Please do." He produced a business card and said, "Call me anytime. Even if you just want someone to talk to regarding financial matters."

"Thank you. I appreciate that. You'll have to excuse me. It's time I get back to the receiving line."

"I understand and please call."

Carol said, "I will."

When Carol had left, Susan said, "Thank you Charles for providing those comforting words to Carol. This is a terrible time for her and I know she appreciates it."

CC said, "It isn't going to be easy for her over the next few months. But maybe the parties involved will see they can't possibly avoid a settlement and come up with one all on their own."

"Does that happen very often?"

"All the time. The parties involved will assess their exposure and liability. If it doesn't look good for them then they will try to settle. And if they feel they can't win, a proposal will come sooner than later. Their insurance carrier's understand the legal system. They know how expensive it is to defend lawsuits. If they sense a settlement is a cheaper way out than litigation, they will put it on the table."

"Should Carol settle?"

"Depends on what is offered."

"I guess Carol will have a lot to think about."

"She will and she will need to be ready to consider any and all offers put in front of her."

Susan looked at him and said, "Why wouldn't she hold out for the maximum?"

"Because you never know how a case is going to be resolved. Sometimes it's best to take a sure thing than to risk some unforeseen factor arising during trial where one might lose everything."

"I guess."

"I'm not saying Carol should settle. I'm saying she should consider. She needs to weigh the facts and her own situation. Then decide."

"That sounds like good advice. I'll try to help Carol understand those points. Do you think you would be interested in helping her if a settlement were to be proposed?"

"As I said to Carol, I provide financial consulting. Sometimes my work requires me to help clients assess an overall situation and to make a decision that's most appropriate given the circumstances. So yes, I'd probably be able to help. If the situation should arise, I hope Carol will call on me."

"I'll see to it. Thank you Mr. Charles Chamberlin. You've been a big help."

"Your Welcome. Now if you'll excuse me, I have to be leaving."

"Certainly. And I hope we will get a chance to talk again."

"You never know."

At that, he rose and left the funeral home.

Riding home, CC decided he would not go to the funeral. He had laid sufficient seed to pursue Carol Tindle as a target in the near future. He would follow the William Tindle situation in the news and on Google for the next few weeks and see what unfolded.

Chapter 11

CC read the obituaries for the next few days. Nothing seemed to catch his attention even though the newspaper carried on average twelve to fifteen death notices per day. As had been the pattern, most of the obituaries were for people over age sixty and as such, they would be outside the parameters CC had established. CC had confidence in his plans and his criteria. He had already netted a nice sum from his first target and he felt no remorse in having executed a successful plan against her. He still had anger in his mind but even that was starting to temper with all that had been happening to him since embarking on the plan to set himself up for the rest of his life. As he thought about it, he was starting to question his plans especially when it came to the women he had affairs with. He even thought he might change his overall goals and decide to work his newfound successes indefinitely. After all, he now had money, sex with beautiful women and a renewed self-esteem that he could do anything. Things were looking up.

After eight days and not having found another suitable target, CC decided he needed to expand the area he had been watching. He decided to get information from the towns just off Cape Cod and see if there were any acceptable targets in those areas. The first area he selected was Plymouth, MA. He entered it into the Internet search engine. When the response came back, he looked for information on newspapers and in particular obituaries. Once he had access to the information he was looking for, he read through the material looking for targets. Going back for a few days with his search criteria, he spotted a few candidates that looked promising.

One in particular caught his attention.

Stephen R. Watkins
Engineer, Plymouth Research Labs

Plymouth – Stephen R. Watkins of Plymouth, formerly of Walpole, died at his home on Thursday.

Steve was born on August 5, 1965, to Fran Watkins of Brewster and Peter Mark Watkins of North Attleboro. Steve graduated from Xavier Brothers High School in 1983, attended the University of Massachusetts, Dartmouth; received a certificate at RETS in Boston; and pursued a career in electronics as an engineering technician. He worked at Plymouth Research Labs.

Steve loved living near Cape Cod. He was a published photographer and successful inventor. He was the holder of several patents involving Internet Electronic Connection Devices. Steve was a computer wiz who often helped his family and friends with their computer issues.

Steve is survived by his wife of 16 years, Maureen (Dupree) Watkins; his mother, Fran Watkins of Brewster and his father Peter Watkins of North Attleboro.

Visiting hours will be held on Wednesday, from 6 to 8 p.m. at the Coastal Funeral Home, 50 Center Street, Plymouth. A funeral Mass will be held on Thursday at 10 a.m. in St. Josephs Church, 35 Long Lane, Plymouth. Private family burial will follow at a later date.

CC thought, "An inventor who held several patents to Internet technology. Those things must be worth some money or Mr. Watkins might just have licensed those patents to some company". He would have to look into that one and see what his research would find.

He entered Steven Watkins into the Google search engine. To his satisfaction, the search returned page one with twenty-five hits and he could see at the bottom of the screen there were another four pages of listings waiting to be viewed. CC selected each item and read them carefully. Some of the listings were of articles written about Steven Watkins inventions. Some of the listings were disclosures of patient licensing of Mr. Watkins inventions to companies. And one listing was an article from Entrepreneur Magazine about Mr. Watkins. The article about Mr. Watkins intimated Mr. Watkins had become very wealthy as a result of his inventions. CC exclaimed, "Well what do you say my dear Mr. Watkins. Do you have money or what?" CC made plans to attend the wake.

On Wednesday evening, he dressed in a non-descript suit and made the forty-five minute trip from mid-cape to Plymouth arriving at the Coastal Funeral Home around six thirty in the evening. There were only a handful of cars in the parking lot at the Funeral Home. At first, CC thought he might have gotten the date or time wrong. He saw a woman standing on the porch of the Funeral Home so he decided to go up and talk to her. As he approached the porch, he said, "Hello, is this where the wake for Mr. Watkins is being held?"

The lady on the porch said, "Yes it is. The wake is right in that way." And the lady pointed to the door at the end of the porch. CC walked to the end of the porch and opened the door. When he entered, there was a podium with a guest book on it and a box of fact cards at the top of the book. CC took one of the cards and read it. It said Steven Watkins, born August 5, 1965, Husband of Maureen, Engineer and Inventor.

CC signed the guest book and then went into the room that contained the casket. There were eight to ten people in the room standing at the front of the room talking. They turned and looked at CC and one of them said, "Can we help you?"

CC said, "I'm here to pay my respects to Steve."

101

The elderly gentleman came over to CC and said, "I'm Peter Watkins, Steve's father."

"I'm Charles Chamberlin. I did some work for Steve recently. I can't believe he's gone."

"The wake doesn't really start for another half hour, but you are welcome to come in."

CC looked down at his watch and said, "Oh, I thought the wake was from 6 to 8 p.m."

"It is, it's only five thirty right now. We are just getting ready."

CC looked down at his watch again. The hands were both almost straight down. He could see it was only five thirty. He wondered how he could have left home too early. He was starting to make some mistakes and that made him nervous. A rather heavy woman approached Peter and said, "Peter, what is going on?"

"Maureen, this is Mr. Charles Chamberlin. He did some work for Steve in the past and he has come by to pay his respects."

Maureen said, "I don't think I'm ready to talk with anyone just yet. Can you ask him to wait until the wake begins."

CC overheard the whole conversation and stepped up to the two and said, "Mrs. Watkins, I am sorry for your loss and I apologize for arriving early. I'll be on my way and leave you to continue getting ready for what will already be an difficult evening for you."

Maureen said, "Thank you. I appreciate your thoughts."

CC turned and walked away. Mr. Steven Watkins might be worth some money but things were not going smoothly and CC decided to pass on the Watkins target.

Arriving back home around seven o'clock. CC powered up his computer and accessed the Internet. He decided to see if there had been any progress in the Tindle case. One of the listings returned from the search laid out the summary case against the construction firm involved in the accidental death. The lawsuit alleged negligence, misconduct and improper management. The suit was asking for $12 million.

As CC was looking at items returned in the search, he glanced over at his phone and saw the message waiting light was blinking. He picked up the phone and entered his number for messages. When prompted, he entered his security code and selected the message waiting option. There was a voice message from Carol Tindle. He selected the option to hear the message.

"Charles, this is Carol Tindle. The construction company that had been involved in the death of my husband has proposed a settlement. My attorney, Mr. Wesley Donleavy, said they have offered to settle for five million nine hundred thousand dollars. I'd like to meet with you tomorrow so I can hear your opinion of the settlement if you can make it. Please call me anytime."

Charles deleted the message and then called Carol. "Carol, it's Charles Chamberlin. I got your message. I'd be happy to meet with you tomorrow to discuss your situation."
"Oh, thank you Charles. I really appreciate it."
"Where would you like to meet?"
"If you don't mind, could we meet at my house? I have all of the information on my home computer and I'd like to be able to reference it during our meeting."
"That would be fine. What time would you like me there?"
"Can you make it for one in the afternoon?"
"See you at one."

The next day CC dressed in his business attire and left his home about a quarter to one. Promptly at one o'clock CC arrived at the Tindle residence. Carol greeted him at the door and asked him to join her in the home office. Entering the office, CC couldn't help but notice Carol was dressed in a pair of pink Capri slacks and a white short sleeve blouse. Her hair had been pulled back into a ponytail and he thought she looked rather attractive.

Carol greeted him and asked him to follow her into her study. CC saw Carol had everything neat and in order. The large maple desk by the bay window had a file in the center of the desk. The computer on the credenza behind the desk was turned on and displayed a list of files. Two Victorian chairs sat in front of the desk. A TV sat off to one side and was turned on to CNN. On the far wall, CC observed numerous certificates, some in Carol's name, some in her deceased husband's name. CC looked at the Certificates for Bill and commented Bill had served his community admirably over the years. Many of the certificates were in recognition to Bill's service supporting the local Little League and other youth organizations.

Carol said, "Bill was very proud of the service he did for the community and those certificates are just a small reflection of his contributions."

Continuing to look around, CC noticed the wall to his right was lined with three cabinets CC figured contained records and important information.

Carol asked CC to take a seat. She started out the conversation by telling Charles her computer contained a file entry for every date she had to go to court along with files documenting anything and everything she felt pertinent to the case. CC was impressed with her organization skills and attention to detail. Turning back to the desk, Carol opening the file on the desk and said, "Charles, I have here a proposed settlement from the insurance company covering the construction company involved in the accident. They are proposing a five million nine hundred thousand dollars cash settlement to resolve the litigation. What do you think?"

"Carol, that's a nice sum of money. What was it you were asking for?"

"Twelve million."

"Well, the proposal is way short of that number."

"My Attorney came up with the twelve million dollar number. I have no idea of what would be a good number or not."

"I think I can help in that area. We can look to the Internet to get a range of similar settlements that have taken place in the recent past. That should give you a better idea of what to expect."

"You can do that?"

"Sure. Let me sit at your computer for a few minutes and see what I can come up with."

"Can I get you something to drink while you are doing that?"

"Do you have any soft drinks or iced tea?"

"I do. Which would you prefer?"

"An iced tea would be nice."

Carol rose and went off to get drinks. As soon as she left the room, CC took a CD out of his briefcase and put it in the CD drive. He typed the commands to load PCTrackR. In just over a minute the software was installed.

When Carol returned with drinks in hand, CC said, "I have found a number of similar cases that have been settled over the past two years. If you'll come over here where you can see the screen, I'll bring some of them up."

Carol went to a closet and took out a folding chair and brought it behind the desk. She opened it up and placed it next to the chair CC was sitting in.

CC said, "Here is a case involving a shipping company where an innocent person was killed by one of their trucks. The case settled for two million eight hundred fifty thousand dollars."

He clicked a few keys and another case displayed.

Carol was looking at something on the desk. CC lightly touched her hand and then pointed to the screen and said, "Here is another case where a carpenter fell to his death when scaffolding collapsed. Apparently the scaffolding was faulty and the supplier's insurance company ended up settling for four point four million dollars."

She followed along listening to his analysis of the information he had retrieved. He clicked a few more keys and yet another case displayed.

"And here is another situation where a cinderblock wall collapsed at a construction site and two workers were killed. The insurance company representing the cement company ended up settling with one party for six point three million dollars and the other for five point eight million dollars."

Carol reached over and put her hand on CC's shoulder. "It sure looks like there are a number of settlements I would need to reference and get to attorney Donleavy."

"Your attorney will probably have even more cases to reference similar to yours. These are only the ones I found using limited criteria. Just off hand from what I saw, the settlements ranged from a low of nine hundred thousand dollars to a high of seven point two million dollars. I must have read over twenty cases that sound like they had issues similar to your situation."

"Well, what do you think?"

"If it were me, I'd have to know that five point nine million dollars would be the end of it. I mean, if you don't think that's enough, then don't settle. Keep in mind the case could go on for quite a while and the outcome might be something other than what you've been offered. It could be more or it could be less."

"I understand what you are saying. I'm going to have to think about it."

"That's the right way to look at it. Talk to your attorney. Talk to people you trust and then make a decision."

"Thanks, that's good advice. If I do settle, will you be willing to advise me as to what to do with the money?"

"Certainly."

"Well then, I'm going to have to think about it."

"When you are ready to talk again, please call."

"I will. And thank you again Charles for coming over and talking with me about this topic. I know Bill would be pleased I confided in one of his advisors before doing anything."

"I'm sure he would be pleased."

At that, CC gathered up his things.

Carol walked with him to the door and as he was about to leave, she embraced him with a hug. She pressed her body to his holding him close and said, "Thanks."

As he drove home he thought, "She's qualified and PCTrackR is ready and waiting."

Chapter 12

Carol Tindle had made a decision. She would accept the five million nine hundred thousand dollar settlement and thus avoid any further proceedings. She felt good about the decision and decided to call CC and inform him.

"Charles, this is Carol Tindle."

"Carol, have you made a decision?"

"I have. I am going to accept the settlement offer."

"I think that's a wise move. The settlement offer is in line with the research you and I did yesterday and taking it now will avoid any further complications."

"That's what I am thinking as well. I know attorney Donleavy is going to get a third and I'm fine with that."

"I am glad for you that you are able to come to terms with the settlement and put this behind you."

"Me too. This whole process had been difficult for me."

"I can imagine. When do you think the settlement will be finalized?"

"Why do you ask?"

"Well, you'll want to get that kind of money invested pretty quickly. If you do, then you can begin to realize the benefits of the settlement sooner rather than later."

"My attorney said I should get a check in a few days. What do you think I should invest in?"

"Let me do some homework and see what looks most promising. I'm going to Florida for a few days and I'll call you when I get back with my ideas. Will that be alright?"

"Where are you going in Florida?"

"I have rented a place in Key West for a long weekend. I think I need a little break."

"Me too. I could use a rest."

"Why don't you join me? I can't promise anything other than sun, rest and relaxation. Plus, Key West has magnificent sunsets at Mallory Square."

"I don't have any reservations. I don't know."

"Let me check into it and I'll call you back."

"Ok. I could use the rest."

CC got on to a travel website and found the seat next to him on the flight down and back had not been taken. He promptly purchased e-tickets for Carol Tindle and had her assigned to the seat next to him. Next he checked the hotel. There were no rooms available. Fortunately, he had reserved a suite that came with a foldout bed in the living room. He would offer it to Carol and see if she was still interested.

CC printed the confirmation for the e-tickets and exited the site. He called Carol back.

"Carol, I was able to get you seats on the same flights I am taking to Key West. We leave Friday at nine thirty in the morning. I wasn't able to get another room at the Key West Hyatt but I have a suite reserved and it has a pullout bed in addition to a bedroom if you don't mind."

Carol thought for a minute and said, "That would be fine. I think I know you well enough to share a place for a few days."

"Then we are all set. I'll pick you up Friday morning at six thirty. That way we can make T.F. Green airport in Providence in time for our flight."

"Good. I'll see you Friday at six thirty."

Hanging up, Carol thought "I can't believe I'm going to Key West for a long weekend with a man so soon after Bill's death."

Carol Tindle, at thirty-one years old, was five feet nine inches tall around 130 pounds. She had brunette hair and a nice figure. She didn't have any standout features but she was attractive in her own way. She always dressed appropriately and carried herself very well. This trip would be the first adventurous thing she did since she got married to Bill many years ago. Carol had decided she needed to get on with he life and a weekend away in a tropical setting with Charles Chamberlin would be her first adventure.

Carol called her best friend Susan White. She said, "Susan, you'll never guess what I am doing this weekend?"

Susan sensing Carol's excitement said, "Ok, spill the beans."

"I'm going to Key West."

"I think that might be a good idea. You can get some sun and rest and maybe you'll meet a nice guy down there."

"I'm going there with a nice guy."

"Who?"

"You know Charles Chamberlin?"

"Yes, I met him at Bill's wake."

"He was gong to Key West for the weekend and I invited myself along."

"You did. That's so unlike you."

"I know. But I have to get on with my life. He is single and a nice guy. Plus he has been helping me out with a few things and I kind of like him."

"Where will you be staying?"

"Charles has reservations at the Key West Hyatt."

"Are you staying with him in his room?"

"He has a suite and he said I can have the pullout bed."

"How convenient."

"Don't say it like that. The whole thing came about in a harmless manner."

"It might have started out that way but it looks like a steamy weekend to me."

"I'm going for some rest and relaxation. I just need to get away."

"Call me right away when you get home. I want to know all about it."

"Oh, I will. Bye."

CC had some business to take care of before the trip. He had to return a call from Katherine Sterns as she was hounding him to get together. He knew what she wanted. But she was really starting to show the pregnancy now and CC wanted to back out of the relationship. He called Katherine back and said, "Katherine, its Charles."

"Oh Charles, I was trying to get a hold of you."

"I have been tied up with business and didn't get my messages until this morning."

"Have you been out of town?"

"Yes. I'm back for today and then I'm off again on Friday for a weekend business meeting."

"That's too bad. I was hoping you could come and spend the weekend with me. I was looking forward to your companionship."

"I'm afraid I am going to have to pass this weekend. Maybe I can get a night free next week for dinner or something."

"I'm sure I'll be very hungry by then."

"I'll call you as soon as my schedule frees up."

"If you have to."

"It's business, I have to."

When CC hung up the phone, he thought he needed to end the contact with Katherine very soon. She was getting too needy and he didn't want to become any more involved.

He retrieved the next message on his phone. It was from Angela Davis. "Charles, I have news regarding the legal proceedings. The court has ruled my husband's will is valid. It looks like I am going to have to hope no one comes forward with anything that might take away my share. For now, I still have the house. I plan on laying low for the foreseeable future. I'd like to have you come over Saturday to meet with me. Plan on staying overnight. Angela."

CC thought. "I want no part of this." He entered Angela's number and got her voice mail. "Angela, this is Charles Chamberlin. I got your message but unfortunately, I'll be out of town on business for a few days and unable to meet with you. I'll call you when I get back into town."

He would have to think of a way to get Angela Davis out of his life completely.

Next, he brought up Excel and opened his Targets file. He put in a new entry for Carol Tindle. He entered two million dollars in the amount field. His rationale was the attorney got a third, CC would take a third and leave the balance for Carol. He scanned the other entries, one for Katherine Sterns, one for Theresa Lee, the completed entry for Sharon Kelly and the new entry for Carol Tindle. He deleted the Angela Davis entry. In all, the tally looked like it would add up to eleven million five hundred thousand dollars for the targets he was working.

Target	Location	Amount	Take
Kelly	Rockland	$2,000,000	$1,500,000
Sterns	Vanguard	$2,500,000	$2,000,000
	ING	$450,000	
	Franklin	$50,000	
	Sterns	$1,900,000	
	401K	$5,100,000	
Lee	Insurance	$1,500,000	$1,000,000
	Lawsuit	$6,000,000	$5,000,000
Tindle	Lawsuit	$5,900,000	$2,000,000

On Friday morning, CC packed the bags into his vehicle and went to Carol Tindle's house to pick her up. Arriving there, she greeted him at the door. Carol was dressed in white slacks with a silk floral top. She had her hair up in a ponytail and looked like she was heading off to summer camp.

"You look like you are ready for the sun."

"I'm not sure if I'm doing the right thing or not but I'm ready to go."

CC picked up her bags and put them in the car. She locked the door and they left for the airport.

During the flight, they got to know each other better talking about family, likes, dislikes etc. CC liked Carol Tindle. She was very organized and straightforward. She didn't pretend to be someone other than who she was. He

112

found talking to her very easy. At one point, he caught himself starting to tell her about his accident. Fortunately, he stopped before telling too much and changed the subject to something else. Carol told CC she was looking forward to some rest and relaxation in the sun. CC said he would do his best to make sure she got just that.

When they arrived at the Hyatt in Key West, CC registered them under his name. A bellman took the bags and escorted them to the suite. As CC was tipping the bellman, the bellman said, "I hope you and Ms. Chamberlin have a pleasant stay?"

"Thank you, we will."

When the bellman left, Carol said, "You registered us as husband and wife?"

"No, I only registered my name. Hotels don't ask that kind of stuff anymore."

"Oh, that's alright. I don't expect to be needing my name down here anyway."

"Well, neither do I but the reservation was in my name so I just left it at that."

"I think I'm going to put on my suit and go down to the pool."

"I'm going to unpack and then I'll join you."

"Shall I order you a drink for when you get there?"

"I'd like that."

Carol went into the bathroom and put on her bikini. Over it, she put on a robe. When she came out, CC couldn't tell what kind of suit she had on but then again, he wasn't looking either.

"See you at the pool." Then she left the room.

CC unpacked his belongings and got into his suit. Then he went down to the pool as well.

He walked around the pool until he saw her sitting on the far side near the boardwalk overlooking the gulf to the west. As CC reached Carol he said, "Wow, you look great in that suit."

This was the first time he saw Carol in anything other than her fairly simple clothes. She had a very nice body. It was trim and nicely proportioned. She had on a thong bikini that accentuated all of the right things.

Carol looked at CC and said, "I hope you like Mojito's?"

"I can't say I have tried them before but I'm game."

They sat and drank. CC said, "These are good."

"I'm glad you approve."

"What here isn't there to approve of? A beautiful woman, warm sunny weather, a great cocktail and this view?"

Carol looking shyly at CC said, "You are making me blush."

"Carol, you shouldn't blush. I hope you are enjoying this as I am."

"I am."

They sat for two hours and had two more drinks each. Finally, Carol said, "I think I had better head to the room. I don't want to get too sunburned on my first day here."

"Me too. I made dinner reservations for us tonight at a nice restaurant on the water."

"I think I'd like that."

Returning to the room, Carol looked at herself in the mirror. She commented to CC, "Look at this. It looks like I spent a little too much time in the sun."

She undid her suit top to reveal a small white line around her back where the strap had been. As she did, Charles came over to her with a tube of lotion and said, "This will help."

"Can you put some on my back for me?"

"Sure."

At that, Carol dropped the bikini strings and allowed CC to rub in the lotion on her back. When he had finished, she removed her top and said, "Can you do the front as well?"

She turned to face him. CC looked at her breasts and said, "If you like."

"I like."

CC put more lotion on his hands and started at her shoulders. He worked his way down being careful not to touch her breasts. As he reached her belly button, Carol said, "I think I'm burned on my legs as well."

CC looked down and said, "Yes, you have some redness on your legs as well."

Carol reached down and removed her suit bottom. She said to CC, "It might be easier if we went into the bedroom and I lay on the bed for you to do my legs."

"What ever you say."

They went into the bedroom and Carol lay on the bed face down.

Charles put lotion on the backs of her legs from just below her butt down to her ankles. When he got there he said, "Roll over." She did.

He applied the lotion to the front of her legs in a similar fashion. When done, Carol could see something pushing out of CC's trunks. She said, "What do we have here?"

She reached out and touched his trunks. She undid the tie and dropped his trunks to the floor.

CC joined her on the bed. They kissed. CC touched her breasts that were now very hard. "Very nice."

Carol reaching down took a hold of CC and said, "I agree."

With that, she guided him. They made passionate love for the next hour.

"Charles, I don't know what came over me."

"Carol, this has been wonderful."

"I have never done anything like this before in my life."

"It's a new life now. You are entitled to happiness."

"I am."

"I'm going to take a shower. Will you join me?"

"Sure."

They took a shower together. They lathered each other's bodies. When rinsing, they touched each other in all the right places. CC became erect again and they made love in the shower. When finally finished, Carol said, "Charles, my life has been turned completely upside down for the last few months. I can't begin to tell you how much this means to me."

"I'm enjoying it as well."

"Do you think we can continue a relationship when we return home?"

"I don't see why not. We are both single and we seem to get along pretty good."

"I thought my life was over when my husband died. But you've given me something to look forward to."

"Carol, I am here and available right now. You needed an out and this trip is providing it. Time will tell about how things will eventually work out."

"You are so right. Thank you for being here for me."

"All kind of coincidence actually."

"Maybe so, Maybe so."

They enjoyed the rest of the weekend. Carol didn't sleep on the sleeper couch once while there. They made love many times. They took in the sites of Key West along with nightly dancing and the Duval Street bar scene. They both had a wonderful time. When the weekend was over, they returned home totally exhausted. As Carol got into her house, her phone was ringing. It was Susan.

Carol answered it and said, "Hello Susan, I just walked in the door."

"Well, how did it go?"

"It was very relaxing. In fact, I am exhausted."

"How was the place?"

"Very nice. We stayed at the Hyatt. It's right on the Bay looking west. Magnificent sunsets."

"And how was Mr. Chamberlin?"

"A perfect gentleman."

"You went to a romantic place like Key West and nothing happened?"

"I didn't say that."

"Well, tell me more?"

"It all started when I got a little sun burned. I had Charles put lotion on my body and one thing led to another."

"Did he make love to you?"

"Many times."

"What's he like?"

"You can't imagine."

"Tell me more."

The two went on for another half hour. Carol described the whole weekend to Susan. She talked about dancing, scenic tours, romantic sunsets, warm days at the pool and about the many intimate times she had with Charles. Susan said, "I'm happy for you."

"It was a nice trip that I needed."

"Will you be seeing him again?"

"Probably. He is helping me with financial consulting."

"Yeah, I forgot about that. Well, keep me informed."

"Will do."

When Carol hung up, she sat there with a smile on her face. Charles was there for her.

Next she checked her mail. There was a notice in the pile from her attorney saying the settlement funds of four million dollars had been deposited into her account at the end of the day last Friday. Carol went to her computer, turned it on and logged into her Bank of America account. She entered her account number and password and could see her balance was $3,995,685.21. The attorney had withheld his third minus the prepaid expenses and deposited $3,994,000 in her account.

PCTrackR made an entry capturing the information.

Chapter 13

Taking stock in his pursuits, CC now had three solid targets he was tracking plus one target where he had been successful in carrying out his plan. While it was taking him longer than he had hoped to come up with the number of targets he desired, the potential dollar total had started to exceed his expectations thanks to the Theresa Lee target.

CC thought about his quest and some things were starting to bother him. He was having fun with some of the women he was targeting. Plus, he hadn't planned on the intimate relationships that had come about. Before the accident, he would not have imagined having relations with women the likes of Katherine and Carol. He was very much attracted to Carol and enjoyed his time with her. Thinking about her and looking at his computer spreadsheet that listed his potential target tally, he began to have second thoughts about going any further. He had already netted one and a half million dollars from Sharon Kelly. He actually thought about sending the uninstall command to the PCTrackR locations he had already established and forgetting about the whole plan.

Then he got a sharp pain in his leg while sitting there and it brought him back to feeling the way he did when he set the plans in motion in the first place. He reasoned if he were able to change his life based on the plans he had devised, once he netted the funds from his targets, he could continue to use the techniques he had developed to get more women. Only by then he would have enough money to fund the lifestyle he desired. He rubbed his leg where the pain had come from and refocused on his plans.

CC picked up the paper and opened it up to the Obituary section. There were thirty-two obituaries in the paper on that day. He scanned the first line of each one to quickly determine if any would qualify in his age range. As had been the case, most of the listings were for elderly people. He ignored the women who were listed and only read further into an obituary if the person was male. About three-quarters of the way through the listings, he identified a Ken Johnson, age thirty-nine that looked promising.
The obituary read:

Ken E. Johnson, 39

Enjoyed cooking; loved nature and traveling

East Falmouth – Ken E. Johnson, 39, died unexpectedly on Friday. Born in East Falmouth, he was the son of the late Ronald E. and Beverly A. Johnson.

His wife Mary (Adams) Johnson, two sons, Zachary and Jacob Johnson of Connecticut, survive him. Also surviving him are his grandmother, Irene Blane of East Falmouth; sister, Judith Woods of Florida; niece, Crystal Pennington of Kentucky; aunt Debra Blane of East Falmouth; cousins; and many friends.

Ken was a gourmet cook, working in many restaurants, from Lincolnville, Maine, to Falmouth, to Naples, Fla. He was a noted gourmet cook author having written numerous books. He always made sure there was plenty of food for everyone. He was loved nature, traveling and reading, especially Naval history. He will always be remembered for his kind heart.

A funeral Mass will be celebrated at noon Monday, at St. Anthony's Church 167 E. Falmouth Highway, East Falmouth. Immediately following, family and friends are welcome to gather at the VFW Hall, Achushnet Post, 180 Shore Road, Bourne.

CC cut out the obituary and placed it on his desk next to his computer. He would look up Ken Johnson on the Internet later on in the day and see what he could find. He made plans to go to the service on Monday morning and work the situation. If things worked out, he would have another target.

On Monday morning, CC went through his routine getting ready for the day. Again, he read the paper looking for more targets. He didn't see anything promising so he focused on his task for the day, qualifying Mary Johnson. He dressed in a business suit and put on a non-descript tie and headed out for the funeral home.

At eleven a.m. he got in his car and traveled to East Falmouth. He had used Yahoo Maps to get driving directions to the church. He arrived there a few minutes before noon. The parking lot was nearly full so he parked in the back of the lot and got out. There were other mourners working their way through the parking lot as well so CC just got in behind them entering the church. He took a seat in the back of the church.

The service was orderly with three people getting up and saying nice things about Ken Johnson. When it was over, the casket with a procession behind it went past CC. He kept his head bowed but did take a quick look at the widow when she walked by.

Mary Johnson looked to be in her twenties. She looked to be tall; around five foot eleven inches tall. She had on a dark overcoat and held a Kleenex to her face as she walked by. CC thought that with not having a wake, he would have to be careful about how he obtained information about Ken Johnson.

When the end of the procession reached his pew, CC got in line with the rest. As everyone lingered outside the church, the Pastor made an announcement that Ken Johnson would be buried in a private ceremony at a later time and everyone had been invited to a gathering at the VFW Hall on Shore Road, Bourne. He indicated his assistant had directions for anyone who needed them. CC took a copy.

The Hall was only a few miles away. CC had no problem finding it. When he got there, he joined the other people who had arrived from the service as well. Walking into the hall he started up a conversation with a man who identified himself as Fred Adams, a cousin through marriage to Ken Johnson.

"Fred, I'm Charles Chamberlin. You must be a relative of Mary's?"
"I am. Mary and I are cousins."
"What a tragedy this is with Ken dying so unexpectedly."
"It was. Ken's career was really taking off. His books were selling all over the place. I think he was even offered his own cooking show on one of the cable TV cooking channels."
"Yes, I had heard something about that."
"Mr. Chamberlin, How is it you knew Ken?"
"I'm a financial consultant by trade. I did some business with Ken over the past few months."
"That must have been fun with all of the money Ken was bringing in?"
"I only provided some advice. Ken already had accounts set up where he did his investing."
"Well, in talking with Mary, your advice must have been paying off because she told me last night Ken had recently made a lot of money with his investments."
"Yes he was doing ok."
"Here comes Mary now, please excuse me while I take a moment to speak with her."

As Fred took Mary's arm and steered her away from the crowd, he began talking to her and pointing in the direction of CC. CC could see the expression of puzzlement on Mary's face when she looked at him. Then she said

121

something back to Fred. Whatever she said caused Fred to come right over to CC.

Fred said, "Mr. Chamberlin, Mary does not know you. She said Ken did all of his financial counseling through a firm in Boston. She is sure he would have told her if he were planning on doing something different. I think you have some explaining to do?"

CC asked Fred to follow him and he walked over to Mary. He said, "My name is Charles Chamberlin. I am sorry for your loss. Mr. Adams has indicated you are concerned with my presence, as you don't know me. I assure you I knew your husband and he had asked me for advice recently regarding some investments. He had told me he had asked his advisors in Boston for a local contact in this area but they indicated they didn't have any offices near by. Then they gave him my name as a reference should he need to call on someone locally." CC took a gamble and said, "I have worked with the people at Fidelity and some of the other Boston Investment firms on numerous occasions. I'm sure they felt I could give Ken what he needed."

Mary said, "So you spoke with the people at Fidelity?"

CC said, "I do all the time. We have a number of mutual clients."

Mary looked at Fred and said, "Well, I guess it's ok. I just didn't recognize Mr. Chamberlin."

Looking at Charles she said, "Will you accept my apology?"

"It's Charles. And no apology is needed. I understand."

Mary said, "After all of this is over, I'd like to call you and discuss what it is you were doing for Ken if you wouldn't mind?"

"That would be fine with me. That's what I do."

"If you would please excuse me, I have other guests to attend to."

"Again, I'm so sorry for your loss."

"Thank you." Then she moved on to other guests.

CC took the time to mingle with some of the other guests gathering information. He learned about Ken's cooking exploits and about his family. At one point, he met a woman named Karen West. She said she was a close friend of Mary's.

CC said, "My name is Charles Chamberlin. I was a business acquaintance of Ken's."

Karen said, "The Johnsons are my neighbors. I've known them for eleven years."

"So you and Mary are good friends?"

"Yes. We do a lot of things together."

"What do you think Mary will do now that she has lost Ken?"

"She had been handling all of the business aspects of Ken's books from her home office. I think she will continue with that for a while. Plus, Mary has to take over the investing side of their finances. Ken used to handle all of that stuff himself."

"That might help take her mind off of things."

"Yes, it should. And in time, I'm sure she will start to get out and restart her life."

"That has to be so difficult to do."

"Well, I'm single so I'll have to get her to tag along with me once she is ready."

CC looking at her said, "Single huh?"

Karen was in her mid-thirties and took very good care of herself. She had shoulder length black hair with a cute button nose face. She looked to be about 5' 7" and had a slender figure. CC thought she must workout regularly as she looked fit.

"Mr. Chamberlin, are you married?"

"No, I'm not."

"Then maybe sometime we could get together for a drink or something?"

"I'd like that."

"How would I contact you?"

CC took a card out of his pocket and gave it to her. He said, "Here. Call anytime."

Karen took the card and looked at it. She said, "I might just do that."

"Well, I have to be going. I hope to hear from you?"

"We'll see."

CC turned and left the hall.

Karen walked over to Mary who had been watching the conversation.

Mary said, "So what did you think of Mr. Chamberlin?"

"Nice dresser. Into finance."

"Karen, you are working the field even at my dead husband's service."

"You've got to be on the lookout all the time."

"Karen, how do you do it?"

"Mary, you are going to have to learn this stuff as well. You are single now also."

Mary thought about it and said, "I guess I am."

Karen produced CC's business card and said, "Here is his card if you want to start somewhere."

"Karen, not here, not now and now so soon."

"Remember what I said, you have to be on the lookout all the time. You never know when opportunity will knock."

"This is all so new to me."

"Honey, you will thank me sometime down the road. Stick with me and good things will happen."

Mary looked at her with apprehension and said, "I don't know if I'm ready for all this stuff."

"You will be. Just give it a few days, then call Mr. Chamberlin."

"I guess."

She put the card away and turned her attention to the other guests.

Driving home, CC thought he had another candidate. He didn't know what Mary Johnson was worth, but he would find out in the near future. He thought about his plans and the current focus was going to be on Carol Tindle and Mary Johnson. He had already qualified Katherine Sterns and Theresa Lee and he will have to do something about Angela Davis. The latter might be good for sex but he wasn't sure about her inheritance and if that didn't work out, having no wealth would disqualify her.

124

He decided to call Angela Davis and end their relationship.

When she answered the phone he said, "Angela, it's Charles Chamberlin."

"Charles, nice to hear from you."

"Angela, I have given it a lot of thought and I don't think I'll be able to see you anymore."

"Why not? Is it because I might be destined to be a poor person."

"That's only part of it. I have other interests and I need to curtail my activities outside of those interests."

"Oh, another woman. I understand."

"It's not what you think."

"I know what it is. I might be headed the wrong way and you would prefer to keep moving in a positive direction."

"I'm glad you understand."

"I understand all right. You found a better situation."

"I'm sorry you feel that way."

"Don't feel sorry honey. If I were in the same situation, I'd do the same thing."

"You sure do have a grip on things."

"I try to do my best. Well, good luck and give me a call sometime if things don't work out."

"Thanks and I will."

Chapter 14

The next day, CC read the paper again looking for his next target. He didn't find any promising prospects. After cleaning up his place he picked up the claim check for the pictures he had taken while in Key West and went to the corner pharmacy to pick them up. He had dropped off the memory stick a few days earlier and the clerk had indicated she would need a day or two to have the pictures printed, enlarged and the ones CC had indicated framed.

When CC presented the claim check, the clerk said, "Mr. Chamberlin, your pictures are ready. They came out very nice."

"Thank you. Did you have any problems with the enlargements?"

"No. I did have to order the special stock you had requested and it came in yesterday. Take a look for yourself."

She opened the folder and took out the pictures and spread them out on the counter. The enlargements were very nice. The extra heavy stock CC had selected gave the pictures a firm look more like posters than pictures. CC told the clerk he intended to frame the enlargements and had found the stiffer paper holds up best when framing. She said he had made a good choice because regular stock paper tends to curl over time even if framed.

When CC was admiring the pictures, the clerk said, "Isn't the woman in that picture Mrs. Tindle?"

"Yes it is. Do you know her?"

"Yes, she is my next door neighbor. I'm Amy Downey. I live at home with my parents next door to Mrs. Tindle."

"When I was looking at these pictures I was wondering when they were taken? I see Mrs. Tindle in some of the pictures in a bikini at a beach somewhere. Didn't her husband just pass away recently?"

"Yes, not too long ago. I was going to Key West last week and she joined me on the trip. She said she needed to get away."

"Looks like she had a good time."

"I tried my best to get her mind away from the bad things that had happened to her recently."

Amy picking up one of the pictures that showed Carol with a drink in her hand making a toast and said, "Well it looks like your efforts paid off."

"I was a business associate of her late husband and I take a personal interest in all of my clients and now Carol is my client."

"How nice of you."

CC paid for the pictures. He put the pictures back in the folder and thanked Amy for her help. She said, "Good luck with Mrs. Tindle."

CC was getting a little annoyed because he thought Amy was getting a little rude. He said, "Thanks." And left the store.

When CC got back home, he called Carol and said, "Hello Carol, its Charles Chamberlin."

"Charles, nice to hear from you."

"I picked up the pictures I took when we were in Key West. They came out great."

"Oh, I'd like to see them."

"When would you like me to come over?"

Carol thought about it. It had not been very long since her husband had died and she said, "I don't know if that would be such a good idea. What will the neighbors think?"

"I met one of your neighbors today at the corner pharmacy. She recognized you in the pictures."

"Oh no, what will they think? Who was it?"

"It was a young girl, I guess about twenty years old. She said her name is Amy something or other."

"Amy Downey, she is my next door neighbor."

"That was what she said."

"What did the picture look like?"

"What do you mean?" CC questioned.

"The one in which Amy recognized me?"

"You and I were on the beach. Remember that night just as the sun was setting. We had been sunbathing and were wrapping up the day having cocktails and you made that toast."

"Yes, I remember. What will they think of me?"

"I wouldn't worry about it."

"Amy will tell her mother and she will tell everyone in the neighborhood there is a loose woman in the neighborhood on the prowl."

"Carol, I think you are getting a little carried away."

"You don't know my neighbors."

"Carol, you are single now. You can do what ever you like."

"Yes, but so soon?"

"Let me come over with the pictures tonight. I'll be a real gentleman about it."

"I just don't know."

"Oh, come on. You and I shared something very special together. Don't let that go."

"All right. Why don't you come over after dinner around seven?"

"See you then."

After CC hung up, Carol called her friend Susan White.

"Sue, it's Carol. When I went to Key West with Charles Chamberlin, we took some pictures."

"So."

"The pictures kind of show me having a good time with another man."

"What do you mean with another man?"

"The pictures showed me in my bikini, drinking and doing things with someone other than Bill. One of my neighbors saw the pictures."

"So what. Bill is gone and there is nothing wrong with you seeing someone else."

"Yes, but so soon."

"Hey Honey, there isn't a time table on this kind of thing."

"Yes, but now my entire neighborhood will know."

"Carol, that's going to have to be their problem. You are entitled to have a life."

"Yes, I know. But I don't have the confidence you do."

"Don't let them get to you. If I were you, I'd have a guy over as soon as I could. That would give them even more to talk about."

"I am having Charles over tonight to show me the pictures."

"Good. Let them see you being friendly with him."

"What do you mean?"

"Greet him outside on your porch with a kiss or something."

"I'm not sure I can do that."

"You slept with him in Key West didn't you?"

"Well yes."

"Then move on girl. They will get over it."

"If you say so."

"I say so."

"Thanks. I'll call you later and let you know how it went."

CC dressed in casual attire, dark gray slacks and a red-blue pinstriped button-down shirt. He wore a pair of black loafers with black socks. Charles arrived promptly at seven o'clock. Carol came out on the porch to greet him and made sure they stood under the porch light clearly visible to any prying eyes that might be looking. She was dressed in a mid-length green skirt with a white halter-top that was a little more revealing than what she normally wore around the neighborhood. She greeted CC as he reached the top step leading up to the porch. She wrapped her arms around his neck and gave him a kiss on the cheek. CC almost jumped back and said, "To what do I owe this greeting?"

Carol said, "Come inside and I'll tell you."

They went inside and Carol told CC about her conversation with Susan and the whole neighborhood would soon be talking about her. She said Amy's mother was the gossip column of the neighborhood and would salivate over having something to talk about.

CC said, "I wouldn't worry about it."

"That's what Susan said."

"Susan has good sense. What else did you talk to Susan about?"

"I talk to Susan about everything."

"Everything?"

"Everything."

"Even about our trip to Key West?"

"Everything."

CC put his arms around Carol and was about to kiss her when Carol said, "I have something I would like to talk to you about."

"What is that?"

"I have decided to accept the settlement from the accident that had involved my deceased husband."

"That's good news."

"It's time to move on with my life and accepting the settlement will allow me to put that behind me."

"Are you sure you can put it behind you?"

"I think so."

"Then lets go out and celebrate."

"I don't think I'm really in the mood to celebrate."

"I'm sorry. I guess that was insensitive of me."

Carol put her arms around him and said, "I know you mean well. I am still getting over Bill dying. I have a stereotype set in my mind of what a widow is supposed to do and being with another man so soon isn't part of that picture."

"Only you can decide when the time is right to move on."

"You are so kind Charles. Thank you for understanding."

"Let me change the subject. I came over here to show you these pictures."

He opened the folder and pulled them out. For the next half hour, he and Carol looked at the pictures and laughed about the good time they had at Key West. The last picture in the pile was the one Amy had seen. It showed Carol in her bikini at sunset making a toast. When she saw it she said, "Charles, that trip was fun. You really helped me during a difficult period."

"I am just glad I was there to help you."

He said, "What are your plans for the settlement money?"

Carol thought for a minute then said, "I don't know yet. What do you think I should do with it?"

"I have been following a few funds recently that look to be positioned to provide a very nice return over the next twelve to eighteen months."

"Do you think I should invest in them?"

"You might want to put some money in them. And put some in fixed investments."

"Can you do that for me?"

"You can do it all yourself right on your home computer."

"Yes I guess I can. Thanks for the advice."

CC said, "Your welcome."

They went back to looking at the pictures again. Carol made coffee. They talked and laughed for another hour and finally CC said he had to go. They said their goodnights and Carol made a point to walk him out to his car and give him a kiss on the cheek. She was hoping her nosey neighbor was looking.

Carol went back inside and got on to her computer. She sent an e-mail to Susan telling her about the evening details including the kisses on the porch when CC arrived and when he was leaving. She told Susan she liked Charles and was looking forward to seeing more of him in the future. Carol was moving on.

PCTrackR made an entry capturing the information.

The next morning, CC rose, made his coffee, took his shower and straightened his place up. He got the daily paper and began to read it. He had a smile on his face recalling his evening with Carol. He wondered where the relationship was going.

As he turned to the obituary page, he saw an obituary that got his attention.

Robert Stevenson, 41

Rockland – Mr. Robert A. Stevenson, 41 residing in South Yarmouth, died Thursday at Plymouth Hospital following complications received in a recent automobile accident.

He was preceded in death by his mother Judy (Kelso) Stevenson and his father Len Stevenson. He is survived by his wife Pamela (Mason) Stevenson, brother Henry Stevenson, and niece and nephews.

Funeral services will be held at Morris & O'Connor Funeral Home, 58 Long Dr. South Yarmouth on Thursday at 1 p.m. Calling hours are Wednesday from 6 to 8 p.m. Please sign a guest book at www.morrisoconnor.com.

CC thought Mr. Stevenson dying from an automobile accident might mean insurance money would be forthcoming. He would go to the wake and check it out.

On Wednesday, he went to the Morris & O'Connor Funeral home a little after six o'clock. When he arrived, there were about fifteen cars in the parking lot. He went inside. Entering the funeral home, he was greeted by one of the attendants who asked if he was family or friend. He said friend. The attendant directed him to a room at the front of the building. When CC went into the room, there were a few people in there sitting and talking to each other. He took a seat in the back. The room was separated by a set of sliding doors that were opened.

On the other side of the doors he could see a few people standing near the casket with a person who was saying prayers. CC thought a family service was being conducted so he just remained at the back of the room. When the prayers were over, the person who had been talking stood and turned around. CC could see the person was a minister. The minister came to the opened doors and thanked the friends for allowing the family a few minutes of prayers and the friends could now pay their respects to the family.

CC got in line. When he got to Pamela Stevenson he expressed his condolences. She didn't recognize him but said thank you. CC went to the back of the room again and stood by the door. Another gentleman standing near by said to CC, "Too bad about Bob isn't it."

"Sure is. He was too young to go."

The man said, "That's what happens when you drink and drive."

CC said, "Oh, I hadn't heard."

"Apparently the accident was Bob's fault."

"That's really bad."

"Sure is. And now Pamela is left with nothing."

"What do you mean?"

"With Bob being laid off and now getting killed in an accident, he left her with nothing. I don't even know if he had any life insurance."

"Well, with not working and all, I'd be surprised if he could afford insurance."

"You are probably right."

"Sometimes things just go completely wrong for some people."

"Sometimes."

Having heard that kind of information, CC excused himself and left the funeral home. He decided any further pursuit of Pamela Stevenson would probably not be worth it.

When he got home, the light on his portable phone was blinking. He picked it up and called in for messages. The first message was from Katherine.

She said, "Charles, where have you been? I have trying to get a hold of you for a few days. Give me a call when you get in."

The next message was from Carol Tindle. She said, "Charles, I want to thank you again for being so considerate. I know I am being a little reserved with Bill dying so recently but please bear with me. I'll call you later in the week. Carol."

CC thought about his visit to her house and how she greeted him and how she said her goodbye. He thought she was rather affectionate. He would have to ask her what was going through her head.

After getting the messages, CC called Katherine. When she picked up the phone he said, "Katherine, it's Charles."

"Charles, I have been trying to reach you."

"I have been out of town for a few days on business."

"I was hoping to have you over for a night."

"Katherine, your pregnancy has to be moving along quite a bit now. Do you think it's a good idea?"

She came back with, "What, do you think I'm getting too fat?"

"It's not that but..."

And before he could say anything more she said, "Then is it another woman?"

"No it's not that either."

"Well, if it isn't any of those things then what is it?"

"I'm just not comfortable given your condition."

"Well it's not like I'm going to get more pregnant."

"I know, but the child isn't mine and I just don't feel right about having sex with someone who is pregnant with someone else's child."

"I guess I see your point. But what can I do about it."

CC said, "Not much for the foreseeable future." He continued, "Katherine, I think it would be best of we just put things on hold for a while."

"I guess. If you say so."

"Why don't you call me after you've had the baby."

"That's months away."

"I know. But that's the way it has to be."

"Ok, good bye. I'll miss you."

"Me too."

When he hung up the phone he let out a big breath. That was behind him. He would monitor things via PCTrackR from here on with regard to Katherine Sterns.

Chapter 15

Things continued as usual for CC for the next few days. One day when he logged on to his e-mail account, he had a number of incoming messages with the subject line of Strokes Included. He knew his day would be filled with breaking down the data streams being sent to him from PCTrackR. He began analyzing the files.

The first e-mail was from PLEE. CC opened the e-mail and promptly saved the attachment as TL Strokes 4 and then opened the file. He could see where Theresa had gone to the website www.troweprice.com. When she got there she entered the ID PLEE and the password of PL020450. Once in the account, she had selected a few options and then logged out.

Theresa had then gone to another website for www.sovereignbank.com. She entered the same ID and password and again it looked like she was checking balances. That was followed by a few e-mails that were sent to family and friends. One of the e-mails was to her attorney where she indicated the six million dollar proceeds of the court settlement should be sent to her in a bank check net of the attorney fee.

Another of her e-mails was to customer service at www.dreyfus.com. In the e-mail, Theresa indicated she had sent in a check for one million five hundred thousand dollars resulting from an insurance policy on her recently deceased husband. She indicated in the e-mail the funds should be put into the account money market fund when Dreyfus received them and she would select her desired investments once the funds showed up in the account.

The second e-mail was from KSTERNS. Again, CC opened the e-mail and saved the attachment as KS STROKES Four file. He opened it. The first thing he saw as an e-mail from Katherine to Andrew. In it, she apologized to Andrew for not calling on him recently. She had indicated she had met another man. She told Andrew she was becoming concerned about getting too involved with her new man, Charles, given her association with him and Sterns and Dunn. She said she didn't want anything to come between Andrew and her that might affect their business interest. She asked Andrew to call her.

Next he could see where Katherine went to her Accounts at Vanguard, Franklin Templeton and at ING Direct. While logged into her ING Direct account, he could see where she requested a transfer of fifty thousand dollars into another account. CC thought about it and figured he would have to do some research on the new account if he were to get those funds down the road. But for now, most of her money was being kept in a place he could gain access.

Then the keystrokes file indicated Katherine logged into her deceased husband's company, www.sternsanddunn.com site. He could see she had selected a few options. He would have to log in to that site and see where the options she had selected had taken her. He printed that section of the e-mail and would come back to it later.

The last thing in the file looked to be a Google search request. Katherine had entered "Charles Chamberlin" into the search request field. That was the last entry in the strokes file. CC wondered what Katherine was doing requesting information on him.

The next e-mail was from CAROLT. CC didn't know why he was getting an e-mail from Carol so soon. He must have set the number of days option to something other than seven. That would explain him getting the e-mail so soon. CC opened the e-mail and selected the attachments tab. He downloaded the file and saved it as CT Strokes One file. This was his first contact with the PCTrackR copy he had installed on Carol Tindle's computer. He carefully went through the contents looking for websites, account numbers and passwords. When he had finished, he had logged the site www.boa.com and the ID CAROLT and password TIN05. He now had the knowledge to start looking at her accounts whenever he liked.

CC liked Carol so that target would present him with an emotional challenge. He tracked the information sent by PCTrackR and it looked like she had looked at her account balance. He would log in to the bank site later and see where the strokes would take him.

To his satisfaction, he could see where she had logged into a site www.smithbarney.com. At that site, she had selected an option and then entered a dollar amount of one million. Then she had selected another option and again entered a dollar amount of one million. When she did the same thing for a third time, CC figured she was investing the suit proceeds into investments. He would confirm the activity once he logged into the account later.

As CC was finishing up with the e-mails, his phone rang. The caller-id indicated the call was from Mary Johnson.

"Mr. Chamberlin, this is Mary Johnson."

"Mrs. Johnson. How are you doing?"

"I'm adjusting. I was talking with my friend Karen West and she gave me your business card and said I should call you."

"She did?"

"Yes. She had indicated you helped my husband with his investments and Karen said I should take the time to get to know Ken's advisors before doing anything with the investments."

"That sounds like good advice to me."

138

"Do you think we could get together to discuss a few things?"

"That would be fine with me. What would you suggest?"

"I could come to your office if that would be ok?"

"That would be fine with me or we could have a dinner meeting at a local restaurant."

"I think I'd like that. It would get me out of these surroundings. Do you have a recommendation?"

"Recommendations are my business. Let me see. Why don't we meet at Alberto's Restaurant in Hyannis on Tuesday night, say six o'clock."

"That would be fine. I think I know where it is?"

"It's just off Main Street so it should be easy to find."

"Ok, six o'clock Tuesday it is."

After hanging up with Charles, Mary calls her friend Karen. "Karen, I took your advice and I am going to meet with Mr. Chamberlin."

"When?"

"We are having a dinner meeting at Alberto's in Hyannis next Tuesday."

"That's a start. Let me know how it goes."

"I will."

Hanging up the phone, CC returned to his computer to check on his targets' accounts. He first selected Carol Tindle. CC logged into www.smithbarney.com. He used the ID CarolT and password TIN05. He could see the account total of just over three million two hundred thousand dollars. The account details were broken down into three funds each having a balance of one million with the remaining two hundred thousand in a money market account. This must have been where she put the accident settlement and this account should provide him with the target amount he had in mind.

Next, he logged into her www.boa.com account. He used the same keystrokes recorded from the captured data file and it returned balances in CDs and a money market account. She had five hundred thousand dollars in CDs and another two hundred thousand dollars in the money market account. CC made entries into his targets spreadsheet file of the information he had obtained.

There were other keystrokes captured in the file but they didn't reference any websites. CC was really only interested in activity that identified assets he might consider as part of his target. He skipped everything that didn't show any promise.

Finishing up with Carol Tindle, CC turned his attention to Theresa Lee. He first logged into her T Rowe Price account at www.troweprice.com. He used the login information of PLEE and password of PL020450. He wondered why she was still using her dead husband's account access information and why the institution didn't insist on her changing it. He would have to watch the incoming e-mails carefully in the future from PCTrackR to see if she changed account information. If she did, and he was sure she would, he would need that information to complete his plans in the future. He put in the same thing PCTrackR had captured and the computer returned a screen showing a balance of just over five hundred eighty thousand dollars in the account.

Then, he accessed her bank account at www.sovereignbank.com. He put in the same keystrokes PCTrackR indicated she had previously entered and it returned a screen showing a balance of $5,916,114.20. This was her working account and he didn't figure he would need this account but he would have to follow the activity to find out where the funds would end up. He selected the history option and entered parameters indicating he wanted to see all activity for the past thirty days. One of the entries was a deposit for five point nine million dollars. The lawsuit had been settled for just under nine million dollars and her portion of the settlement funds had been deposited.

Lastly, he accessed another of her investment accounts at www.dreyfus.com. Again, entering the same keystrokes Theresa had entered, the computer returned a screen showing this account had a balance of one million nine hundred twenty thousand dollars. Checking the account history, he could see an entry for a one million five hundred thousand dollar deposit from an insurance company. The life insurance policy had come through.

CC felt good about his future. His plans were starting to come together. The assets of his targets were known and within his reach. If only he could get another two or three, he could put his plans into motion and be set for the rest of his life.

He turned his attention to Katherine Sterns. He first logged into the website www.franklintempleton.com. He used the information he had obtained some time ago and it worked fine. He had entered KSTERNS in the ID field and KS812 as the password. He was returned with her account information. She had fifty thousand dollars in the account. He checked the www.vanguard.com site next and it had the balance of two point five million dollars. Lastly, he checked her www.ingdirect.com account and it had changed since the one million had been sent to Franklin Templeton, and an additional fifty thousand withdrawn. It had a balance of four hundred thousand dollars in it. She had started to make investments in the Franklin Templeton Account and move funds out of ING Direct. The only other change to the account had been the crediting of interest.

The last thing he did under the category of Sterns was to check the www.sternsanddunn.com site. Once logged in, he could see all of the business accounts for the company. When he selected the bank accounts tab, he could see it had a few thousand dollars in the checking account and another thirty four thousand dollars in a companion money market account. Every time he looked at the accounts for Sterns and Dunn, the balances would be all over the place. He figured there was just too much volatility in the business accounts to make the risk worth taking. He had already thought he would leave the business accounts alone and reconfirmed that position again.

Katherine would get to keep whatever investment she had in Sterns and Dunn intact.

CC knew from Katherine she had inherited Sam's interest in Sterns and Dunn. She had told him the company was worth millions and it had received three million dollars in Key Man insurance when Sam had died. He knew there must be money here somewhere. He just couldn't find it in one big chunk. He tried all of the tabs on the company finance page but was not able to find out where the insurance money had been placed. He had made up his mind he would stay clear of the operating accounts as they were probably monitored on a daily basis. But if he could find the place where the insurance lump sum had been placed, he might go after it. He could see in the accounting details file that large amount withdrawals had been made shortly after the insurance proceeds had been deposited but he would need the actual check to determine where the funds were going. There was no indication in the journal as to where the funds were being sent. CC wondered if Andrew Dunn was doing this purposely to keep something from Katherine.

When he didn't find the data he was looking for, he signed out of his e-mail account and went on to other business.

CC updated his summary data file with all he had learned and confirmed. His plans were coming together. He had identified candidates, met them, gained their confidence and been able to get the detailed data he would need down the road when it came time to complete his plans.

Thinking about his targets, CC thought he would have to be careful as time went on so he would not jeopardize his plans. Katherine Sterns presented a problem because she was very aggressive. He didn't like being so intimately involved with a woman who was pregnant with another man's baby. In fact, he found it distasteful. The only thing that kept her in consideration was she did have a sizeable sum of money available to him he felt he could easily access.

Theresa Lee was very straight forward as a target. He didn't have any invested emotions or involvement with her. The result was CC figured that target would be the easiest for him to pursue. After all, she was getting a large lawsuit settlement and had already received a nice insurance policy payout.

Carol Tindle was another story completely. CC really liked Carol. After their trip to Key West, CC found himself thinking about her more and more. Carol was a low key individual. She didn't put any pressure on anyone. She was interesting and pleasant to be around. She wasn't loud or flashy and CC liked that. Plus, under all the simple clothing she usually wore, existed a physically attractive person. The more he thought about her he considered including her in his future once he fully executed his plans. He was unsure exactly how he would do that, but if she came along with him, he wouldn't have to take any of her money and still have the luxury of access to it. That situation began to weigh on him.

Chapter 16

Later that afternoon, CC got a call from Katherine.

"Charles, its Katherine. I was wondering if we could get together tonight to discuss a few things."

"Katherine, I thought I made it clear I can't be involved with you at this point in your life."

"Charles, I'm not calling to get you into bed. I want to go over a few things with you."

"What did you have in mind?"

"I've been thinking about my interest in Sterns and Dunn and would like to get some advice."

"My last appointment is at four o'clock. We could meet after that."

"Why don't you come to my place after you're finished. I'll make dinner."

"I'll see you then."

"Bring something to drink if you would."

"Any preference?"

"No, you pick it."

"Ok, see you around six."

CC knowing her state of pregnancy stopped and picked up two bottles of mineral water on his way to Katherine's. Arriving at her house just after six, he handed her a bag when she opened the door. Katherine was dressed in black slacks, a crisp white blouse with french cuffs, and black ballet flats. She didn't have any jewelry on. CC thought her appearance was rather not-Katherine-like. Looking inside she saw the mineral water and said, "Nothing stronger?"

"I didn't think it was fair, given your condition."

"You didn't have to deprive yourself just because of me."

"It's not a problem. I'm here to discuss business anyway."

"Well, come in. Dinner will be ready in a few minutes."

CC followed her to the kitchen and opened one of the bottles of mineral water. He filled the two wine glasses she had already set out on the counter and put them on the table that had been set for dinner. Katherine was busy taking up the steamed broccoli. After putting that in a bowl, she took a roasting pan out of the oven. She had made oven roasted chicken. She asked Charles to cut up the chicken. When he finished, she poured a cream sauce over the chicken and asked him to put it on the table. While he was doing that, she poured the cooked rice into a bowl and put it on the table. Then she went to the refrigerator and took out a bowl that had a pre-made salad in it and put it on the table. They took their seats and began to eat.

"This is really good. What is the sauce?"

"It's an old family recipe. If you want it, I can write it down for you."

"I'd like that." Charles paused, put his fork down, and then looked directly at Katherine. "Katherine, what is it you were thinking relative to Sterns and Dunn?"

"Well, when my husband died, the firm got millions in Key Man insurance. Since then, I haven't had much involvement in the operations of the business other than to spend time with my new partner Andrew Dunn."

"And isn't he doing a good job?"

"Yes he is. But I don't know if I should keep my interest in the firm or look for someone to buy my interest out."

"Have you talked to Andrew about this?"

"No I haven't. I wanted to get your advice before I said anything. Once that cat's out of the bag, there's no saying *'never mind'* is there?"

"What are you thinking? Do you want to sell to Andrew or someone else?"

"Andrew would be my first choice. But what if he doesn't want to buy me out?"

"Do you have any indications he might not be interested?"

"No, but I'm unsure of how to approach this topic with him. I don't want to get him annoyed with me. He is in control of the business and he could affect it."

"That's true. Or he might beat you to the punch and sell out from under you."

"I hadn't thought about that possibility."

"Would you like me to speak to him?"

"No, I think I should be the one to talk with him about this subject."

"Can't you keep your interest in the business and just monitor things from here?"

"Well, I can access the company's electronic information that had been made available via the Internet from here. But that doesn't give me any insight about what's actually going on."

"What kind of things do you have access to?"

"I have access to the company e-mail system. I get the newsletters they send out. I can see the finance books. And I have access to the company's bank accounts. Anything I can't see from here, I can ask for."

"You have access to their bank accounts? From here?"

"Well, not really me, but Sam had an ID and password I can use to see the company's electronic files like bank account and other things."

"What kind of other things?"

"Oh, their 401k plan, their insurance information and other finance things."

CC thought Katherine might have access to wherever the Key Man insurance payout ended up and she might not even know she had that kind of information.

He said, "Do you have access to the company line-of-credit information at the bank?"

She said, "Yes, I can see references to a LOC at one of the sites I have been on."

CC said, "Have you ever found any references to savings, money market or other accounts where the company might keep reserve funds?"

Katherine thought for a minute and said, "I have seen references to a rainy day fund. But I'm not sure exactly where I saw that information."

CC didn't respond right away. He thought Katherine might know where funds are being held in reserve that he would be interested in but she might not recognize what they actually were. CC said, "You know, some of these accounts like a rainy day fund might contain significant sums of money you might be entitled to."

"How so?"

"Well, if the company has money set aside somewhere, you might be entitled to get at it before it can be spent given you want out."

"I don't know how much money is there but I'll have to find out."

"That might be a good idea before you say anything to anyone."

"I'll let you know what I find out."

"That would be a good idea." He would investigate later.

CC didn't know how far the relationship with Katherine and Andrew actually went. He had his suspicions based on her comments, and behaviors, in the past. She was definitely aggressive and open-minded. He thought to himself as he ate and then said, "Katherine, if you sold your interest in Sterns and Dunn, what would you do?"

Katherine said, "Well, after I have this baby, I would be free to spend all of my time with you and not have to worry about the business anymore."

CC wasn't ready for that statement. He said, "Raising a child is a pretty big deal. I'm not sure my lifestyle would be a positive influence on a child."

Katherine said, "Oh, I'm sure you would be a good father."

CC wished he had brought something stronger after that comment. He said, "Me, a father. I'm not so sure. I have been on my own for quite a long time and I'm not sure I'm ready for something like that."

"I'd make it worthwhile" exclaimed Katherine.

CC just looked at her and didn't respond.

After an awkward moment, Katherine said, "We could raise a family. I could make you dinner every night. And we could have wonderful sex whenever you wanted it."

"Not sure. Surely not. Sure."

"What?"

"Not sure about a family. Definitely not in for home cooked dinners every night. But sex whenever I wanted it from you would be a definite plus."

"Charles, this is a real dilemma."

"No dilemma. Why don't we leave it as it is and see where things go once you have the baby?"

"Because I need something to ground me. This pregnancy is making me nervous."

"I can't make any commitments right now. I'll have to think about it."

Katherine changed the subject back to Sterns and Dunn. She said, "I think I'll call Andrew tomorrow and talk with him about my getting out of that business."

"Be cautious about how you phrase your words. You don't want him to get concerned about your intentions. Try to find a way to approach the subject that won't alarm him. You might want to consider bringing in the child factor and securing the child's financial future. Also, many businesses have corporate documents that dictate the activities that have to take place in order to add or remove a partner. You could just ask to see the corporate documents, generally."

"That's a good idea. Andrew would understand that concept."

"And then try to get Andrew to consider buying your interest. Tell him you would be willing to consider any proposal he might come up with."

"I'll do that."

Finishing dinner, Katherine told Charles to leave everything on the table, she would get it later. She came up from behind him and put her arms around him. She pressed his chest and said, "Why don't you come with me to the bedroom. I'd like to express my appreciation to you."

"While I'd like that, I have an early appointment tomorrow and I have some preparation to do. I'm going to have to reluctantly pass."

"It's me being pregnant is why you're saying that."

"Well, there is that, but I do have a meeting early tomorrow and I do have to prepare for it."

"Well, then how about just another hour?"

CC said, "I really have to get going."

Katherine sounding disappointed said, "Charles, I'm still hungry. I need you tonight."

"Another time."

He got up and started for the door.

"Are you sure you can't stay?"

"I'm sure. Let me know how your talk goes with Andrew?"

"Ok. I will."

At that, CC took the opportunity to open the door. Katherine came over to him and gave him a big kiss. He returned it and then closed the door.

When CC left, Katherine went to her computer. She logged into www.sternsanddunn.com. When she gained access to the proprietary section using Sam's ID, she selected the financial information tab. She selected the Reserve tab and looked at the information being returned. It read "$3,425,558.71." She had found the rainy-day fund. So had PCTrackR.

The next day, Katherine called Andrew. At first, Andrew was skeptical about taking her call but he did. He said, "Katherine, how are you?"

"Fine Andrew. I was calling you to see if you had some time for me this week."

Andrew now being cautious with Katherine said, "What did you have in mind?"

"Do you think you can come over one night this week?"

Andrew thought he might know where this was going and said, "What is it you would like to talk about?"

"I'd like to talk about the future."

"Can you be more specific?"

"Well, with having this baby and all, I'm starting to think about the future."

Andrew said, "That's a good idea. How can I help?"

"I'm not sure how much involvement I'll be able to have with the business and all once the baby arrives. I'd like to talk with you about those things and seek your advice."

"When then would you like to meet?"

"You pick the night. I'm free most of the week."

"Ok, how about Thursday?"

"Thursday is fine. What time should I expect you?"

"I can be there around seven. Will that work?"

"That will be fine." As she hung up the phone, Katherine remembers the documents Charles had mentioned. "Oh well" she thought, "Maybe I'll mention it on Thursday."

When Andrew hung up the phone he thought about what she had said. He started to think this might be the right time to try to buy out Sam's interest. Maybe he could suggest she consider selling her interest to him. Then he would own the whole business. His mind started working on the ways he might buy her out. One of the first things he thought of was the rainy-day fund as a component of a buyout package. He thought about the company line-of-credit and he could get another half million there if he needed it. Then he thought he might be able to borrow some from the bank. The business was worth over ten million so he would have to come up with

150

six million or so to buy her out. But then again, maybe Katherine didn't even know that.

The next day when Andrew got to work, his computer manager, Chris Bond, asked to talk with him. He told Andrew there had been recent outside access to the company website. At first, Andrew didn't understand the magnitude of what Chris was saying but when he said the ID and password had belonged to Sam, Andrew became concerned. Chris went on to tell Andrew the person logged in as Sam had gone completely through the company electronic files accessing everything from accounting journals to the rainy-day money market account information. Now Andrew became alarmed. Was it Katherine? That was probably the least of his worries, although he was worried regardless.

He said, "Chris, can you shut down Sam's ID and password?"

"I can. Do you want me to do that?"

"Yes. Do you know who is using Sam's information?"

"The source was Sam's home computer. I think it was his wife."

"Well, she is entitled to that information. After all, she is now the majority owner in the business. I had better talk to her before you shut down access. If it's her, she has every right to have access."

"Well, not only does she have access using Sam's ID, but she can also transact business with that ID."

"Maybe we should issue her an ID and password of her own but one that allows her to view information only."

"That would be easy to do. I'll take care of it right away."

"Give me the information when it's set up and I'll talk with Mrs. Sterns about it. Meanwhile, don't shut down Sam's ID. Wait until I give you the word."

Chris said, "Will do." Then he left Andrew's office to get things going.

Andrew was going to have to speak with Katherine about the use of Sam's ID. Then he thought if he could interest her in selling, he might be able to avoid a potential confrontation. Timing and how he approached these issues would be very important. He didn't want to offend her and then try to buy her out. She might make things difficult for him. "What to do, and when to do it", thought Andrew.

Chapter 17

Carol Tindle called her friend Susan White. She just had to tell her about her feelings for Charles.

"Hello Carol. How are you doing?"

"How did you know it was me?"

"I could see your number on my caller ID."

Carol then went on and told Susan about the suit settlement. She said, "I'm settling for just under four million. That should give me enough to live on for the foreseeable future."

"If you invest it right, that should be enough to last your lifetime."

Carol then added, "Well, Charles is helping me with the investments and I have confidence in him."

"Have you followed up with any references on Charles?"

"No. But I got to know him very well on our trip to Key West and he has good ideas."

"I'm sure he does, but you should not mix money and sex. If things go bad with one, they will definitely go bad with the other."

"Oh you are just saying that."

"No, I don't believe in mixing business and pleasure like that."

"I know you're only looking out after my interest. But I believe Charles can help me with both needs."

"Well, don't say I didn't warn you if things don't work out."

"I won't, and I probably won't even tell you," laughed Carol. "By the way, the private eye company you gave me was a big help in finding all the places Bill hid our money. And the retainer fee was reasonable. They should be able to clean everything up within the year."

"Would I ever steer you wrong?"

Carol didn't answer right away.

"I think I'm falling in love with Charles."

"Be careful Carol. You just buried your husband. You might be getting these feelings on the rebound, especially after having had that weekend in Key West."

"We had a lot of good chemistry down there. I think it's for real for both of us."

"You had a lot of sex down there. He wined and dined you. You needed some sweaty physical contact and he provided it. Recognize the weekend for what it was."

"You make it sound so naughty Sue."

"Sex is always naughty in my book. If it weren't, then why do it?"

"You do have a way with words my friend."

"No sense mincing them. Now, about Charles, take it slow and see where things go."

"You're probably right. I'm in no hurry."

"You'll need to date a few guys over the next year or so. Make sure you have the right guy before you jump in."

"I will. But I still think he's the right guy."

"You are hopeless. But let me know how it all works out."

"I will. Gotta go. Bye."

"Bye."

When Carol got off the phone with Susan, she called Charles.

"Charles, can we get together on Tuesday night to talk for a bit?"

"Tuesday. Let me see."

She could hear him leafing through papers. "No, Tuesday night doesn't work for me. I have a dinner meeting that night with a client."

"What time do you think you will get done?"

"I don't know. Can't we make it another night?"

"Sure, how about Wednesday?"

"I'm open on Wednesday night."

"Then I'll make a reservation at a restaurant for seven. Pick me up at six thirty."

"That works for me."

"See you Wednesday night Charles. Bye."

"See you then. Bye."

On Tuesday night, CC met Mary Johnson at Alberto's for a dinner meeting. The hostess seated them in a quiet corner table CC had requested. They ordered two espresso martinis, something Alberto's is famous for, and CC loved the coffee beans that floated on top. Mary was dressed in a sunflower yellow dress that just skimmed her knees. She had a thin gold necklace, with a single pearl that peeked from between the top buttons of the dress. The matching pearl post earrings made the outfit very summery and cool. When the waitress left to place the order, Mary spoke.

"Charles, I'm going to receive a life insurance payment on a policy Ken had taken out. Since you're in the local area and had been giving Ken advice, I thought I would ask you for your opinion on how to handle the distribution."

"How much money are you expecting?"

"Well, from what the agent told me, Ken had a term insurance policy in the amount of one million dollars."

"That will be a nice amount to add to the other investments."

"It will. As you already know, Ken had quite a few funds with Fidelity. Plus he gets royalties on his cooking ventures, the books, shows, equipment etc."

"I know about a few of his funds, but from the sound of it, he had many other things going as well."

"He did. I don't know if I should be consolidating some of the investments and things or not."

"When you get a number of investments working for you at the same time in different places, it can become overwhelming."

"That's how I'm starting to feel."

"Well, I might be able to help you in that area."

"What do you have in mind?"

"If you can get me information about all of the things Ken was involved in, I can help you put together a cohesive financial plan that will be more straight forward, easy to understand, and easy to follow."

"That would be helpful."

"Then round up what you can and then call me when you're ready to have me start an analysis."

"Ok, that sounds good to me."

CC changed the subject. "I understand the seafood pasta dish is excellent here."

"I think every dish they have here is excellent. I'm going to have the vegetarian lasagna though. If I'm going to be bad and have a martini, and one of their freshly baked rolls, I've got to have vegetables somewhere."

CC thought about it and said, "I think I'll order the seafood pasta."

They ordered and continued to talk about things other than Ken or finances. The seafood pasta was just as good as everyone said. Charles ate every bite, even soaking up the last of the spicy sauce with one of the homemade rolls that still sat in the breadbasket.

After dinner Mary said, "Charles, I'm really glad we had the opportunity to get together."

"Oh, why is that?"

"You're very easy to talk to and you're very knowledgeable on a number of subjects."

"When you're a financial consultant, your work takes you into many different scenarios."

"I'm sure it does. Tell me again, just how did you get to know Ken?"

"Ken had been doing most of his investing directly with Fidelity. He wanted to have someone he could meet with without having to go to Boston, and a friend of mine at Fidelity referred him to me."

"That was nice of your friend."

"You'd be surprised how that happens more often than not."

"I guess."

"Ken and I met a number of times to talk about opportunities he was interested in. Sometimes it involved Fidelity, sometimes it didn't. Like when he wanted to branch out into starting a local restaurant under his name."

"He didn't mention that to me."

"Probably because when I did the research for him, it showed he would be better off opening a restaurant in the Boston area than on Cape Cod. He dropped that idea."

"I had no idea."

"Ken had a good nose for business. He would evaluate the upside and downside and make a decision. That was probably what allowed him to amass a nice nest egg." CC thought this technique of sharing an unknown fact about the deceased was a great way to answer questions such as Mary's. After all, now that Ken is gone, who's going to know?

After dinner, they ordered after dinner drinks. She had an Irish coffee; he had Bailey's on the rocks. Mary made a toast.

"To a good evening, good advice, and good company."

"I can't argue with that."

They laughed a little and made small talk for the balance of the dinner meeting. Finally Mary said, "Well, thank you Mr. Charles Chamberlin. This meeting was certainly worth it."

"I'm glad you feel that way. If you can get me that information we discussed by next week, I'll begin to work on it and get back to you promptly."

"I'll do that."

CC walked her to her car. He noticed it was a chilly evening. Mary pulled her white sweater tighter around her waist, as CC wrapped a warming arm around her shoulders. They hugged briefly and said their good nights. "She's a pleasant person" CC thought to himself.

When Mary got home she called her friend Karen. "I had a dinner meeting with Charles Chamberlin tonight. What a nice man, and so good looking, too. I have good feelings about him."

"Did you have him over after dinner?

"No."

"Why not?"

"I think it's too soon."

"If you aren't going after him, maybe I should."

"No, too soon for me. But come on Karen, give me some time."

"Maybe I'll try him anyway," Karen taunted.

"Whatever. You let me know if you get anywhere."

"I'll keep you posted. Oh, I have another call coming in. I'll call you tomorrow Mary."

"OK. Bye."

The next morning, CC went through his routine again. He had a number of things in the works and wasn't really looking for another target when he noticed an obituary for a Ronald Pierce.

Pierce, Ronald J.

Ronald J. Pierce, age 39 of Bourne, MA, formerly of South Yarmouth, passed away on Tuesday. Beloved husband of Ann (Woodward) Pierce, devoted son of Teresa C. (Asbury) Pierce and the late F. R. Pierce, Sr., brother of Thomas H., Maureen S; also survived by his aunt Marie Asbury, nieces, nephews and cousins.

Ron was a well-known Realtor on Cape Cod. He headed the local Century21 real estate office in Bourne and was the owner of numerous resort properties on Cape Cod.

Relatives and friends are invited to his Funeral Mass on Friday, 10 a.m. St. Pius Church, Bourne and Overlook Cemetery, Bourne. Calling hours Thursday 7 to 9 p.m. at Nickerson-Bourne Funeral Home, 40 Central Blvd., Bourne, MA.

In lieu of flowers, donations can be made in his memory to the Barnstable County Regional Cancer Ctr. 501 Main Street, Hyannis. www.nickersonbournefuneralhome.com.

CC speculated if Mr. Pierce was in real estate and had been the owner of a number of resorts on Cape Cod, he must have a decent net worth. He went to his computer and entered the name "Ronald Pierce". The Google search returned over ten pages of hits. Mr. Ronald Pierce had been in the news many times. He had become a very successful businessman in the resort properties community. Scanning the articles, CC could see Mr. Pierce owned five prominent resorts in Bourne, Falmouth, Hyannis, Cotuit and Sandwich. In addition to articles about Mr. Pierce and resort properties, there were numerous articles describing Mr. Pierce's experiences in real estate. He had sold a number of business properties and upper scale homes. One article even described Mr. Pierce as one of Cape Cod's mega millionaires.

Busy or not, CC would definitely follow up on this potential target.

On Thursday at six o'clock CC left his house for the wake in Bourne. He figured it would take him forty minutes to drive there so he allowed a few extra minutes to find the place. He thought he knew where the funeral home was so he didn't request directions from Map quest. When he got to Bourne, the funeral home wasn't located where he thought. He stopped at a gas station and asked for directions. Not a very "manly" thing to do, CC thought, but he didn't want to be late. The place was only a few miles from where he stopped.

Entering the funeral home, the wake was very crowded. In keeping with the information he had read from his Internet search, Mr. Pierce knew a lot of people. Some of the people in the room wore their work blazers. He could tell this by the emblems on the breast pocket announcing the most prominent real estate firms on Cape Cod. CC got in line to pay his respects. Arriving at the front of the room, he was greeted by Mrs. Ann Pierce. She was dressed in a sleeveless black dress and comfortable looking black ballet shoes. She wore a simple gold chain necklace that held a heart pendant with the letter A engraved in it. She wore simple diamond stud earrings and had her hair pulled back with a barrette. Her demeanor seemed typical of a grieving widow; swollen eyes from crying and a crumpled tissue in her hand.

CC took her hand and said, "I'm Charles Chamberlin. I'm so sorry for your loss. I knew Ron through my business."

Ann looked at CC and said, "Thank you for coming Mr. Chamberlin."

CC moved down the line to the next person and said a similar "I'm so sorry".

When he reached the last person in the line, he extended his hand to say I'm sorry and Andrew Dunn greeted him.

Andrew said, "Charles, you knew Sunny, I mean Ron?"

CC was taken aback a little but said, "Yes Andrew, I did."

"My firm handled the books for Ron's enterprises. He was a young and successful businessman, and it's too bad he passed away. Stick around for a while Charles. I'd like to talk for a few minutes. I'm going to take a break soon."

"I'll be in the back of the room or outside getting a breath of air."

"I'll come find you."

CC wondered what Andrew's connection to Ron was, but he was almost afraid to ask, because if CC actually knew Ron, perhaps he should already know the connection. CC moved off to the back of the room. He observed Andrew greeting the mourners. He seemed to know many of the people by first name. CC would have to be careful in how he handled his conversation with Andrew.

Around twenty minutes later, Andrew found Charles just outside talking to a couple of men who were in the real estate business.

Andrew said, "Charles, Katherine has told me good things about you."

"Oh she has?"

"Yes. She said you've been very helpful walking her through many of the financial obstacles a widow faces and in providing her advice going forward."

"I'm glad my clients say those nice things about my business."

"Yes. She said you have hidden talents you are shy about bringing out but she has been working on you and feels your future looks very promising."

"She said all that did she?"

"Well, that's the short version."

"If you say so. I'm flattered."

"Not to change the subject, but Mrs. Pierce is going to need financial consultation and advice in the near future. Would you mind if I referred her to you?"

"Not at all. I'd be delighted to help her. As I mentioned earlier, I did some consultation to her husband over the last few years, so I'm already familiar with some of the details. My business grew considerably as a result of his referrals. It would be like repaying an unpaid debt helping her."

"Then I'll speak to Ann and I'll see if we can all meet at my office once she's able to function. As you could see she's not exactly focusing. "

"I noticed. That would be fine with me."

"Well, I have to be getting back. Nice to see you again."

"Same here."

CC went home and created a paper file with printed marketing material for his consulting business. He also put in some spreadsheets and pie charts describing a few business ideas, cost/benefit analysis, and descriptive information about CC's experience. He labeled the file *Chamberlin Consulting*. He would keep the file in his car in case an opportunity presented itself to put it in Ron Pierce's home office files. Next, he created a file that described a new resort idea that was currently under development in the Hyannis area. He labeled that file *Resorts* and put it in the car as well.

On Friday, he attended the funeral and burial. He saw Andrew again at the church and cemetery. "Charles, we're having a little get together at Ron's house after the burial. Can you come over for a while? I'd like to formally introduce you to Ann."

"Sure. I don't have another appointment until two this afternoon."

"Good. Just follow me when we leave." Andrew gestured towards a black Cadillac Escalade as he spoke.

"Will do."

CC followed Andrew to the Pierce residence. When he got out of the car, he took the files he had put in the car with him. Entering the house, Andrew took him aside and said, "Charles, Ann's still a little upset so keep that in mind when I introduce you to her."

"Of course she is. I understand."

Andrew left for a minute and came back with Ann Pierce. CC recognized her from the wake. Andrew said, "Ann, this is Charles Chamberlin. Charles is a financial consultant and he is currently representing some of my clients."

CC took her hand and said, "Again Mrs. Pierce, I am so sorry for your loss."

"Thank you Mr. Chamberlin. So you and Andrew have a number of clients in common?"

"We do."

Andrew said, "Excuse me Ann. I'll leave you and Charles to speak privately"

"Yes. Thank you, Andrew."

Andrew left and Ann said, "Mr. Chamberlin."

"Please call me Charles."

"Ok. Charles. My husband was involved in a number of different financial matters. I'm sure I don't even know the extent of all of them. Andrew said you have a good reputation and you provide solid advice. He said you have a number of clients who are widows."

"I have many different clients. It just seems the people I have in common with Andrew are mostly widows."

"Well, that's not a bad thing because you've probably seen things from a widow's perspective. That's a real plus."

"I hadn't thought of it that way. I guess I just view each client as unique."

"Anyway, I'd like to be able to call on you for advice when things settle down. Are you taking on new clients?"

"I'd be honored to help you in any way I can. I owe Ron for some of the doors he opened up for my business. In fact, I have a file here that should be returned to his office."

He held the file up for her to see it. She could read the file labeled *Resorts*.

"Is that something you were working on with Ron?"

"Yes. You know that new resort that's being developed down by Hyannis?"

"Yes, Ron talked about it often."

"I don't know if he got into that one, but he had me do some research work for him about it. I'd like to give you the file to have it put back in his office."

Ann pointed to a set of closed french doors, "That's Ron's home office. Why don't you just put it on the desk in there."

"Ok. I'll be right back."

As CC was opening the office door, he glanced back at Ann. She was now talking to three women. He entered the office. Coming around the back of the desk, he put the *Resorts* file on it. He then pulled open the right hand desk drawer, saw file folders, and slipped the *Chamberlin Consulting* file where it fit alphabetically. He then pressed the on button on the monitor sitting on the desk. He moved the mouse and the screen came to life half filled with icons. He took a CD out of his pocket and put it in the drive. He clicked on the Start button in the lower left corner of the screen, and clicked on the CD. Then he clicked the install icon. Within a few minutes PCTrackR was installed. Again. He clicked the home icon in the internet line. When the Yahoo home screen appeared he entered the name of the resort in Hyannis into the search window. The screen that came up indicated the new property was taking pre-construction applications and had a number of pictures showing the progress.

Just then, the door to the office opened. Andrew walked in. He walked over to the desk and said, "Charles, what are you doing in here?"

"I had a file to drop off and Ann said I should leave it on the desk."

"Yea, I heard. But what are you doing on Ron's computer?"

"I was just looking up one of the properties I had done some work on for Ron."

Andrew could see the screen was showing the Hyannis-Nantucket Resort home page. CC picked up the file and said, "This is the resort I had researched for Ron."

Andrew took the file and opened it. The first page he saw inside showed the same image of the Hyannis-Nantucket Resort on it. It was followed by a few spreadsheets with names, pictures and numbers on them. CC said the lists represented potential purchasers of Resort shares Ron had been pursuing.

CC pressed the off button on the monitor. He said, "Let's return to the others. I can look up the rest of the information when I get home."

While CC wasn't sure, Andrew was really not suspicious of Charles. The paper file on the desk appeared to be legitimate and the screen he observed matched the file, and what Charles said he was doing. Plus, all he had heard from Katherine about Charles was very glowing.

"Charles, can I get you a drink?"

"Sure, scotch and soda."

They left the office. PCTrackR, of course, was staying behind.

Chapter 18

Thirty-eight years old, five foot seven inches tall, 135 pounds, slender with a nice figure, Ann Pierce had become a wealthy, young, beautiful widow. CC thought she was way too young to be a widow but sometimes that happened. Having all the wealth her husband had amassed had allowed her to live a life style second to none. She drove a high end Mercedes 500. She dressed in the latest fashions. She had her long blond hair freshly highlighted and trimmed once a month. Manicures and pedicures were weekly treats. She belonged to the best golf and fitness clubs in the area. She lived in a large home that while not a mansion was bigger than she needed, and beautifully appointed. The landscaping was professionally done, as was the interior designs.

Ann had been educated at Boston University where she majored in English. While attending college, she met Ken at a frat party at MIT. He was enrolled with a finance major, business management minor, and a lot of ideas about making it big when he finished college. The two dated off and on for two years and then when Ken was in his senior year, he asked her to marry him. The year following her graduation, they were married. By then, Ken had taken the real estate exam and was licensed as a realtor.

During the early years, he sold every piece of property he could get his hands on. He was the real estate person of the year three years running. By the time he was in his late twenties, he had already earned his first million. Ann made sure their life style kept pace with Ken's income. She made sure he dressed the part and drove the nicest cars. When Ken had dinner meetings, Ann would accompany him to the finest restaurants in the area. In fact, Ann would take care of all of the details for all of the social events. In a few short years, she was a well-known member of the "in crowd".

She worked charity events by organizing them and acting as emcee on numerous occasions. When dignitaries would come to the region, Ann made sure Ken got an invitation. She knew the value of rubbing elbows with the right people. When Ken decided to get involved in resort properties, it was Ann's connections that helped him with some of the obstacles he faced dealing with the local government bureaucracies. She had the contacts with the husbands and wives of the parties with whom Ken did business.

Their lives became so active; they decided to put off having children. Then, by the time Ann was thirty-five, she had decided children were not in the cards. She liked her life style and so did Ken. Their discretionary spending and social calendars were just too much of an anti-kids factor. They were the couple on the go, involved in just about everything. Then it all came crashing down when Ken had an aneurysm. He was in the hospital for two days. Doctors were unable to clear the clot in his brain with medication and could not operate given the location of the clot. On the second day, Ken died.

CC didn't know if it was fortunate or unfortunate he had met Andrew at the wake. Andrew said good things about him and set up a meeting for the next week where CC could make a pitch to Ann. He would have to think about the situation more and decide how to approach it. He just wasn't sure how close Ann and Andrew were. His caution was elevated.

CC had the weekend to think about Ann Pierce. He would formulate a strategy by Sunday evening. In the meanwhile, he had been invited to join Carol Tindle at a party on Saturday night. He had decided to go thinking it would be fun to do something with Carol. Just as he thought he'd go into weekend mode, the phone on his desk rang.

"Charles, its Andrew. I know this might be short notice, but Mrs. Pierce is pretty anxious to get her financial house in order, and was interested in having a meeting, with you, at my office Monday morning. Are you available?"

Charles quickly flipped his desk calendar over to Monday. He was available all day. "I am, Andrew. What time?"

"Make it ten. You know where the office is. I'll see you there."

Charles wasn't sure he did know where the office was, but with technology today, it would be easy enough to find.

On Saturday, CC dressed in casual clothes. He wore a button down shirt with a sweater vest and had on a pair of dark slacks. At a little before seven, he picked Carol up at her house. Carol was dressed in dark brown corduroy slacks and a short sweater in Tiffany blue. She had it buttoned half way, and an ivory camisole peaked from the top button. CC complimented her.

"Carol, you look nice tonight.

"Thank you Charles."

As the two got into his car, he said, "Which way?"

Carol looked at the invitation and said, "Take a left at the corner and the second right after that. Then look for number twenty-two on the right side of the street. It's a gray colonial."

"Left, second right, then number twenty-two. Got it."

They arrived at the home where the party was being held a few minutes later. There were a few cars in the driveway and a few lining the street.

Carol said, "Looks like most of the other people are already here."

"How many are you expecting?"

"I don't know exactly. Maybe twenty. Charles, don't you like crowds?"

"Oh, I like them, I just don't know if I brought enough business cards with me."

"No business please. This is supposed to be a relaxing night out."

"What if someone asks me what I do, for my number?"

"Tell them you are a con-artist and don't use phones."

"Right. I'll come up with something."

The party was in full swing. Carol introduced Charles to her friends who were having drinks and chatting. After making two martinis, CC handed one to Carol and she made a toast to him. "To a fun filled evening."

"To one of many."

They sipped their martinis and joined the others. A group of twelve were all around a table playing a game called L, R, C. It's a pretty straightforward game where three dice are used. The dice have an L, an R, a C and a dot on them. Each player joins the game with three dollars. Each of the players take turns rolling the dice and take their instructions from what shows up on the dice. A player gets to throw up to three dice depending on how many dollars the player has left. If a player rolls a dot, an L and a C, for example, that player puts one dollar in a pile in the center of the table and passes one dollar to the player to that person's left. The dot is neutral and does not require any action. If a player has no dollars left, that player cannot roll any dice until someone to their left or right rolls an L or R giving the person with no dollars one or more. This process continues until only one player is left and all of the other players have either put their dollars in the center pile or given them to the last player standing. The last player with money gets all the money in the center. You won't get rich, but the game is fun. Charles and Carol joined in the next game.

Within twenty minutes, the only players left in the round were Carol and Charles. Everyone commented it was beginners luck. Charles had said he felt lucky that night and Carol had better watch out. Carol had three dollars left and CC only had one. It was his turn to roll. He rolled one die, because he only had one dollar, and it came up a dot. Carol took all three dice and rolled three Cs. Charles howled and said, "I told you I felt lucky."

He collected the pile of ones and put them in his pocket. Carol told him she would make them both another martini to celebrate his winning.

They stepped out of the game and went into the next room to have their drinks.

"Charles, I'm really having a good time."

"Me too. But I'm going to have to slow down on the martinis. I have to drive home later."

"Oh, it's only around the corner. You can stay at my place tonight."

"Am I going to get lucky more than once tonight?"

"We'll see."

The two chatted with the other partygoers for another few hours. The guests were all in various states of intoxication, with the designated drivers speaking to each other away from the crazy people. While CC and Carol partied with the crazy people, when midnight arrived, CC was ready to hit the road. "It's getting pretty late. I have some things to do tomorrow. Do you think we can get going soon?"

Carol, who had had a bit too much to drink by then said, "Sure Charles. Give me a few minutes."

Driving home, they talked about the fun they had at the party. Arriving at Carol's house, Carol said she had too much to drink and she needed to lie down. CC looked at her and smiled. Parking the car in her driveway, CC had to help her get inside. While he went back to close the front door to the house, Carol went down the hall to the guest bedroom, which was the last room on the left side of the hallway.

Charles followed her. When he got inside the room, he closed the door and joined her on the edge of the bed. He sat down next to her. Charles put his arms around her and kissed her on the cheek.

"I need to get some sleep," she said.

"Here, let me help you get changed."

169

He started to undo the buttons on her sweater. Carol didn't resist. After he undid the last button, the camisole slipped easily over her head.

He reached around behind her to undo her bra. At first he had trouble getting the clasp to let go so Carol reached around and assisted him in undoing it. He moved her bra away and gently held her breasts. Her breasts were full and firm. After a few minutes of fondling, CC reached over and undid the catch on her pants. Next he unzipped her pants and reached down. Carol sighed. Carol leaned back either enjoying the attention or getting ready to pass out.

As she lay back, she was within easy reach of CC. She undid his pants and reached in. They had each other for the next few minutes when CC noticed Carol had stopped moving. Looking over at her from his position, he could see she had indeed passed out. He slowly got up off the bed. He made an attempt to right her clothing and then covered her with the bed blanket. Then he picked up his things, kissed her on the cheek and left. He just smiled as he locked and closed the front door to the house behind him.

When Carol woke the next morning, she was in her guest bedroom. She was somewhat dressed from the night before. Her blouse was undone as was her bra. Her pants and underwear were off one leg. The bed was a mess with pillows and blankets thrown all around, some on the floor. She wondered what happened.

She called Charles at ten.
He answered and said, "Good morning Carol. How are you doing?"
"I have a headache."
"I don't doubt that."
"What happened last night? I don't remember anything after we left the party."
"Well, you had too much to drink and decided it was time to call it a night."
"I really don't remember much. What happened?"

170

"You needed some help so I helped you get into bed."

"But in the guest room?"

"That's where you ended up so that's where I left you."

"Why are my clothes half on and half off?"

"You were struggling to get them off and asked me to help you."

"So what happened?"

"I was having trouble getting your bra off. Then you helped me and together we got the clasp undone."

"Didn't you have too much to drink, too?"

"Not really. I stopped earlier in the night. Remember we talked about it last night?"

"No I don't remember. But then again, I don't remember much."

"Then while I was trying to help you with your slacks, you took advantage of me."

"I did?"

"You did. We were in the middle of enjoying each other when you passed out."

"I passed out?"

"Yes you did. So I tried to make you comfortable and then I locked up and left."

"What time was that?"

"I think it was one or one-thirty."

"And you drove home?"

"As I told you, I had some things to be done today and you were out of it. I figured the best thing for you would be a good nights sleep. So I left."

"Did we have sex?"

"Not in the traditional sense."

"I would have liked to wake up with you next to me this morning."

"So would I and I hope to make that happen soon."

"I'd like that. Why don't you do the things you need to do and come over when you're done?"

"I don't think I can make it today. I have stuff I have to spend some time on, and I have no idea how long it will take me to get ready for the upcoming week. I'll call you later on in the week as soon as I can free up time where we won't be interrupted."

Carol, pouting, said, "Alright."

"Bye, and get some rest."

"Ok."

Chapter 19

On Monday morning, CC changed his routine as he had a ten o'clock meeting at Andrew's office to meet with Ann Pierce. CC had spent Sunday afternoon gathering his information and preparing his presentation for Ann. Since Andrew had given CC such a glowing recommendation, CC thought he had a good chance of landing her as a client. If he were able to convince her to utilize his services, then CC might be able to steer some of the investments into items that would lend themselves to easy liquidation down the road. Ron Pierce definitely had lots of money. Now it was all in Ann's hands and she was seeking advice. Poor thing.

CC decided to put off his usual duties of reading e-mails and his other regular computer investigative work until after his morning meeting. He gathered three copies of his assembled marketing materials, put them each in a softbound folder and put the finished products into his briefcase. He had prepared a PowerPoint presentation to visually illustrate his organization and comprehension skills relative to Ron's portfolio. The last page identified a number of possible considerations for Ann to think about going forward. CC was ready for the meeting.

At ten CC was greeted by Andrew as he entered the Sterns and Dunn office. Andrew indicated Ann was in the restroom and they could begin as soon as CC was ready. CC got himself a cup of coffee and flipped on his laptop. He brought up the presentation on the monitor, and made sure it was ready to go. When he turned around, Ann had entered the conference room.

"Mr. Chamberlin. It was nice of you to come."

"Please call me Charles. And the pleasure is all mine. I look forward to sharing my ideas with you and Andrew."

"Thanks for coming Charles. I'm sure your advice will be beneficial for Ann, and it will help me to better understand your services in case any of my other clients have similar needs."

CC didn't know why Andrew was being so helpful. He barely knew him. But from what he gathered, Katherine had said very good things to Andrew about him and she had benefited from his financial advice already. What CC didn't know was whether Ron Pierce was one of Sterns and Dunn's larger clients if not the largest single client. Andrew's strength was in accounting. In the past, his deceased partner Sam had handled these kinds of things. CC thought, "Is Andrew looking for a partner?"

Andrew asked CC to begin. Over the next half hour, CC went through the various holdings that could be in Ron Pierce's portfolio. He covered Stocks, Mutual Funds, Bonds, Residential Properties and Resort Properties. CC indicated Andrew would be better positioned to talk about the value of the various holdings and his focus would be on a strategy going forward. One of the first things he did was ask Ann how much involvement she wanted to have with the various holdings. She indicated that while she was involved in the social aspects associated with some of the resort holdings, she didn't have a keen working knowledge of some of them and would prefer not to have to get into a level of detail that would take up her time.

When CC got to the last page in his presentation, the first consideration was "Sell." The second consideration was "Partner." The third consideration was "Third Party Manage." And the last consideration was "Self Manage." CC looked at Andrew. His expression was that of indifference. Ann on the other hand had a frown on her face.

CC said, "Ann, you look puzzled."

"Well, I understand "Sell" and I should probably consider serious offers for the residential and resort properties. I assume you could help me with the other investments?"

CC said, "I could or any qualified advisor could."

Then she said, "But the other two, Third Party Manage or Partner are choices I hadn't considered."

CC said, "There are firms that perform Third Party Management. Think of it like a Time Share Company or a Property Manager. And as far as Partnering, I'm sure there are entities out there that would love to be a partner with you in the Resorts in Ron's Estate. You could retain ownership, and derive income from the investments, but have the Partner deal with the things you aren't interested in. You'd always have the asset, and down the road, who knows."

Ann said, "What would I have to give up to pursue either of these two choices?"

CC said, "You would probably have to give up some ownership percentage and probably have to give up routine management decision making."

Ann said, "I don't know if I want to be involved in day-to-day operations anyway."

CC said, "So that really wouldn't be a problem."

Ann said, "What would I get in return?"

CC said, "You would continue to be majority owner. You would probably continue to get a nice income stream plus the tax benefits."

Ann looked to Andrew and said, "Andrew, what do you think?"

"Ann, if it were me and I didn't really want to be involved in some of the holdings, I'd look to see what I could get for them. If the price were right, I'd sell now. You could always take the proceeds, invest otherwise, and derive an even better return or income stream, without the headaches of ownership at all."

Ann said, "Thank you Andrew for being so candid. I think that's what I would like to do."

CC said, "You should be able to get a very nice price for the resort properties. I gather from my research they are all in great shape and have strong bookings."

Andrew said, "I can attest to that. Ron did a superb job with the resort properties. Their occupancy rate is over ninety percent."

Ann said, "How should I go about selling those holdings?"

Andrew said, "I have some contacts I can call. I had dealings with some of these people when I worked with Ron doing the books for the Resorts. I'm sure they'll be interested or know of people who are interested."

Ann said, "Great. Charles, if it looks like the properties can be sold, can you provide me with your thoughts about what I should do with the proceeds?"

CC said, "Yes, I can. When you have some idea of the levels of funds you would be getting out of a transaction, we can start to look at considerations at that time. You have to be comfortable with your risk tolerance at that time as well."

Ann said, "It looks like we have a plan. Charles, what kind of business arrangement can you offer me?"

CC said, "For this kind of work, I work on a retainer basis. My fee is twelve thousand five hundred dollars per month for up to forty hours and then two hundred fifty dollars per hour after that plus expenses. We can work on a month to month basis."

Ann turned to Andrew and said, "Does that sound fair to you?"

"I'd say it's definitely competitive. If anything, Charles is on the lower end plus his offer isn't taking a percentage."

Ann said, "What do you mean a percentage?"

"Some advisors want a percentage of funds under management or a percentage of funds being considered for investment."

Ann said, "That could be a very big number couldn't it?"

Andrew said, "Sure could."

Ann turned to CC and said, "Mr. Chamberlin, you have a deal. Get me your contract you need signed and I'll execute it."

CC said, "Great. I look forward to working for you."

Returning back to his office, he felt good about the meeting. He would send Ann a contract and begin working for her as a financial consultant. He would steer her into selling the Resort properties and the other residential properties. His goal was to get as much of her assets into fairly liquid holdings as quickly as possible.

He logged on to his computer and brought up e-mail. He had a number of incoming e-mails in the list of which a few had "Strokes Included" in the subject line.   With PCTrackR installed at four target sites, he should be getting these files regularly now.

The first e-mail he opened from PCTrackR was from CAROLT. He downloaded the attached file and stored it as CT Strokes 2. When he opened the file, he began to evaluate the contents of the keystrokes that had been captured. It looked like she had been looking things up on eBay® because he could see www.ebay.com followed by the words "Caribbean cruise". It looked to him like she was researching a trip.

The next entry was to www.boa.com. It was followed by CAROLT and then by TIN05. A few single keystrokes had followed and then an entry to www.SmithBarney.com appeared. It was also followed by the same CAROLT and then TIN05 as the previous entry. In each instance, there were only a few keystrokes captured. She must have been looking at her account balances without making any changes.

The next entry was e-mail to Charles Chamberlin. The e-mail said she had a good time at the party on Saturday and she had been looking into Caribbean cruises and wanted to know if Charles was interested. He thought about it for a minute and a smile appeared on his face. He was definitely interested.

The next entry was another e-mail. This one was to her friend Susan. In it she told Susan about going home with Charles after a neighborhood party and she had too much to drink. She had written that when she woke up the next morning, her clothing was half on and half off and Charles had left. She didn't have any recollection of what happened. She ended the e-mail telling her friend she thinks they had sex but she really didn't know. CC would have to bring her up to date as to how the night ended.

The last entry in the attachment file was e-mail to Cape Cod Investigative Services from Carol. In her e-mail, she had indicated a check for fifteen thousand dollars was being sent. CC wondered what that was all about. He got a sick feeling in his stomach. She had requested the written report of their findings be mailed to her home address. He would have to figure out a way to bring it up with her.

When he finished with his e-mails, he used his computer to check on his targets' accounts. He first selected Carol Tindle. CC logged into www.SmithBarney.com. He used the ID CAROLT and password TIN05. The three point two million dollars was still there. He logged into her www.boa.com account. The CD amounts had increased due to interest crediting as did the money market account, but the money market account also had a withdrawal for twenty thousand dollars leaving a balance of one hundred eighty thousand dollars. He figured she must be living off the money market funds and needed money to pay bills. CC made entries into his targets spreadsheet file of the information he had seen.

CC looked at the next e-mail in his in box. It was from his attorney. He opened it. His attorney indicated the suit against Sharon Kelly had been settled. He wrote he had received a check for two hundred thousand dollars and he would withhold his retainer plus out of pocket expenses, and would send the balance of one hundred thirty three thousand dollars on to CC's Cayman account. CC smiled, "It's good to be the victim, sometimes."

The next e-mail was from Mary Johnson. She told CC in the e-mail she had attached a file identifying all of Ken's holdings. She said the balances were as of the last statements Ken had put in his files and she would provide him with the account information when they get together next. CC clicked on the attachment and downloaded an Excel spreadsheet that had been attached. He labeled it mjohnson.xls.

The last e-mail that was not junk mail was also from PCTrackR. He opened the file. It was from APIERCE. He saved it as AP Strokes 1. She had logged into www.ingdirect.com and had used PIERCEA as an ID and Part as the password. He would make a note of it in his files. She had requested something to be done with an amount of one hundred thousand dollars. He wrote down the keystrokes so he could figure it out when he accessed the account.

When done, CC brought up Microsoft Word and selected a file named "sample agreement." He filled in the blanks identifying Ann Pierce as the client and the fee structure he had discussed with her. The text describing the services stated Chamberlin Financial Services would be providing personal consulting services to Ann Pierce in the areas of Stocks, Bonds, Mutual Funds and Real Estate. CC saved the file as Piercecontract.doc. Then he went back to his e-mail account and addressed an e-mail to Ann. In the text he indicated a written agreement of their relationship was attached and if she had any questions, she should call him. If not, she should print two copies and sign both. He said once the agreements were executed, to call him and he would make arrangements to pick them up. He said he would sign both documents when he got them and give one original back to her for her records.

Finishing up with his administrative duties, CC checked his calendar. He should be getting files from PCTrackR KSterns and PLee soon. He saw the light on his phone blinking, messages he hadn't retrieved. He picked up the phone and called for messages. There was one from Katherine. She was asking him if he could come over and help her install her new computer.

After deleting the message, he called Katherine.

"Hello Katherine. I just got your message. So you got a new computer?"

"I did. I'm in the process of trying to get my files moved from the old machine to the new one and I am having some trouble with my financial institution data."

"What kind of trouble are you having?"

"I don't seem to be able to get the sites to load properly so I can just click on an icon to gain access. I think they're called shortcuts?"

"That's a pretty easy thing to do. When would you like me to come over?"

"Could you come by today?"

"I think I could do that. What time?"

"Any time will be fine. How about I make you dinner?"

"You don't have to do that. I'll see you this afternoon." He put the PCTrackR CD in his briefcase, and headed for home. It would probably be easier to install a new version of PCTrackR than to try and move it from one PC to the other.

Chapter 20

When CC got home, he checked his e-mails again. He only had one, from Ann Pierce, that had an Excel file attached. When he opened the attachment, he saw an inventory of all of the investments of her husband, Ron. Since he had obtained an ID and password from the strokes file he had received earlier from PCTrackR, CC decided to go to a few of the investment sites and see if he could gather any additional information.

He went to the www.troweprice.com site and logged in as *PierceA* with a password of *Part*. To his satisfaction, he gained access to the account. Under *My Accounts*, a number of mutual funds were listed with current balances.

New Era	$243,546.77
Emerging Markets Stock	$171,541.21
Latin America	$332,336.89

CC looked at the summary line and it showed $747,424.87. CC would track these funds for future potential.

Next, he went to the www.ingdirect.com site and again entered the same ID and password. He was granted access and the account returned balance information of $2,110,052.68.

The last liquid fund he found in Ann's e-mail he could quickly access was to the www.bankofamerica.com site. Using the same ID and password, he gained access. Two accounts were listed. One a checking account and the other a companion money market account. The checking account had a current balance of $18,854.40 and the money market account had a balance of $700,000. With such an even amount, CC guessed the money market account must have just been set up and the funds recently deposited. He selected the history option and it confirmed his suspicion. The funds were transferred into the account just a few days earlier, probably the same day as the funeral. Ann had been busy getting the accounts into her name and moving some assets around.

Some of the other assets in the spreadsheet, such as the residential properties and resorts, would take further research to assess their value. He had time and had already identified a nice asset base from which to work.

Shifting gears, CC picked up a pad and pencil, and started to jot down ideas he would use later to work on Katherine's thought process relative to Sterns and Dunn. There had to be a few million more at stake. CC thought they would be easy pickings, but only if Katherine continued to have access to it. He looked up at the telephone, and saw the light was blinking, indicating he had messages waiting. Seems messages were waiting for him everywhere today. Calling in, he had a message from a Mr. Ted Miller. Miller identified himself as Mary Johnson's financial advisor. He wanted to talk with CC about the Johnson situation. CC thought the word *situation* was odd, as he wasn't aware of any *situation* with Mary.

CC wrote done Mr. Miller's phone number, and retrieved the next pending message. It was from Ann Pierce. She said the Agreement for Services was acceptable to her, and she had signed both copies. She asked Charles to call her so they could make arrangements to have him sign them. He deleted the message, and called Ann back.

"Ann, this is Charles Chamberlin."

"Hello Charles. I'm glad you returned my call so quickly. I have the signed agreements ready for you to sign."

"I can come over and pick them up if that's alright with you."

"Why don't we get together somewhere tomorrow night for dinner. I have some things I'd like to review with you."

"Six o'clock would be good for me."

"I think I can be ready by then."

"Do you have a place in mind Ann?"

"No, you pick it. Can you pick me up?"

"Sure, I'll make a reservation somewhere for six-thirty and pick you up at six."

CC had other messages but he decided he'd retrieve them later. He had to find out what this Mr. Miller wanted, get to Katherine's for her new computer installation, and he had to get ready for his dinner meeting with Ann.

CC called Mr. Miller. The receptionist answered, "PriceWaterhouse Boston. How may I direct your call?"

"I'd like to speak with Mr. Ted Miller."

"One moment please." CC could hear the call being transferred, and listened for a moment to a generic on hold musical medley. "Was that Pink Floyd?"

"This is Ted Miller. How can I help you?"

"Mr. Miller. My name is Charles Chamberlin. I'm returning your call."

"Chamberlin. Yes. My client, Mary Johnson had told me about your discussions with her relevant to her assets."

"I'm not in the habit of discussing client information with anyone other than the client."

"My policy as well Mr. Chamberlin, but Mrs. Johnson isn't your client."

"Pardon me?"

"She told me about your dinner meeting and your request for detail information regarding her assets. Her husband had set up trust funds through me prior to his death. I am the trustee of the accounts. Mary is the beneficiary or benefactor of those assets, but I am the trustee. Anything she wishes to have done with those assets must go through me."

"That's not how Mrs. Johnson represented her situation." "Ah", CC thought, "Here is the *situation* Mr. Miller referred to". "If I had known I would've respected your position in the discussions."

"Well, as you can understand, she is under a lot of stress and may not even understand her limitations in that regard."

"So what you're telling me is back off. Right?"

"That kind of sums it up."

"I understand. Mrs. Johnson won't be hearing from me again."

"Thank you Mr. Chamberlin. I appreciate your cooperation in this matter."

"Not a problem Mr. Miller. But certainly…." Before CC could finish the sentence, Mr. Miller had ended the conversation.

CC didn't want to bring any unnecessary scrutiny, especially from someone who might be able to reveal his plan before he was able to complete it. He had already identified a number of promising targets, and he didn't need Mary Johnson to screw it up. He deleted all the files he had established on his computer with her information.

Later that afternoon CC went to Katherine's and helped her with the new computer. He put the icons in for the same sites she had on the old machine. When she wasn't looking, he installed PCTrackR on the new machine and activated it. When Katherine came back and sat next to him at the computer, he was just finishing up the install and she asked him what he was doing. He had just hit the delete key on the PCTrackR icon when she said, "What was that icon for?"

"I activated your security features on this computer the same as what was on the old machine. I'm just cleaning up your desktop so you don't have to see these things all the time."

She looked at the monitor and saw it did in fact look exactly like the old one. "That looks exactly like my old desktop. This transition should be easy."

"Some of the icons might be in a different order, but it's basically the same."

"I think I can take it from here."

CC got up from Katherine's computer and said, "I think you're all set."

"Thank you Charles, you saved me hours of unnecessary frustration."

"No problem. On a separate subject, I was talking with Andrew Dunn today with another mutual client and he asked to speak with me for a few minutes when we were done."

"And?"

"Well, Andrew told me you mentioned something about considering selling your interest in Sterns and Dunn."

"Yes, I did mention it to him. We're supposed to get together later in the week to discuss other things as well."

"Andrew is concerned you have access to some of the sensitive information at the company and they will probably be restricting your access in the near future."

Matter of factly, Katherine said, "Well, as of today, I am still the majority owner in the company."

"Yes that's true, but he's concerned proprietary information not meant for public consumption will get outside the company."

"Who does he think I'll share the information with?"

"He didn't say. I can understand where he's coming from though because you're not really involved in the day-to-day operations. Even though you are legally entitled to view the information, you really have no business reason for viewing it."

"True, but I would never jeopardize my investment."

"I'm sure Andrew doesn't think you would purposely jeopardize the company, he's just being cautious."

"What do you think I should do?"

CC thought for a minute and responded, "If you want out, then let me work with Andrew on your behalf. I could represent you in selling your interest."

"Andrew and I have been through so much together, why wouldn't he just want to deal with me directly?"

"I don't think he doesn't want to, but it isn't a good practice to represent yourself in a transaction involving so much money. I'm sure, if you're serious, Andrew will have someone else representing him in the transaction."

"I guess. Well, I'm not opposed to you talking to Andrew on my behalf."

"I have some experience in these kind of matters. Let me follow up with him and see what he's thinking."

"Ok. Oh, is Ann Pierce the other client you have in common?"

"Yes, do you know her?"

"Yes. She, Ron, Sam and I played golf together in a charity golf tournament last year. We probably got paired up because no one else had brought his wife with him."

"Probably."

"I don't know her very well, but I do know who she is."

"I'd appreciate it if you didn't mention anything about being a client of mine."

"I get it. Professional integrity kind of thing."

"Something like that."

"Well, if I do talk with her, I won't say anything about us."

CC wasn't sure what she meant by that comment. As far as he knew, Katherine wasn't an *us* kind of girl. "Well, I have to go. I have another appointment this evening."

Katherine, disappointed said, "I wasn't aware I was just another appointment. Can't you stay for a while?"

"I've been here for over an hour already. What will the neighbors say?"

"They already think I'm a loose woman. So who cares?"

"I really do have to be going."

"If you have to. When can I see you again?"

"Call me after you've met with Andrew."

"Ok. But remember Charles, all work and no play makes you a dull boy."

Charles, sensing this was a warning shot, leaned gently towards Katherine and kissed her cheek. "A promise of better times. I'm sorry."

Katherine turned, and closed the front door behind her, without another word.

Getting back home, CC remembered Carol's investigative activity. CC was concerned she had someone investigating him. He didn't know what the investigation was about but was concerned enough he decided to take immediate action to carry out his plan on the Tindle accounts.

He logged into www.SmithBarney.com and utilized her ID, CAROLT, and password, TIN05. The screen showed her account balance of just over three million. He clicked on the Transfer Funds function and directed two million be transferred to his offshore account. When prompted to select either Immediate or Scheduled for the timing of the transfer, he selected Immediate. The request was processed, and a confirmation screen was returned. He would verify the transfer later.

Next, he sent an e-mail to CAROLT that had instructions embedded in it to de-activate PCTrackR. The e-mail sender field identified the e-mail as coming from Smith Barney service center. It confirmed the account had a current balance of $3,212,667, which was no longer the case, but CC didn't want Carol to know that, obviously. The e-mail was composed to look like a form statement letting her know what the current balance. But in reality, it would kick off an erasure of the PCTrackR programs. By tomorrow, CC would get the confirmation of the deposit to his account and all traces of PCTrackR would disappear from her computer. "Poor Carol", CC thought.

CC's strategy in not taking all the funds was to make it look like someone who has access to the account was siphoning off pieces. If an investigation began, it would be those persons who would be looked at first, namely Carol. It would take more time for authorities to figure out the account holders were actually the victims. The distraction would buy him some time, not that he really needed it. There was absolutely no trail that would lead to him.

He had had himself a $2,000,000 payday.

Chapter 21

The next day, CC read the papers looking for another target or two. He felt confident he would succeed in finding six or seven targets that would net him over ten million dollars once his plan was fully executed. The first two targets worked out to his satisfaction although he liked Carol Tindle and was sorry to sever his ties with her. He didn't find any suitable targets in the paper so he continued his routine and powered up his computer.

Checking his e-mail, he had an incoming e-mail from CAROLT. When he opened it, the message said Deactivation Complete. He felt confident PCTrackR had been successfully erased from her computer leaving no trace of his involvement. He logged into his offshore account and to his satisfaction saw a transfer had come in overnight for two million dollars. His plan had been successfully completed, again.

CC updated his spreadsheet where he had been keeping track of the fruits of his plan. His total take was now up to over three million five hundred thousand dollars. It might take another month or two and he would be able to find the rest of his targets and disappear never having to worry about finances again. He wrapped up his computer session and began to work on his files. He had planed on having dinner with Ann Pierce that night to discuss things so he had some homework to do. He opened her file and looked at the details.

While he was preparing for his dinner meeting, his home office phone rang. "Chamberlin Financial Services, Charles Chamberlin speaking. How may I help you?"

The caller-id said the incoming call was from Cape Cod Investigative Services Co.

"Mr. Chamberlin, my name is Robert Delano. I work for Investigative Services Company and I have been looking into a few matters for a Mrs. Carol Tindle."

"How may I help you Mr. Delano?" CC could feel the hair on the back of his neck stand on end.

"Do you know anything about any funds being transferred out of the Tindle bank account yesterday?"

"No. Why would you be calling me? Has something happened to Carol?"

"She's fine although someone transferred two million dollars out of one of Mrs. Tindle's accounts yesterday and it wasn't her."

"Who else has access to the accounts?"

"She didn't think anyone other than she and Bill Tindle had the access information to get into the accounts."

"Is it possible Mrs. Tindle moved the funds somewhere but doesn't recall?"

"She called us and asked us to investigate the matter for her so I don't think she did it. This transaction happened yesterday, so it's not like she forgot." Mr. Delano didn't want to be too specific with this Mr. Chamberlin, so if he was involved, knowing too many details might trip him up.

"I had talked to her about investments, but she didn't provide me with the information to access her accounts. We were working more on future activity rather than current assets."

"Do you know of anyone else who might have access to her accounts?"

"No, Mr. Delano, I had only recently started to talk to her about finances. I'm a financial consultant, as you may already know. Did you ask her if she had given the account access information to anyone else?"

"Not specifically, but I will."

When they hung up, Mr. Delano called Carol Tindle and asked her if she had given anyone access to the accounts. She said no, and as far as she was concerned, only she and her husband Bill had known the access information.

"Carol, this is very important. Two million dollars in funds were transferred out of the Smith Barney account last night. Only you and your husband had the ID and password to be able to get at those assets and we know he didn't do it. That leaves only you. Did anyone else have access to the account ID and password? Could Bill have set up a future transfer before he passed?"

Carol said, "I don't think so. He'd have no reason to, and I never gave the information to anyone, but I also don't know if Bill ever did."

"Well, someone has transferred funds out of the trust and I'll find out who."

"Are the funds insured?"

"No, they're not. They are only insured if the company you invested with goes belly up. Theft is not part of the protection. "

Carol, becoming nervous, said, "Can you make sure the rest of the funds are secure?"

"I've already taken care of that matter. The IDs and passwords on all the accounts were changed today from my office."

"Will you tell me what the new ID and password are?"

"I will. But for now, if you don't need access to the funds, let's leave them frozen. It might make it easier to find out how they were fraudulently accessed to begin with. If the breach originated from your home, it could happen again if you use the new codes from there. Do you understand that?"

"I do Mr. Delano. Those funds are investment oriented, so I don't need access."

"If you need anything from the account in the meanwhile, call me."

"I understand, keep me informed if you will."

Mr. Delano said he would.

Promptly at six Charles picked up Ann Pierce at her home. She greeted him at the door with a handshake, put on her blazer that had been draped across her arm and then picked up a folder off a corner table in the foyer. "I'm ready to go."

As they started towards Hyannis, Ann said, "Where did you pick for dinner?"

"Albertos. Have you been there?"

"Yes, I like the place."

"It has a few quiet corner tables and I've reserved one so we can have some privacy while talking."

"Sounds good to me."

When they arrived at Albertos, they were seated in a corner that did offer a little privacy. When they were being seated, CC looked across the room and saw Katherine Sterns sitting at a table with Andrew Dunn having dinner. CC said to Ann, "I see Andrew Dunn likes Albertos, too."

Ann turned and looked over her shoulder. "Perhaps we can share a drink after dinner. I have some things I'd like to speak with you about in confidence now that we are working together."

"You mean I'm working for you?"

"I don't like to think of it that way. I'd rather say we're working together." Ann then pushed herself away from the table.

She went over to Andrew and to say hello. Charles followed. When they got to Katherine and Andrew's table, Andrew stood and said, "Ann, Charles, nice to see you here."

He then turned to Katherine and said, "Katherine, you know Charles, do you know Ann?"

"Yes, we have met in the past. How are you Ann?"

While Ann, Katherine and Andrew politely chatted, Charles nodded to Katherine, who didn't respond at all, in any way. Ann and Charles then politely departed to resume their business dinner as the waiter brought fresh drinks to Andrew and Katherine, a beer and soda, respectively. Ann and Charles returned to their table, and sat down with their backs to the room. Katherine couldn't see or hear what was going on and it bothered her.

At one point, Charles excused himself and started for the restroom. Katherine saw CC get up and excused herself from Andrew. She said she had to go to the restroom. She waited outside the men's room for Charles to exit.

When he came out, she said, "So, this is how you're spending your evenings? She's pretty and not pregnant?"

"It's not like that Katherine. And that's a crude statement. She's a client of mine, a recent widow as you know, and I'm just beginning to do financial work for her."

"I'll bet you are. Charles, you have to know I want to be with you."

"Katherine, you're here with Andrew. I'm here with a client. It can't be anything other than that right now."

Katherine sensed an opening and said, "Does that mean there will be a time for us?"

"Why don't you have a nice evening with Andrew and I'll call you in a few days."

"Andrew doesn't satisfy me like you do. Plus, he's trying to distance himself from me as quickly as possible."

"How can you say that? He's here with you for dinner isn't he?"

"He's being polite because soon we'll be in negotiations for my part of the business, and being nice to me might pay off big time for him."

"Why do you always think there's an underlying motive for everything?"

"Because there almost always is."

"I'll call you in a few days." He walked past her and rejoined Ann at the table.

When ordering for dinner, CC asked Ann, "Would you like a wine with dinner?"

"No thank you. I don't drink."

"I didn't know that."

"I had some issues with alcohol some years ago and haven't had a drink since."

"I'm glad its worked out for you."

"It's ok. I have my fun in other ways."

"Care to share?"

"After we're done here, we'll see how the evening goes."

"You're a mysterious woman."

"Not really."

Then Ann picked up the folder she had brought with her and produced the two agreements CC had sent her. She handed them to him. He took out his pen and signed both copies and dated them. He gave her one executed copy and folded the other and put it in his jacket pocket. "Well, I'm working for you now."

"Good. Let's talk."

Over the next two hours, they had dinner and discussed all of the investments Ron had assembled. They talked about the positive and negative side of each asset and what it might mean to her if she kept an asset or sold an asset. When done, Ann looked at Charles and said, "Wow, if I liquidate some of these holdings over the next few months I'm going to have one big tax bill this year."

"Yes, you will. But most of it will be long-term gain. That will mean you pay the most favorable tax rate. Still, you want to make sure you at least set aside the tax obligation somewhere safe so you don't spend it, and then get burned April 15."

"The good news is I'll get to keep about eighty percent of what I get for those assets I liquidate."

"Yes, and you can take those funds and do whatever you desire."

"I just don't want to be involved in real estate. Too many headaches."

"As we discussed, you could have someone else handle all of the work."

"Yes that's true. But I'd rather have the funds and do other things. I'm more into the passive investments I guess."

"I understand that perfectly." CC stabbed at his chocolate drizzled tiramisu as he spoke.

"That's enough shop talk, let's get out of here." Ann put her fork down next to the crumbs of her lemon meringue pie.

CC asked the waiter for the tab. When it came, Ann said she would pay for it. Charles said, "No way. I'm old fashioned. I'll pay."

"Have it your way. But when you run out of money, don't come crying to me."

When they left, CC looked over to where Katherine and Andrew had been sitting. They had already left.

On the way back to Ann's home, Charles asked her, "So, it's after dinner. Are you going to tell me how you have fun?"

"Why don't you come in when we get to my house and I'll show you how I relax."

"Still the mystery. Ok. You have my curiosity."

"Oh, I'll get that too."

After they were in the house, Ann went to the back of the house and asked Charles to follow. She opened a set of French doors to a patio. The surroundings were very intimate and secluded. She walked over to a hot tub and asked Charles to help her remove the cover. It pivoted easily on its frame. Ann pressed a few buttons and the hot tub came to life. The lighting around the patio was low level but enough to see.

She began to remove her clothing and said to Charles, "This is one of the ways I relax. Join me?"

"Looks good to me."

"You like hot tubs?"

"I wasn't talking about the hot tub."

He took off his clothing and they both got into the hot tub. It was very nice. The temperature of the water must have been around one hundred three degrees. The swirling action of the water felt soothing on his body. As he sat back in the in-water recliner formed by the hot tub framing, Ann came over to him and kissed him. He returned the kiss and in a few minutes they were all over each other.

CC said, "Would you like to move to a drier place?"

Ann said, "Have you ever made love in the water?"

"I can't say I have."

"Then this will be a new experience for you."

She moved on top of him and allowed him to enter. They moved in one motion together in the water. At one point, CC thought he might end up going under and drowning. Ann had taken complete control. She sat up on him and worked up and down creating waves in the hot tub. He reached for her breasts, not for pleasure but for safety. Finally, she reached climax and lay down on him.

"Did you climax at the same time?"

CC lied and said, "I sure did."

"What did you think?"

CC lied again and said, "That was a wonderful experience. And a first for me." To himself he thought, "I hope that never happens to me again."

"Lets try it again soon."

"Next time, I get to pick the place. Maybe dry and stationary?"

"Where's your sense of adventure Charles?"

"I think I lost it in the hot tub."

"Let me get us some towels." Ann pulled herself out of the tub, her tanned skin glistening in the moonlight. CC started rethinking this whole hot tub thing. Ann was very good looking. It was clear to him she either came from good genes or took care of her figure. Regardless of why, her skin was smooth and pulled taut across her muscles. Her stomach, her legs, her shoulders; they were all flawless.

"Should I follow you Ann?"

"Yes. We can take a quick shower and wash off the chemicals."

"That sounds good to me." CC wondered what kind of husband Ron had been, seeing as his wife was very anxious to put him in the past. Maybe it was one of those kind of marriages.

Ann let him shower first and then she stepped in behind him. Ann allowed Charles to lather her whole body. At one point she leaned back on him and said, "What is this?"

She turned around, and as Charles lifted her face to his, and then lifted all of her to his height, she wrapped her legs around him, allowing him to try again. "Permit me to assist you," he said. He leaned back against the tiled wall, and found a rhythm that seemed seamless with the rain shower over them. She was still wrapped around him and he slowly moved his hands lower on her back. Then he worked his magic, and they both climaxed at the same time.

Ann and Charles took towels hanging outside the glass doors, and dried off quietly, each gently drying each other's back. "Now, wasn't that relaxing Charles?"

"I liked it better the second time."

"That's because doing it in the water takes time to get used to."

"That and I thought I was going to drown."

"Well, there is always the possibility," Ann laughed.

The two got dressed. Charles said he had a very nice evening and he was looking forward to working with her again.

She said, "This was just the beginning. I'm sure we will have many things to talk about and papers to sign."

CC wasn't exactly sure what she meant but he hoped it didn't involve water. He told her he would begin researching all of the issues regarding her holdings and he would be ready in a few days to meet with her again to discuss the next step.

"I look forward to hearing what your thoughts are relative to my assets."

Evaluating her assets as he stood there, CC said "I've got some ideas already."

"I'll bet you do. And I have some creative ideas regarding compensation."

CC said in a higher pitch, "I'll bet you do."

She escorted him to the door and gave him a big kiss before he left. As he turned out the door, into the cool evening, she smacked him on the behind for good measure. CC was still smiling as his hand reached for the car door.

Chapter 22

It had been a few days since CC had found any obituary that looked promising. But on this morning, as he had his coffee and read the paper, one of the obituaries caught his eye.

Paul Jacobs – MD

Harwich - Dr. Paul Jacobs, 46, passed away yesterday after a long battle with cancer. He was born in Rockland, MA on September 19, 1961, and lived in Harwich for the past fifteen years. Dr. Jacobs was managing partner of Mid-Cape Neurology Care Center in Hyannis.

He is survived by his wife, Sarah (Cohen) Jacobs of Harwich, mother Elaine Jacobs of Harwichport, MA. His father, Dr. Paul Jacobs, Sr, predeceased him.

Dr. Jacobs was active in the community. He hosted numerous charitable events and was most generous in donating his time helping others. He was the author of numerous books on the subject of Neurology, which showcased his expertise and elevated his reputation throughout the industry.

Funeral services will be held Tuesday 10 a.m. at Doane Beal & Ames Funeral Home, 260 West Main St. Harwich. Burial will be at Hilltop Cemetery, Harwich. Calling hours are Monday 7 to 9 p.m. at Doane Beal & Ames Funeral Home.

For directions, please visit: www.donaebealames.com.

What caught CC's attention was the fact this doctor had written a number of books. That might mean he had money. Plus, everyone knows successful doctors have money. He would have to add Mrs. Jacobs to his potential target list.

On Monday night, CC dressed in khaki slacks, white button down shirt, and brown loafers. It was a very crowded event. The funeral home could probably hold a hundred and fifty or so and arriving, CC observed a line of more than thirty cars waiting for a parking space. He went past the funeral home and parked on a side street. He walked up to the funeral home and had to wait in a line that extended out the door by a dozen people.

Standing in line, CC spoke to a man in front of him. "Looks like everyone came out to pay their respects to Dr. Jacobs tonight."

The man turned, "Paul was well liked. Not only was he involved in his practice but he supported many of the local charity events in the area."

CC said, "I'm Charles Chamberlin. I had some business dealings with Dr. Jacobs."

The man held out his hand and said, "I'm Dr. Gregory Lamb. I worked with Paul at the Center."

CC, knowing he never met the man before, said, "Paul may have introduced me to you once when I had a meeting with him at the Center. You look familiar."

"Paul was always introducing us to someone. I don't remember you, but that doesn't mean anything. When was it you came to the center?"

CC thought and said, "Some time last year. I don't remember the exact date."

"I must have been new there at the time because I only started there a little over a year ago. Paul may not have included me in his private circle at that time" Dr. Lamb winked.

Dr. Lamb thought for minute and said, "Did you do some work on the facilities expansion for Paul?"

"I'm in financial consulting, not construction."

"Oh, I was just thinking Paul was so involved in the expansion of the Center when I joined. He always had people in for meetings."

"I had met him talking about finance issues. Some of our discussions involved business financing. As I recall, we did talk about how to structure the expansion."

"Did you provide the financing for the expansion?"

"No, I was only a consultant. I advised Paul on financial things."

"Have you worked with any of the other partners?"

"No. Paul was my only contact."

"That was so like Paul. He kept most of the finance stuff to himself. We only got to see the quarterly reports for the practice. He ran a tight ship from a financial point of view."

"Yes, I'd say he did."

The line was moving along slowly and they had finally gotten inside the building. A man was exiting the building passing Dr. Lamb when Dr. Lamb said, "Michael. How is she doing?"

The man stopped and said, "She's holding up ok. But I think the crowd will get to her in a little bit. There are so many people here."

Dr. Lamb said to the man, "Dr. Michael Kraft, this is Mr. Charles Chamberlin. Mr. Chamberlin was a financial consultant to Paul."

Dr. Kraft extended his hand and said hello. CC took his hand and said, "Nice to meet you."

"Dr. Kraft is now the managing partner at the Center now that Paul is gone." He looked at CC and said, "Mr. Chamberlin had helped Paul with some of the financing issues when the Center did the expansion last year."

Dr. Kraft said, "Paul pretty much handled all of the finance issues for the Center so I don't know much about that end of it. But I'm going to have to come up to speed quickly."

"If I can be of any assistance, please call me." And he handed Dr. Kraft a card.

"Thank you, I may do that. Greg, I'll see you tomorrow."

The line continued to move along and eventually CC reached the receiving room. At the front of the line was an attractive lady standing by the casket greeting each person. She stood by herself. Dr. Lamb gave her a kiss on the cheek and whispered something to her. She gave him a quiet thank you. Then she turned her attention to CC. He extended his hand and introduced himself.

He said, "Mrs. Jacobs, I'm Charles Chamberlin. I knew your husband through my business. I'm very sorry for your loss."

Mrs. Jacobs said, "Thank you for your kind words."

CC let go of her hand and moved on. He stopped in front of the casket as if to say a prayer and then moved to the back of the room.

Standing there, a lady who was crying quite a bit stood next to him. He picked up a box of tissues from the table and asked her if she needed them. She said, "Oh, thank you. I can't believe he's gone."

CC said, "Yes, it's a tragedy. So young."

"I'm Linda O'Donnell. I was Paul's secretary."

CC extending his hand said, "Charles Chamberlin. I'm a financial consultant. I did some work with Dr. Jacobs in the past."

Linda said, "He was so good to everyone."

CC said, "Yes. Especially the charities."

"All the time."

"How long were you with him Linda?"

"Over eleven years."

"Then you were there when they expanded the Center?"

"Yes. But I missed some of that year when I had my son."

201

"Maybe that's why I don't recognize you, because I had met with Paul at the Center a few times last year advising him with some of the financing issues."

"That could be. He had a temp in while I was on maternity leave."

"Well, you probably saw some of the paperwork from my firm, Chamberlin Financial Consultants?"

"If it happened when that temp was there, we might not even have a file. She was terrible."

"Oh, I hope that's not the case. I would hope the new managing partner would be able to call on me if the Center needs help in the future."

"If you have a business card, I'll check the files when I get back into the office."

CC handed her a card. "If you don't find my file, let me know and I'll get you enough information so you can create a new one. I'm sure I have copies of letters and e-mails I sent, and obviously originals of documents Paul provided to me."

"That will be fine. And thank you for taking my mind off things, even if only for a few minutes. This is so hard."

"No problem, it was nice to meet you Linda."

CC exited the funeral home having gained quite a bit of information about Dr. Paul Jacobs. Some of the contacts might prove valuable in the future. He had an in and now had to work it. One of his first tasks would be to call on Dr. Kraft, the new managing partner. He would call him at the end of the week.

Returning home, he turned on his computer. He logged into his e-mail account and had an incoming e-mail from Mary Johnson. The message said she had updated the file containing information on Ken's holdings and was sending the update to him. It had an Excel file attached. When he downloaded it and opened it, it was an inventory of all of Ken Johnson's holdings. CC selected the reply tab on the e-mail and wrote to Mary, "Mary, I have had contact with the Trustee of Ken's Trust, a Mr. Ted Miller. Mr. Miller indicated he is in control of all of Ken's assets and you should deal only with him with respect to any issues you have regarding Ken's assets. For that reason, I have deleted the file you sent me and I am referring you to Mr. Miller should you need any assistance."

He pressed the send tab and hoped he wouldn't hear from her again.

When done with the e-mail, he put in a call to Andrew Dunn. He knew it was late but he wanted to leave a message for Andrew to call him in the morning. To his surprise, Andrew answered the phone.

He said, "Sterns and Dunn, Andrew Dunn speaking."

"Andrew its Charles Chamberlin."

"Charles, what's up?"

"I wanted to leave you a message to call me in the morning. I didn't expect you to be at the office at this time."

"I have some things I'm working on that have been keeping me here late some nights. Things have been pretty hectic since Sam died."

"I can imagine. I was calling to talk with you about Katherine. I think she is ready to sell her interest in the firm. She has asked me to represent her in discussions with you."

"I figured that was coming. When we saw you the other night at Alberto's, I could sense she had something to say but didn't."

"Did she talk about selling?"

"Not directly. But she hinted she wanted to travel more and her attentions would be re-directed once the baby was born."

"How interested are you in buying her out?"

"If the price is right, I would certainly consider it."

"I'd like to get a better understanding of the business value before I bring anything to her."

"That sounds fair. What did you have in mind?"

"I'd like to come to the office when it's convenient for you and to take a look at the books, benefits, holdings etc. Anything that would be involved in the valuation of the business."

"Let me check into that tomorrow and I'll call you."

"That would be fine. I'll wait to hear from you."

"How long do you think you'll need in order to formulate an opinion to be able to speak with Katherine?"

"I should be able to get back to you in a day or two after I get the data I need. It's only preliminary discussions at this point."

"That should work fine for me. I just don't want this to drag on for a long period of time. I'm having a difficult enough time keeping up with my tasks and with those Sam used to handle. And if you would Charles, please don't say anything to Katherine about this until we can speak again?"

"I won't mention anything to Katherine until after we speak."

"Well, you know she has her ways. And if she gets even the slightest inkling you're doing analysis on the business, she'll be all over you. And I mean that both figuratively and physically."

"I know what you mean."

"You have to be careful. She seeks more than just representation. If you can keep your contact with her to daytime, you'll probably be fine."

"Yes. Thanks for the heads up. It sounds like you're speaking from personal experience."

"Let's just say she knows how to get what she wants."

"I hear you."

Chapter 23

Sarah Jacobs at forty-four years of age, five foot eleven inches tall, weighing about 130 pounds, with shoulder length brunette hair, brown eyes and a perfect figure, could be a model. Sarah worked in a local advertising agency as a public relations advisor. She had received her degree in Marketing from Boston University. After college, she worked for a number of firms in the Boston area performing various functions in marketing. She had met Paul while working as a marketing consultant for a pharmaceutical company in the Boston area. The two dated for a few years, married and she relocated to Cape Cod.

Sarah and Paul resided at 27 Shore Drive, Harwich, MA. Sarah became involved in many of Paul's charitable endeavors and eventually took over the public relations and some of the marketing leadership tasks for a few of his more prominent pursuits. The two were a formidable team in raising money. He was the consummate professional doctor, and she was the well-organized brilliant strategist in public relations.

The Jacobs' are known throughout the area as one of the leading philanthropic couples of the current times. Any charity that had the Jacobs participation easily met goals in both fundraising and benefits. Sarah Jacobs had promised to continue the good work she and her former husband had been so successful at in the past.

For entertainment, Sarah liked all outdoor sports. She was an avid skier in the winters. In summer, she could be seen daily walking the beach in Brewster. Most mornings, Sarah and her dog, Doc, could be seen walking just inside the tidemark on the sand. She had said this was her peaceful time allowing her to prepare for her day and get the exercise she needed to keep so fit. After her morning walk, Sarah would go to the Cape Cod Health and Fitness center on Hookum Rock road in Dennis for a half-hour workout. In the winters, she would go there for an hour and a half, as most times it would be too cold to walk the beach. Something about being pelted with flying sand didn't appeal to her.

On weekends, Paul would occasionally join Sarah and Doc for their beach walks. Now, Sarah would be alone for just a short while. It wouldn't be too long before someone would take a keen interest in her. With her looks, smarts and money, she would be highly sought after.

Dr. Michael Kraft called Sarah. "Hello, Sarah, this is Michael."

"Oh, hello Michael. How are things with the Center?"

"Pretty good. I'm getting into taking over the things from Paul's job. I was contacted by one of the Local Charities, the Cape Cod Humanities Organization, and asked if someone from the Center would be filling in in place of Paul when their Silent Auction dinner is held in a few weeks. I wasn't sure how to respond."

"Paul chaired that event for Cape Cod Humanities for years. I helped him with the public relations chores, but that was the extent of my involvement."

"Do you know of anyone who might be able to replace Paul?"

"I'm not sure anyone can replace Paul. He was so good at what he did."

"That's for sure. Well, I have to come up with someone by the end of the week. Can you let me know if anyone comes to mind?"

"Let me think about it. I'll call you back if I think of anyone."

"Thanks. I really appreciate it."

Sarah hung up the phone and thought for a moment. No names popped into her head. She thought about Paul's passion for the charity group and about his contacts. It would be very difficult to come up with someone to replace him. She would try to come up with a name.

When Michael Kraft hung up, Linda O'Donnell came into the office and said, "Dr. Kraft, I have been going through Dr. Jacob's files and there are some finance matters you might want to look at."

"What do you have?"

"Well, Dr. Jacobs had told me he wanted to make some changes to the 401k plan for the Center and this file was one of the ones in his TO DO pile."

She handed the file to him. Opening it he said, "Did he give you any indication of what he wanted to do?"

"He had me gathering information about changing some of the mutual fund choices that are available to participants."

"I don't know much about that end of the business. Maybe we should get some outside help."

Linda thought for a minute and said, "I talked to a gentleman at the wake who had done some financial consulting for Paul in the past. He might already know what Paul's plans were. Would you like me to call him?"

"That would be a good start. What's his name?"

"Charles Chamberlin of Chamberlin Financial Services in Hyannis."

"I think I met him at the wake. Yes, call him and see if you can arrange a meeting."

"I'll call him and see what can be arranged."

"Thanks."

Michael looked through the file. He recognized the fund names because he had been contributing to some of them in his own 401k. He read Paul's notes. They didn't make much sense to him. He would have to rely on professional help in handling that aspect of Paul's position.

Linda O'Donnell called Chamberlin Financial Services. "Mr. Chamberlin. It's Linda O'Donnell from the Center. We met at Dr. Jacobs' wake."

"Ms. O'Donnell. Yes. I remember speaking with you."

"I'm now working for Dr. Kraft. He has taken over the duties Dr. Jacobs had. I was speaking with him about changes Dr. Jacobs had been pursuing for the Center's 401k plan and we thought about calling you in hopes you could provide the Center some professional help in making changes to the plan."

"What did you have in mind, Linda?"

"Dr. Jacobs had me gathering information about expanding the number of mutual fund choices available to the participants of the fund. I think Dr. Kraft wants to continue to pursue these changes."

"What is it you or Dr. Kraft would like me to do?"

"He would like to arrange a meeting to discuss the changes. Do you have any time available?"

"Let me see." CC flipped a few pages of his desk calendar forward. "Yes, I have an opening on Thursday, eleven o'clock."

Linda looked at Dr. Kraft's calendar on her computer and said, "That looks like it will work for Dr. Kraft as well. I'll write it in. Where can I reach you if he can't make it."

"You can call me at 508-394-2231. That's my cell number. Anytime is fine."

"Right now, that time is alright, but sometimes he gets called in on an emergency and has to interrupt his schedule."

"I understand. Just call if something comes up. Otherwise, I'll be at the Center at eleven."

"Thank You Mr. Chamberlin. I'll inform the doctor of the appointment."

"One more thing Linda. Have you been able to find a file in Dr. Jacobs records for the past consulting work I did for him?"

"No, I've looked in all of the places where those things were kept and I've not found it. By any chance had you talked to the Paul recently?"

"Why do you ask?"

"Well, sometimes he worked a lot from home, at night and on weekends. He may have brought some files home.

"If you can't find the files, I can provide you with copies of some of the past efforts I performed for Dr. Jacobs."

"Oh, I don't think that will be necessary. But that's nice to know in case the need arises to look at any of the past efforts. I'll just start a new file and place a reference note in it stating you have the documentation of past engagements at your place of business."

"Thank you Linda. I think that'll work fine."

"If you need anything else Mr. Chamberlin, just give me a call. Otherwise, we will expect you on Thursday.

"Thank you for your assistance Linda. I'll be there on Thursday."

With that, Charles went about his tasks for the day and included preparation for the meeting with Dr. Kraft as part of his routine.

On Thursday, Charles went to the Center to meet with Dr. Kraft. He was escorted to a very plush office that was well lit. The entire back wall of the office was floor to ceiling glass overlooking Nantucket Sound. The name on the door still said Dr. Paul Jacobs. When Charles entered, Dr. Kraft came from behind the desk and extended his hand.

"Thank you for coming Mr. Chamberlin. I'm in the process of taking over for Dr. Jacobs. The whole process has been rather overwhelming."

"I can imagine. How can I help you?"

"Well, one of the things in Paul's, I mean Dr. Jacobs pile was to make changes to the Center's 401k plan. And since I don't have much experience with those kind of things and knowing you did some financial consulting to Dr. Jacobs in the past, I thought you might be able to help us."

"What kind of things precisely was Dr. Jacobs pursuing?"

"It looks to me like he wanted to change the mutual funds available to the plan's participants."

"That isn't unusual, but most companies get lazy, set up a plan and pretty much leave it alone."

Shaking his head, Dr. Kraft said, "I don't know much about that but Dr. Jacobs had his secretary doing some research and he wanted to make some changes for some reason."

"Well, with all of the things happening in the financial markets recently, he might have wanted to get into some better investment choices. Some people feel the market is getting soft. There are investments you want to avoid in such markets."

"Possibly. But he didn't talk with the other partners about it. Usually, Paul would come up with some recommendation, make a presentation to the other members and we would all go along with it. He had made us so much money in the past, we all just came to rely on his savvy."

"Can you have Ms. O'Donnell provide me with the plan information and Dr. Jacob's notes. I'll analyze the material and get back to you with my thoughts."

Picking up the folder, Dr. Kraft said, "Here's what we have. Take a look at it and get back to me if you would."

"I can do that. Would next week be fine?"

"That would be fine with me. And I want to thank you Mr. Chamberlin for coming down. One other issue I'd like to discuss. Ms. O'Donnell said your file somehow got lost when we had a temp filling in for her. What kind of arrangement did you have with Dr. Jacobs?"

"My fee is composed of a retainer I work against plus expenses. The initial retainer is ten thousand dollars and it usually covers the first month or two of work initially. The set up phase of any relationship is the most labor intensive. Then, I'll bill monthly for hours worked and out of pocket expenses after the retainer is exhausted. Paul was already into the monthly billing process, but it might be more appropriate to restart with the retainer again. There will be legwork and research that has to be done. My relationship with you will be new."

"That sounds fine with me. I'll instruct Ms. O'Donnell to request a retainer for you today and you should have it in a few days. Can you send me a basic agreement for all of this?"

"Sure. I'll get it to you right away."

"Thanks. I really appreciate your coming on board to help me with this."

"You're welcome. Let me go and get started."

When CC got home, he opened the file Kraft had given him, and started to read. Dr. Jacobs had made notes about the funds the 401k offered. He had written percentages in the margin next to each fund. CC would have to research the funds to see if he could figure out what the percentages meant. On what started as a blank page, Dr. Jacobs had written a few notes listing Emerging Markets, China, Asia and Latin America. A few mutual fund companies, Vanguard, Fidelity, T.Rowe Price and Dreyfus were all listed as well. CC guessed Dr. Jacobs had been considering expanding the fund choices to funds in the categories listed on the page. Since the current 401k only offered Vanguard Funds, CC thought maybe Dr. Jacobs wanted to change investment firms as well as offering more choices or possibly he was using the other firms as comparative information. He'd have to look into the terms of the 401k for changes to the managing company.

He then pulled up a blank agreement for his services and filled in the blanks with the detail information for the Center and filled in Dr. Kraft's name in the authorization box. He printed two copies of the agreement and signed both. Then he put them in a folder and addressed it to Dr. Kraft. He would drop them off for the doctor to sign later on that day.

He went to the www.vanguard.com site and looked up a few of the funds that had been listed in the file under the current 401k plan. When he brought the funds up, he paid particular attention to the performance numbers and discovered the percentages Dr. Jacobs had written in the margin were the same numbers that showed in the one-year performance category. He checked all of the funds and the numbers matched. Then, CC looked up some of the funds had been hand-written and found that on average, these funds had returned more than double what the funds currently in the 401k had achieved. It was clear to CC Dr. Jacobs had intended to change the plan to make funds that had been returning better returns available to the participants. CC researched the funds from the other institutions and created a spreadsheet of the funds Dr. Jacobs had been considering listed under each institution. At the bottom of each category, he created a summary average for each fund category. He would use this information when he returned to speak with Dr. Kraft. CC made printouts of all of the funds Dr. Jacobs had been looking into.

Next, he analyzed the information regarding the participants. Dr. Jacobs had just fewer than two million dollars in the 401k plan. Dr. Kraft had about one point one million in it. The other participants combined had about three million in the plan. That meant the 401k for the Center had over six million dollars in it. CC thought that would make a good haul for him. But, he wasn't sure what the consequences would be going after something other than individual assets. After all, targeting individuals such as widows allowed him to pursue weakness and fear. These things might not be present in business assets. He would have to give the thought careful consideration. Then again, with this opportunity, no one was watching the details anyway. That in and of itself was the biggest weakness.

At minimum, he could go after just the late Dr. Jacobs portion. The funds hadn't been distributed to the widow yet so all he had to do was get to her and then he might be able to tap into the Jacob funds.

Chapter 24

CC received a special delivery in the mail via FedEx. It was his copy of the agreement papers he had expected to be getting back accompanied by more information about the details of the 401k package he had discussed with Dr. Kraft. He filed the agreement in his business file cabinet and began to read the information that had been sent.

Detail records for all of the 401k plan participants had been included. The documents were computer printouts Dr. Kraft's secretary must have printed the day before. Also included were performance charts for the new funds Dr. Jacobs had been considering. A note was attached indicating once Charles had completed his analysis; Dr. Kraft would like to have another meeting.

CC laid everything out and decided it would be a reasonable approach to pursue expanding the Center's 401k fund choices with some of the funds Dr. Jacobs had been interested in. He selected the Latin America Fund, the Energy Fund and the Asia Fund as the three that seemed to be doing the best. He used his computer to prepare a presentation and report about these funds. When finished, he had prepared a favorable recommendation he would present to Dr. Kraft. The report showed that making a few changes, the plan participants would be able to consider investing in a few of the more aggressive funds in the marketplace that had been outperforming all of the rest. The Funds CC was recommending were outperforming the current Center's 401k funds by more than three fold. CC was pretty sure Dr. Kraft would be pleased with his report.

CC called the Center and asked for Dr. Kraft's office. Linda O'Donnell answered the phone.

"Dr. Kraft's office, Linda O'Donnell speaking. How may I help you?"

"Linda, this is Charles Chamberlin. I have completed my analysis. Your note indicated I was to call and schedule another meeting with Dr. Kraft when I was done."

"I know he is anxious to get your report. I think he wants to impress the other Doctors here because he told me this morning to let him know as soon as you called."

"Well, I'm ready. I can come in as soon as he would like me to be there."

"Hold on a minute and let me see if I can catch him now."

CC was put on hold while Linda spoke with Dr. Kraft. She came back on the line after a minute and said, "Can you be here this afternoon a little after three?"

"Sure. Should I bring anything?"

"He asked you to bring four copies of your report and be prepared to speak to the group. They have their weekly partners meeting this afternoon and I think he wants you to talk to the whole group."

"Doesn't he want to hear what I am going to have to say first?"

"I don't think so. Things have been kind of crazy here lately and I think he wants to just show the group he is getting things under control."

"Ok. I'll be there at three with copies."

"Is there anything you will need for the meeting?"

"No, I'll bring everything with me I'll need."

"Just ask for me at the front desk and I'll come get you."

"Will do."

CC spent a few hours preparing for his presentation. He created a PowerPoint presentation for the group and made handout copies for the attendees. After a few hours, he sat back and looked at his preparations. He was ready to meet with the group of doctors at the Center.

At three, CC arrived at the Center and asked for Linda O'Donnell. She was paged and came to the reception desk to get him. She said the Doctors were in the meeting room and he should go right in. Upon entering the room, Dr. Kraft, who had been sitting at the head of the table greeted CC and introduced him to the group. CC made his presentation. It was well received by the group. The Doctors talked about what the changes might mean to their account balances if the new fund choices continued to perform as they had in the past. CC reminded them these were riskier funds and they should use caution when investing in them. Dr. Lamb said he would have a few hundred thousand more in his account if the new funds had been available to him when he had joined.

When CC had finished, the group took a break and Dr. Kraft spoke with CC outside the conference room.

"Charles, Dr. Jacobs had a sizeable investment in the funds in our plan. I'm not comfortable talking about his interests to his widow Sarah. Do you think you would be able to speak with her about his, I mean her assets in the plan?"

"I could do that. If you would have Linda call her and let her know I'll be calling her about the plan and then let me know Mrs. Jacobs has been notified, I'll follow-up with her."

"I'll speak with Linda after the meeting. Thank you for coming Charles, I really appreciate it."

"I'll go ahead and contact the 401k Plan Administrator and start the ball rolling to get the new funds available. You should see something from the Administrator in a few days and then the group can consider exchanging or investing new contributions into the new funds at that time."

"Charles, you've been a big help. Thanks again."

"You're welcome. I'll report back to you from time to time and let you know how things are going."

"Please do."

CC left the Center thinking this had been a very productive morning. Maybe he would expand his plans to include some of the Doctors' money that was invested in the 401k plan. Then again, why not just pursue the widow Jacobs? After all, she had inherited a nice sum of money. He decided he would wait to get the call from Linda and then pursue Sarah Jacobs.

It didn't take long. Linda O'Donnell had left him a voice message before he had even got back to his office. The message said she had called Sarah Jacobs at Dr. Kraft's instruction and Mrs. Jacobs said Charles could call or come to meet her at her house at any time. Charles didn't have anything else planned for the next morning so he decided he would look in on Sarah Jacobs at that time.

Getting near the end of the afternoon, CC decided it would be a nice day to take a walk on the beach and watch the sunset. Things were going along pretty well. His practice was busy and his plans for wealth were looking better and better. He drove to the east side of Susuit Harbor and parked in the lot. He got out and walked through the dunes down to the beach. The sun was still fairly high in the western sky but it was starting to cast soothing color patterns on the partly cloudy sky. He began to walk to the east along the high tide line.

A little way off in the distance, he saw a woman playing with a dog on the beach. She would throw a ball out into the water and have the dog retrieve it. He continued to walk along smiling and whistling pleased things were going so well. As he approached where the woman and dog were, the dog ran up to him and dropped the ball at his feet. He reached down to pick the ball up. As he stood, the woman approached and said, "I'm sorry my dog disturbed you."

CC said, "No problem." He reached out to hand her the ball.

"Aren't you Mrs. Jacobs?"

"Yes, I know you from somewhere don't I?"

"Yes, I'm Charles Chamberlin. I met you at your husband's services. Again, I'm sorry for your lose."

"Oh, yes, now I remember. Thank you."

216

He handed her the ball and she threw it into the surf. She said, "Doc fetch." The dog raced out into the surf to retrieve the ball. As CC was looking out at the dog he said, "In fact, I was about to give you a call to talk about some matters involving your deceased husband's practice."

"You were? What's it all about?"

"Well, Dr. Kraft has retained my firm to handle some changes to the 401k plan for the Center. Your husband had a sizeable investment in the plan."

"Yes, I am aware of that."

"Dr. Kraft has me making some changes to the plan for the other partners and wanted to make sure you were made aware of the changes and given to opportunity to participate in the changes as well."

"That was considerate of him."

"He is really swamped with having all the new duties and he had my firm do the research, analysis and report for the changes. When I met with the partners, they signed off on the recommendations and Dr. Kraft asked that I get in touch with you."

"That's what I understood when I talked with his secretary, Linda O'Donnell."

"Isn't it coincidence we met?"

"Linda said you would be calling. How did you know I would be here?"

"I didn't. I like to take a stroll on the beach from time to time, especially at the end of a busy day. Kind of clear my head."

"I know what you mean. I come here every chance I can with Doc. It takes my mind off things."

Doc came running up and dropped the ball at their feet. CC picked it up and threw it down the beach just into the breaking waves. Doc scampered after it.

"What is it you would like to speak with me about?"

"My recommendation to the partners was to open up three new mutual funds in the 401k plan. The new funds offer much better returns but also carry more risk."

"What kind of better returns are you talking about?"

"On average, the new choices have returned about three times what the current choices had been returning."

"And the added risk?"

"The funds are in the international marketplace. That means they will fluctuate. The funds can be affected by world events and by things going on inside the countries in which the investments are made. Sometimes news is not as forthcoming as one might desire."

"Do you think I should consider changing where some of Paul's investments are held?"

"That's something you have to decide. He did have a sizeable portfolio. You might want to consider giving some portion of the funds the chance at better returns."

"I don't really need any more money. But if Paul was looking into it, then there must be something to it. Let me think about it and I'll get back to you."

CC took his wallet out of his pocket and extracted a business card. He handed it to her and said, "Call me anytime."

"I will. And thanks for the information. It must be fate we met like this. Paul must be speaking to me from the grave."

"I'd say more like coincidence."

She called Doc and he came running. She took the card and ball and started to walk in the opposite direction. Turning back she said, "I'll call you Mr. Chamberlin."

"Bye Doc, Bye Mrs. Jacobs."

"Call me Sarah. Come on Doc."

Walking away, she thought about CC. "What a nice man. He was tall, good-looking, successful and with no ring on his finger, apparently single. And he likes walking on the beach at sunset." She thought about his response. "Coincidence? No. Fate." She would call him again. It was time to start looking for another man.

CC walked back to his car. How could things get any better? He had never had so much success in his life. Here he was with money in the bank. His business had clients paying nice fees. Beautiful woman were in his life. He had a plan that continued to prove worthwhile. Life was looking better and better.

When he got back home, the light on his phone was blinking. He had a call from Andrew Dunn. Andrew's message said he had gathered the information they had spoken about and he would like to meet with CC on the next day. He said he had an open schedule from nine to eleven if CC could make it. CC deleted the message and called Andrew's office. He got Andrew's voice mail and said he would be there at nine.

The next morning CC arrived at Sterns and Dunn offices promptly at nine. Andrew showed CC the materials he had gathered. The documents inventoried the assets of Sterns and Dunn. There were equipment lists, financial documents, customer lists and other things outlining the assets of the firm.

CC said, "Do you have all of this summarized somewhere so I can get a feel of what we are talking about?"

"Yes." Andrew produced an excel spreadsheet that covered a few pages. CC went to the last page first.

"I see here you are showing the firm to have a little over six million in assets?"

"Yes, that's what all of this adds up to."

"I'm sure once everything is audited, then I'll be able to bring a number to Katherine and see if it's what she is looking for."

"That would seem right. Did you have someone in mind to do the audit?"

"I have some contacts with people who do this kind of thing. If it looks like we are going forward with the firm buying Mrs. Sterns out, I'll have someone get in touch with you."

"That would be fine."

"One thing that's puzzling me is the overall value of the firm."

"Why is that?"

"Well, if there was a three million dollar Key Man policy on Mr. Sterns, the proceeds from that policy don't seem to be represented here?"

Andrew sat back kind of surprised. "What do you mean?"

"Well, while doing my research for Mrs. Sterns, I came across insurance policies that existed on Mr. Sterns. Didn't the company receive a death benefit when he died?"

Voice shaking a little, Andrew said, "It did. The firm used some of the funds to pay down debt and for other expenses."

"Three million dollars?"

"Yes. There were things that needed to be settled."

"Were there any unusual things paid out of those funds? Like bonuses or anything like that?"

"The firm has regularly paid out any excess cash that was on-hand after expenses had been paid. The partners would get the funds at year-end anyway."

"What kind of bonuses was paid out of the Key Man policy?"

"Routine partner bonuses."

"Andrew, did you get a bonus?"

"Yes I did."

"How much was the bonus for?"

"One million five."

"And how much went to Sam?"

"I'm sorry, I don't understand what you are asking? Sam is dead."

"Well let me put it another way. How much went to Katherine?"

"Nothing. She is not working here."

"Maybe she isn't. But she is entitled to his share."

Andrew didn't like where this was going. CC told him he expected the audit would clearly show the Key Man payment and the disbursements. He was sure the audit would also disclose the past pattern of bonus payments. Andrew would have some explaining to do or he would have to inflate the value of the business to compensate for the bonus money Katherine didn't receive.

CC finally said, "I'd say the asset value of Sterns and Dunn is more like nine million. I think that's where your offer to Mrs. Sterns should probably come in."

Andrew's response was measured. "I'll have to take a look at it again and get back to you."

"You do that. Meanwhile, I won't say anything to Mrs. Sterns. It might make her angry and we know she can be aggressive."

"Thank you. I'll get back to you."

"Andrew, if the business is worth say nine million, sixty percent of that belongs to Katherine. That works out to about five and a half million. What you have here plus the key man proceeds puts the business value in that ballpark."

"But the business doesn't have the key man proceeds on hand. As I said we used it in the course of our business."

"Andrew, I think any reasonable authority might have a problem with how those funds were handled. Especially since Sam's shares didn't get a penny of it. Those funds should have been kept in the business for ordinary planned operations. Not disbursed to the remaining shareholders. You used the proceeds like they originated from a term life insurance policy, not a key man policy. I think you might find it difficult to explain if that were brought up by an attorney, let alone to have to explain it to Katherine."

"I guess I can see your point. I'll have to think about it."

"Do the right thing Andrew. Then she will go away and you will have the business. I'm not even factoring in the new accounts or the expected growth. If you propose a five million buyout, I think she will go for it."

At that, CC closed his briefcase and saw himself out.

Chapter 25

It had been some time since CC had an e-mail from Katherine Sterns computer or from Theresa Lee's computer. He had set them up for bi-monthly transmission. The Ann Pierce files were coming in every five or six days and that frequency allowed him to stay on top of the situation easier. When he logged on to his computer the next day, he had three incoming e-mails with the subject line of Strokes Included. He figured the day would be a busy one spent breaking down the data, saving what was valuable and then following up on the information captured and updating his plan.

He selected the file from Katherine's computer first. He was interested in getting the file, as it was the first one since he had helped her install her new computer. He downloaded the file and saved it as KS Strokes Five. Then he opened the file. The first activity he saw looked familiar, as PCTrackR had captured the activity he had entered while at Katherine's right after he had installed the software on the new computer.

KS was doing some research on Sterns and Dunn. She was trying to get information about the Key Man Insurance payment that had been made to Sterns and Dunn. She had logged into the company website and had logged in as SADFIN and a password of ASST4US. Katherine didn't find any particular account listed that would indicate where the insurance proceeds would be found. She went into the accounting system located on the finance page and selected the history option. Once in history, she entered the dates for the ninety days following Sam's death. She must have found what she was looking for because she exited the site without doing anything else.

The next entry in the file was an e-mail to Andrew. In it she wrote, "Andrew. I have reviewed the company financial information recently and want to make sure any significant expenditures outside the business plans Sam had in his home office for the current year are run by me as majority owner in the firm. I'm taking this precaution to ensure the integrity of the company finance situation remains within the confines of the published business plan and statements. If you have any questions, please call me."

CC wondered what that was all about. Maybe Katherine was making sure Andrew or someone else didn't run down the finances of the company before a deal could be worked out.

The next item in the file was an e-mail to her friend Dotty Masters. In it she told Dotty things were looking up with Charles. She also said she was looking to sell her interest in Sterns and Dunn. Andrew wasn't interested in her any more. She told Dotty she was looking forward to their upcoming trip to Boston and the pregnancy thing was starting to get to her.

The next data captured by PCTrackR was a series of Internet inquiries regarding baby care and baby supplies. It looked to CC like she was starting to think seriously about having the baby. At the baby care sites, she had looked into health care, feeding and assistance. Maybe she was thinking about getting a Nanny for the baby?

Another e-mail to Dotty Masters followed next. It must have been the day after Katherine saw Charles at Alberto's with another woman because in it she told Dotty she saw Charles with another woman at a local restaurant and it looked like the two were being cozy sitting in a corner of the restaurant. She wrote to Dotty the pregnancy thing was really starting to put a dent in her social life.

The Dotty e-mail was followed by a search at www.google.com. The search criteria entered had been "Charles Chamberlin". It looked like she reviewed the information returned and then entered another search for "Chamberlin Financial Services". What could she have been looking to discover?

Next, she went to websites www.ingdirect.com and www.franklintempleton.com. It looked like she was reviewing the account information as there were few actions taken at either site.

The last entry in the KS Strokes Five file was another e-mail from Katherine to Dotty Masters. The keystrokes from Katherine indicated she was getting very depressed. She needed to get out of the house. The upcoming trip to Boston for the weekend couldn't come soon enough. She wrote to Dotty that Dotty should be prepared for a partying weekend.

He made notes on a scratch pad of the things he wanted to pursue. He closed the file and deleted the e-mail from his in-basket.

Next he opened the e-mail PCTrackR had sent from Theresa Lee's computer. He downloaded the file and labeled it TL Strokes Five and then opened the file. He hadn't had any contact with Theresa for a few weeks and wondered what she had been up to. His curiosity was getting the best of him.

The first entry was an e-mail from Theresa to her attorney thanking him for resolving the lawsuit. She also thanked him for handling the financial aspects and for depositing her portion of the settlement into her account. She wrote to him she had been pleased with the services performed by the law firm and if there was anything that needed to be done, he should call her.

The next data captured showed her accessing her accounts at www.sovereignbank.com, www.dreyfus.com and www.troweprice.com. She had requested a transfer of fifteen thousand dollars from her Dreyfus account to her Sovereign Bank account. CC guessed she was using funds from the accounts to pay for her living expenses. He didn't know if she had a job and would research her Sovereign Bank account to see if he could identify a regular income stream. CC thought he would go easy on a widow who didn't have a regular income stream and had to live off her inheritance.

The data that followed indicated Theresa had been going in and out of her computer virus software. She had performed a scan. Then she had cleaned up cookies and temporary history files. Then she had gone to the control panel and started deleting applications from her computer. CC guessed her computer had a virus or something and she was trying to fix it.

These actions were followed by an e-mail to www.computermechanic.com. She was writing to the service department asking if she could bring her computer in for service. She asked someone to call her and let her know when it would be convenient to bring in the computer. CC wondered if the service people at Computer Mechanics would find PCTrackR?

Finding no more data to be analyzed in the file, CC closed it and deleted the e-mail from his in-box.

The third e-mail he opened was from PCTrackR on Ann Pierce's computer. He downloaded the file and labeled it AP Strokes Two. Then he opened the file and began to examine the contents.

Ann had accessed her accounts at Bank of America and ING Direct. She must have been checking on her balance because there were no additional keystrokes at either site. The next thing captured was an e-mail to him. He could see the same e-mail again he had received a few days ago where she sent him the Excel file identifying Ron's holdings.

The next data captured was an e-mail from Ann to Andrew Dunn. In it she wrote she was happy with the services Charles Chamberlin had been providing. She thanked Andrew for introducing them. She wrote to Andrew that Charles had some recommendations for her that seemed sound, reasonable and fairly safe. She wrote he would be seeing some of the recommendations being implemented in the near future and Andrew should call on Charles if he had any accounting questions about the changes.

With no other significant data being identified in the file, CC exited the file and deleted the e-mail from his in-box. The last e-mail was from Andrew. He said he thought things over and was prepared to pay KS four point one million dollars cash for her interest. He asked CC to call him and talk before he said anything to Katherine.

When done with the e-mails, CC went to the www.sovereignbank.com website and accessed Theresa Lee's account. He selected the history option and requested the history for the past six months be displayed. He carefully reviewed the data displayed looking for deposits being made on a regular basis for the same amount. To his satisfaction, he saw a regular deposit of eighteen hundred dollars being made into the account around the first of every month. Theresa was getting an income. He thought that was good because he didn't like her and wanted to take her for as much as he could. He laughed and said out loud, "Let's see her live on eighteen hundred for awhile."

Finishing with the Lee issues, CC focused on the data he had written down from Ann Pierce. He went to www.boa.com and the balances had not changed since the last time he checked. He logged out of that account and then entered www.ingdirect.com. He entered the same ID and password and was granted access. He selected the account balance tab and saw she had over two point one million in the account. He logged out of that account and checked on the TRowePrice account. Even though Ann had not accessed that site, he wanted to make sure the funds stayed pretty much the

226

same. They had. A balance of just under seven hundred a fifty thousand remained. Now done with his research, he brought up his excel spreadsheet of potential targets and updated the amount fields under Ann Pierce.

It had taken hours for CC to dissect the data captured by PCTrackR from Katherine, Theresa and Ann. He looked at the balances of all of his targets and was satisfied with what he saw.

Target	Location	Amount	Take
Kelly	Rockland	$2,000,000	$1,500,000
	Settlement	$200,000	$133,000
Sterns	Vanguard	$2,500,000	$2,000,000
	ING	$400,000	
	Franklin	$50,000	
	Sterns	$5,500,000	
	401K	$5,100,000	
Lee	Insurance	Paid	
	Lawsuit	Settled	
	TrowePrice	$580,000	
	Sovereign	$5,939,921	$5,000,000
	Dreyful	$1,905,000	$1,000,000
Tindle	Lawsuit	$5,900,000	$2,000,000
	Bank of Am	$779,224	
Pierce	Bank of Am	$718,000	$500,000
	TrowePrice	$747,000	$500,000
	ING Direct	$2,110,053	$1,500,000

CC saved the excel file. He was potentially now looking at a total of between thirteen and fourteen million dollars. His plan was looking better and better.

The last thing CC decided to do for the day was to call Andrew. He had something he needed to say.
"Andrew, its Charles Chamberlin."
"Charles, how are you doing?"
"Andrew, I'm calling because I am concerned about something that had come up with Katherine."
"What might that be?"

"When we last talked, you and I discussed the potential value of Sterns and Dunn. I brought to your attention the Key Man insurance payment. Well, Katherine has now brought that up with me."

"What did she say?"

"Katherine said there was a Key Man insurance policy on her husband and that paid three million dollars to Sterns and Dunn when he died. So she knows about the policy. She thinks you are trying to keep that money out of a potential sale."

"As I had told you, the company did get a payment from our insurance carrier."

"Katherine thinks somehow that money didn't make it into the company properly."

"Well it did. And as I previously said, we have used it for our regular operations."

"Yes, I remember. A lot went for bonuses. Is it all gone at this point?"

"I don't think it's all gone, but I did put it to good use."

"Katherine thinks it might be possible that things were done with the insurance money that wasn't on the up and up. I didn't tell her about the bonuses."

"I don't know what she would be referring to."

"She thinks the funds might have been used improperly and possibly devaluing her interest in the business. And she might be right."

"That's a pretty serious charge."

"You should be aware she has asked me to evaluate the company business plans and financial projections Sam had in his office at home regarding the company for the current year."

"Why does that mean anything to me?"

"Because if the plans and projections indicate how the company is to be run and you are doing something else as a result of the insurance proceeds, then you and the firm might be liable for any adverse effect your actions have on her interests."

"Do you think she might take action against the firm?"

"I don't know. But you know how she can be. When she sees something that gets her attention, she is relentless."

"I see what you mean. I am preparing to make her a reasonable offer, do you think she will take it?"

"That will probably depend on what you offer."

"I was thinking four million."

"Let me see. When we last spoke, I estimated the value to be over nine million. She owns sixty percent. Her share would be more in the range of five and a half to six million. You might want to reconsider your offer."

Andrew didn't say anything for a minute or two. The silence was telling. He knew he was trapped and if he didn't propose a number that included the Key Man money, she would balk. Finally, he broke the silence.

"Charles, I need to do some homework and speak with some of the people here."

"Do what you have to do. But if I were you Andrew, I wouldn't take too long. Katherine is an impatient person."

"I know, I know. I'll get back to you."

Chapter 26

The next day, CC did his regular routine again. After getting ready for the day, he checked the paper obituaries for another suitable target. He didn't find anything to his liking so he moved on to other activities. Going to his desk in his home office, he noticed the light blinking on his phone. He had messages waiting. When he called in, there was a message from Andrew Dunn asking that he call. Charles entered the number for Sterns and Dunn. The receptionist forwarded the call on to Andrew's office. Andrew's secretary was busy away from her desk. Andrew answered the call himself.

"Andrew Dunn speaking."

"Andrew, this is Charles Chamberlin. I'm returning your call."

"Charles, thank you for calling. I wanted to talk to you today about the proposal to buy out Katherine."

"What did you have in mind?"

"I have met with the other partners and our bankers. We are prepared to offer Katherine five and a half million for her interest."

"How would it be structured?"

"The firm could pay her three million in cash and we are looking for her to take back a note for the other two and a half million."

"I think she wants to make a clean break. If that's the case, she will want all cash and up front."

"I don't know if the firm could handle that. Our bankers said they could float a loan for two million but that's it."

"Katherine knows about the Key Man policy. That plus the bank loan would give you what she is looking for."

"Some of the Key Man monies were used in the operations of the company."

"She told me what you had told her. I don't think your explanation meant anything to her."

"Well, that may be so, but I can't ask for the money back?"

"But you could put back the bonus you got."

Andrew hesitated for a minute thinking. Before he could say anything else, CC said, "Andrew, who would end up owning Sam's interest in the business?"

"The other partners and I agreed we would put Sam's interest into Treasury."

"Then that would mean you would become majority owner. Would it not since you were second to Sam owning thirty percent of the business?"

"I guess that would be true?"

"Andrew, you are being coy. Your thirty percent would triple. After the transaction were done, you would own ninety percent of the firm."

"So what is your point?"

"I think you should pony up that big bonus you cut yourself. Then combine it with the loan from the bank. After that, you would be closing in on what Katherine is asking for."

"I'll have to talk to the other partners and get back to you."

"Andrew, I don't want you to think I'm being difficult, but I have to professionally represent my client."

"I understand. Let me get back to you."

"Ok. I'll wait to hear from you before I say anything to Katherine."

CC went about his tasks doing research. He recalled Katherine had requested a Google search on Charles Chamberlin so he decided to see for himself what she had learned. He brought up the Google search engine and entered the information. It returned a few pages of information. He started to read.

There was information about his firm Chamberlin Financial Consultants and a number of articles about his firm. Most of the items referenced advertisements he had placed in the local papers for his business. There were a few references to anything more than a year old. The search engine results didn't seem to show any appreciable history for Charles Chamberlin. Katherine clicked on a few of the items returned in the search. There wasn't anything particularly revealing in the information returned from the search. CC wondered what Katherine was looking for.

Next, CC brought up the home page for the Cape Cod Times Online. He scanned the information looking to see what the headlines were for the day. One article caught his attention. It read, "Local man killed in freak accident." The article went on to tell about an accident that occurred at a local marina where a crane cable had snapped killing a worker who had been assisting in the effort to perform maintenance on one of the big boats in the Hyannis harbor. Somehow, the worker had been hit by the broken cable and thrown to the ground with such force his neck had been broken. The report indicated the man died instantly. What caught CC's attention was the boat being worked on belonged to a very prominent person, Henry Krandel.

It was well known Mr. Krandel had been the catalyst in the development of the new commercial complex on Route 132 where the new Stop-and-Shop and Home Depot stores are located. Mr. Krandel was a developer and owner of the twenty-seven acre site. The property had been estimated to be worth over ninety million dollars. Being in the news often, CC knew Krandel had a lot of money. He sensed someone getting a big settlement from the accident.

The article had identified the man killed in the accident as Mr. Davis Reese. CC went back to the newspaper obituaries and looked to see if Mr. Reese had been listed. He had not. CC would look again tomorrow.

Late in the afternoon, CC got another call from Andrew.

"Charles, it's Andrew Dunn. I have talked to the people here and I think we can meet Katherine's number."

"Well, I'm sure she will be happy to hear that information."

"It will put a little strain on the firm, but we feel confident we can close on the transaction in a few weeks."

"Great. I'll convey your offer to Katherine. I'll call you back as soon as she gives me an answer one way or the other."

"Charles, make sure she understands the firm can't go any further."

"I think she'll be happy with those terms. I'll call you as soon as I know something."

"Please do."

Hanging up, CC smiled. He entered Katherine's telephone number.

"Katherine, its Charles. I have good news."

"What is it?"

"I want to surprise you with the news, are you open for dinner tonight?"

"Well, I can be. What time do you want to pick me up?"

"How about seven? Should I get a bottle of champagne chilling for you?"

"No, that's OK. It wouldn't be nearly as much fun drinking it without you. We'll save that for a few months from now, when you can share it with me."

"That's fair. How should I dress?"

"Fancy."

"So much mystery. I can't wait."

"Ok, I'll see you around seven."

Katherine had been upstairs in her house when she had answered the call on her cordless phone. She pressed the call end button and jumped for joy shouting Yes, Yes. Then she lost her balance at the top of the stairs and tumbled all the way down the steps landing at the bottom. She had hit her head on the way down and lie unconscious sprawled out on the floor.

CC went about his business wrapping things up at his place. A few minutes before seven, he left and went to Katherine's. When he arrived, the outside light was not on. He thought it strange because she was expecting him. He walked up to the front door and rang the bell. Nothing. He tried it again. No one answered. Then he knocked on the door. Katherine didn't answer. Wondering what was going on, CC moved down the porch and looked into the window. The lights were on in the living room. As he looked back to the left, he saw a set of legs lying on the floor at the bottom of the stairs.

He went back to the front door and turned the knob. Fortunately, the door was not locked. He opened it and rushed in. He went to Katherine who lay unconscious at the bottom of the stairs.

He yelled to her. "Katherine, can you hear me?"

Nothing. He put his ear to her mouth. Her breathing was shallow and barely audible. He picked up the cordless phone lying next to her. The battery had popped out and he couldn't find it right away. He ran into the kitchen and using the phone on the wall, he dialed 911. The operator came on the line and asked him to state his emergency. He told the operator who he was, where he was and his friend must have fallen down the stairs or something because she was laying at the bottom unconscious. The 911 operator said help was on the way.

CC ran back to Katherine and tried to wake her. He gently touched her face trying to get her attention. He didn't want to move her because he was concerned he would make her injuries worse. Sitting there, he said, "Don't die on me like this. It'll spoil my plans."

Katherine moaned and started to come around. She opened her eyes and saw Charles was trying to help.

"Just lie still. You have taken a fall. Help is on the way."

"Charles. It's you. How did you get here so fast?"

"We were getting together at seven. Don't you remember?"

"Is it seven already?"

"It is." They could hear the sirens coming down the street. Charles told her to remain still until the paramedics could examine her. When the paramedics came into the house, they rushed right over and asked what happened. Charles told about his call to Katherine a few hours earlier and the two were going to get together to celebrate the good news. Then he told about arriving at seven and finding her like this.

An officer now standing behind Charles said, "So you just arrived on the scene and found her like this?"

"Yes. She was so excited when I talked to her around five. She must have slipped and fallen."

"Are you sure you didn't have anything to do with her falling down the stairs?"

"Absolutely sure. I was on the other end of the line talking to her from my house."

The officer wrote a few things down in a pad he held. He took down CC's name, address and phone number and said he would be talking to him again after he had a chance to speak with Mrs. Sterns. The paramedics finished their exam and said they had to transport her immediately to the hospital. One paramedic was overheard saying to the other that Mrs. Sterns was pregnant and the baby might be in jeopardy. CC asked what hospital they would be taking her to and was told Cape Cod hospital in Hyannis. That made sense since anything happening east of Hyannis meant you went to Hyannis Hospital.

Katherine was loaded on to a stretcher and put in the ambulance. They raced off lights flashing, sirens whaling down Route 28. CC closed the door to the house, got into his car and followed.

235

At the Hospital, CC went to the emergency room. He asked about Mrs. Sterns. The receptionist asked if he was a relative. He said no but he had been the person who discovered her at the bottom of the stairs in her home. The receptionist said the hospital could only allow relatives in and no one would be able to see her for some time as she was rushed into surgery.

CC thought, "Surgery. That doesn't sound good."

He decided to call Andrew Dunn and ask him if she had any other relatives in the area. CC got the answering system at Sterns and Dunn. He entered Andrew's extension.

"Andrew Dunn."

"Andrew, I'm glad I caught you. I'm at Cape Cod Hospital with Katherine. She had an accident."

"What happened to her?"

"She apparently fell down the stairs."

"Is she alright?"

"No, she is in surgery right now. The doctor said they are going to have to try to deliver the baby."

"It will be premature, won't it?"

"Yes, but that's irrelevant now. The doctor said the baby is in distress from the fall."

"Is there anything I can do?"

"I hope so. The hospital won't tell me much because I'm not a relative. Do you know if she had any relatives in the area?"

"Gee, Sam was the only one I am aware of. I don't know if she has any relatives or not."

"What can we do?"

"I'll come right down and see if I know any of the people there. Maybe we can get some information that way."

"Ok, see you soon."

Andrew wrapped up what he was doing in a few minutes and left for the hospital. Arriving at the Emergency Room, he quickly found Charles. The two went to reception and asked to see the resident administrator. Fortunately, the administrator who was there was someone Andrew knew. He explained the situation and he and Charles were led inside the Emergency Room to a waiting area. They talked to a doctor

236

who said she had just come out of surgery and it would be about an hour before they could talk to her. They both waited nervously.

"Charles, so what do you think happened to her?"

"I don't know. I talked to her around five. We were going to go out for dinner tonight so I could tell her about the deal. She seemed real excited."

"I hope she and the baby are ok."

"Something is up if she had to be rushed into surgery. We'll have to wait to hear it from her as no one wants to tell us anything not being relatives."

They sat silently. After another half hour, the doctor came back again and said; "You can see her but only for a moment. She has had a traumatic shock to her body and she needs her rest."

They entered the room and the first thing they both thought was she had lost the bulge in her belly. Katherine lying on her back looked at them and said, "I lost the baby."

"What happened Katherine? I talked to you around five and you seemed alright."

"I was so excited, I must have slipped and fallen. I was upstairs when you called. I remember talking on the cordless phone and jumping up and down."

"Somehow you fell all the way down the stairs. I found the cordless phone next to you but the battery had fallen out."

"The next thing I remember is your face yelling at me to wake up. Could I have been lying there for hours?"

"You were unconscious when I arrived. So I guess so."

Andrew came forward and said, "Katherine, I'm so sorry."

She touched her belly and tears came to her eyes and gently rolled down her cheeks. The doctor came in again and said the two would have to go and allow her to get her rest. Charles said he would be back tomorrow to visit and asked her to have the Doctor notify the reception that it would be all right for him to visit.

The doctor looked at Katherine and she shook her head with a yes answer. He said, "I'll see to it."

As they were leaving both told her to rest and get better.

As they were leaving, Andrew said, "I'll continue to work on the deal. Things are going to be tough for her for the next few days. Let me know if I can do anything else."

Charles extended his hand and said, "Thanks for coming down Andrew. I know this meant something to her. If anything comes up regarding the sale, just let me know."

"Will do."

Chapter 27

When Andrew got to his office the next day, he asked his secretary if she had a phone number where he might reach Sam's friend Tom Bowman. A few months after Sam's death, Tom and his family moved south. Andrew's secretary said she didn't have a number but thought she had an idea of how to find them. At lunch, she went to the Bridge Bar and asked to speak with Dave the bartender. Dave had been in the kitchen getting something for a customer and when he came out, Andrew's secretary spoke with him.

"Dave, my name is Angela D'Angelo. I work for Andrew Dunn. Andrew was a partner of Sam Sterns who recently passed away in an ice fishing accident."

"Yes, I know who Mr. Dunn is. He came in here a few times with Sam. How can I help you?"

"I'm trying to get in touch with Mr. Tom Bowman. He was Sam's friend. I remember hearing at the wake Mr. Bowman had frequented this establishment often and I was hoping you might know how I could get in touch with him."

"Let me understand this. You are trying to reach Tom?"

"Yes. Something has happened to Mrs. Sterns and Mr. Dunn wanted me to try to contact Mr. Bowman."

"Wait a minute and let me see if I can find a number."

Dave went to the back of the bar and opened a few drawers looking for something. Then he turned around with a small book in his hand and came back to Angela.

"Here it is. Let me see what I have for Tom."

He went through a few pages and then said, "Tom moved to Virginia with his family not too long ago and he left a number with me in case someone wanted to reach him."

He took a piece of scrap paper and wrote it down and handed it to Angela.

"I hope this helps you."

"It's a start. Thank you for your help."

"No problem. You said something happened to Mrs. Sterns. What happened?"

"She had an accident and lost her baby."

"I didn't know she was pregnant. That's just terrible. Losing your husband and then your baby in the same year."

"It's tragic. Mr. Dunn is trying to locate the next of kin to Mrs. Sterns."

"I talked with Sam and Tom many times here at the bar and I don't think either Mr. or Mrs. Sterns had many living relatives."

"I know he had an uncle from Seattle because I talked to him at the wake but I didn't meet anyone there who said they were related to her."

"You are right about the Uncle. I remember that. But now that you mention it, I didn't talk to anyone who said they were a relative of hers."

"I'll pass the information you gave me on to Mr. Dunn. Again, thanks for the help."

Angela left the bar and went back to the office. She called the number Dave had provided.

"Hello, this is Tom Bowman."

"Mr. Bowman, its Angela D'Angelo, Mr. Dunn's secretary at Sterns and Dunn on Cape Cod, Massachusetts."

"Hello Angela, how are you? What can I do for you?"

Angela said she was fine and she was calling on behalf of Mr. Dunn.

"Mr. Bowman, Mr. Dunn is trying to locate the next of kin to Mrs. Sterns."

Tom said anxiously, "Has something happened to Katherine?"

"Yes, she had an accident and is in the hospital."

"What happened?"

240

"She apparently fell down the stairs at her home. The result is she lost the baby."

"Oh no. I know she was looking forward to having the baby. It was Sam's only real legacy."

"Mr. Dunn is working with the funeral home to make the arrangements and it would be easier if a relative were here."

Tom didn't answer for a few seconds and then said, "I don't know. Sam had told me Katherine was an only child and her parents had died a few years ago. I don't ever remember him or her saying she had any relatives. As a matter of fact, when they were married, the only relatives from her side were her parents who were still living at that time."

"So you don't think there is anyone Mr. Dunn could call?"

"Not that I could come up with."

"I know Mr. Dunn was trying to handle this without having to ask Katherine but it looks like there is no other way."

"I guess not."

"Well, thank you Mr. Bowman for the time. I'll tell Mr. Dunn what you have told me."

"Sorry I couldn't help more."

Angela hung up the phone and went into Andrew's office.

"I talked with Mr. Bowman and he didn't have any names for you to follow-up with."

"I guess I'll have to ask her."

"Everyone I talked to said the only relatives anyone ever knew were her parents and they are both now dead."

"Ok. Thanks Angela for your help. I'll take it from here." Andrew would have to bring the subject up with Katherine even though he didn't want to talk to her more than absolutely necessary.

CC read the paper the next day and did find an obituary for Mr. Davis Reese. It read:

Davis Reese, 39

Provincetown – Davis Reese, 39 died unexpectedly yesterday as a result of a commercial accident. He was born in Springfield and was a resident of Provincetown for the past four years. He was employed by Mid-Cape Rigging.

His partner J.D. Parsons survives Mr. Reese. His mother Violet Reese and his brother Donald Reese, both of Springfield, also survive him.

Services will be at 10:00 a.m. today from the Doane Beal & Ames Funeral Home, 729 Rt. 134, S. Dennis. Calling hours are today from 9 to 10 a.m. Mr. Reese will be cremated at a later date.

CC thought he didn't have much time but if he rushed, he could make the wake before the service began. He quickly dressed and went to South Dennis. He arrived at the funeral home at about nine forty. He went inside. As he entered the greeting room, the scene took him by surprise. There were about thirty people in the room. The striking thing is they were mostly men. In fact, the only woman was an elderly woman in the front of the room. CC got in line to pay his respects and when he got to the front of the line, he told the woman he was sorry for her loss. She looked at him and said, "Thank you for coming. Who are you?"

"I'm Charles Chamberlin. I was a friend of Davis."

She turned to the person and said to him. "J.D. this here is Mr. Chamberlin. He says he knew Davis so you must know him."

J.D extended his hand and said, "Mr. Chamberlin, I'm J.D Parsons. I was Davis's partner. How did you know Davis?"

"Davis had talked to me a few times about some financial matters. I'm a financial consultant."

"Funny, he never said anything to me."

"He had been looking at making some investment changes and sought some advice from my firm."

"I didn't know he had any investments."

Violet Reese approached the group. She was an elderly woman probably in her late sixties or early seventies. She was dressed in a black dress that nearly touched the floor. She had a black hat on with a black scarf. Her wire rim glasses sat near the end of her nose and she looked over them as she began to speak.

Violet interrupted and said, "Davis was a secretive person. I'll bet there are things no one knew about him."

J.D. looked at her like she was a little crazy and said, "I think I knew Davis as well as anyone."

Violet said, "Oh you can never know someone completely. Everyone has a dark side."

J.D. turned back to CC and said, "Did you end up doing anything for Davis?"

"No. I was supposed to meet with him again this week when I saw the story in the paper about his accident."

"Well, those people who were involved in the accident are going to pay. I'm going to sue all of them. They are responsible for his death."

CC thought this wasn't the time or place to pursue this any further. Emotions were already running high. He said to J.D. "Here is my card. Give me a call if I can ever be of assistance."

J.D. took the card and said, "If I get a big settlement, you'll be hearing from me."

CC moved on and out the door. He was hoping he would never hear from J.D. Parsons. In fact, he almost ran out of the place, as he was concerned someone would see him and label him.

Since he was already out, CC decided to go to the hospital to visit Katherine. When he got there, Andrew was already in the room speaking with her. He stood outside the room for a few minutes and listened to what was being said. He heard Andrew tell her he had tried to locate her next of kin. He said it would be easier if a relative of her were there to make the arrangements for the baby's burial but he couldn't

243

find a relative. Katherine had responded with, "Andrew, I don't have any relatives that are living. Both of my parents died some time ago and I am an only child."

He had asked her, "Don't you have any relatives?"

"Not any close ones. I'm sure I have a second cousin or something like that somewhere. But I haven't had any contact with anyone from my family since my parents died. And that was nearly ten years ago."

Andrew went on to tell her she would have to authorize the arrangements for the baby. He told her about how Angela had gone around trying to find a relative and eventually spoke to Tom Bowman. When she heard Tom's name, she sat up in the bed.

"Tom Bowman, what did he have to say?"

"Nothing really. He didn't know of anyone either."

"You know, Tom could be the baby's father."

Andrew's eyebrows rose and said, "Really?"

"Yes, I had a relationship with Tom just before Sam died."

"And you had sex with me when he was missing?"

"Yes, that's true. Then you could be the father."

"Is there anyone else?"

"There was always Sam. But I don't think it could have been him."

Andrew didn't say anything more for a few minutes. The two just sat there in silence. CC took the opportunity to walk in. When he did, Andrew stood and said he had to be going. CC asked him if arrangements were being made for the baby and he said they were. Then Andrew left.

CC took a seat and said to Katherine, "So how are you feeling today?"

"Better. But I'm sore all over."

"You took a pretty bad fall."

"And lost the baby."

"Yes. It's too bad it happened. Speaking of the baby, I couldn't help but overhear you speaking to Andrew when I came in. Something about Andrew possibly being the baby's father."

244

Katherine thought for a minute and recalled she and Andrew had been sitting in silence for a few minutes before CC entered. He must have been standing outside the room for a few minutes before he entered if he heard the comments. She said, "I had a thing with Andrew when Sam went missing."

"Then he might be the baby's father?"

"Could be. I don't know. I never did have a DNA test performed."

"Don't you think you should have it done now?"

"Why would I want to do that?"

"Well, if he is the father, there might be legal implications. I mean the baby might have had some claim to his wealth."

That got Katherine's attention. Her voice rose a bit and she said, "Do you think there might be something in it for me?"

"I don't know. But think about it more, you might not want to do anything until the sale of Sam's interest in Sterns and Dunn has completed."

"You make a good point. I'll keep it in the back of my mind until after the sale is done."

"You get some rest and we'll talk more tomorrow."

"Thanks for coming in to see me."

"Your welcome."

CC left the hospital and went to his office. His phone was blinking when he got to his desk. He called for messages and had one from Sarah Jacobs. She asked him to call. He returned her call and when she answered he said, "Sarah, its Charles Chamberlin."

"Hello, Charles, I was wondering if you had walked the beach recently?"

"Yes, I walked it yesterday afternoon."

"Oh, I have been walking on mornings. Have you gotten around to getting information about the 401k plan?"

"Yes, I have a report ready for you and would like to meet and explain it to you. I have already presented the report to the other doctors at the Center and you are the only one I haven't spoken to."

"What was the reaction of the doctors at the Center?"

"They were very receptive to the changes Paul had been pursuing. In fact, I have already arranged for the new funds to be available starting tomorrow."

"Can you come over this afternoon and update me?"

"Sure, what time would you prefer?"

"How about three?"

"See you at three."

Then at three p.m. CC arrived at the Jacob residence on Shore Drive. Sarah asked him to come in. She had prepared coffee and a plate of cookies. They sat in the living room where CC went through the report explaining the advantages and risks of the new funds to be offered.

"Sarah, do you have a computer in the house you use for e-mail and things?"

"Yes, it's in the den."

"You can use it to look up the new funds for more information and articles. If you can give me a few minutes on the computer, I can show you where to find some of the information you can use to make a decision and monitor the funds."

She rose and asked him to follow. They went into the study. She pressed the on button on the computer and said it would take a minute or two to bring the computer up. While it was doing that, she told CC she would make a fresh pot of coffee and be right back. He said that would be fine and he would bring up the sites that contain the information he was referring to while she got the coffee. When she left the room and after the computer came up, CC pulled a CD from his pocket and installed PCTrackR on Sarah's computer. He was just finishing up the install when she entered the room.

"Here we go." He exclaimed.

Sarah came around to stand behind him and the screen changed to the Yahoo home page. CC pointed out the Finance label on the screen and clicked it. Then when the Finance screen appeared, he showed her how to enter a fund in the symbol box. He used "Flatx" as an example and the screen changed to Fidelity's Latin America Fund. He went through the exercise explaining to her how to find information. Then he asked her to sit at the computer and to look up the three new funds were being added to the 401k plan. Sarah became proficient at viewing the data in a few minutes.

"So, you now have the tools you need to learn about the new funds."

"Yes, I can't believe all of this information is so readily available."

"That's what Paul knew. And he thought it was time for everyone at the Center to start getting better returns."

"I'm going to look at this information and see what changes I want to make."

"I think that's a good idea."

"Thank you Charles for coming over and showing me all of this."

"That's what I'm supposed to do if I'm doing my job properly."

"I'd say you are doing it well."

"Thank you for your confidence."

He put his empty coffee cup down and got up. Sarah said, "Let me take that." She took the cup and coffee to the kitchen. When she did, CC ejected the CD and put it back in his pocket. Sarah returned and walked him to the door.

"If you have any questions about anything you don't understand, please call."

"I will. And again, thank you."

CC left. PCTrackR was up and running at the Jacobs household. He would get what he wanted in due time.

Chapter 28

CC had plenty of things going on in his life. His business was thriving. He had identified a total of five targets to date and had successfully executed his plans against two of the targets. One of his clients who was also a target had just lost a baby. One target had a sizeable inheritance and he intended to take most of it. Another target had inherited a significant amount of real estate and it was now up for sale. A huge sum of money could come from the sale. CC might have access to it. And he had just started the qualification process for another target. She was the wife of a successful doctor and the good doctor had stashed away a nice nest egg.

Evaluating the potential of his targets, CC thought he would pursue only one more target. As soon as he could find a suitable candidate and identify how to get access to the assets, he would put his final plan in motion. It took a few days of reading the obituaries in the paper and scanning the online obituaries in the areas just outside the reach of the Cape Cod Times, but he finally found one he thought had potential.

Joseph Thomas Ronaldi

Harwich - Joseph Thomas Ronaldi, 47, president of the Seaside Savings and Loan, died unexpectedly on Friday. He is survived by his wife, Rhonda (Lewis) Ronaldi; his mother Helen and father Ted Ronaldi.

Mr. Ronaldi founded Seaside Savings and Loan in 1980. He built the business into one of the largest Savings and

Loan Institutions in the region. Mr. Ronaldi was actively involved in civic endeavors and public office having held numerous positions in the local government in Harwich.

Visiting hours are from 7 to 9 p.m. on Saturday and Sunday at Doane Beal & Ames Funeral Home 260 Main Street, West Harwich. Services will be held at St. Mary's Church in Harwich Monday at 10 a.m. followed by burial at Overlook Cemetery.

Founder of a Savings and Loan, President of the Institution, one of the largest savings and loans in the region, this man had to have money. CC made note of the wake and decided that possibly Mrs. Ronaldi would be his final target.

On Saturday night, CC dressed for a wake and proceeded to West Harwich. Arriving at Doane Beal & Ames Funeral Home, the place was packed. CC commented that it looked like the paper had it right. This guy knew a lot of people and many of them were here to pay their last respects. CC had to park on the street, as there was nothing open in the lot.

Walking up to the funeral home, there was a fairly large crowd milling around outside the funeral home. CC took out a smoke and reached for a match. He didn't have one. He stood at the edge of the crowd trying to get a feel for them. He needed to begin his information gathering. The first person he talked to was an elderly gentleman who was standing off to the side by himself.

"Got a light?" Asked CC.
"Sure." The man said.
"This came as a total shock, Joe dying and all."
"Sure did. He will be missed."
"My name is Charles Chamberlin."
"Len Cummings."
"Nice to meet you Len. How did you know Joe?"
"I worked for Joe at the Savings and Loan. Started with him in nineteen eighty actually."

249

"You don't say. So you have seen it all with him."

"Yeah, pretty much."

CC took a drag of his cigarette and blew the smoke into a stream as he looked up to the sky. Len coughed and said, "Where are you from Mr. Chamberlin?"

"I have a financial consulting practice in Hyannis."

"Did you do some work with Seaside?"

"Some of my clients have over the years. I met Joe through a few of them."

"Oh, do you have accounts with Seaside?"

"No, I do all of my business in Hyannis."

"Yeah, Joe wanted to open a branch in Hyannis next year. I don't know if the bank will get around to doing that or not now with him gone."

"Who will be taking over for him now that he is gone?"

"I'm not sure. Joe had majority interest in Seaside. The owners will have to find someone or maybe it's time to sell to one of the larger firms that have been pursuing Seaside."

"Maybe it's time. I know Joe had been following up on some of the interest because he had asked my opinion about one of the suitors."

"Oh, which one was that?"

"I'm not sure I can reveal the interested party as there are disclosure issues that need to be considered."

CC had just played his first card. He let on he had some form of association with Joe Ronaldi, which he did not. But Les seemed to buy it. The secretive nature of non-disclosure worked as well. He would have to remember that one for the future.

"Mr. Cummings, what do you think about having one of the larger firms buy out Seaside?"

"I think it would make Mrs. Ronaldi even richer than she is already. Joe had worked himself into a very nice position with Seaside. I think he was bringing down over five hundred grand a year in salary and bonus. Plus, he had built up a substantial fortune over the years from his interest in

250

Seaside. My guess is Seaside would bring in over a hundred and fifty million. Not bad for a guy who had started out with really nothing in '80."

"Too bad he isn't going to get to spend it."

"Yeah, she stands to get thirty million just for his share."

"Oh, I thought you said he had controlling interest in Seaside?"

"He did. He owned twenty percent. He brought in institution investors who owned forty percent collectively and Joe represented them. That gave him controlling interest. The nearest individual owner to him was Milt English over there. He owns ten percent."

"I see what you mean." CC extinguished his cigarette and said goodbye to Mr. Cummings.

Mr. Cummings went inside ahead of CC. CC stopped at the door and turned to Milt English.

"Mr. English, Charles Chamberlin."

"I'm sorry, I don't remember you."

"Joe spoke about you and some of the other investors from time to time. I run a financial consulting practice in Hyannis and I recently did some research for Joe regarding investors."

"And how did my name come up?"

"It didn't. Joe had asked me to look into some of the larger institutions that wanted to purchase Seaside. Part of my assignment was to assess the potential impact on the current investors. Your name was right at the top of the investors list, right after Joe."

"Mr. Ronaldi didn't mention anything to me."

"We hadn't finished the analysis when this happened. I'm not sure where it will go now."

"Just curious, what kind of numbers was Joe looking at for a potential sale?"

"I can't go into that here but it was significant."

CC could see Mr. English in thought. He didn't know if Mr. English was thinking about the potential windfall or about CC. Then Mr. English said, "I know Seaside needs to find a new leader soon. When that happens, I'll make sure that person makes the sale one of the top priorities."

"Do you have any ideas as to who a successor might be?"

"Not at this point. Those institutional people Joe brought in will have ideas of their own. And Joe's wife Rhonda will end up with his interest. Since Joe was the Institution, I'll bet everyone looks at this as an opportunity to get out quickly."

"But Seaside is growing and expanding."

"Yeah, all under Joe's direct supervision. And now that's gone."

"I guess you're right. It would probably take some time for another person to come in and take over."

"Joe just had that touch. Everything he touched turned to gold. I think it's time to cash out."

"You have a point. Well, it has been nice talking to you Mr. English."

"Milt. Call me Milt. Nice talking with you also."

At that, CC turned and went inside the funeral home. As he entered the building, a man standing at the table that contained the guest-signing book said, "Mr. Chamberlin, nice to see you again."

CC turned to see Carl Pruit, one of the managers of the funeral home.

"Mr. Pruit, you remembered my name?"

"Yes, kind of a habit. I'm in the people business. Remembering names and faces is a hobby of mine. It comes in handy in my line of work."

"I guess what you do would require you to remember people. I just thought of a wake as something people would rather not remember."

"You wouldn't believe how competitive this business is. Some of our business is reactionary, but some of it results from knowing where to be when things happen."

"What do you mean?"

Mr. Pruit told CC to come with him for a minute and he lead him down the hall and into an office. Inside, there was a scanner, a television, a computer and a few phones.

Mr. Pruit said, "We listen to the police scanner all the time. When an accident happens where someone dies, we get on the phone and find out what we can and then try to get the business. We also use the computer to scan stories that indicate who might be gravely ill or who had been in a serious accident and we follow the results closely."

"I never thought of it as a competitive business."

"And we have our literature spread all over the area especially at places that would be logical for what we do, like the hospitals, the police departments, the nursing homes, places like that."

"So you actively pursue your clients?"

"Look Mr. Chamberlin, there are only a few things that are certain in this world and death is one of them. It might not sound so nice, but death is my business."

"I guess if you put it that way."

Mr. Pruit lead CC out of the office and back down the hall. While walking he said, "So, you're here for another wake so soon after the last one?"

"Yes, unfortunately, Mr. Ronaldi was another client I had done some work for."

"So are you here to pay your respects or to protect your client relationship?"

"I guess it's a little of both. I just didn't think of it in those terms."

"Not many people like to talk about death. But for those who remain, life goes on."

"I guess it does. Well, you'll have to excuse me if you would. I need to pay my respects and get going."

"Sure. Nice to see you again Mr. Chamberlin."

CC felt uncomfortable about his conversation with Mr. Pruit. He was being seen too much at funeral homes. He hoped Joe Ronaldi would work out and this would be his last time to gather information this way. His plan had to come to conclusion soon. CC got in the receiving line and waited his turn to pay his respects. When he reached Mrs. Ronaldi, he

253

told her how sorry he was Joe had died. She thanked him for coming. He said his private thoughts in front of the casket and then exited the funeral home.

On Monday, he went to the church and attended the service. Then at the cemetery, he was standing talking to Mr. English when Mrs. Ronaldi walked up to them. She said, "Milt, we need to talk about Seaside sometime soon."

Mr. English said, "Yes, I agree. I had been talking with Mr. Chamberlin here about Seaside. Do you know each other?"

"We met at the funeral home."

"Mrs. Ronaldi, my condolences." Milt extended his hand to her and shook it limply.

Mr. English said, "Mr. Chamberlin had been working with Joe gathering information about a possible sale of Seaside."

"I know he had expressed some interest in selling Seaside to me, but he didn't say how far along he was in the process before he died."

"He was still in the information gathering phase but he did have some discussions with a very large savings and loan institution as I recall."

"Well, someone is going to have to take over while we sort all of this out. Milt, you are next in line as investor who knows something about the bank. Why don't you step in on an interim basis?" she said.

Milt English had worked for Joe since Seaside began so he knowledge of Seaside was only second to Joe. With having Mrs. Ronaldi's backing, Mr. English wouldn't have much of a difficult time stepping in for Joe. "I can help out on an interim basis. But I don't want to make it permanent."

"How about we make it short term until the sale of Seaside can be flushed out?" Rhonda was surprisingly inquisitive.

"I could go along with that. Maybe Mr. Chamberlin here can help me with the analysis and bring me up to date."

"I'd be happy to assist," answered Charles.

"So it's settled. Milt, you take over on an interim basis. Mr. Chamberlin can help you get your arms around the sale. Lets meet in a few days and see where we are at."

"Sounds ok to me," answered Milt.

"Me too" responded CC.

The three went their respective ways.

When CC got back home, the light on his phone was blinking. He called in for messages. There was one from Katherine. She sounded weak and shaky.

"Charles, I appreciate all you're doing for me. I was just lying here thinking about my accident and I recall you telling me something about spoiling your plans. What were you referring to? Give me a call when you get in."

CC thought about it for a minute and had to come up with something. He called her back.

"Katherine, how are you holding up? I got your message. You asked about some of the things we talked about when we were waiting for the emergency help to arrive at your house after the accident. One of the things I talked about was what I had envisioned as plans for you for the future."

"What did you mean spoil your plans?"

"Oh, nothing. I had planned to take you to dinner for a celebration."

"What were we going to celebrate?"

"The sale of your interest in Sterns and Dunn. Andrew agreed to the full amount you wanted. It should be completed in a week or two."

"Oh, was that all?"

"That's all. Katherine, you become a very wealthy woman with that sale."

"I already have enough money."

"You have some, but raising a child can be expensive."

Then CC realized what he had just said and tried to be compassionate.

"I'm sorry Katherine, that was insensitive of me."

"That's ok. I know what you mean. But I already have quite a bit of money as you well know."

255

"You have a few million. And yes, that money can provide a nice income. But with the sale of your interest in the company, you will have a very nice income for the rest of your life."

"I guess."

"Let's not talk about it any more, not until you are up and around and feeling better."

"How are the burial arrangements coming for the baby?"

"Everything's set. The service and burial will be the day after tomorrow."

"I can't thank you enough Charles. You and Andrew have been wonderful in all of this."

"I'll let you get back to your rest and I'll see you at the funeral home."

"Thanks again."

Chapter 29

Rhonda Ronaldi was an attractive woman at forty years old. She had brown hair and brown eyes, a silky complexion and visited the salon every week. Rhonda worked at the town library managing the facility, not that she had to work, but she enjoyed the quiet time offered by a library and it gave her something to do. A side benefit of working there allowed her the opportunity to meet many people in town the result of which her husband used to his advantage at the bank and in his political ambitions. At many a dinner or party, Rhonda was able to introduce Joe to the right people who could influence his business and political pursuits.

Rhonda was always the impeccable dresser. She wore only the highest quality clothes in the latest styles. If there were ever a person who dressed and looked like a picture from a fashion magazine, it was Rhonda. Her days at the library had honed her speaking skills to be that of a soft spoken person who got right to the point. It must be something that comes with working with a level of detail found in a library.

Rhonda grew up in a Unionville, Connecticut. On a vacation to Cape Cod one summer, she had met Joe at Sundancers Bar in West Dennis while out with some of her girl friends. Joe and Rhonda had hit it off right from the start. Joe had asked Rhonda if he could see her again and she said he should call her if his plans brought him to Connecticut. As chance had it, he had a business trip planned to Connecticut a few weeks later. When he got to there and put a call in to her home, he was told she was out for the night at the Olive Bar at the main intersection in Unionville. Joe got directions and went to the bar. When he got there, Rhonda was at the bar with a group of friends listening to a guitar player who was off in the corner. Joe tapped her on the shoulder and she was so surprised, she gave him a big hug and kiss. Then she introduced Joe to her friends. From that point on, the two would spend many weekends together either on Cape Cod or in Connecticut until Joe finally proposed to her one night about six months later while at the Olive Bar. They were married the next spring and Rhonda moved permanently to Cape Cod.

The Ronaldi residence on Smith Road in Harwich was a very large Colonial style home. It had five bedrooms, a three-car garage, four bathrooms, a home office, a study, and an enormous wrap-around deck surrounding three full sides of the home. On Cape Cod a house like this was easily valued in the millions. Rhonda drove a brand new top-of-the-line Lexus, cream in color on the outside, dark brown leather interior. Joe had driven a Lincoln Navigator that was now parked in the garage until Rhonda could figure out what to do with it.

Rhonda had a few hobbies she enjoyed. When the weather was nice, she and Joe would golf whenever time permitted. During winter months, the two would try to get away for long weekends to the Caribbean or skiing in Vermont. But the thing that took up most of her free time was entertaining. Joe had business or political meetings nearly every night and he relied on Rhonda to take care of planning whatever activity was needed for the occasion. Working at the library gave her time and access to take care of the social needs supporting Joe's ambitions.

With Joe gone, Rhonda was going to have to follow-up on Joe's business interests and bring them to conclusion. She got the business card CC had given her out of her pocketbook and called.
"Chamberlin Financial Services."
"Hi, is this Mr. Chamberlin?"

"Yes it is. How may I help you?"

"Mr. Chamberlin, this is Rhonda Ronaldi."

"Mrs. Ronaldi. It's good to hear from you. What can I do for you?"

"We spoke at my husband's service the other day and had agreed that you and Mr. English, I mean Milt, were going to look into the sale of the Seaside Savings and Loan that my husband had been pursuing."

"Yes, that was my understanding."

"Well, while I feel confident Mr. English is capable of handling the business issues associated with the sale, I'm not sure I should have him representing my interest."

"I'm not sure I understand what you mean?"

"Joe built Seaside into what it is today. He had a considerable investment in it both financially and emotionally. Milt has the experience but I'm not sure he shares Joe's emotional ties to the place. I don't want to sell just for the sake of selling. I want to make sure its for what its worth."

"I understand. If you are not under duress to get the sale done, then taking the time is a smart thing. "

"In any event, I want to make sure Seaside gets the proper consideration in any potential sale."

"By that you mean the most value I assume?"

"Yes. And in that regard, I'd like to retain your firm to see to it my interests are best represented."

"Would Mr. English take that suspiciously?"

"I'll explain it to him. I don't think he'll have a problem with it. He can run the business on a day-to-day basis and construct the deal. You can assist based on your prior relationship with my husband and your new relationship with me."

"I guess that could work."

"I'm sure it can. What do I need to do to secure your services?"

"I can bring over an agreement for you to look at and if it's acceptable to you, we can go from there."

"That would be fine. When can I expect you?"

"How about this afternoon, say four?"

"Then four it is."

CC went to his computer and brought up a blank consulting agreement. He entered the information identifying Rhonda Ronaldi as his client and laid out the specific terms of their relationship. He updated the schedule for his fees, and then saved the document. Confident the document would do, CC printed two copies and put them in a folder. He saved the changed document to a new CD and put the CD in his briefcase when he had finished.

At four p.m. CC arrived at the Ronaldi residence on Smith Road. Driving up to the place he thought the house was impressive. They certainly had money. The place was well landscaped and large by Cape standards. When he rang the doorbell, Rhonda greeted him.

"Mr. Chamberlin, thank you for coming."

"No problem. I'm happy to help."

"I talked to Mr. English today and he is onboard with your role. He understands my position wanting representation and was happy to oblige."

"Then it looks like things are falling into place."

"Yes. Come in. We'll use our home office."

The two went into a spacious office at the back of the house. The walls were lined with books many of which focused on the topic of finance. Another wall contained a large flat screen television turned on to MSNBC. A large mahogany desk with two side chairs in front and a hi-back leather chair behind it sat in the center of oversized picture windows looking out onto a garden.

"Joe liked to work here. He had his computer and his TV. The man was addicted to anything to do with finance."

"His reputation was most certainly appreciated in the community."

"Yes, his political ambitions were for the town to be a picture perfect community. And he used his connections and finance background to make it the best he could."

"That's what I had heard from everyone I talked to and it's how I'll always remember him."

"Mr. Chamberlin."

"Call me Charles."

"Ok, Charles. What do you propose for an arrangement in representing my interests?"

"My services are usually provided on a retainer basis of ten-thousand dollars up front from which I'll draw at a rate of two-hundred fifty dollars per hour plus expenses. When the retainer is exhausted, my services would continue on a time and materials basis billed monthly in arrears."

"That could end up costing quite a bit of money couldn't it?"

"That would depend on how long a sale would take and how much involvement I would have to have in bringing the sale to conclusion. My experience says the upfront retainer should be sufficient to consummate a sale."

"Is there any other compensation arrangements you would consider?"

"Sure, I'd consider working on a commission basis if that would be preferable."

"What would that look like?"

"I'd consider something like a real estate structure. Say five percent of your eventual take in the sale."

"Would I have to put any money up front?"

"Being that I have knowledge of the situation already, I'd be willing to represent your interest on a strictly back-end or commission basis. I would only get paid when the deal completes. It's open ended, which means the sale may take place five years from now, and I would still get the commissions."

"I'd like to pursue that path if it's acceptable to you."

CC didn't have that agreement with him but if he could use her computer for a few minutes, he could modify the one he had to reflect those terms and print it right there. Then they could sign it.

"That would be fine with me," Rhonda said.

CC opened his briefcase and took out two CDs. He walked to the computer workstation and sat down. He inserted one CD in the drive and started to type.

"Can I get you a cup of coffee or something while you're updating the agreement?"

261

"Yes, please. Can I get it black with two sugars?"
"Sure, I'll be right back."

When she left the room, CC installed PCTrackR. He quickly went through the setup and in a few minutes it was up and running. He removed the CD and inserted another CD in the drive. He opened Word and started making changes to the Services Agreement. When finished, he printed two copies of it and closed the programs he had opened on the computer. Rhonda came back into the office just as the second document copy was printing.

"Here's your coffee. Black with two sugars."
"Thanks. The modified Agreement reflecting the commission structure is printing now."
CC took a sip of the coffee and then picked up the two copies. He separated the two from the stack of paper he had taken off the printer and stapled both copies. He handed one copy to Rhonda and picked the other copy up for himself.

"I've made the changes we discussed. You can see the changes here on page one and page three."
"Yes, this looks fine. Should I sign here on page four?"
"If everything looks in order, then we can both sign and it's done."
Rhonda picked up a pen and signed both copies. CC did the same. He handed one copy back to her and put the other along with the CDs back into his briefcase.
"That's done." He said.
"I look forward to hearing from you about the sale as soon as you can meet with Milt."
"You'll be hearing from me pretty quick. I expect Milt will want to move things along rather quickly."
With that, they both rose and Rhonda escorted CC to the door.

Driving home, CC recalled Cummings telling him Seaside would probably go for one hundred fifty million and Mrs. Ronaldi would get thirty million. His cut of five percent

262

would net him one and a half million. This might be even better than hacking into her accounts. Getting one and a half million legitimately. Now that was something he would have to think about.

CC called Mr. English when he got back to his office. The two discussed strategy and the next steps. Milt told CC a deal for the regional Seaside Savings and Loan was heating up. He had only been in the office one day and the calls were already coming in. Milt told CC the President of Provident Savings and Loan had called and had indicated they had been in discussion with Joe about the possible sale of Seaside to them. He indicated Provident had been working out a deal in the range of one hundred sixty million cash just prior to Joe's death.

"They're one of the suitors Joe had been considering."

"Were there others?"

"Not as far along, but there were a few others."

"Do you think Joe had expected to get an offer from Provident?"

"I'm pretty sure. As I said, he had me looking into how a sale would translate to the shareholders. And I was working with an amount of one hundred fifty million."

"If Joe was considering Provident, that would be good enough for me. I'll go along with his lead. I'll call Provident back and keep the ball rolling."

"Is there anything you would like me to do at this time?" asked CC.

"No, I can handle it. Just report back to Mrs. Ronaldi and I'll keep you informed."

CC thought Milt just wanted to get all he could for his interest as quickly as possible and he was right. CC had bluffed his way through up to this point and he saw no reason to interfere. Rhonda Ronaldi would get thirty-two million and he would get five percent of that number. Everyone would be happy and he didn't have to commit a crime to get his share.

After the call, CC turned his attention to the day's mail. There was a letter from William Tindle's bank. The letter explained that two million dollars had been transferred

263

from the account of Mr. William Tindle and the firm of Cape Investigative Services was pursuing the matter of the missing funds. The letter went on to say Cape Investigative Services would be contacting persons and businesses having contact with Mrs. Carol Tindle during the past ninety days and asked that Mr. Chamberlin cooperate with the investigation. Of course he would.

Chapter 30

The service for Katherine's baby was a sad event for her. Charles and Andrew stood at her side throughout. Some of the people from Sterns and Dunn attended along with a few of the Katherine's neighbors. There were a few flower arrangements around the casket and there was one from Tom Bowman that had a message on it that said, "My deepest sympathy, Tom."

The small casket, only about three feet long, clearly looked out of place sitting among the arrangements. Katherine had named the baby Sam after her deceased husband. The entire service and burial didn't take more than an hour and a half. Katherine was the last person to leave the casket. As she turned to leave, she looked up and there stood Tom Bowman. He had tears in his eyes. Lisa had not accompanied him. He held out his arms towards Katherine and she walked up to him and embraced him. He whispered in her ear, "I'm so sorry Kat. I knew how much you were looking forward to having our baby."

"I'm sorry too, Tom. So I guess you figured it out."

"Yes, it didn't take too much calculating to figure out the baby was a result of our night together."

"I just couldn't bring myself to say anything at the time of Sam's death. How it would have looked."

"I guess you're right. What do you intend to do now?"

As the two were embracing, Charles approached and asked Katherine if everything was all right.

"Everything is fine Charles. This is an old friend of my husband's. Tom Bowman, this is Charles Chamberlin."

"Charles, nice to meet you."

"Tom."

"Charles, can you give me another few minutes with Tom? He's come all the way from Virginia and I have a few things I'd like to talk to him about."

"Sure." Charles turned, looking over his shoulder, and left.

"Tom, I know you were the father of the baby. I hadn't been having sex with Sam for some time and I had already stopped having my period when I got together with Andrew. I'm glad I got to tell you about it and hope this will put closure on our relationship for both of us."

"Kat, you know what happened on the ice with Sam, I did it all for you."

"What do you mean?"

"You know. The whole ordeal. I did it all for you. You know how much I wanted you to myself."

"What are you talking about Tom? Exactly what happened on the ice that you did for me?"

"Everything I did to Sam's body was so I would be able to get back to you. I had to do those things to Sam in order to get myself rescued. Otherwise, Sam's death would have been for nothing."

"Sam's death was for nothing. The authorities closed the case out as an accident; a stupid, random, bad luck accident. Isn't that how it happened?"

"I guess you're right."

"Well, then this service puts closure to our relationship. I hope you can go back to Virginia and completely resume your life with Lisa."

Tom stood back, kissed Katherine gently on the cheek, and realized he had no future with her. She had moved on. Charles came back up to Katherine and escorted her to a waiting car. Tom went to his rental car and got in. He went back to his hotel room, packed his bag and left Cape Cod hopefully for the last time.

At the car, Katherine told Charles and Andrew she was going to take some time off and go visit with a friend, Dotty Masters. She would probably be gone for a few weeks, but she gave them both a number where she could be reached if something needed her attention. "Charles, would you drive me home so I can pack?"

"Absolutely. I think it's a great idea."

Katherine turned and hugged Andrew, and then climbed into the car. Charles went around to the driver's side of the vehicle, and waved to Andrew as he turned to his car.

On the way, Charles tried to figure out how to start the conversation about the sale of her interest in Sterns and Dunn.

"Katherine, I know you probably don't want to talk about it today, but with your going out of town, we should talk about the sale of your interest in Sterns and Dunn."

"Charles, I really don't want to talk about it today. My mind and heart are just not ready."

"I can certainly understand where you're coming from, but how would you like me to proceed while you're gone?"

"I'll sign a power of attorney over to you and if you can close the deal for me, go right ahead."

"I can certainly do that if you're sure that's what you want."

"It is and I'm sure you'll do the right thing."

"I'll bring over the power of attorney for you to sign this afternoon. I'll take care of the sale on your behalf, and if the transaction closes while you're gone, I'll deposit the funds into a money market account in your name."

"That would be fine."

As they turned the corner on to Katherine's street, Charles asked about Tom Bowman.

"So, what was up with Tom Bowman?"

"He was Sam's best friend. They did everything together that guys do."

"Wasn't he with Sam when he died?"

"Yes. That's one of the things we talked about."

"That was a while ago. What did he say today?"

267

"He said he did it all for me."

"What did he mean?"

"I'm not sure. He said he had to do those things to Sam in order to be rescued."

"That's weird. Do you think he killed Sam?"

"Why would you say that?"

"Well, what do you think he was talking about?"

"I think he was talking about having to mutilate Sam's body in order to be able to write the message on the ice."

"That's one interpretation, but what if he was trying to tell you he killed Sam to get the blood, to write the message, to be rescued so he could be with you?"

"I never got that impression."

"You haven't said much about him to me, but I know you mentioned he was infatuated with you at one time."

"Well, I did sleep with him once and he was the baby's father."

"Katherine, I think there might be more going on here than you think."

"Do you think I should do anything about it?"

"I don't know. But be careful. If you think he's going to hang around and make life more difficult for you, let me know. I can help."

"Thanks Charles, but he's going back to Virginia and I don't expect to hear from him again."

"For your sake, I hope not."

They pulled into Katherine's driveway. "Want some company?"

For the first time, Katherine said, "No, I don't feel up to it."

"Why don't you get done what needs to get done, and then get some rest? I'll come back later this afternoon when you feel better."

"I think that's a good idea. Thank you Charles for all you've done."

"Get some rest."

Katherine got out of the car and went into her house. Her nosy neighbor was watching through a window with the shade partially open. Katherine didn't give her a look. She just went inside.

Charles went to his office and prepared the paperwork for Katherine to sign. Once he had the signed notarized form, he would be able to finish the sale with Andrew.

Later that afternoon, Charles took the form to Katherine for signature. When he knocked at the door, Katherine answered but didn't ask Charles to come in.

"I have the power of attorney here for you to sign."

"Ok, let me get a pen." Katherine retrieved a pen from a drawer in a small table next to the door. She looked at the document. "Do I need to read it before I sign?"

"It gives me the power of attorney to represent you in this transaction only. It's pretty straight forward, but you can read it if you like. I'll come back."

"I'll just sign it now for you."

Charles stood in the doorway while she signed it. As he looked around the foyer, he saw Katherine was already packed; two suitcases were by the door ready to go.

"Katherine, just sign over your name and I'll notarize it. That's all you'll have to do."

"Thanks again Charles for doing this."

"I see you're ready to go."

"Yes, I'm leaving within the hour."

"When do you think you'll come back?"

"I don't know. I need some time to re-center myself. Dotty said I could stay as long as I'd like. I guess I'll be there for a few weeks, but I have no definite schedule."

"Well, if I can do anything, please call."

"You're already doing so much for me. If I need anything, I'll call."

He gave her a kiss on the cheek. Then he picked up the document and left. He went right to the offices of Sterns and Dunn. When he arrived, Andrew asked him to come into his office.

269

"Andrew, Katherine has given me the authority to represent her in the sale of her interest in Sterns and Dunn."

"Isn't she going to attend herself?"

"No, loosing the baby has had such an effect on her, she has signed a power of attorney over to me and asked that I conclude the sale with you."

"Can I see the authorization?"

"Certainly." Charles produced the authorization. Andrew took a few minutes to read the document. Everything looked to be in order.

"This was signed today."

"Yes, as you know, she's leaving town for a few weeks, and it made more sense to keep this moving along, rather than let it sit until she gets back."

Andrew picked up his phone and asked his secretary to come in. When she did, he asked her to get the paperwork for the purchase of Katherine Stern's interest in Sterns and Dunn.

The secretary left for a few minutes and returned with a folder. Andrew asked her to remain as a witness to the transaction. He took out a stack of forms and laid them on the table. There must have been a dozen documents to be signed. He and Charles signed each one, Charles signing and indicating POA after his signature. The secretary signed each document under the witness section. When done, Andrew stood and extended his hand to Charles.

"That concludes the sale."

"That and a check for five and a half million."

"Yes. I'll instruct my bank to wire transfer the funds to Katherine's account."

"I'd prefer if you would give me a bank check and I'll take care of the funds on her behalf. She instructed me to open a new money market account with the proceeds."

Andrew looked puzzled. He asked the secretary if she could get a bank check. "Yes, I can, but I won't have it until tomorrow."

"If I give you an account in Katherine's name, can you wire transfer the funds today?"

"I don't see why not," said Andrew.

"I'll call you as soon as I get the account information and I'd appreciate it if you would make the transfer."

"We can take care of that." Andrew looked at his secretary and said, "If I'm unavailable when Mr. Chamberlin calls, please take down the account information and make sure I get it today."

Charles stood and said, "Well, I guess that takes care of it then." He put all of the signed forms in his briefcase.

"I'll keep one copy and you can have one copy for Katherine."

"No, I'll keep all the originals until the funds are transferred into Katherine's account."

"Mr. Chamberlin, don't you trust me?"

"I have learned in business you don't take unnecessary risks especially when large amounts of money are involved. I'll give you your signed copies when the funds have been transferred."

"Have it your way."

"Then, let me get going and get her account information to you so this deal can be wrapped up."

Charles left and went to his office. He went to Cape Cod Bank and Trust and opened a money market account in Katherine's name. He had to show his power of attorney to get the bank manager to open the account but once he explained the situation, the bank manager was only too happy to help out. Charles told the bank manager there would be a five and a half million dollar transfer coming into the bank in a few hours and he would be calling back to confirm the transfer. The bank manager smiled, said she would await his call, and handed Charles her business card.

Charles then called Andrew's office and conveyed the information. Andrew's secretary said he was in a meeting and the transfer would be done as soon as he finished. A half hour later, she called back and said Andrew had made the transfer. Charles called the bank manager who confirmed the funds had been received by the bank and deposited into the new money market account. Charles asked the bank manager to ensure the account was secured and only he or Mrs. Sterns were to have access to the account. He stressed under no circumstances were the funds to be accessed unless by one of the two. The manager assured Charles the account was secured and his directions would be followed explicitly.

After hanging up, Charles went back to the offices of Sterns and Dunn and dropped off their signed documents. The deal was done.

Returning to his office, he noticed the light blinking on his phone. There was a message from Milt English asking Charles to give him a call. Charles returned the call.

"Mr. English, this is Charles Chamberlin."

"Charles, thank you for getting right back to me. I'd like to arrange a meeting so we can discuss the sale of Seaside."

"When would you like to meet?"

"Can you be here tomorrow?"

"What time?"

"How about ten o'clock tomorrow morning?"

"I'll be there. Is there anything I should bring?"

"No, I have a tentative offer from Provident I would like to review with you and get your opinion of."

"Ok, see you at ten."

Charles reflected on the activity for the day. One deal closed for Katherine Sterns. Another deal was pending for Rhonda Ronaldi. He began to think he might be able to make a decent living doing the kinds of things he had become involved in.

The next day, CC and Milt met to discuss the Provident offer. Milt went over the details and asked Charles what he thought. Charles indicated the offer was in line with what they had previously discussed and there were no surprises in it.

"Milt, I think this offer looks pretty good."

"I was hoping you'd say that. I plan on making a presentation to the board this week and I was hoping you'd meet with Mrs. Ronaldi and give her a similar pitch."

"Why don't you just have her attend your presentation?"

"Because I don't want her to influence the board members. She isn't Joe and I'm not sure what her acumen is relative to these kinds of things. The board can be brutal in their feedback during the review process. I'd prefer she be handled separately."

"I think I understand. You would like me to give her the presentation at the same time though, right?"

"That's right. You can bring up my actual presentation from the company's website."

Milt provided Charles with a piece of paper that told him how to get at the presentation.

Charles had agreed to meet with Mrs. Ronaldi. Milt and Charles would speak when both presentations had been given. If everyone approved, the deal could probably be concluded in a week or two.

Charles left and called Mrs. Ronaldi when he got back to his office. He asked if they could meet the next day and she agreed. The next day, Charles went to Mrs. Ronaldi's home to give her the presentation.

Rhonda Ronaldi answered the door looking like she was going out to dinner. She had on a pink and green silk dress in a tropical print and delicate black slides. A single pearl necklace and pearl studs completed the look.

CC took out the instructions and brought up the Power Point presentation on the computer. For the next half hour, he went through the slides explaining the deal. When done, Mrs. Ronaldi said, "I think that looks pretty good."

"I'd say. Your share of one hundred sixty million dollars will be thirty two million dollars. I think that's a little better than the number we had been expecting."

"Yes, it looks like about ten million more overall and two more than I thought I would get."

"That's right. Do you have any questions?"

"Are there any strings attached to the deal?"

"Not for you. Your interest is a pure cash transaction. When the deal closes, you won't have any lingering obligations."

"Then I'm all for it. Will you let Milt know?"

"Yes. He's expecting to hear from me. Now, it will only take me a few minutes to clean up this stuff I put on your computer."

"How long do you think it will take the legal eagles to put this thing on paper?"

"Oh, I would guess at least a few weeks. It's a lot of money, and both parties want to be protected. It's a litigious society we live in these days, and lawyers get paid by the hour."

"Unfortunate, but true. I'll be in the kitchen getting us something to drink."

She left the office and CC went to the Control Panel. Under the Add/Remove Software listing was PCTrackR. Perhaps he should remove it now. After all, he was already getting a one million six hundred thousand dollar commission on the legitimate transaction. Did he need more? As Rhonda came back in the room, two champagne flutes in her hands, CC closed the window, and shut the computer down.

As Rhonda and Charles toasted, Rhonda said "To a victorious future without lingering obligations."

"To a victorious future" Charles smiled, "and fast lawyers."

Chapter 31

When CC had installed PCTrackR on Sarah Jacobs's computer, he set the interval for capturing information to seven days. This meant he would get information every week until he issued the e-mail to erase PCTrackR. At the end of the first week, he received the first e-mail. He downloaded and saved the attached file as SJStrokes One, and then CC opened the file.

He could see in the data captured where he had shown Sarah how to find fund information, as the sites he had visited when he consulted with her were the first items in the file. Next, he saw where she logged into her bank account using the ID SJACOBS and password Sarah01. He wrote down the ID and password in a notebook he had been keeping on all of his targets' access information. There were no additional keystrokes captured while at the bank site so CC figured she was just looking at her balance. Next, she logged into www.vanguard.com. She used the same ID and password. Now, CC had what he needed to gain access to her accounts. While at the Vanguard site, she selected an option that transferred one hundred thousand dollars from a money market account and to purchase stock in a precious metals fund. She had taken his advice, and was starting to invest some of her funds; she trusted him and that was a good thing.

Next, Sarah went to www.thecenter.com. A string of characters that must have been her husband's ID and password followed the web address: PJACOBS followed by PJ0919. CC would have to investigate that site after he finished with her file because even though he knew it must be related to the facility where Paul worked, he wasn't sure how much confidential information Sarah would or could have access to through it.

After visiting the Center's website, Sarah went to Hotmail and wrote an e-mail to Milt English. "Milt, I have every intention of selling Paul's interest in The Center. I have retained Mr. Chamberlin to advise me on financial matters and he will be contacting you in the near future regarding the sale and Paul's 401k account. Please treat him as my representative. Thank you."

Another e-mail was addressed to CChamberlin@yahoo.com: "Charles, I have advised Mr. English I have retained your financial consulting services. Please contact him and gather the information you need regarding the sale of The Center, and Paul's 401K. When you have had a chance to review the information, we can meet and discuss what to do next. Thank you, Sarah."

The last e-mail entry in the captured data file was addressed to a Cmathews@yahoo.com. "Clair, I am finally getting my arms around everything here, but I have to say, they didn't teach us how to deal with these things back in college. I have retained a financial consultant to help me out with the money issues like selling Paul's interest in The Center and figuring out the investments he had. Charles, the consultant, has already been a big help, even if it's just a little peace of mind he's provided. I hope to be able to come and visit you in Florida in a few weeks. Hope all is well, Sarah."

There were a few more websites in the captured data. It looked like Sarah was doing some surfing because the sites came one after the other with no detail action taken at any of the sites. Reaching the end of the captured data file, CC closed it and looked at the information he had written down. The first order of business was to visit the vanguard site. He entered the ID and password he had written down and was granted access. Once there, he observed Paul had invested in a few international funds. The total value of the funds was just over three hundred forty five thousand dollars. CC wrote that down. Then he went to www.thecenter.com. The site contained description information about The Center practice and what services they offered. In the lower right hand corner was a tab labeled "Center Employees". He clicked the tab. It brought him to another screen that asked for a password. He entered Sjacobs and Sarah01. A response came back "Invalid ID or password". Then he realized he should have used Paul's information. So, he entered PJACOBS and PJ0919. That information was accepted. The next screen that came up showed a list of options ranging from Benefits, to Holiday Calendar, to 401k Information. He selected the 401k tab. The information returned showed Paul had amassed a considerable retirement account, one million two hundred ten thousand dollars and change. "A nice target", CC thought to himself. He wrote the information down for his files and moved on to other things.

Going through his other e-mails, CC saw other PCTrackR e-mails from all of his remaining targets. He started with the e-mail from Katherine Stern's computer. He downloaded the file and labeled it KS Strokes six and then opened it. He saw a number of websites Katherine had visited and it looked like she had been shopping online. "What a surprise" CC thought to himself. There was also an e-mail from Katherine to her friend Dotty Masters which didn't surprise him either. In it, Katherine told Dotty she appreciated Dotty's offer to stay with her for as long as she needed. She was depressed and hurt physically, and she was looking forward to the visit.

Another e-mail was from Katherine to Andrew. It looked like Andrew was suspicious of Charles having power of attorney for her as Katherine wrote she had given authority to Charles because she felt confident he would do the right thing. Katherine also indicated to Andrew she and Charles didn't have a "thing" going on and she resented Andrew feeling that way. Katherine told Andrew in the e-mail she thought he was just jealous. She knew he was with other women and he had not come to sleep with her in a while. She told him to get over it. She trusted CC.

Another e-mail was from Katherine to Charles. It addressed the concept of diversification Charles had been suggesting to Katherine. In it, she wrote she intended to spread some of her investments around so they would not all be held at one place. CC had suggested that to her recently especially now that the sale of Sterns and Dunn was completed. After CC read this e-mail, he went back into his Inbox and deleted the same message that had come through the normal way.

Going back into the KS Strokes six file, an e-mail followed with reference to the website www.ingdirect.com. Katherine had logged in using her ID KSTERNS and password KS812. She had entered a T, and then 75000. It looked to CC like she was moving some of her funds around. He would have to investigate the destination further to determine what she was actually doing. She had sent funds to Franklin in the past, but she had also taken out fifty thousand and he never did know where that went.

When he finished with the data captured by PCTrackR from Katherine, he clicked the new message tab on his e-mail application and read a copy of an e-mail Katherine had sent to Andrew. She had copied Charles on it for some reason. In it she informed Andrew she was consulting with Charles about investing the proceeds from the sale and from the assets Sam had left her. She indicated to Andrew that if he had any questions he should contact Charles directly, but to copy her on communications. This must be the e-mail Andrew was reacting to, but it seemed curious to CC he had not seen in the Strokes file where it had been written. Katherine must be using more than one computer.

The rest of the data stream in the Strokes file didn't look like it would reveal much. Most of the information seemed to center around search engine requests and an occasional visit to a non-financial website.

CC decided to see what the Franklin Templeton thing was all about. He entered the web address, and once there, he entered the ID and password he had for Katherine's account. He was granted access to the site and once in, he could see where she had recently deposited another seventy-five thousand dollars. That must have been from the ING account. She was a quick learner.

The next incoming e-mail was from the PCTrackR at Ann Pierce's house. CC downloaded the file and saved it as AP Strokes Three and then opened it. There were a few e-mails from Ann to family members that CC had met at the wake. The information was mostly thanking them for their kindness and for being there for her. After the thank you e-mails, there was a reference to sites www.boa.com, www.ingdirect.com, and to www.troweprice.com. Following each website was the same information. She had entered PierceA followed by Part1. "That must be her ID and password", CC thought to himself. He wrote it down. He would visit the sites when he finished with the captured data file and see what changed, if anything.

After these sites, she had sent an e-mail to Andrew thanking him for the introduction to Mr. Chamberlin. From what she got out of the meeting with them, Mr. Chamberlin looked like he could provide her with the advice she needed. She indicated to Andrew she would follow-up with him as things progressed.

The captured data file ended there. CC closed the file and went to the web sites. At each site he entered her ID and password. At the Bank of America site, her checking account was down to eleven thousand, but her money market was over seven hundred thousand, probably because of interest. Going to the www.troweprice.com site, he used the same ID and password and saw the total balance under the account was up to eight hundred thousand; the market was being good to Ann. The last site CC brought up was www.ingdirect.com. Again, he used the same login information and saw the account still had just over two million dollars in it. "Another worthwhile target", CC thought to himself. He wrote down the balances so he could update his target information when he was all done.

The next e-mail was also from PCTrackR, and was from Rhonda Ronaldi's house. He clicked on the attachment and downloaded it. When downloaded, he saved it as RR Strokes One and opened it.

As was the case with the other widows, CC could see e-mails being sent to family and friends thanking them for their support during this difficult time. There were a few e-mails from her to Milt English regarding the sale of Seaside and one to Charles. In it she wrote she really appreciated his guidance and felt sure he would help her in achieving the best deal for Joe's stock in the bank. Of course he would, it was in his best interest too. Once again, Charles deleted the "normal" e-mail reflecting the same information.

Following the e-mails, PCTrackR reported Rhonda had visited the site www.pimco.com. CC was familiar with the company because it was a financial institution. At the site, she had entered Ronaldi followed by 10762. CC wrote the information down in his target notebook.

Finding no other data in the captured file, CC closed it, and entered the www.pimco.com address. At that site, he entered Rhonda's ID and password and was granted access to her account. She had already had the account changed to her name and password since her husband's death. It had a balance of over two million seven hundred fifty thousand dollars. CC thought it was a nice target amount but his commission would be more than enough from this one. She had treated him with respect and he appreciated that. He had already decided the only thing he would take from the widow Ronaldi, or rather earn from her, would be the commission.

As he finished up with the incoming e-mails from PCTrackR, CC opened up his targets spreadsheet and updated the information he had gathered. The target plan had become rather impressive over the past few weeks.

Target	Location	Amount	Take
Kelly	Rockland	$2,000,000	$1,500,000
	Settlement	$200,000	$133,000
Sterns	Vanguard	$2,500,000	$2,000,000
	ING	$400,000	
	Franklin	$50,000	
	Sterns	$5,500,000	
	401K	$5,100,000	
Lee	Insurance	Paid	
	Lawsuit	Settled	
	TrowePrice	$580,000	
	Sovereign	$5,939,921	$5,000,000
	Dreyfus	$1,905,000	$1,000,000
Tindle	Lawsuit	$3,212,667	$2,000,000
	Bank of Am	$779,224	
Pierce	Bank of Am	$711,000	$500,000
	TrowePrice	$808,332	$500,000
	ING Direct	$2,114,000	$1,500,000
Jacobs	Vanguard	$245,000	$245,000
	The Center	$1,210,000	
Ronaldi	Commission	$32,000,000	$1,600,000
	Pimco	$2,750,076	

Looking at his spreadsheet, CC was prepared to haul in over $16,000,000.

But something puzzled him. He hadn't gotten any e-mails from Theresa Lee's computer in weeks, maybe even a month. Either the software had been found and removed, or it wasn't working. That would be strange if PCTrackR didn't work at just one location, and did at the others. Maybe he should make a courtesy call to Mrs. Lee. Perhaps she could use his help.

Chapter 32

CC had gone to the grocery store to purchase a few things. Upon returning home, he noticed the message light on his phone was flashing, so he put his bags down on the counter, picked up the phone, and called in for messages. There was only one message waiting, and it was from Cape Cod Investigative Services. The caller, a Paul Kenshaw, asked that he call him when he got the message. He left a phone number. CC wrote the number down and then deleted the message.

CC called Mr. Kenshaw. The phone rang three times when it was finally answered.

"Cape Cod Investigative Services, How may I direct your call?"

"Mr. Kenshaw, please."

"One moment."

"Paul Kenshaw, how can I help you?"

"Mr. Kenshaw, this is Charles Chamberlin returning your call."

"Thank you Mr. Chamberlin for returning my call so promptly. I was calling to speak with you for a few minutes about the Tindle matter."

"Certainly. What's up?"

"Well, as you know, some funds are missing from an account of Mrs. Tindle's and my firm has been investigating the incident."

"Yes. I've spoken already with a Mr. Delano of your firm. How can I help you today?"

"Carol Tindle says she had spoken to you about her finances after her husband passed away. Did she not?"

"Yes, she had talked to me a few times about her situation."

"And you and Ms. Tindle took a long weekend away together shortly after her husband's death, right?"

"I had planned a long weekend away before I met Carol, and when I mentioned to her I would not be in town for a few days, she asked where I was going. When I told her, she said she could use a few days away so I invited her along."

"And the two of you shared the same room while you were down there?"

"I had a suite at a hotel and she stayed in my room with me."

"Did you sleep in the same bed?"

"I don't see how that's any of your business?"

"It might not be, but some of the six million dollars she received from her husband's estate is missing. We have tracked it to a bank in Grand Cayman but the bank is not being very cooperative in providing information regarding the owner of the account."

"Isn't Grand Cayman one of those places that have a policy of not disclosing that kind of information?"

"It is, but we have our ways of getting the information we want. That's why people hire investigators."

"Well, I don't know any more than what you've already brought to my attention, and I don't really appreciate your sarcasm."

"Do you have any accounts in any Grand Cayman banks Mr. Chamberlin?"

"Even if I did, I'm not obligated to tell you."

"Let me ask you something else Mr. Chamberlin. How successful is your consulting practice?"

"I think you're getting into my personal business a little more than I'm comfortable with, so if you'd like to pursue these kinds of questions, I'd suggest you call my attorney."

"We're sorry you don't want to cooperate with us, Mr. Chamberlin."

"Oh, I don't mind cooperating. It's getting into my personal life and my business details I object to. I have talked to you about information specific to Mrs. Tindle, but anything beyond that just isn't any of your business."

"Well, Mr. Chamberlin, if it turns out you had anything to do with the missing funds, we'll find that out and a whole lot more."

"Are you threatening me?"

"Not at all. Not at all."

"Well then, goodbye. If you have any further questions, call my attorney."

CC hung up the phone. Cape Cod Investigative Services probably can get information the average person couldn't. He would have to do something about laying a false trail for them to follow.

After he had hung up the phone, he dialed his office number to see if there were any messages waiting at the office. There were two, one from Andrew Dunn. Andrew said he got the e-mail from CC about helping Katherine with her investments. Andrew said he was a little concerned about CC advising her in that regard. He wanted to make sure the tax and accounting implications would be properly addressed. He told CC he would speak with Katherine about any concerns he had. He then went on to talk about Ann Pierce. He said she had told him she was very satisfied with the work CC had been doing. He concluded telling Charles he'd like Charles to call him when he got a chance.

The second message was from Carol Tindle. In the message she said she wanted to see Charles again. She said she was fond of him and she thought they had chemistry together. She asked Charles to call her so they might arrange a time to get together. CC deleted the message, and then called Carol.

"Carol, this is Charles."

"Hello Charles, I was hoping you would call me back. Do you think we could get together tonight?"

"I don't think so. I had a call today from Cape Cod Investigative Services, a Mr. Kenshaw."

"I don't know him. I've been talking with the owner, a Mr. Delano."

"I had talked to Mr. Delano on another occasion, but this time, Mr. Paul Kenshaw called and asked a lot of personal questions about me and my business."

"I'm sorry to hear about that."

"Apparently, they got the impression from speaking to you that you and I have been having an affair."

"An affair? I didn't say that."

"Did you tell them we went to Key West for a long weekend together just after your husband's death?"

"Yes, but..."

"Did you tell them we slept together?"

"Not in so many words."

"Did you tell them I have been giving you investment advice?"

"Yes, but..."

"There aren't really any buts, Carol. These people think there is something fishy going on between you and me and I think they suspect something about your husband's death."

"What do you mean? I didn't even know you when my husband died."

"But you told them I knew Bill."

"Yes, but that's because you told me that."

"I did, but now they're suspicious about his death."

"I'm sorry Charles, I didn't mean to get you involved in all of this."

"Now, I'm a suspect in the disappearance of some funds that have apparently gone missing."

"I never said anything to Mr. Delano suggesting you are in some way involved with the missing funds."

"Well, that's the impression those folks have now."

"Can you come over tonight so we can talk about this further?"

"I don't think so Carol. In fact, I think it would be best if we didn't see or talk to each other for a while. I'll be happy to transfer responsibility to another financial planner, and to help that person come up to speed on our plans."

"But Charles, I had become so fond of our relationship."

"That's just how it has to be for right now Carol. Call me when this whole missing money thing is settled."

"But Charles…"

He hung up the phone before she could continue any further.

CC called Andrew back to talk about Katherine's transactions. He got Andrew's voice mail. CC left a message that he had advised her to speak with Andrew about the tax consequences and Andrew should be consulted on every significant money matter so as to not create a situation that would end up having a negative impact on her financial status. He asked Andrew to call him when he got a chance.

He hadn't hung the phone up for a minute when it rang. It was Andrew.

"Charles, Andrew here."

"Andrew, I just left you a message."

"I was in the john, but I heard what you said. I'm glad you told Katherine to make sure she checked with me before making any big moves. She has some tax consequences she will need to consider when she makes any financial decisions for the next few years. So, I'm glad you told her to do that."

"I kind of figured there would be some things she wouldn't know much about. Has she done something in particular you're concerned about?"

"Not yet, but I know she has a lot of money laying around right now and she needs to be careful about her tax situation as she does things with the money."

"That's kind of what I told her. I hope she takes the advice seriously."

"Well, she thinks I'm jealous of your relationship with her. She went as far as to tell me that. My concern has nothing to do with whom she sees or doesn't see. But I feel I have a fiduciary responsibility, and I don't want to be held accountable for something I have no control over. If she doesn't keep me in the loop, I'll have no control."

"My relationship with her? What's she talking about?"

"I assume she means the two of you are seeing each other outside of business. Not true?"

"She's my client. We've had a few dinners together and I like her, but I'm not sure I'd define it as a relationship."

"Well, she thinks it is. When Katherine gets something in her head, she's a very determined person and she will use everything available to her to get what she wants."

"You sound like you're speaking from experience."

"Let's just say I know her all too well."

"I don't look at my time with her as other than that of a client that from time to time has shared a night out."

"I'm glad to hear that. I'm sorry to bring this to your attention, but I was getting a little concerned."

"Don't be. I think I can handle it, and I'll definitely keep you informed."

"Let's keep the lines of communication open. I think we could both benefit from keeping it that way."

"Sounds good to me."

"On another matter. Ann Pierce has told me she is very happy with the work you've been doing for her."

"I'm glad to hear that."

"Well, keep up the good work. I'll talk to you in a few days."

"Ok."

CC was going to call Katherine but he remembered she had gone to visit with her friend Dotty Masters. His conversation with her would have to wait until she returned.

Thinking about the situations that had come up, CC wondered if the time was right to put the final steps of his plan into action. He had already executed the transaction phase of his plans for the first two targets. He had another four targets identified and had already obtained the access information he needed to activate his plan against them. The only thing holding him back was getting paid the commissions he had earned from the Ronaldi target. If he finished his plan now, he would have to disappear for a while, and that would prevent him from getting the commissions.

He decided once the commission funds reached his account, he would execute the final phase of his plan. Patience was a virtue, true, but it was also a factor in his newfound anxiety.

Chapter 33

Katherine had gone to visit her friend Dotty Masters. She had known Dotty since college, as they were assigned as roommates in their freshman year and the two took to each other right away. They liked the same things, including music, clothing and men. When they graduated, Dotty moved back home and Katherine moved to Cape Cod with her fiancé, Sam Sterns. The two maintained their friendship through the years and from time to time would go on vacations together with their significant others or just go and visit one another at their respective homes. Dotty had come to Cape Cod when Sam died and was there to comfort her friend in time of need. Dotty had been a little put off when she came to the wake and funeral because Katherine had been spending an inordinate amount of time with Andrew Dunn. In fact, Katherine had put Dotty up at the All Seasons hotel instead of having Dotty stay with her. Dotty didn't say anything to Katherine at the time, but she wanted to have a long talk with her at some point. She didn't believe in letting hurt feeling fester, because they could ruin a good friendship. Honesty was always the best policy as far as Dotty was concerned.

Dotty picked Katherine up at the airport, and on the way to Dotty's house, she broke the ice regarding Andrew.
"So, Kat, wasn't Andrew Sam's business partner?"
"Yes he was, now he's my partner."
"I could see that when I was there for the service."
"I didn't want to be alone and Andrew was there for me."
"Did his being there for you start with Sam's death?"

"What do you mean?"

"Well, did you have an affair with him before Sam died?"

"Dotty, you know me well. You know I have this thing for men."

"Yes, unfortunately I know too well."

"Are you still upset because I slept with your former husband?"

"No, but you know you didn't have to sleep with him while I was engaged to him."

"He came on to me."

"And you've never been able to refuse a man, have you?"

"I just like sex, that's it."

"I didn't even know. If you hadn't told me about your affair, I would never had known."

"I know, but I didn't want you to think his fling with his secretary was the first time he wandered. You might have been willing to forgive that one transgression."

"Yes, it was an eye opener. In fact, I think my talk with you is what gave me the courage to finally call it quits."

"That wasn't my intention, but you needed to know."

"Enough about my past, what about this Andrew?"

Katherine went on to tell Dotty how she had called him. She said she didn't know whom else to call and he was all too willing to come over. Then when he did come over, she said it didn't take much to lead from one thing to another. Drinks, mood music, lower the lights and let go of inhibitions. That was how Katherine described their getting together.

Katherine told Dotty all of the details. The two especially liked to talk about how each of their lovers went about it. Katherine said Andrew was very smooth. He had a way about him. She told Dotty that before she even knew it, the two of them were naked exploring each other. She even suggested Dotty might want to meet Andrew sometime and see things for herself.

Then Katherine went on to tell Dotty about the insurance money and her inheritance in Sterns and Dunn. She told Dotty that Sam had provided very nicely for her and she got a nice offer from Sterns and Dunn for her interest in the business. Andrew impressed her in bed and at the beginning she couldn't get enough of him.

"So what's happened?" Dotty wondered.

"Two things happened. First, Andrew can't seem to limit himself to one woman and second, Charles Chamberlin."

"So Andrew was a one time thing?"

"No, I wanted to see him as much as I could. He fulfilled all of my needs for a while."

"Then why did you look elsewhere?"

"I didn't. I met Charles at the wake. He had some business dealings with Sam and came to the service when he heard of Sam's death. I needed some advice on some of the things going on after Sam's death so I called on Charles to help me. He's a financial planner."

"And from the sound of it, he helped you?"

"Yes. He's sophisticated, so polished. And very good in bed."

"And doesn't it all boil down to that?"

"Not completely, but it sure makes things easier."

"How has he helped you outside of bed?"

"He helped broker the sale of my interest in Sterns and Dunn. He got me the price I wanted while the firm wanted to settle for less."

"Well then I guess he's a keeper."

"Sure is. But I'm not sure I can keep his interest forever. He has other woman clients. I've seen him with them. I think he only takes on attractive woman."

"Are they widows also?"

"I don't know. But wouldn't that be interesting."

"Do you think he's sleeping with them, too?"

"I'm not sure, but if I were them, and I was, I would be. Oh wait, I did." The two women laughed like teens for what seemed like fifteen minutes, tears running down their cheeks.

Arriving at her house, Dotty said, "Well, here we are. Lets get you inside and settled."

Back on Cape Cod, Charles had dropped his habit of reading the obituaries looking for new targets. The group he had gathered would serve his plans adequately. Plus, it was getting difficult to manage the relationships with all of the women at the same time. He was glad he had already completed two of his targets because he would probably slip up if he tried to handle all six at once. It had been a few days since he had any e-mails from PCTrackR. It had been even longer since he had contact with Theresa Lee. He decided to call her.

"Theresa, this is Charles Chamberlin. How are you doing?"
"Charles, I was thinking about you recently. How have you been?"
"It hasn't been that long. What a week or two?"
"I'd say more like three weeks."
"Well, I've been busy. I've had a lot to do with a few clients closing deals and all of the legal stuff that goes along with that."
"I hope you made yourself some money doing all of that."
"I did indeed. Have you been able to get your computer figured out?"

She thought for a minute. She didn't think she had told him about the virus problem she had with her computer. She had to go to a local computer firm to have it fixed. She wondered how he could know.

"How did you know I had a problem with my computer?"
CC had to think fast. "I was at the Plaza on Main, where the Computer Mechanic's office is, and I thought I saw you walking out with your laptop. I was having lunch with a client next door or I would have said hello. I just assumed if it was you, and you had brought your computer in, you must

have needed some technical help. I've used them in the past as well when I get viruses, or my computer starts bogging down." Charles just hoped this explanation was plausible enough she wouldn't be suspicious.

"Oh. Yes. Bob fixed a few things with the machine. He said he had to take some software off of it that my husband Peter must have installed that looked like it was keeping track of what I was doing when I used the computer."

"What was that?"

"Something called UTIL0802. I think Peter had it installed on the computer when he had it at his office. Bob recognized the program. He said it was a package called PCTrackR and Peter could keep track of what anyone entered into the computer without the person using the computer even knowing it. I guess Peter didn't trust someone at his office."

"I don't think I've ever heard of being able to do that."

"Yeah, I guess most people don't know about software like that. It can run background and unless someone knows what they're looking for, they wouldn't even know it was there."

"I'll have to remember that one. Theresa, I'm calling to talk to you to see if there is any chance of my firm being able to assist with any of your financial investment needs."

"You may know I had a lawsuit filed against the person who was involved in the accident that killed my husband. The suit just settled and I have the funds already invested."

"Oh, have you retained a professional to assist you with your investing?"

"No, I've been doing it myself."

"Do you think you would be interested in some professional help?"

"Not at the present time. I'm actually more comfortable doing it myself."

CC knew from his past access to her accounts most of the funds were sitting in a money market account. He tried to be a little more aggressive.

"You can't be getting a very good rate from the money market account."

"How did you know I have the funds in a money market account?"

He didn't know what to say. She hadn't told him about that. Then he added, "Or in Bonds. I'm not saying you have your money in a money market account but most people put settlement funds in money market accounts when they get them. It gives them time to evaluate real investment options."

"Well what would you suggest? I'm not very risk tolerant, and need to live on these funds for a very long time."

"I'd like to come by and show you some things my firm might be able to do for you. Is there a time that would be convenient?"

"Let me think about it and I'll get back to you."

"Ok. May I call you in a few days if I haven't heard from you?"

"That would be fine."

CC thought he could find a way to get PCTrackR reinstalled on her computer. If he didn't, he would be taking a risk she would start moving her funds to someplace he didn't know about and even worse, change the login information on the accounts she already had. Then he wouldn't be able to get at her funds. Maybe he should just go after her money sooner? "No" he thought. "I'll develop a PowerPoint presentation for this meeting I want to have with her, and as long as I can put the presentation on her computer, I'll bury PCTrackR into the copy."

Having finished his call to Theresa Lee, he opened his e-mail account. He had two incoming e-mails with the subject of Strokes Included. One was from Sarah Jacobs and one was from Rhonda Ronaldi. There were a few other e-mail files including one from Cape Cod Investigative Services. His last conversation with them didn't go well so he wondered what they wanted this time.

First, he opened the e-mail from Sarah Jacobs's computer. He clicked on the attachment and downloaded the file, saving it as SJ Strokes Two. Then he opened the file. The first string of data he recognized, she had gone to website www.vanguard.com. At the site, it looked like she was updating her account information at Vanguard because the data captured by PCTrackR showed her bank account number. It looked to CC she was setting up the ability to use electronic funds transfer to move money between her bank account and the mutual fund account. He would check that out when he logged into Vanguard.

Next, PCTrackR had captured an e-mail to Dr. Kraft. "Dr. Kraft, I'm satisfied with the information Mr. Chamberlin has presented to me with respect to the sale of my interest in The Center. Please proceed with the transaction. When you think the deal is ready to close, please contact Mr. Chamberlin as he is representing my interest." A second e-mail to Charles followed. In it, she told Charles she had instructed Dr. Kraft to proceed with the sale of The Center and Dr. Kraft would be contacting Charles when the deal was about to close. She told Charles she would discuss it further with him when they got together.

There were other things captured in the Strokes e-mail but none of the information meant anything to Charles.

Next, he opened the e-mail from Rhonda Ronaldi's computer. He selected the attachment and downloaded it. Then he saved it as RR Strokes Two. Opening the file, he could see where Rhonda had sent an e-mail to Milt English. In it she told Milt the details of the sale of Seaside to Provident looked fine to her. She reiterated that Mr. Chamberlin was representing her interest in the transaction and any and all questions should be referred to him.

That e-mail was followed by a few e-mails to people at the library. It looked like Rhonda was coordinating the scheduling of people to work at the service desk. None of the information that followed the e-mails meant anything to CC so he closed the file.

When finished with the PCTrackR e-mails, he recorded the information in the Targets Spreadsheet. Looking at the details in the spreadsheet, CC saw the amount he was targeting from his victims totaled over sixteen million dollars. That amount would be enough to set him up for the rest of his life, anywhere he wanted. Actually, everywhere he wanted.

Opening the e-mail from Cape Cod Investigative Services, Mr. Kenshaw had requested Mr. Chamberlin contact them and speak with Mr. Delano. Mr. Kenshaw indicated in the e-mail there had been developments in their investigation they would like to speak with Charles about.

He called Cape Investigative Services.

"Cape Cod Investigative Services, How can we help you?"

"This is Mr. Chamberlin. Is Mr. Delano available?"

"One moment please."

"This is Mr. Delano, Mr. Chamberlin, thank you for getting back to me. Mr. Kenshaw shared with me the details of the discussion you had with him last."

"I told Mr. Kenshaw if your firm had any other questions you should contact my attorney."

"I don't think that'll be necessary. From what Mrs. Tindle has told us, she had not given you any information regarding her or her husband's accounts. Whoever moved the funds from the one account had to have the access information. You're not a suspect."

"I never should have been considered a suspect. I'm offended."

"I'm sure you can understand our position. Everyone who had contact with Mrs. Tindle is a suspect in one form or another until we apprehend the culprit."

"Is there something you want from me now? I had an e-mail that asked that I contact you."

"No, I just wanted to tell you we're pursuing leads, and Mr. Kenshaw indicated you were pretty upset when he spoke to you."

"I was. He was getting into personal matters I didn't feel were relevant to his investigation."

"I'd like to apologize on behalf of my company."

"Thank you. I appreciate that."

When he hung up, CC thought he would still need to do something that would get the Investigative Services on to another trail anyway. Just in case. He looked up the website address of the bank in the Cayman Islands. Once there, he clicked on the tab to open a new account. When the template screen came up, he entered "Wesley Donleavy" into the name field and entered the address of Wes Donleavy's law firm into the address field. He filled in the rest of the personal data with information he made up. He sent an e-mail to the Customer Service contact indicating a transfer would be forthcoming to open the account. He specified an initial deposit of ten thousand dollars would be sent via a wire transfer. The Cayman Island bank issued a new account number and CC wrote it down, along with the ID and password he had specified.

Having finished the account setup, he logged out as Mr. Donleavy, and logged back in as Charles Chamberlin. From the Home page, he clicked the Transfer tab, and a Funds Transfer page was presented. In the From Account field, he clicked on his account number. In the To Account field, he entered the new account number of the account he had just set up. In the Amount field, he entered ten thousand dollars, and clicked the Transfer Immediately button. Just like that, a new account in Mr. Donleavy's name was set up with a balance of ten thousand dollars. CC logged out of his account and logged back into the new account. He selected the Account Balances tab. When the screen returned, he printed a copy of it. Then he selected the Account Information tab. A screen was returned showing all of the account holder personal data including ID and password. CC printed a copy of that data also. Then he put the printouts into an envelope and mailed it to Mr. Donleavy's law office

Finishing up, CC went to meet with Milt English. He told Milt Rhonda was agreeable to the current deal. Milt said the board was also. Milt said he would get the company's attorneys to draft the Sale Agreement documents and consummate the deal. Milt asked if CC would take care of getting Rhonda's signature when the documents were ready. CC said he would get them promptly.

CC left Milt's office, and stopped at Rhonda's on the way home. She was excited to sign the documents. "Charles, Thank you for making this happen."

"I'm just glad I was able to expedite the matter for you."

"You certainly did. And I think you negotiated a deal that exceeded my expectations."

"Timing is everything with these kinds of deals."

"No, I mean it. I never dreamt I would get this much."

"Your husband worked very hard, and as a result you've benefited."

Rhonda's eyes became moist. "It's too bad Joe isn't here to share this moment."

"Yes it is but I'm sure he would be very pleased knowing you're set for the rest of your life."

"I guess."

"Rhonda, I'd like to take you to dinner to celebrate your fortune."

"Charles, I accept the dinner invitation, but the treat is on me."

"That's kind of you, but I'm a gentleman and I insist."

Rhonda thought very highly of Charles. He not only represented her in the transaction, but also has been a complete gentleman throughout everything. She wondered if he might be interested in seeing her after the business deal concluded.

"Ok, I accept your dinner invitation and gallant offer to pay."

The two went out for a night on the town. Charles dressed in a sport jacket with brass buttons, over a light blue shirt and dark gray trousers. Rhonda wore a knee length blue floral skirt, a white, sleeveless v-neck blouse made of organza, and brilliant blue tanzanite drop earrings. Her hair was swept up in a simple chignon, with short wisps framing her face. Charles thought she looked inviting, but he would keep that sentiment to himself. The two went to the Ocean House on

Nantucket Sound for an upscale dinner. While at dinner, a friend of Katherine's from her gym saw the two of them. They were laughing, and leaning towards each other to talk intimately, and sharing a bottle of Dom Perignon. Charles made a toast, and the two clicked glasses. Katherine's friend did all she could to try to hear what Charles and Rhonda were talking about but her table was a little too far away, and they were speaking too quietly.

At one point, Rhonda went to the ladies room, and Katherine's friend followed. While at the sink pretending to freshen herself up, Katherine's friend spoke.

"This is a very nice place isn't it?"

Rhonda turned to look at the lady and said, "Yes it is."

"I see you're having dinner with a very attractive man. He looks familiar. I think I may know him."

"His name is Charles Chamberlin. Does that ring a bell?"

"Yes, now I remember. He is an acquaintance of a friend of mine, Katherine Sterns."

"Oh."

"Yes, I recall meeting him at Katherine's husband's funeral."

"His funeral, huh?"

"Yes, he did some work for Katherine as I recall."

"That could be. He's a financial advisor. Well, nice chatting with you. Don't want to leave my date too long."

Katherine's friend waited a minute, and then went back to her table. As she sat down she could see Rhonda pointing at her and Charles looking her way. She waved and Charles waved back. Katherine's friend requested the check and then left. As she got into her car, she pulled out her cell phone, and called Katherine's cell.

"Kat, its Sue."

"Hey Sue, what's up?"

"I was just having dinner at Ocean House and I saw that friend of yours from the funeral. That nice looking man..."

"Charles Chamberlin?"

"Yeah, that's the one. He was there with a nice looking woman, a Rhonda something or other. They were having dinner."

"Well, he does have other clients."

"Maybe, but this one said she was there with her date. And they were toasting something I couldn't hear about. There was champagne involved, and I'm not sure anyone would wine and dine a client at Ocean House."

"Charles would."

"Maybe, but didn't you tell me you started seeing that guy after your husband's death?"

"I'm seeing him, both business and pleasure."

"Well, he's seeing someone else as well and it looks like all pleasure."

"Thanks Sue for giving me the info. I'll take it from here."

"Anything for you Kat. You've been good to me in the past and I'd like to return the favor. We women have to watch each other's backs."

"Sue, setting you up with those guys when we had girls night out doesn't require any repayment."

"You might not think so. But I'm really shy and I don't have your good looks to bring in the good looking young guys."

"You're making me out to be some kind of cougar or something."

"I don't mean it negatively Kat, but you've opened doors for me with a few men that wouldn't have been opened otherwise."

"Isn't that what friends are for?"

"I guess so."

"Then you don't owe me anything. Although I do appreciate the heads-up."

"If I hear or see anything else, I'll let you know."

"Thanks Sue."

"Your welcome."

When Katherine hung up the phone, she thought about what her friend Sue had told her. She knew about Charles

300

having other female clients, but she didn't want to know about other lovers.

Chapter 34

A few days later, the deal for Seaside Savings and Loan closed. Charles attended the closing on Rhonda's behalf. The documents had been signed by her previously, and only now had to be counter executed by the Provident representative. Milt English was there representing all Seaside parties. The attorney for Provident Savings and Loan handed CC a certified check for thirty two million dollars. CC told Milt that Rhonda would be very happy with the sale and he was meeting with her that afternoon. Milt thanked Charles for his assistance and indicated the Board of Directors for the Savings and Loan appreciated his handling of a vulnerable party.

That afternoon, CC met with Rhonda at her home. She was all smiles as she greeted him at the door. Her khaki capri slacks were snug and revealing, but not as much as the peach colored tank top she had on.

"Charles, how did it go?"

"Smooth, not a single problem."

"Good."

Charles opened his briefcase and pulled out the check. "Here you go."

"Wonderful. I'll deposit it today. Where would you like me to put your commission? One million six hundred thousand, right?"

"Right. If you don't mind, can you have it wire transferred to this account?"

He provided her with a slip of paper that had an account number on it.

"I'd be happy to have my bank make the transfer. Charles, I can't begin to tell you how you made this transaction almost a pleasant experience."

"I'm glad you feel that way."

"I wasn't sure how I would handle all of this. Joe's passing made me feel almost helpless."

"If it means anything, I think you've handled yourself superbly."

"Thank you."

Charles reached over and softly touched her arm. "If there is anything else I might help you with, please don't hesitate to call on me."

Rhonda put her hand on his and said, "I most certainly will call you once all of this sinks in. I was somewhat mystified after Joe's death. Thanks to your help, I now have a new life to look forward to."

"I only did what you hired me to do."

"You are being too modest. You represented my position in the transaction admirably. I don't think anyone could have done a better job."

"I'm glad you feel that way."

"Thank you again, Charles."

"Well then, I'll be on my way."

CC closed his briefcase and rose. Rhonda approached him and gave him a full body hug and kiss on the cheek. He said goodbye and left the house. On the way back to his office he had a big smile on his face. He even considered dropping his plans for the other targets and trying to get in better with Rhonda Ronaldi. After all, she was an attractive widow with a lot of money. He had a few million now from the first couple of targets and now a nice commission. Maybe he was on to something in this new career of his.

Arriving back at his office, he noticed the light was blinking on his phone. He had messages waiting. He called in for them. The first one was from Katherine Sterns. She had told Charles a friend of hers had seen him at dinner with another woman. They looked chummy, in fact very touchy feely. She told him she thought the two of them had something between them but after her friend's call, she must have gotten the wrong impression.

The next voice message was also from Katherine. She told him she apologized for the prior call. She really didn't have any right to question what he was doing and asked that he call her at Dotty's. She provided him with the number.

Finishing with the waiting messages, CC decided to call Katherine at Dotty's. When the phone was answered, he said, "Is Katherine there?"

"May I ask who's calling?"

"This is Charles Chamberlin. Katherine is expecting my call."

"Oh hello Mr. Chamberlin. I'm Dotty Masters, Katherine's friend."

"Hello Dotty. Nice to put a voice to the name."

"Same here. I'll call Katherine. She's having coffee out back."

"Thank you."

A few minutes later, Katherine picked up. "Charles, thank you for calling."

"Katherine, how are you doing?"

"Better, the rest has helped. Charles, I want to apologize again for the voice mail."

"No need to apologize. I understand you're emotional with all that has happened recently."

"I just kind of get that way with men."

"Well, there really wasn't anything going on that you should be concerned about. One of my clients, Rhonda Ronaldi, had just closed a big deal and I had represented her. We were out celebrating the deal."

"I'm glad to hear that. My friend said it looked like you two were having a real good time."

"Well, it was a happy occasion. And my client has had a difficult year. She lost her husband not too long ago and the sale of the business he had built up over the years was good news for her."

"So she is a widow too?"

"Yes, unfortunately."

"Well, thank you for calling and telling me all of this. It means a lot to me."

"You're welcome Katherine. When do you think you'll be coming home?"

"Probably next week."

"Then I'll see you next week when you get back."

"I'm looking forward to it. I hope we can spend some time together once I get back."

"Just give me a call."

"I'll do that."

CC hung up the phone. He would try to spend some time with Katherine when she returned. Their relationship had been a good one. He liked spending time with a very attractive woman and she could do things that made him feel very good.

Sometime during the day, the package Charles had sent to Attorney Wesley Donleavy arrived at Donleavy's law office. The receptionist, who received the mail, put it into a stack with the rest of the incoming mail and packages. At some point during the day, she sorted the mail and put the envelope into the mail slot for Attorney Donleavy.

CC turned his attention to e-mails. He logged in and had a few e-mails with the "Strokes Included" subject line. He thought about the exercise he had gone through a number of times with his targets and he had learned quite a bit of information thanks to PCTrackR. He opened the first e-mail.

The message was from the Sterns computer. He downloaded the file, saved it as KS Strokes Seven and opened it. The file had information where Katherine had used Orbitz to book a flight to Dotty's. It also contained an e-mail from Katherine to Dotty giving her the details of her flight arrival. Another e-mail was to Andrew Dunn telling him she would be out-of-town for a week or two. She told him she would get in touch with him when she got back from her trip. Other than that, there were no other things worth evaluating. Katherine had gone to Dotty's and PCTrackR had nothing else to report. CC deleted the e-mail.

The next e-mail was from Ann Pierce's computer. He clicked on the attachment, downloaded it and saved it as AP Strokes Four file. Then he opened the file. Ann had logged into www.ingdirect.com and transferred three hundred thousand dollars to Bank of America. Then the captured data showed a few inquiries to websites that didn't mean anything to CC. That was followed by data going to www.boa.com. At that site, Ann had selected an option and entered five years and entered an amount of three hundred thousand dollars. CC would have to check out her accounts and see what she was up to. He didn't want her putting too much money into accounts that weren't liquid, and he sure wasn't waiting five years for his piece of her pie. There was other data in the file but it didn't mean anything to him so he closed the file and then deleted the e-mail.

He went into the Bank of America site and entered Ann's login information. When her account appeared, he selected the history option and looked at the trail of what had happened recently. He could see where she had transferred in three hundred thousand dollars from ING Direct and she used the funds to purchase a five-year CD. Damn. Trying to get at a CD before maturity might be difficult.

Not seeing anything any thing else to alarm him, he logged out of the account and updated his Targets spreadsheet. He saved and closed the file.

Once again, there were no e-mails from Theresa Lee, but now he knew why. Not having her information made him feel almost blind, but if her login information hadn't changed, he could still access her accounts. He would do that today just to make sure things were still accessible.

Having finished his e-mails, he opened his Targets spreadsheet file. He had entered amounts next to some of the accounts of his targets reflecting what he planned on taking. It looked like the time to execute the final part of his plan was approaching. He had previously decided once the Ronaldi deal had closed and he had his commissions he would go after the rest of the funds. His first order of business would be to check on all of the accounts and ensure the information he had on each target account was up-to-date. Then he would systematically begin with the women he had the least amount of contact with and go after the funds one target per day for the next few days.

He would close out the Lee target first. Not having any contact other than his recent call and the early files from PCTrackR, CC figured it was least likely that going after Theresa Lee's funds would present any difficulty. He logged into her Dreyfus account and issued a wire transfer to his Cayman Islands bank account for one million dollars. Next, he logged into her Sovereign Bank account and issued a wire transfer for five million dollars. The last thing he did was send an e-mail to PLEE where he masked the sender and instead put in Sovereign Bank Customer Service. Within the e-mail was the embedded command to delete PCTrackR from her computer.

He would log into his Cayman Islands account tomorrow and see if the transfer went through.

Chapter 35

The next morning, CC got on his computer and logged into his account at the Grand Cayman Bank. He could see his balance had increased. Significantly. He selected the history option, and the list returned indicated he had three transfers over night. One was from Lee's Dreyfus account for one million dollars, one was from Lee's Sovereign Bank account for five million dollars, and the last was from Rhonda's account for his commissions, one million six hundred thousand dollars. He logged out.

Having accomplished the Theresa Lee goals, he turned his attentions to the next person on his list. The target for today would be Ann Pierce. He logged into her Bank of America account using the information he had saved and was granted access to it. There he selected the Transfer option, entered his Grand Cayman Bank account number into the Transfer To field and let the Transfer From account default to her bank account. He entered five hundred thousand dollars into the Amount field, and then pressed the Make Transfer button. The system asked him to confirm the transaction and he pressed the Continue button. The system indicated the transfer had been scheduled for that night. "This is too easy" CC thought.

Next, he logged in to her account at the ING Direct site. He again used the information he had stored and was granted access. He completed the transfer process similar to the last, but entered an amount of one million five hundred thousand dollars. The system came back and indicated the transfer would take place sometime in the next three days.

"Three days? Why three days?" CC wondered. Did ING Direct have some extra layer of security built in for transfers? He went back to the Transfer screen and selected the Help tab. When it came up, he searched on 'transfer time" and the system came back with the following explanation. "Fund Transfers require ING Direct to verify sufficiency of funds being deposited into or withdrawn from ING Direct accounts. As a result, this transaction can take up to three business days to complete. Every transaction requires electronic confirmation before successful completion." What could that mean? Would ING Direct contact Ann Pierce to confirm the transaction? He would have to wait a few days and see what happened.

Last, CC entered Ann's TRowePrice account, and transferred five hundred thousand. No hiccups this time. The transaction was confirmed online.

He had completed his target activities for the day and focused his attention on the incoming e-mails. There was a file from Rhonda Ronaldi's computer with "Strokes Included" in the subject line. He selected the e-mail and clicked on the attachment. He downloaded the file and saved it as RR Strokes Three and then opened it.

Rhonda had written an e-mail to a computer service company asking them why her computer response time was so slow. She indicated there were a number of applications and processes running when she selected the Control-Alt-Delete keys and she didn't recognize many of them. She asked someone from the computer service company to return her call and provided them with her phone number. She wrote she had purchased the computer from them within the past year and she had an Extended Service Warranty that had been purchased along with the computer. If necessary, she was willing to bring the computer to the store.

CC was a little concerned about this new development. If Rhonda had the computer savvy to know how to look at what applications and processes were running, she might be able to discover UTIL0802 either by herself or through the computer service company. He hadn't made up his mind yet about using Rhonda as a target, but was leaning towards taking just the commission he had earned and leaving the rest to her. Even still, having anyone discover UTIL0802 running on her computer before he had completed his entire plan might compromise the balance of the plan if they could figure out what UTIL0802 was all about. He didn't want to send the PCTrackR uninstall command through an e-mail, as he had done in the past. If the PC was at the shop, they might get the e-mail intercepted before it could run.

CC decided to call Rhonda as a follow-up to the transaction in which he represented her.

"Rhonda, this is Charles."

"Hello, Charles. How are you on this beautiful day?"

"I'm good Rhonda. I was just following up to make sure you had no problems depositing your check, or initiating the wire transfer." Even though Charles already knew the money was in his account, he needed a way to speak with her about her computer and possibly get in the house to delete 'his little friend' from the hard drive.

"I have instructed my bank to wire transfer your commissions to the account you provided, but I did it later in the day so it may have taken an extra business day to process. It should be taken care of by the end of today and if it isn't, please let me know Charles."

"Thank you, I appreciate it. And I'm happy for you that everything worked out smoothly and quickly."

"Me, too. But I wish I could say the same about my computer."

"Not smooth and quick, eh?" Sometimes CC wondered how he always got this lucky.

"The thing is so slow. I only purchased it less than a year ago and for some reason, response time is very slow."

"Maybe it has a virus or something."

310

"I don't think so, I run all of the latest anti-virus software. I have a firewall through the router I use and have another one on each computer. I think it's something that's running background chewing up storage. It only started a week or two ago. Up until then, my computer was very quick in responding."

"Did you install any new software recently?"

"No. But I have noticed there are some things running on the computer that weren't there a few weeks ago, and they run all the time."

"What kind of things?"

"There's something labeled UTIL0802 I don't recognize. I've called my computer support at the store where I purchased the computer and asked them if they know anything about that program."

"UTIL0802. That sounds like an application followed by a version number. Would you like me to look into it for you?"

"It might be some kind of Adware or something else that somehow worked its way on to my computer. I'll run my scan program today and see if it takes it off."

"That would be a good start. And let me know if it doesn't work. I could take a look at the computer for you."

"No, I've already written to the service department about it. I wanted to make sure I put it in writing because I paid for the Warranty so I expect them to honor it. Plus, I wouldn't want anything I do at this end to void it. Let me see what they say about the response times."

"Alright. But if you need help, please don't hesitate to ask. I know quite a bit about computers and I might be able to help."

"Thank you Charles, that's very nice of you. I'll keep you posted anyway, and you let me know if there's any problem at the bank with your transfer."

"I will."

Rhonda called the service department of the store where she purchased the computer when she hung up with Charles. Once transferred to the Technical Support Department, she identified herself and her Extended Warranty

311

Program number. The technician asked if her computer was currently turned on, and if the Internet was up. If it was, he needed her permission to access it from the store. Rhonda checked to make sure the computer was up and logged into the Internet, and then watched as the technician went through some diagnostic steps remotely. Rhonda could see where the technician looked at everything that was running, and where he cancelled some of the user applications that were running. Then the technician came back on the phone, "Mrs. Ronaldi, I have temporarily removed or isolated some of the applications running on your computer to see if they were the problem. Would you try a few of the things you had been doing when you noticed the degraded response time?"

"Yes. By the way, that's so cool that you can do these things right from your store."

"The technology has been around for a while where we can take control of your computer right from here. That way, you don't have to bring the computer in, we can provide you with quicker service, and the costs of repair are reduced."

"Do you think you found something that would degrade my machine?"

"Yes, there were a few things running you don't need. One was an Adware program, another was a keystroke monitor program and there were a few other things that would slow your computer down. You can always use them if you want, but they don't have to run all the time. "

"A friend of mine said there might be an Adware program there or some other kind of thing running background that would degrade response."

"The UTIL0802 program is something that keeps track of everything that's being done on your computer. There are a number of these programs around such as Web Watcher, Spy Agent, PC Pandora, Guardian Monitor and others. They can be purchased over the Internet and usually cost less than a hundred dollars. It's the kind of thing parents put on their computer to keep track of what their kids are doing when they are unsupervised."

"How would that have gotten there?"

"Someone would have to have installed it."

"I don't recall installing anything like that."

"Maybe your husband did?"

"My husband recently passed away. But I have no idea why he would have installed anything like that on the computer?"

"Do you have children he may have been concerned about?"

"No. We had no children. He wasn't a paranoid, or technically savvy man, so I can't imagine him doing that."

"Anyhow, the program has been deactivated. It will automatically start up again the next time you reboot your computer so you may want to delete it from the computer permanently. Just use the Control Panel Add/Remove Programs feature and you can delete it."

Rhonda tried a few things and her response time was back to normal. She thanked the technician for the assistance and concluded the support call. Later that day, she called Charles back.

"Charles, I won't need any help with my computer. The technician at the store where I purchased the computer was able to fix it."

"What did he find?"

"Something called UTIL0802 was running background. The technician said it was really slowing the computer down."

"So you had it removed?"

"No, the technician only deactivated it temporarily. He said I would have to delete it or it will start up again the next time I turn my computer on."

"Did he say he found anything else?"

"Nothing as invasive, but he said someone had to install the UTIL0802 on the computer for it to get there. I didn't do it and I can't imagine my husband had it installed."

"Were you having any problems where your husband might have been suspicious of you?"

"No. Not that I was aware of."

"Well, at least you know what was slowing the machine down and now it's fixed."

"That's true. I'll have to get rid of that program."

"Do you know how to do that?"

"The technician told me how to do it. I'll see if I can get it removed later on today."

"Well, if you need any help, let me know."

"I will. I just wanted to let you know I found the problem and it has temporarily been fixed."

"That's good to hear. A warranty program that has paid off. Who would've thought? You're probably the first."

The two friends laughed, although CC would have been happier if she deleted the offensive program right then, while he was on the phone.

Returning to his computer, CC had another e-mail in his in box with the Strokes Included subject line. The file was from Sarah Jacobs' computer. He selected the e-mail and selected the attached file. He downloaded it and saved it as SJ Strokes Three and opened it. The file showed where Sarah had gone to her Sovereign Bank account, her Vanguard account and to the website for The Center. At each site, she had entered her account ID and password. At the Vanguard site, she had selected something new as there was additional information following the login information followed by a dollar amount. CC would have to log into her account after reviewing the e-mail to see what she was doing.

The file contained web site addresses for EBay, Amazon and a few other sites. "She was either shopping or looking for something", he thought. When he reached the end of the file, he deleted the e-mail and decided to call Sharon. But first, he would look at her Vanguard account and see what she was trying to do.

CC logged on to www.vanguard.com. When the site came up, he selected the login tab and entered Sarah's ID and password. Once the account information came up, he selected the history option. There were no new entries in the data returned. He next went to the Pending Orders tab and selected it. Sharon had a transfer pending for a hundred thousand dollars. She was moving funds into a new mutual fund. He made a note of the order. He logged off the site and picked up the phone.

"Sarah, this is Charles Chamberlin."

"Charles, how are you?"

"I'm fine. I was calling you to see if you've started to diversify your assets from our last discussion. I have a bead on a few up and comers you might be interested in."

"I have. Earlier today I started to move some of my assets into other investments. I think I've done all the investing I want to do for right now. But thanks for thinking of me. I'd love to be kept informed on new opportunities."

"Good. You don't want to have everything invested in the same thing. If you diversify, you will buffer yourself from the downside of any one investment going down."

"Yes. I'm taking your advice. I understood what you had told me and in a few days I should be all set."

"Let me know if I can be of any further assistance, and I'll put you on the Newsletter mailing list."

"Thanks Charles. And you'll be the first person I call when I'm ready to take another step in this crazy world of finances."

During that same day, a Senior Vice President of Smith Barney called the Hyannis Police Department to talk with them about the missing funds from Carol Tindle's account, and spoke with Detective Ben Rogers.

"This is Detective Rogers of the Hyannis Police. I understand you'd like to talk to us about a situation where one of your client's funds has gone missing?"

"Yes Detective. My name is Mitchell Vernon. I'm Senior Vice President of the Smith Barney branch here in Hyannis. One of our clients, Carol Tindle, has reported a significant sum of money is missing from her account."

"How much money is missing?"

"Two million dollars."

"That's quite a bit of money. Can the bank verify the amount?"

"Yes. The transaction is part of her account history. She knows when the fund were removed, but not by whom."

"Does she have funds with other institutions?"

"Yes. Recently, she had begun to move her funds to other institutions and that's when the funds disappeared. Prior to that, her husband, who recently died, had done all the banking. She said it looks to her, from her transaction history, the money may have gone to another bank. She doesn't have another bank account."

"Have you contacted the other bank?"

"No. When another institution is involved, we turn the matter over to the appropriate authorities. It becomes a federal matter, and I believe we have to contact local authorities to initiate the federal support. That's why I am calling you."

"Can you provide me with the name, account number, date of transactions and any other information you feel might be pertinent to the missing funds?"

"Yes, we can provide that information. Where would you like me to send it?"

"Please forward the information to me in an e-mail. My address is detbrogers@hyannispolice.com."

"I'll have it done right away. And Detective, you will keep me involved won't you? If our site has had a hacker, we obviously need to notify all of our accountholders."

"Sure Mr. Vernon. I'll let you know what we find out."

"Thanks. I'd appreciate it."

Hanging up, Detective Rogers spoke with his Captain about the situation. Captain Lewis told Rogers he had recently spoken with Detective Tomlinson of the Dennis Police Department and he was investigating a similar situation. Lewis told Rogers to include Tomlinson in his investigation in case they could each benefit from the other's work. If there was one person perpetrating these crimes, that person needed to be stopped.

Chapter 36

First thing the next day, after taking his shower and making coffee, CC turned his computer on and went to the Grand Cayman Bank web site. He entered his ID and password and accessed his account. The balance had increased by another two million five hundred thousand dollars. Checking the history option, he could see transfers from Bank of America for five hundred thousand dollars, one from ING Direct for one million five hundred thousand dollars, and one from TRowePrice for five hundred thousand. His concern about the message from ING Direct was unwarranted, and he was relieved. The funds transferred the next day and he didn't have to wait three days nor did it look like anyone had to be contacted to confirm the wire transfer.

Before logging out, he selected the Transfer option and transferred all but one thousand dollars out of the account and into his Swiss bank account. Making this second transfer gave CC a greater level of confidence the funds would never be found. He logged out and then went to check e-mails.

He had a couple of incoming e-mails. One was from Rhonda Ronaldi's computer with the subject line of Strokes Included. He had made the decision to leave Rhonda's fortunes alone. The commissions he had received from doing legitimate business with her would be all he would get from her. Plus, too many things were going on with her computer, so CC decided to send an e-mail to her computer anyway and deactivate PCTrackR.

He selected the new message tab. He entered her e-mail address and entered "Some Helpful Tools" into the subject line. In the text portion, he entered, "Rhonda, here are a few tools you might want to take a look at to help you improve your computer response time. I have used them and they have removed some of the clutter that had slowed my computer down. Let me know if they help. Charles."

One tool was a scan tool that identified Adware and other nuisance applications that might be on a computer. Another tool cleaned up unused files that might be sitting in temporary storage. The third tool would look at user applications and present them to the user for a decision to keep or delete the application. Embedded in the e-mail was a command to delete PCTrackR from Rhonda's computer. As long as Rhonda opened the e-mail, the embedded command would execute, even if she did nothing further with the tech tools.

After sending the e-mail to Rhonda, CC went to the Vanguard site to take what he could from Sarah Jacobs' account. It only had two hundred forty-five thousand to begin with, and now she was making other investments and transfers. Access to the 401K funds, while the bigger pot of the two she had, would probably not be possible. Someone at the company would have to be involved and that would get too messy. So, CC just took all of the Vanguard funds, and transferred it to his Cayman account. Next, he initiated the program delete e-mail. Using Sarah Jacobs' e-mail address, he entered "Vanguard Customer Service Notice" into the subject line and then entered text indicating Sarah's account was being upgraded to Preferred Customer Status and she would get another e-mail in a few days once the upgrade was completed. The e-mail went on to tell Sarah if she had any difficulties with her account during the upgrade, she could call customer service with her questions. The message indicated that as a Preferred Customer, she would be entitled to increased benefits such as highest interest rates available to only Preferred Customers in checking and money market accounts in addition to preferred CD rates. Again, embedded in the e-mail was the command to deactivate and erase PCTrackR from Sarah's computer.

Finishing his e-mails, CC logged into his Swiss bank account and checked the balance. It showed thirteen million seven hundred thirty-two thousand dollars as a balance. His Cayman account wasn't shabby either, with a balance of two hundred forty-six thousand after the Jacobs transfer. He was well on his way to completing his plans. He logged out of his Swiss account and opened up his Excel spreadsheet. Then he opened his Targets file and updated the information.

Only one target remained untouched. CC had successfully taken funds from his first four targets, Kelly, Tindle, Lee and Pierce, and would have funds coming in from a fifth target, Sarah Jacobs. Rhonda Ronaldi wasn't really a target anymore as the funds he was expecting from her were actually earned and had already been received. Only Katherine Sterns was left. CC wanted to see her again and decided to wait a few days before completing his plans. He also wanted to try to get closer to Rhonda Ronaldi. "With her wealth and not having taken anything from her", CC thought "there might be possibilities in their relationship." He'd have to think about it.

Getting close to completing his plan, he started to think about what he would do once all of the targets had been fulfilled. He decided to start to clean up things at his home and at his office. For the balance of the day, he went to his office and started to clean up the files and paperwork. He returned home and started to do the same with his computer. He deleted all the files for Kelly, Tindle, Pierce, and Lee. He gathered up all of the paper files for these targets as well and threw the paper into the trash. He put all of the paper files for Jacobs and Sterns in a separate pile he would throw out once those targets were fulfilled. He left all of the Ronaldi files and paperwork intact where they were but purged them of any information related to PCTrackR and its associated e-mails.

Later that same day, when Sarah Jacobs turned her computer on and logged into her e-mail account, she had an e-mail from Customer Service at Vanguard. The e-mail told her about being upgraded to Preferred Status and about the benefits that would come with the upgrade. She was pleased Vanguard would offer her these benefits and was not concerned about the account. She didn't know funds had been removed from her account. She made a note on her desk calendar to check her account in a day or two and see if the upgrade had been completed.

Meanwhile Detective Rogers of the Hyannis police who had been contacted about the Tindle matter, called Carol Tindle. He introduced himself and told her the Smith Barney Vice President had contacted him on her behalf.

"Detective Rogers, I've retained Cape Cod Investigative Services to investigate the situation. I have talked with a Mr. Delano there and they're trying to determine exactly what happened. You might want to talk with Mr. Delano."

"Do you have a number for this Mr. Delano?"

"Yes."

"Thank you Mrs. Tindle. I'll contact him and see what they have. I would like to have you come to the station to provide us with additional information if you don't mind. Any paperwork you have on the account's activity, or information from the bank regarding balances and activity. Can you do that?"

"I'd be happy to come down. When would you like me to be there?"

"Would tomorrow ten o'clock be alright?"

"That would be fine with me. I'll see you tomorrow."

"Thank you Mrs. Tindle. I'll expect you at ten."

Hanging up, Detective Rogers called Cape Cod Investigative Services. "Cape Cod Investigative Services. How may I direct your call?"

"This is Detective Rogers with the Hyannis Police Department. I'd like to speak to Mr. Delano."

"One moment Detective and I'll connect you."

"Mike Delano speaking."

"Mr. Delano, this is Detective Rogers with the Hyannis Police Department. Mrs. Carol Tindle has informed me your firm is investigating missing funds from her Smith Barney account. Are you familiar with this situation?"

"Yes, my firm has been retained by Mrs. Tindle to look into the matter."

"Well, now the Police are involved too. We're investigating another case similar to Mrs. Tindle's and the sooner we get them both resolved, the better."

"Understood, and I agree. My firm will help in any way possible. We've been hired to trace the path of the funds and determine where the funds eventually landed. If during our investigation it's determined criminal activity has taken place, it's our policy to turn the matter over to the police at that point. What would you like to know?"

"For starters, what have you found out?"

"Two million dollars was transferred out of an account at Smith Barney belonging to Mrs. Tindle. The account had been set up shortly after Mrs. Tindle had inherited the funds from her recently deceased husband's estate. The interesting thing was the Smith Barney account had a balance just under six million dollars in it and only two million dollars was transferred out. Our thinking is this isn't a theft but rather funds being transferred somewhere else to set up another account. Otherwise, why wouldn't a thief take the entire balance?"

"I see your point. But that would seem to indicate Mrs. Tindle is somehow involved. Where were the funds transferred to?"

"In speaking with the personnel at Smith Barney, we have determined the funds went to a bank in the Cayman Islands."

"Then you should be able to find out from them who owns the account."

"It isn't that easy. Cayman Island Banks are like Swiss Banks. They won't tell you anything and unless you have the bank account number, ID and password, you can't get anything from them."

"So what are your plans?"

"Since the funds in question are considerable and since Mrs. Tindle is taking the position she didn't move the money, Smith Barney has given us some latitude in pursuing the matter. We think we might have a way of getting the information we need but I'm not ready to talk about it just yet. If you can give me a few hours, we should be able to say whether our idea will fly or not."

"I guess a few hours won't hurt. I'll work at the Smith Barney end to see what else we can get from their files. Can you get back to me if your idea looks like it will work? I'd like the Police Department involved in all aspects of the case."

"Sure. Where can I reach you?"

Detective Rogers gave Mr. Delano his cell phone number and told him to call anytime. The idea Cape Cod Investigative Services had come up with was an interesting one. Paul Kenshaw, one of the investigators, came up with it; one of their field agents would go to Grand Cayman and try to get a job working at the bank. If the agent was able to get inside, then she might be able to gain access to the bank's client information and find out where the funds ended up. How many two million dollar transfers happen in one day? All Kenshaw was waiting on was information from the Cayman Islands Bank regarding job openings. He had sent an inquiry on behalf of their field agent, Maureen Lang, indicating she had recently moved to Grand Cayman and was seeking a teller position having come from a similar position back in the Massachusetts.

Mike Delano called Paul Kenshaw to see if he had received a response yet.

"Paul, did you get anything back from Cayman yet?"

"No, but hold on. I'll check my e-mails."

Kenshaw logged into Maureen Lang's e-mail account and had a response from the Grand Cayman Bank in her inbox. The e-mail read, "Thank you Ms. Lang for your inquiry. As a matter of fact, Cayman Islands Bank does have openings for Teller positions at three of our branches on surrounding islands and openings in our headquarters on Grand Cayman. We would like to have you come in for an interview at the main office the day after tomorrow at eleven in the morning if that would be possible. Please confirm the time via e-mail or by calling our headquarters office. Also, please bring a resume with you to the interview."

Kenshaw said to Mr. Delano, "Good news Mike. The Bank in Grand Cayman wants Maureen there at eleven the day after tomorrow for an interview. They indicated they have a few openings. I'll get Maureen on the next flight."

"Good work Kenshaw. Let me know how things are progressing."

"Will do."

After hanging up, Mike called Detective Rogers.

"Detective Rogers, This is Mike. Delano. I have some information for you."

"What do you have?"

"It looks like our idea might work out. We looked into sending a person to Grand Cayman to get a job at the bank where the funds were sent, and we heard back from the bank today. They have openings."

"Do you plan to send someone down there soon?"

"Yes, an interview has been set up for the day after tomorrow at eleven. If all works out, our person will be on the job right away."

"Can you keep me informed?"

"When we know something, you'll know something."

Detective Rogers called Detective Tomlinson of the Dennis police department and updated him about the Cape Cod Investigative Services role. The two talked about their cases for a few minutes. Tomlinson said his case looked like it had funds going to the Cayman Islands also. He said the victim in his case had been a recent widow and some of her assets have been sent to Grand Cayman Bank.

"Do you know what the account number was that was used to receive the funds in the Cayman Islands?"

"Yes, I have it here somewhere." Tomlinson went through his papers and found what he was looking for. He read the account number to Rogers.

"That's the same account used to receive the Tindle funds."

"So there is one perp or one group."

"Looks that way."

Detective Rogers asked if all of Tomlinson's victim's funds had been transferred or only a portion. Tomlinson said most, but not all of the account balance had been transferred. That puzzled Rogers and he explained why to Tomlinson. Tomlinson agreed with Cape Cod Investigative Services' reasoning that if the Tindle matter was a crime, all of the funds should have been taken. Tomlinson thinking out loud said, "Maybe the person taking the money isn't done with Mrs. Tindle's assets yet."

"I guess that could be a possibility."

"I'm going to have to have Mrs. Tindle's other accounts watched closely to see if any other transactions take place. Maybe that will produce more leads."

"I'll let you know what happens with the Cape Cod Investigative Services information from Grand Cayman."

"Please do. And I'll call if there are any changes at this end."

Chapter 37

The next morning, Detectives Rogers and Tomlinson met at the Dennis Police Station on Route 134. Rogers had spoken with Mrs. Tindle and Cape Cod Investigative Services personnel. Tomlinson had spoken with Mrs. Kelly. The two began to compare notes.

Tomlinson said, "Mrs. Kelly was taken for one and a half million. It originated from her Rockland Trust account. She was a recent widow. When I had asked her if she had met anyone new since her husband's wake, she said no. The only people who were new in her life were the result of an automobile accident she had with a Charles Connors shortly after her husband's death. Who ever took the funds from her account, didn't take all of the money in the account. We've checked into Connors and the settlement check from the accident was deposited into his personal account. His bank account only had a balance of a little more than the settlement amount. The history in his account shows no significant amount of funds for the past year. We've classified Mr. Connors as an unlikely suspect."

Rogers said, "Mrs. Tindle and Smith Barney hired Cape Cod Investigative Services to look into the funds missing from her account. To date, two million dollars have been transferred out of her Smith Barney account. That amount was roughly a third of the total value of the account. Since the entire account was not taken, the Investigative Services thought it might be possible Mrs. Tindle did something with the funds. However, the transfer of funds went to an account in the Cayman Islands. You and I also confirmed the account number at the Cayman Bank is the same for both transfer transactions."

"Mrs. Tindle indicated she met a few people at her husband's wake who she had not known before. One person was a Charles Chamberlin. She said Mr. Chamberlin was a business acquaintance of her husband's and he offered to provide her with financial consulting. He owns a business in Hyannis called Chamberlin Financial Services."

"Have you checked this guy and his business yet?"

"No, but it's on the top of my list."

"So we have a couple of victims who have had funds taken and sent to the same account in the Cayman Islands. What other similarities do they have?"

"Did they travel in the same circles, same functions, gyms, stores or anything else in common?"

"I think we'll have to talk to them in more detail and see what they had in common."

"I agree. Let's try to do that today and get back together tomorrow morning at eleven o'clock."

"Also see if you can get someone from Cape Cod Investigative Services to join us for the meeting tomorrow."

Rogers said, "I'll give them a call."

Maureen Lang took the morning flight to Miami and then on to Grand Cayman Island. She arrived early in the afternoon. She checked into a local hotel within walking distance to the Grand Cayman Bank's home office. She took out the resume the Cape Cod Investigative Services had given to her before she left and began to memorize the facts. She would need to be able to convince the interviewer she was for real during the interview. Cape Cod Investigative Services had successfully solicited the assistance of a local bank in preparing the resume and job requirements information. If anyone were to follow-up on Maureen Lang, the personnel department of the bank would say she had worked there as a teller. She did, in fact, as a teenager work at a bank as a teller. That would help.

That same day, Brewster Police got a call from Senior Vice President Earl Fox of Sovereign Bank. The call was directed to Detective Mike Akron.

"Mr. Fox, this is Detective Akron. How can we help you?"

"Detective Akron, I am Senior Vice President of Sovereign Bank. We have a situation where some funds have been transferred without permission from one of our client's accounts."

"How much are we talking about?"

"It looks like five million dollars."

"That's a lot of money. Have you talked with the client in detail?"

"Yes. Mrs. Lee brought it to our attention. She said she got an e-mail from the bank telling her the bank was making some changes and her account might be affected but it would be all set in a day or two. When she logged into her account a few days later, the funds were gone."

"Do you suspect anyone at the bank?"

"Not at this point in time. The funds were transferred to an offshore bank."

"Have you followed up with that bank?"

"Yes, we contacted the bank in Grand Cayman but they don't disclose any client information to anyone. We tried to reverse the transfer but the reversal was rejected for insufficient funds."

"What does that mean?"

"It means the funds have already been moved somewhere else. If the bank security has been breached, the bank will have to make good on at least part of the funds."

"I'd like to come over to the bank to gather more information. Do you think you can meet with me this afternoon?"

"Yes, I have an appointment at one and that should be wrapped up by two."

"I'll see you at two then."

Hanging up, Detective Akron asked around the office to see if anyone had any information about similar situations. The desk sergeant told him that during the morning briefing, the Captain had covered a situation in two other Cape towns where large sums of money had mysteriously disappeared. When Akron asked about the towns, the Sergeant looked back through the morning shift notes, "Hyannis and Dennis". Akron wrote down the towns and then used the online Police directory to get the names of the detectives in each town who had been following up on the cases. This case might require putting heads together.

Detective Akron called Detective Tomlinson. When he spoke to Tomlinson, he was told about Mrs. Tindle and Mrs. Kelly. Tomlinson asked, "By any chance does your case involve a recent widow?"

"Yes. Mr. Lee recently passed away, within three months. Why do you ask?"

"I'm not sure yet, but it looks like we have someone going after widows who have recently come into large sums of money."

"Have you established a theory at this point?"

"Not completely. But in the case I'm pursuing and in the case Detective Rogers of Hyannis PD is pursing, victims had funds transferred to an account in the Cayman Islands."

"Wow. That's where Mrs. Lee's funds were transferred according the bank officer at Sovereign Bank."

"Do you have the account number of the transfer?"

"No, but I can get it."

"Listen, Rogers, a local Investigative Services company and I are meeting tomorrow at eleven here at Dennis PD, do you think you or someone from your Department can be there?"

"I'll be there. I'll get more details about my victim today and bring that information with me."

"Good. See you tomorrow at eleven. I feel like we're getting close."

Detective Akron called Mr. Fox back at Sovereign Bank. He asked a few more questions and obtained the account number of the transfer. He got Mrs. Lee's phone number from Fox and said he would be calling her. He called Theresa Lee.

328

"Mrs. Lee, I am Detective Akron of the Brewster Police Department. I spoke with Mr. Fox, Vice President at Sovereign Bank about your missing funds. He indicated you are missing five million dollars. Is that correct?"

"No, I'm missing six million dollars. Another one million is missing from an account I have at Dreyfus."

"You're missing funds from two different institutions?"

"Yes. Someone took most of the funds from both accounts."

"You say most of the funds. Not all?"

"Each account has a balance of around nine hundred thousand dollars left after the transfers."

"So who ever took the money didn't take it all?"

"That's right."

"Do you have any idea of who might do this?"

"No. But it has to be someone who either knows me or knew my husband. The person had to know about our assets and accounts."

"I'd agree. Who would have access to that kind of information?"

"Let me think. Peter did. He's our accountant. I did, or course, but I can't think of anyone else."

"Did you have the information written down anywhere that would have indicated your account numbers, IDs and passwords?"

"No. But Peter may have written it down somewhere?"

"Do you think you could try to find out if there is anything in his personnel effects from work that might contain that kind of information?"

"I'll go through his office today and see what I can find. I have his briefcase and his business information book here at the house."

"Let me know if you find anything."

"I will. And can you call me if you find out anything?"

"Yes."

"Thank You Detective, I really appreciate it."

CC had been having a good day. He had checked his accounts and everything was going according to plan. The funds had been transferred from his target accounts to his Grand Cayman account and he had transferred the balance to his Swiss Bank account. There was only one target left. He logged onto his computer and went to Katherine Sterns' account at Vanguard. He logged in using her ID and password and was granted access. He processed a transfer of two million. He checked the balance and the account would be left with five hundred thousand dollars in it. She should be able to live on that, and whatever else she had left.

Next, he tried to log into the Sterns and Dunn website. He wanted to check on the balance in the 401k account to make sure Katherine would continue to have access to the millions that had been there the last time he had checked. However, the ID and password he had entered was denied access. Someone had changed the login. CC thought his timing was right. Someone was getting close to discovering his plan.

He logged into his e-mail account and entered Katherine's e-mail address. He changed the source e-mail from his own, to that of Sterns and Dunn. In the subject line, he entered "Changed ID and Password". Then in the text portion, he entered a message that indicated the ID and Password used to gain access to the 401k account information had been changed. He indicated the new information would be coming in the mail. He embedded the PCTrackR deactivation command in the message and pressed send. Katherine would get the e-mail, read it and not suspect anything. After all, she had obviously changed the login information recently.

Sure enough, later that day, Katherine got the e-mail and read it. She didn't understand why she was getting the e-mail. Andrew had already spoken to her about accessing company information and he had told her the ID and Password had been deleted from the system. In fact, he had told her the funds from the 401k account would be transferred to Franklin Templeton per Katherine's instructions. She called Andrew.

"Andrew, it's Kat. I just received an e-mail from Sterns and Dunn indicating I would be getting a new ID and Password for Sam's 401k account."

"That's news to me. I had the funds transferred out of the 401k into Franklin Templeton a few days ago. Are you sure?"

"Yes. The e-mail said I would be getting the new information in the mail in a few days."

"Something's wrong. We don't send that information in the mail. Who sent you the e-mail from here?"

"It didn't have any name other than Sterns and Dunn in it."

"Do you still have the e-mail?"

"I just deleted it. But I'm sure it's still in my Delete box."

"See if you can get it back and forward it to me."

"Ok. Call me if you need anything else."

Katherine went back into her e-mail account and got the message back. She forwarded it on to Andrew and also printed a copy for herself. About twenty minutes later, Andrew called her back.

"Katherine, I got the e-mail. It isn't from us. I had one of our technical people look at it and he said the e-mail sender information has been altered. He also said there is something at the bottom of the e-mail that looks like it's issuing an embedded command."

"I printed a copy of the e-mail and I'm looking at it now."

"Look at the end of the message. Do you see the line EXEC DEL UTIL0802?"

"Yes, what does that mean?"

"My tech says it's some kind of embedded command. He thinks it's issuing a command to delete something."

"What kind of thing?"

"He isn't sure but it has something to do with a program called UTIL0802."

"What is that?"

"Tech's not sure but he thinks it might be a program running in background on your computer. Do you know if you have a program called UTIL0802 on your computer?"

"I'm not sure but I'll have it checked out."

"Be careful, something isn't right with that e-mail. Let me know if you find anything. Someone might be phishing for information from your computer. It's not unusual, but I'm surprised it's somehow connected with Sterns and Dunn."

"I'll call if I see anything of interest."

When she hung up, Kat went to her computer. She logged into her Franklin Templeton account and saw the transfer from the 401k account was there. She logged into her Vanguard account and it looked all right. She pressed the CTL ALT Delete keys at the same time and a list popped up of everything currently running on her computer. She scanned the list looking for the UTIL0802 program but it wasn't there. Not finding anything wrong, she turned her computer off. Someone told her once if the computer wasn't on, nothing bad could happen to it. Who told her that?

Chapter 38

At eleven o'clock on the next morning, the detectives from the three towns met at the Dennis Police Station on Route 134. Mr. Delano from Cape Cod Investigative Services also attended. Detective Tomlinson led off the introductions followed by Detective Rogers, Detective Akron and finally Mr. Delano. Detective Tomlinson asked Detective Akron if he had the opportunity to speak with Mrs. Lee. He had talked to Mrs. Lee, and had visited the bank branch. He did have additional information.

"Did Mrs. Lee indicate if she had met any new individuals at her husband's wake?"

"Yes, Mrs. Lee met a number of people at the wake she didn't know. Only one person took a special interest in her situation and followed up with her. His name was Charles Chamberlin."

Detective Rogers said, "The victim in the case I'm investigating, Mrs. Tindle, also had met Mr. Chamberlin at her husband's wake. In fact, shortly after having met Mr. Chamberlin, she went away with him for a weekend trip down south."

Detective Tomlinson said, "Do you think the two are working together?"

"I don't think so." Said Rogers. "She only met him at her husband's wake. During a subsequent conversation Mr. Chamberlin said he was making a trip down south and Mrs. Tindle kind of invited herself along."

Mr. Delano said, "My firm has investigated the trip the two took. Mr. Chamberlin had only booked a flight for himself and had reserved a room for one. Her story was consistent with the facts as we know them."

Detective Tomlinson said, "So we have this Mr. Chamberlin having met each of the widows at their husband's wake. But the victim in the case I am investigating doesn't know Mr. Chamberlin. And she didn't meet anyone new at her husband's wake."

Detective Akron asked, "Do you have any leads in your case Detective Tomlinson?"

"No. We can't seem to find anything other than the account where the funds had been transferred. In both my case and in Rogers, the funds went to an account in the Cayman Islands."

Akron said, "The funds of my client were sent to Grand Cayman also. Here is the account number they were sent to."

Detective Akron said, "Plus, the victim in the case I'm pursuing had two accounts at different institutions affected."

Detective Tomlinson said, "Two different institutions, then somehow, the person transferring the funds is getting inside information about the victims assets."

Mr. Delano went to the board and asked each detective give him the victim's name, amount of funds transferred, and institution involved in each case.

Detective Tomlinson began. "Mrs. Kelly, one and a half million, Rockland Bank and Trust."

Detective Rogers said, "Mrs. Tindle, two million, Smith Barney."

Detective Akron said, "Mrs. Lee, six million, Dreyfus and Sovereign Bank."

Mr. Delano noted that all of the victims were widows. Two of the three had met Mr. Chamberlin as a result of their husband's wake and funeral. Only Mrs. Kelly had no known contact with Mr. Chamberlin. All of the transfers of missing funds had gone to Grand Cayman. Mr. Delano asked if anyone had a photo of Mr. Chamberlin. No one did. Tomlinson said he would like to get a picture of Mr. Chamberlin to present it to Mrs. Kelly and see if it was anyone she recognized. They all agreed they would try to get their victims to provide a description of Mr. Chamberlin and have them ready for their next meeting.

At the front of the room, Mr. Delano said, "My firm has sent a person to Grand Cayman in an attempt to gain information about the person whose account is the recipient of the transfers. We were able to manufacture a credible background for our field agent who had been hired by the Grand Cayman Bank that received the funds. At this moment, our Agent has started working for the Grand Cayman Bank as a teller. We hope she will be able to uncover the identity of the account owner very shortly."

Detective Rogers said, "Since this Chamberlin fellow has shown up a few times, see if you can get your person to check for his name. Also, perhaps he's a local fellow and we can just open a phone book to find him."

Detective Tomlinson said, "And have her see if any of these names show up as well." He handed a list of names to Mr. Delano.

"Connors, Donleavy, and Stoner."

Akron said, "Who are these people?"

"Connors is a person Mrs. Kelly had been involved in an automobile accident with. She had hit his vehicle and he ended up injured. Donleavy was her attorney who represented her in a lawsuit brought by Mr. Connors. Stoner was an investment advisor for Prudential who had some business dealings with Mrs. Kelly."

Akron said, "So you think one of these people might be our clever thief?"

"I don't know. But I'd like to know if any of their names show up at Grand Cayman Bank."

Mr. Delano said, "I'll be speaking with my person down there tonight. I'll ask her to look for any of these names."

Detective Tomlinson stood. "Ok gentlemen. We have some work to do. Let's see if we can get a general description of this Mr. Chamberlin. With any luck, one of the victims might have a photo. Can we all meet here the day after tomorrow at three?"

They all indicated the time and date would be fine.

CC had logged into his Cayman Island Bank account. The funds from Katherine Sterns had arrived. He transferred the funds to his Swiss Bank account. He had already sent the e-mail to Katherine to delete PCTrackR from her computer so that task was done. While he was at his computer, his phone rang.

"Charles, it's Katherine."

"I was just thinking about you."

"Oh really? I'm back and I'd like to see you tonight."

"Tonight." He hesitated. "I have plans for the evening already and I don't think I can break them."

"Well, when your plans are done, why don't you come over to my house?"

"It might be rather late."

"That will be fine with me. Plan on staying the night."

CC didn't really want to go there. He had already raided her account and it was apparent to him she didn't know about it yet. He said, "Can't we make it another night?"

"Oh all right. Call me tomorrow. I really want to see you."

"I'll call tomorrow."

After she hung up the phone, she went to her computer and logged into her account at Vanguard. She noticed her balance had dropped dramatically. Stunned, she selected the history option and it indicated a two million dollar transfer had been made overnight. She called Andrew Dunn.

"Andrew, I just looked at my account with Vanguard and someone took two million dollars out of it last night."

"Are you sure?"

"The account balance has been reduced by that amount and when I look at history, it shows a transfer for that amount."

"Where did the funds get transferred to?"

"I don't know. The history only shows an account number."

"Well, the account number must have the routing information as part of the information that's been captured.

336

Go back and see if you can get the information, then call Vanguard and tell them you have funds missing."

"I'll do that."

"If they don't know anything, or can't help you, call the police."

She hung up and went back into the account and got the information Andrew told her to get. She then called Vanguard and reported the missing funds. The representative from Vanguard said they would freeze the account immediately and begin an investigation. They suggested she call the police.

Katherine Sterns called the Dennis Police Department. Her call was directed to a Detective Jenkins.

"Mrs. Sterns, this is Detective Jenkins. You might remember me. I assisted you when your husband was missing.

"Hello, Detective Jenkins. Yes, I remember you. Your job title is different. Congratulations, I suppose. I'm calling because some money has been stolen from one of my accounts. It's been transferred to someone else's account, and it wasn't done by me."

"You mean someone has stolen funds from an account of yours?"

"Yes. The people at Vanguard, where the money had been deposited, suggested I contact the local police and report the missing funds."

"Let me have the information you have and I'll get back to you."

Katherine gave him the information. Two million dollars transferred from her Vanguard account to an unknown account. She gave him the number.

"Do you have any idea who might have taken the funds?"

"There are people at my husband's former place of business who knew about the account and then there is my attorney, accountant and financial consultant. They all know about my finances."

"Can you provide me with the names of all of these people? And if you could, please send them to me in a e-mail so I have the proper spellings."

"I can do that. You should get the information this afternoon. What's your e-mail address?"

"It's fjenkins@dennispolice.com. Thank you Mrs. Sterns. I'll look for the e-mail."

When the call ended, Detective Jenkins went into Detective Tomlinson's office and said, "Do you remember the case we had some time ago where that fisherman died?"

"Yeah, what was his name?"

"Sam Sterns. Well, I just had a call from his widow. Someone has misappropriated some funds from her?"

"Wow. I'm working on another case where another local widow had funds taken. And two other districts on the Cape are working on similar cases. I hope this isn't just the tip of a very big iceberg. What kind of information did she give you?"

"She said someone transferred two million dollars out of an investment account she had with Vanguard."

"Did she have any idea who might have taken the money?"

"She's sending me a list of possible suspects today. What do you think?"

"Show me the list when it comes in. I'd like to see if any of the names match up with the case I'm working on or with any of the other cases. I'm already meeting with the detectives from Brewster and Hyannis."

"So, someone might have targeted Mrs. Sterns just like the victims in the other cases?"

"Could be."

"I'll bring you the information when it comes in."

Later that afternoon, Jenkins brought the e-mail in to Tomlinson. He looked over the list. The first few names didn't register but when he saw the Financial Consultant name of Charles Chamberlin he said, "Bingo."

"You got something?"

"Sure do. This guy Chamberlin is the same guy involved with the victims in the Hyannis and Brewster cases."

"What about your case?"

"I don't have a connection yet. But the funds all went to the same account in Grand Cayman."

"Wait a minute. Mrs. Sterns gave me the account information from the transfer out of her account. It's on my desk. Let me get it."

Showing the account number to Tomlinson, Tomlinson said, "Same account."

"So, Mrs. Sterns has been targeted by the same person."

"Or persons. We don't know much more than that right now."

"Did this Chamberlin guy have any contact with your victim?"

"Not that we know of yet. Mrs. Kelly doesn't know anyone named Chamberlin."

"I'm trying to get a description of Chamberlin to review with Mrs. Kelly to see if it matches up with anyone she might know. If you could, ask Mrs. Sterns if she could describe Mr. Chamberlin for you."

"I can do that."

"Let me know what she says."

"Will do."

Detective Jenkins went back to his office and called Katherine Sterns.

"Mrs. Sterns, it's Detective Jenkins again. One of the names on your list has surfaced to the top."

"Which one?"

"Charles Chamberlin."

"Charles. Why him?"

"I can't say at this time. But could you provide me with a description of Mr. Chamberlin?"

"I can do better than that. I have a picture of him."

"You do. Could I get a copy of it?"

"Yes. I can drop it off at the Police Station this afternoon."

"Thank you Mrs. Sterns. That would be very helpful. Also, Mrs. Sterns, when you come in, I'd like to talk to you for a few minutes."

"Of course. I'll ask for you when I get there."

Maureen Lang got the job at Grand Cayman Bank. She started the following day. On her first day on the job, she tried to learn as much as she could about new accounts. She asked the other tellers how new accounts could be set up and was told they could be done in person or more likely, the accounts could be set up over the Internet. One teller told her they had a tab on their master menu that showed all accounts opened in the past seven days. This was important because anyone requesting fund transfers or withdrawals during the first seven days of opening a new account would have to wait in order to gain access to the funds. The Bank had a policy of ensuring the funds were actually in their possession before they would allow for any movement of the funds. Once the initial account setup had been completed, which took about seven days, then funds could be transacted daily. The new accounts tab was the first place where Maureen Lang looked. When the screen came up, only the account numbers were visible. She asked the other tellers how they could tell whom the client was and she was told only after entering a valid account User ID and password would the name information appear. Only bank management had full access to the personal information. Maureen had hit a snag.

That night, when she talked to Mr. Delano, she told him what she had learned. He provided her with the list of names the detectives had given him and the account number all of the transfers was made to. She would investigate using the account number tomorrow.

Chapter 39

Maureen Lang went to work the next morning. As a teller at the Grand Cayman Bank, she was a quick learner. Activity was rather slow during the morning hours and Maureen decided to spend her idle time learning more about the bank's computer system. From the main screen, she went through the various options. The system was broken down into Teller Services, Private Banking, Commercial Lending, and Administration categories. All her work involved using the Teller Services option. She went through the other categories taking note of all the things available under each option. When she got to Administration, there were a number of sub-categories for Accounting, Human Resources and Research. She selected the Research sub-category and discovered this was where information could be obtained about clients and accounts. Under the new accounts category, the system asked for either a name or account number. She entered the account number that had been provided by her office in Massachusetts. The system returned a screen that asked for an ID and Password. She didn't know what to enter, as she had not been given an ID or Password to access this kind of information. Using the Back button, she entered the names Mike Delano had given her.

The first name she entered was Tindle. The system returned the message "No Match Found". Then she entered the name Chamberlin. The system returned the message "No Match Found". She entered Connors and again there was no match. Then she tried Stoner and the system returned the same thing, "No Match Found". She was getting frustrated not getting any hits at all and entered the last name she had been given, Donleavy. To her amazement, the screen came back with a line that showed the name Donleavy and an account number. She wrote it down.

After getting out of the Research category, Maureen searched out her supervisor. "Ms. Donahue, I've been doing some self teaching using the computer system, and I wasn't able to access the account information. Did I do something wrong?" Her supervisor informed her that only employees who had been at the bank for more than ninety days were allowed to have access to the most secure business at the bank. Maureen was told the bank conducted an extensive background check on each new employee after the initial hire and that getting an ID and Password that would allow access to the entire computer system of the bank required all employees to successfully pass the extended background check and an evaluation by internal security sixty days after being on the job. Her supervisor told her that was a precaution to prevent employees who might be curious or devious from working their way into the bank's operations.

That afternoon, when Maureen took her lunch break, she called Mr. Delano.
"Mr. Delano, this is Maureen Lang."
"Hello Maureen, how's your new position working out?"
"The bank has a series of pretty complex procedures to make sure information does not get out of their control. Only employees that pass an extended security background check and evaluation are granted full access to the bank's complete computer system. That process usually takes about ninety days."
"Are you saying you would need to be there for ninety days to get the information we need?"
"I have found out a few things, but it looks like I can only get the specific information you request if I stay here that long and successfully pass their inspection."
"I don't think our client is willing to front the expense for that long. What have you found out so far?"

"I was able to gain access to a Research section of the computer system. There I was able to enter the list of names you provided and only one of the names got a hit."

"So Chamberlin got a hit?"

"No, Donleavy returned with an account number. But the account number was a different number than the account number you had provided to me."

"Your saying you got a hit on the name Donleavy but no hit on Chamberlin?"

"That's right. And I didn't get any hits on any of the other names."

"Were you able to look at the account under the Donleavy name?"

"No, that's where the extra security kicked in. To get into the account specifics, you have to have a special bank ID and Password or the actual User ID and Password for the account. And I'm not eligible to get the special bank ID and Password for ninety days."

"I see. Well, that's certainly interesting, although I don't know what it means yet. I'll bring up what you've found with the police at our next meeting. I'll get back to you with what we want you to do next."

"Ok. I've got to get back to work now. My lunch break is just about over."

"Thanks Maureen. Keep up the good work."

First thing that morning, the Bourne Police department had gotten a call from the local Bank of America Office. Office manager Helena Rodriguez of Bank of America had spoken to an upset customer, Ann Pierce, when the bank opened for business that morning. Ann had gone to the bank because when she had checked her account online, her balance had been reduced by five hundred thousand dollars. When the bank manager looked into the matter, she saw where a transfer had been made to a unknown account for that amount a few days earlier. When she looked up the transit information contained in the transaction record she found out the funds were sent to an offshore bank. Pierce told Rodriguez she didn't initiate the transaction and didn't have an offshore bank account anywhere. The theft complaint got transferred to Detective Arnold of the Bourne Police Department.

"This is Detective Arnold, how can I help you?"

"Detective, my name is Helena Rodriguez. I am the office manager at the local Bank of America branch. One of our clients, Ann Pierce, is here with me and has reported that a large sum of money has been taken out of her checking account without her authorization."

"How much money are we talking about?"

"Five hundred thousand dollars. Her husband recently passed away and she has been working through settling his estate. She said she only discovered the missing funds as a result of attempting to get the money invested."

"Can you put Mrs. Pierce on the phone?"

"Sure."

"This is Mrs. Pierce."

"Mrs. Pierce, you say five hundred thousand dollars has been taken from your checking account without your authorization. Is that correct?"

"Yes. I only discovered it this morning and I immediately came here to the bank to see what was going on. The date of the transaction was two business days ago."

"Have you had that sum in your account for a long period of time?"

"Not really. I've been working my way through my recently deceased husband's estate. It has taken some time to get the insurance and his assets all settled. I use my checking account to clear all of the funds that are released to me. The funds that were taken had recently been deposited as a result of insurance policy proceeds."

"Do you have any idea who would want to do this to you?"

"No. I didn't think I had any enemies. Could the insurance company have taken the money back?"

"Mrs. Rodriguez indicated the funds were transferred to an offshore bank. I don't think the insurance company would do that. Mrs. Pierce, what number can you be reached at?"

Ann Pierce provided the Detective with her address; home phone number and her cell phone number. She told the Detective she could be reached anytime on her cell.

Hanging up, Detective Arnold discussed the case with his Captain. The Captain told him there had been a rash of these kinds of things going on in other towns on Cape Cod and information could be found in the Cape Cod Daily Police Information release that came out each morning from the regional State Police Department. Detective Arnold went back through the information releases for the past two weeks and found the reports from Hyannis, Dennis and Brewster all revealing similar cases. He called the Hyannis Police Department and asked to speak with the Detective Division.

"This is Detective Rogers, how can I help you?"

"Detective Rogers, this is Detective Will Arnold of the Bourne Police Department. I'm investigating a case of missing funds from a person in my town. My Captain indicated other departments on the Cape have been investigating other cases that look similar to our case and your department along with Dennis and Brewster were listed in the Daily Information Releases during the past couple of weeks."

"Yes, we have a case where a widow was the apparent victim of a crime where someone has taken funds from her. I am in contact with the other PDs and their cases are very similar to the one I am pursuing. In each case, funds were transferred to an offshore account. Do you have the account number identifying where the funds went?"

"Yes." Detective Arnold read off the account number.

"That's the same account. It looks like our guy has another victim."

"Do you have a suspect identified at this point?"

"We have a number of possible suspects. Some look better than others. Listen, the detectives from the towns who are investigating the various crimes are getting together this afternoon at the Dennis Police Department. Do you think you could make the meeting?"

"What time?"

"Three o'clock."

"I'll be there."

345

At around two thirty, Katherine Sterns went to the Police Station. She asked for Detective Jenkins.

"Thank you for coming down Mrs. Sterns. I appreciate you dropping the picture off for me."

"No problem Detective. Here it is. You said you wanted to talk. What's up?"

"I do hate to bring this subject up, but the investigation into your husband's death has never been closed. The Coroner indicated the autopsy was inconclusive in determining the actual cause of death due to the condition of the body."

"What do you mean?"

"Well, Sam's body had been cut up pretty badly and organs removed. It looked to the Coroner like he died of hypothermia but the Coroner couldn't tell if there were any other contributing factors."

"Other factors. Like what?"

"Sam's body had cuts into major organs that could have occurred before he died."

"I thought the Corner's report said he died of hypothermia?"

"It did. But Sam may have been seriously injured before the hypothermia set in. And since most of the blood had been drained from his body and some of his major organs removed, it was impossible for the Coroner to verify with any degree of certainty exactly what transpired and the order of events."

"Detective, when I recently lost my baby, Mr. Bowman attended the service and said something to me afterwards that seemed really strange. He said "I did it all for you". At the time, I wasn't sure what he was talking about and I'm not sure now. Do you think he murdered Sam?"

"Would he have had any motive to kill your husband?"

"I had sex with him a few weeks before my husband's death. Somehow he interpreted the sex to be something more than that."

"So you admit to having sex with him while your husband was still alive?"

"Detective, you sound like a prude. Sex isn't in the closet anymore."

346

Detective Jenkins was quiet for a minute. "If you don't mind Mrs. Sterns, I'd like to have a discussion with my superiors and see what they think. There might be more to your husband's death."

"I can't imagine Tom killing Sam based on a one night fling."

"Mrs. Sterns, you never know what's going through a persons head."

"If you say so. Is there anything else?"

"No, not at this time. I'll let you know if we decide to reopen the case."

"Please do."

"Mrs. Sterns, anything is possible. I try not to make any judgments until all the facts are in. When Mr. Bowman spoke with you at your baby's service, do you think he was talking about killing Sam or about having to cut up his body and use his blood to write the distress message on the ice?"

"I'm not sure."

Detective Jenkins escorted Mrs. Sterns to the door just as the other detectives were arriving for their meeting.

At three o'clock, the detectives gathered at the Dennis Police Department. Detective Rogers started the meeting off and introduced Detective Arnold. Arnold told the others about the crime that had been reported to him that morning. He gave the name, amount and confirmed the funds had been transferred to the same offshore account as confirmed by Detective Rogers.

Detective Tomlinson reported that another victim in Dennis had been targeted. He introduced Detective Jenkins who told the story about Sam Sterns and about the crime committed against his widow, Katherine Sterns. When Jenkins finished, Tomlinson looked to Detective Arnold and said, "Detective Arnold, does your victim have any other accounts at any other financial institutions?"

"I don't have any specific information, but I'm sure she does," said Arnold. "She indicated to me she had been working her way through her husband's estate and she had discovered the missing funds when she tried to invest some insurance proceeds."

"You might want to check and ask her to review all of the places where she had money. Detective Akron will tell you about his case where the victim lost money at different institutions" said Tomlinson.

"Really?"

"That's right. The victim in the case I'm investigating had funds taken from Dreyfus and Sovereign Bank."

Arnold asked, "How could a thief get access to different accounts at different institutions and apparently in different towns?"

"This guy is pretty slick. We're starting to develop a profile and we think the perpetrator or perpetrators target widows whose spouses had been in a position of wealth," said Tomlinson.

"That's an interesting scenario," remarked Arnold.

Tomlinson looked at the man sitting at the end of the table who had not said anything up to this point. "Mr. Delano, do you have anything to add at this point?"

Mr. Delano stood and said, "I've heard from our agent in Grand Cayman and we have uncovered something."

"What have you learned?" asked Detective Rogers.

"Well, our agent has been able to research the names I got from our last meeting. One of the names had a positive hit."

"Which one?" stated Akron with eyebrows raised.

"Mr. Donleavy. He was the attorney for Mrs. Tindle. He had represented her interest in a business transaction."

"What about Chamberlin?" asked Tomlinson.

"Nothing, and nothing on any of the other names," said Delano. "Plus, my person on site said she can't get more detailed information for ninety days. The bank apparently has some security precautions in place where employees can't get into the most protected customer information the bank has until they pass a security background check and an evaluation after a few months."

"Why can't we get a subpoena and get the information?" asked Akron.

348

"Because it's an offshore Bank. They're not subject to the domestic bank rules. Grand Cayman offers the same kind of secrecy to clients Swiss Banks are noted for offering," said Tomlinson.

"Then we don't have enough for an arrest warrant, then do we?" asked Rogers.

"Not yet, but we have more to go on," said Tomlinson. "And unfortunately, more victims means more information."

"My firm is going to have to pull our agent out of Grand Cayman. My client only authorized the expenses for a week and they have indicated they won't fund ninety days" said Mr. Delano.

"Let's focus on the Donleavy guy. Find out if he had any contact with the other victims," said Tomlinson.

"Ok," said Rogers. "Can we get the information and get back together again the day after tomorrow?"

Everyone said ok. They agreed to meet at three o'clock the day after tomorrow but at the Hyannis Police Department.

Chapter 40

Sarah Jacobs turned her computer on and went to her Vanguard account. She wanted to see what benefits and changes were being offered now that her account had been updated to a preferred status. What she saw shocked her. The balance in her account was zero. She was taken aback and immediately selected the Contact-Us tab to look up the phone number for customer service. She called the number. When the representative answered, she explained about getting the e-mail. She indicated waiting a day to log back in to see what changes had been made to her account. That was when she noticed the missing funds. The representative asked for the account number and looked it up while she had Sarah on the phone. She said, "Mrs. Jacobs, I see here you did a fund transfer for two hundred and forty-five thousand dollars two days ago."

Sarah said, "I most certainly did not do any such transfer. What are you talking about?"

"If you look at the recent history option on your screen, you can see where the fund transfer was made."

"I didn't transfer anything out of my account."

"If you didn't, have you made sure no one else had your account information?"

"Look, I got an e-mail from your customer service department telling me my account was being updated to a preferred status. Then when I log into my account a few days later I discover all my money is missing. I think something is wrong at your end. Maybe the update didn't run correctly."

"That's not what the records are telling me. Someone made an authorized fund transfer out of your account. That could only be accomplished if someone knew the account number, ID and Password. And by the way, we don't have any kind of Preferred Customer program being offered at this time I'd suggest you contact your local police department. We will assist them in any way if they need our help. "

"Oh, I plan on doing just that. You'll be hearing from me again."

The customer service representative reported to the fraud department at Vanguard that a client had called in and reported funds missing. The fraud department would be responsible for following up on the claim.

Sarah Jacobs called the Harwich Police Department. She was connected with the Detective division and spoke with a Detective Lou Munson.

"Mrs. Jacobs, my name is Detective Munson. I understand you're reporting someone has robbed you. Is that correct?"

"Yes Detective, I have an account at Vanguard and when I checked on it earlier today I discovered two hundred and forty-five thousand dollars was missing."

"Have you talked with the people at Vanguard about the missing money?"

"Yes, they said someone transferred funds out of my account two days ago. It wasn't me and I don't know of anyone else who would have had access to that account other than my husband and he died."

"Is it possible he gave that information to someone else?"

"I don't think so. He always told me to make sure I kept that kind of information to myself and if I had to write it down, to make sure it was kept in a secure place."

"Well, that was certainly sound advice. But someone got to your account."

"Yes and it wasn't me."

"What other information can you give me, such as other accounts, advisors, accountants, those kinds of things?"

"What are you thinking Detective?"

"It's too early to draw any conclusions, but I'll want to follow-up with any and all persons whom might have had access to your finances. Think about it and write down all that you can. Is there anything else you might be able to tell me at this time?"

Sarah went on to explain about the e-mail she got from customer service. She told Detective Munson about being upgraded and she had to wait a day or so for the changes to take place. Then when she checked her account earlier that day, the funds were missing. Detective Munson said he would begin an investigation and get back to her.

Detective Munson was a friend of Detective Tomlinson of the Dennis Police Department. They had gone through the police academy together and had maintained a friendship ever since. While they were playing golf last weekend, Tomlinson had told Munson about the cases being pursued regarding funds missing from recent widows. Munson called Tomlinson to tell him about the call he had just fielded from Mrs. Jacobs.

"Tomlinson here."
"Ken, it's Lou."
"Lou, you looking to set up a rematch?"
"Not today buddy. I just took a call from a Sarah Jacobs. She reported having some money stolen out of one of her investment account."
"How much did she say she lost?"
"Two hundred and forty-five thousand."
"Did she say where it went?"
"Just that it was transferred two days ago to some account she knows nothing about."
"See if you can find out what the account number was the funds were transferred to. The other cases in the other towns all had the funds going to the same account offshore."
"Ok. I'll get back to you."
"Lou, I'm getting together with the other detectives handling the other cases this afternoon at three at the Hyannis PD. Why don't you come?"

"I could do that. How about I pick you up at two thirty?"

"See you then."

Detective Munson called Sarah Jacobs back and asked her if she had the account number where the funds were transferred. She said she did and gave him the number. She asked him if he knew something about the missing funds and he said he was pursuing leads. He would get back to her.

During the day, Detective Jenkins called on Katherine Sterns. When she answered the door, she was dressed in a pair of denim shorts; a very short pair of denim shorts. A chocolate brown halter-top showcased her golden tan, and shapely shoulders. They were the result of time in the gym, he could tell. Her hair was pulled back into a ponytail giving her the look of a very attractive athletic woman not long out of college. Jenkins wanted to just stand there and take in the view, but he forced himself to focus on her eyes only. He was dressed in his usual detective uniform: black slacks, black shoes, light blue shirt, sleeves rolled up to the elbows, no tie.

"Can I help you, Detective?"

"I'm sorry to bother you at home Mrs. Sterns, but I wanted to talk to you about your case."

"Oh please come in, and call me Katherine. Have a seat."

"Thank you, and you can call me Frank."

She led him to the sofa and sat on the cushion next to him.

Frank explained that the police had leads and they had a few suspects. He asked questions about where Katherine did business including banking, accounting, legal and financial consulting. He took notes about everyone Katherine talked about. He asked her if she had a computer at home and if she used it to access her accounts at the different institutions with which she did business. Her response was yes. When Frank asked her about Charles Chamberlin, she had only good things to say. She told him about how Charles had helped with her

353

selling of her husband's business interest and that he had definitely earned his fee. He asked how she had paid him and she said she paid him by check. Katherine offered to get the cancelled check, and Frank wrote down the account number written on the back of the check. He would research the account later. He asked if she had any ongoing contact with Mr. Chamberlin and she said she did. She expected to have dinner with him within the next few days.

Frank returned the cancelled check to Katherine.

"I'm going to put this back and get myself some water. Would you like anything to drink Frank?"

"No, thank you. I think I've got new information here I'd like to start working with."

When Katherine got back, she leaned over to put her glass on the table in front of Frank. As she did this, Frank looked up and was met with a full shot of Katherine's chest. The halter-top fit, but not so tight as to prevent a show, and without a bra, even her nipples could be seen. When Katherine stood up, she could see Frank was transfixed on something other than her face. "Mission accomplished," she thought to herself.

"OK, I've got to go." Frank could feel his face flush.

"Don't make yourself so scarce Frank. I'm sure there is quite a bit we can talk about."

"I'll keep that in mind. Thanks for the information."

"Anytime."

Detective Tomlinson called on Sharon Kelly. He asked the same kind of questions Jenkins had asked of Sterns. Tomlinson made notes of her responses. When he talked with her about financial consulting, he mentioned Charles Chamberlin. The name didn't mean anything to her. When Tomlinson asked if she had a home computer, she said she did and she used it regularly.

Detective Rogers called on Carol Tindle. Like the other detectives, he went through the same line of questions the detectives had developed as a group. He made notes about everything said. He made a special note about the lawsuit settlement where Attorney Donleavy got three million dollars.

354

When he mentioned Charles Chamberlin, Carol smiled. She told him she had the utmost respect for Charles. He had helped her with the lawsuit, with investments and personally. She too did business online with her financial institutions from her home computer.

Detective Arnold called on Ann Pierce. The first thing Ann told Detective Arnold was she was missing another one and a half million from an account she had at ING Direct, and five hundred thousand missing from her TRowePrice account. She said they were all transferred to the same account, as were the other funds. When Detective Arnold mentioned Charles Chamberlin, Ann had nothing but good things to say about him. He had helped her sell her husband's real estate interests and had yielded a very nice profit for her. She was very grateful for his professionalism. Detective Arnold ask her if she was somehow involved with Mr. Chamberlin. She looked down and said she had been out with him a few times. When he asked if it was anything more than that, she said she felt uncomfortable talking about personal matters.

Detective Akron called on Theresa Lee. He had asked similar questions to those asked by the other detectives. When he asked about Charles Chamberlin, Theresa said Charles had helped her sort out the financial mess she was left with when her husband died. She said he had helped her get her finances in order and he was instrumental in helping her make sound decisions she was comfortable making. Akron asked her if she had a computer in her home. As she talked about her computer she said she had trouble with it in the past and had used Computer Mechanics, a firm in the area, to fix it for her. When he inquired further, he discovered they had identified an application called PCTrackR had been installed on the computer and it had been capturing everything that was done using the computer. When Detective Akron asked what she knew about the program, Theresa said she thought her deceased husband had installed the package on her computer but she really didn't know for sure how it got there. Detective Akron ended up with two pages of notes from his meeting with Mrs. Lee.

Maureen Lang returned from the Cayman Islands and reported in to Mr. Delano. They discussed what she had learned. She said she could see where Donleavy had opened a new account but couldn't tell how much money was in either the account or where it had come from. About the only thing she did find out was that the account number was different from the account that had been used in the crimes.

"I think its time for us to make a visit to Mr. Wes Donleavy's office," Mike said.

The two went to the Attorney's office and explained the situation to Attorney Donleavy. Donleavy denied knowing anything at all about the Cayman Island Bank account. He had been on vacation for three weeks in Europe, and his passport could prove that. The receptionist knocked on the open door to Donleavy's office.

"I'm sorry to interrupt Mr. Donleavy."

She put a large stack of newspapers, magazines and envelopes onto his desk. The top envelope had a handwritten address and return address, which obviously wasn't too strange, but the return address was Grand Cayman Bank. Banks almost always had preprinted return addresses, or a window that showed the typed address.

"I think you may want to open that top envelope."

"This is strange," Donleavy said. He pulled two sheets of paper out of it, looked at both, and then he handed them to Mr. Delano.

"I think you have some explaining to do."

"That's not my account."

Mike handed the paper to Maureen.

"These are screen prints from the Grand Cayman Bank's website. Whoever printed these has an account with the bank," said Maureen.

"Mr. Donleavy, I think you need to turn this information over to the police."

"I'll cooperate with the police in any way I can."

"You might want to contact the Dennis Police Department and speak with a Detective Tomlinson. He's investigating the Tindle case."

"I'll do just that."

At the next meeting of the detectives, they went around the room and talked about what they had learned from each of the victims. When it was Jenkins' turn, he produced the photo of Charles Chamberlin and provided each of the other detectives with a copy. Tomlinson was anxious to show the picture to Sharon Kelly. She was the only victim without a connection to this Chamberlin. Why? Why had he not taken all of the funds from some of his victims but almost every dime from others? Something just didn't sound right. The victims who had business dealings with him all respected him. It sounded to the detectives that at least two of the victims had been involved with Mr. Chamberlin. Just what was it this guy had on them. A few of the victims had paid Mr. Chamberlin for his professional work and it appeared he had done a good job. Could Chamberlin be a victim, too? Was someone using his name? In a few cases, he had used their home computers but even with all this information, they didn't have the right information to act legally. They didn't want to tip this guy off prematurely. With the money he had stolen, he could flee.

It was decided one of the detectives would need to learn about the PCTrackR package to determine what role it might have played in the crimes. Jenkins volunteered to find out about PCTrackR and to learn as much as he could about it. He even purchased a copy and installed it on a computer at the station. He contacted the company that developed and now sells the software and learned about the detailed workings of the package from the company's programmers. In just a few hours, he had installed the package, trapped everything he had done on the computer and printed out a report that played back everything he had done. He would bring the information to the next detectives meeting.

Following the meeting, Detective Tomlinson made another visit to Sharon Kelly. He produced a photo from his jacket pocket and showed it to her.
"Do you recognize this person?"

Sharon looked at the picture and said, "I most certainly do. This is Charles Connors. He's the person that sued me as a result of an automobile accident."

"You're sure his name is Connors?"

"I'm sure. My insurance company paid him a few hundred thousand dollars to settle the suit."

"Well, isn't that interesting."

"What does Mr. Connors have to do with my missing money?"

"Do you mind if I take a look at your computer?"

"No, it's in the study. It's already on. I usually leave it on all the time, unless there's a bad storm."

Tomlinson went to the computer and pressed the Control, Alt and Delete keys. A list of processes running on the computer was displayed. He scanned the list looking for the PCTrackR program. It wasn't there.

"Are you looking for something specific?"

"Yes, we think someone has been committing crimes against widows in the area using a computer program to get account access information."

"And you think its Mr. Connors?"

"It seems your Mr. Connors has been doing things under a different name. He also goes by the name of Charles Chamberlin."

"Even if it is the same person, how could he have gotten my account information?"

"We don't have all the answers yet, but we're getting close. Let me get back to the station and I'll get back to you. In the meantime, if you should see or speak to Connors, don't say anything. We're not ready yet and we don't want him to run. Thank you for your help Mrs. Kelly."

"I just hope you're able to get my money back."

"We're trying."

On the drive back to the station, Detective Tomlinson called Detective Jenkins and told him what he had found out. It might be time to take action, if it wasn't already too late.

358

Chapter 41

The meeting held at the Hyannis Police Department seemed to be a turning point in the case. Detective Tomlinson introduced Detective Munson to the others. Munson provided a brief review of the Jacobs case. The other detectives asked a few questions and it was quickly agreed Jacobs was another victim of the same perpetrator. Detective Munson took a seat and listened to the other detectives. One by one, they went around the room and reviewed the information obtained from the follow-up meetings each had had with their victims. When Tomlinson spoke, he confirmed Mrs. Kelly identified the photograph of Charles Chamberlin as being Charles Connors. The two were one and the same person. Delano updated the information the detectives had been keeping on the victims and added Sarah Jacobs, Ann Pierce and Katherine Sterns to the list.

Detective Arnold told the others the victim he was following up on had indeed had funds at another institution taken. He said Ann Pierce had other accounts at ING Direct and TRowePrice, and she was missing one and a half million dollars and five hundred thousand dollars, respectively, from those. Delano added up the total and said it looked like over fourteen million dollars had been looted from the accounts of the widows over the past few weeks. The detectives all looked at each other and were amazed at what had been pulled off.

Detective Tomlinson was the first to speak following Delano's tally.

"Gentlemen, I think we all agree that this Charles Chamberlin aka Charles Connors, is our man. It looks like he had been getting his information from the victims themselves although the victims didn't know they were providing the it. Detective Jenkins went ahead and purchased a copy of the computer software package we think Chamberlin used to secretly obtain the information on the victim's accounts. I'd like to ask Jenkins to give you the details how it all worked."

Detective Jenkins stood at the head of the table. He had a laptop computer with him he used to illustrate his findings. "Detectives, I purchased a copy of a computer software program called PCTrackR. It's one of a number of computer software programs out there that can be installed on any personal computer and it can be used to keep track of everything that's done by anyone using that computer. Keystrokes are recorded and from time to time, the program is capable of sending the captured information to a remote destination via an attachment to an e-mail. The person receiving the e-mail can easily figure out what a person using the computer was doing. Once the perpetrator got hold of the information, he or she could re-play the keystrokes on another computer and gain access to our victims' accounts. It's really a fairly simple process. The PCTrackR program runs in background on the computer it was installed on. A user of a computer that had the program installed on it wouldn't even know it was there."

Detective Arnold said, "That sounds like it might be what happened to our victims but how did the perpetrator gain access to all of the victims computers?"
Detective Jenkins said, "He must have somehow gained access to the victims computers at one time or another."
Detective Akron said, "When I looked at Mrs. Lee's computer, I didn't see the PCTrackR program running on it."
Jenkins said, "Did you look for a program labeled UTIL0802?"

Akron said, "Yes, I was told that was the identifier I should look for when the Control, Alt, Delete keys are pressed and the list of applications appears."

"Then you were looking for the right program," said Jenkins.

Detective Rogers added, "I didn't find anything on the Tindle computer either."

"Somehow, the perp must have figured out a way to get rid of the program once he or she was done with the software. If he had any kind of personal relationship with the victim, and we know he did with some, he could have access to the computer when he visited."

Detective Tomlinson said, "In speaking with Sterns, she told Jenkins she is expecting Mr. Chamberlin over for dinner one night this week. Maybe we should think about how to set a trap for him."

"What'd you have in mind?" asked Detective Munson.

"It looks like Mr. Chamberlin met these widows as a direct result of their husbands' recent deaths. That was the case for all of the victims except Mrs. Kelly, and he met her in an automobile accident. In that situation, he was Charles Connors."

"Do you think there are other victims out there Mr. Chamberlin targeted?" asked Detective Akron.

"I don't know," said Tomlinson. "I think it might be worthwhile to contact the funeral homes in each of our towns and show the picture of Chamberlin to them. If he showed up at any other wakes or funerals, someone might have recognized him."

"That might take a few days. What if he's done and gets wind of our investigations?" asked Detective Arnold.

"This guy is on a roll right now. As Delano has indicated, he had already successfully stolen over fourteen million. He left millions in the accounts of the victims we know about. I'd bet he comes back for more or is already working other victims," said Tomlinson.

"You have a point," said Rogers.

"Then lets see if we can catch this guy in the act. Pay particular attention to any death that has happened recently where the deceased appeared to have some wealth. Let's see what we can come up with," said Tomlinson.

Katherine Sterns called Andrew Dunn and told him about the police investigation. She also told Andrew they asked questions about Charles Chamberlin. Andrew told her he had recommended Charles to some of his other clients and he was getting nervous if Charles were involved, his other clients might be victims as well. Katherine suggested he call Detective Jenkins with the other clients' names.

After ending the call with Katherine, Andrew called Detective Jenkins.

"Detective Jenkins, this is Andrew Dunn. I think I met you some time ago when my business partner, Sam Sterns, died."

"Mr. Dunn, yes, we have met in the past. How can I help you?"

"I was speaking with Mrs. Sterns today and she told me about your investigation into her stolen money. She said you seemed to be interested in a Mr. Charles Chamberlin?"

"Yes, that's true, but it's an active investigation so I'm not at liberty to discuss the details further."

"Well, I had recommended Mr. Chamberlin to some of my other clients and I'm concerned he may have stolen from them, too. I might be able to help you."

"What do you mean?"

"Well, not long ago, someone tried to access my company's 401k assets. It might have been the same person who took Mrs. Sterns money."

"Why do you think so?"

"Because the ID and Password used belonged to my former partner Sam Sterns. The access was attempted after his death."

"That's interesting. Do you think the person trying to get access got the information from Mrs. Sterns?"

"In talking with Katherine, I got the distinct impression that you feel Mr. Chamberlin was getting his information from her as a result of her using her home computer."

"You seem to know quite a bit, Mr. Dunn."

"I only know what I have found out from Katherine. Why don't you let me re-activate Sam's 401k ID and Password. I can give the information to Katherine and let her make it available to Mr. Chamberlin the next time she talks with him. Then if he goes after the account, you've got him."

"Aren't you concerned he will get the funds in your account?"

"No, I'll work with the institution where we have the funds and have the funds put into another account. They could change our current account to have a hold on any transfers so nothing would leave."

"That might work. Let me speak with the other detectives and I'll get back to you."

"Please do. And another thing, I remember when I first met Mr. Chamberlin. We went to Mrs. Sterns house after the service and Mr. Chamberlin took a look at her computer while we were at her house. I left him alone in Sam's home office for a few minutes when I went to get drinks. He could have installed something on her computer while I was away. A second client, Ann Pierce, has also used Chamberlin, and I caught him on her computer after the funeral, too."

"That's good information. Thank you Mr. Dunn. I'll get back to you."

Two hours later, Detective Jenkins called Andrew Dunn back. Jenkins told him the detectives all agreed this might be an opportune time to catch Mr. Chamberlin in the act. Andrew was told to reactivate the account and provide the information to Katherine. Detective Jenkins told Andrew he had spoken to Mrs. Sterns and she knows her role. She had already had plans to have Mr. Chamberlin over for dinner and she had worked out a way to make the information available to him. Andrew agreed with the plan.

That night, CC went to Katherine's for dinner. He thought it would be more than just dinner as had been the case

363

in the past. This was really the first time they would be spending time alone since her return from Dotty's. CC brought a bottle of white wine with him. Katherine greeted him at the door. He gave her a kiss on the cheek and handed her the bottle of wine.

Katherine had prepared a dinner of broiled swordfish, broccoli, wheat grain fettuccine and a fresh garden salad. CC opened the bottle of wine and poured them both a glass. They ate dinner and talked about her time off at Dotty's. At one point, Katherine said she was trying to get into the Sterns and Dunn site to check on the 401k funds Sam had there. She said she was having trouble figuring out what her options were and asked Charles if he could help her. They went into the office and turned the computer on. When it came up, she went into the Sterns and Dunn website. She selected the Benefits tab and then the 401k tab. She entered the old ID and Password Andrew had given her and was returned with the information about Sam's 401k. Katherine looked at the screen and asked Charles how she would go about getting the funds transferred out of the account and into her name.

CC was a little astonished by her questions because he had recently tried to gain access to that account and was denied. Plus, he knew Andrew had tight financial control of the firm's assets and he was sure Andrew would have talked to her about Sam's 401k funds shortly after Sam's death. Surely he would have talked to her about the funds after the buyout. Something didn't seem right. What had changed? CC told Katherine she should speak to Andrew about getting a IRA account set up in her name and getting the assets transferred without taking possession. He could make some suggestions if she wasn't comfortable with Andrew's choices at the company.

She seemed satisfied with his explanation. They turned the computer off and returned to the living room. The two sat on the couch and talked for a few minutes. CC leaned over and turned the light at the end of the couch off. Then he turned back to Katherine and put his arms around her. He reached in to kiss her and she was standoffish and cold. "What's the matter Kat?"

"Maybe I'm just out of practice."

He put his hand on her breast and said, "Let's get you back into practice."

He kissed her again and started to undo her blouse. She resisted and said she didn't think she was ready for sex just yet.

Just then the phone rang. Katherine got up and went to the kitchen to take the call. CC could just barely hear her from the couch, so he got up and stood outside the kitchen. "He's here now. I asked him to take a look at Sam's 401k account." There was a pause and then she continued, "I think he saw the ID and password I entered."

When she came back into the room, she said it was Dotty Masters and she told Dotty she would call her back at a later time.

Something was definitely up. CC said, "I think you might need some time to get re-acclimated. Let me get out of here and give you some space. Call me when you're feeling more like yourself."

"Thank you Charles for being so considerate. I'm sure I'll be back to my old self in a few days."

"I hope so and I look forward to it."

With that, they wrapped up the evening. Not what he expected. Not by a long shot.

Charles guessed Katherine had spoken with Andrew while he was there and Andrew must be concerned Charles had learned the ID and password to be able to access the 401k account. When he got home, he turned his computer on and went to the www.sternsanddunn.com website. He went to Benefits, then to the 401k screen. He entered the ID and password Katherine had entered and was granted access. He selected the Transfer function and tried to enter his Grand Cayman account number in the Transfer To field but the computer would not accept the account number. When he couldn't get it to work, he quickly logged out.

The next morning, Andrew got a call from his technical people who said someone tried to access the 401k account during the night. The person tried to do a fund transfer and the originator information captured by the computer was CC4ME. He didn't have to guess. He knew Charles had tried to get the 401k funds. Andrew called Detective Jenkins to tell him about the discovery.

Chapter 42

After having completed the sale of Seaside Savings and Loan, Rhonda Ronaldi was very pleased with Charles Chamberlin. She made sure his commissions were sent promptly to his account. A few days later, Charles called Rhonda, "Rhonda, I'm going to be taking a trip for a few days down to the Caribbean Island of Grand Cayman. If there's anything you need me for, leave a message on my phone and I'll get to it when I get back."

"When do you think you'll be back?"

"I'm only going for four days so I'll be back early next week."

"If you don't mind my asking, are you going by yourself or with someone?"

"I don't mind. I'm going by myself."

"Would you like company?"

"Would you like to go?"

"I could sure use a break."

"If you want I'll call the resort and see if I can get you a room."

"Don't you already have one reserved?"

"Why yes, but I just thought..."

"Please Charles, we're both adults. If you don't mind, I'll just stay with you."

"I'd really like that."

"Then what time should I be ready to go?"

"I plan on leaving at ten o'clock on Friday. I'll get you a plane ticket and pick you up on my way."

"I'm looking forward to it. I'll see you Friday."

Charles called the airline and was able to get Rhonda a seat next to him on the flight. He called the resort and asked if they had a suite open and if so, would they upgrade his reservation. The resort concierge said the honeymoon suite was available for the dates he was coming down and it would be ready when he arrived. He asked what the amenities of the suite were and was told it had a private balcony overlooking the bay, and the balcony had a hot tub on it. The room had a king bed and had been created with romance in mind. He told the concierge the description was perfect and he was bringing a special woman with him he wanted to impress. "Can you have a bottle of chilled champagne in the room on my arrival?" The concierge said it would be taken care of and if he needed anything else when he arrived, he could just call the concierge desk.

Things were looking up. He had earned a nice commission and had a trip planned with an attractive woman. Charles went to his refrigerator and took out a pack of black sea bass he had purchased the day before from the fish market. He opened a bottle of Pinot Grigio and poured himself a glass. He turned on his deep fryer and mixed the Wondra flour, salt and pepper with a few tablespoons of water. When the oil was hot, Charles put a diced potato into the basket and dropped it into the crackling oil to test the heat. Perfect. When the fries were done, he dipped the fish in the Wondra batter, and then into the fryer. While the fish was cooking, he made a simple salad of romaine and cherry tomatoes and put it on the table along with a bottom of balsamic dressing. When the fish was finished, he placed it on paper towels on a plate, flipping it twice to soak up the extra oil. He then put the fish on his plate, and took the tartar sauce out of the refrigerator and to the table. He was sitting down to one of his favorite dinners.

When Friday morning arrived, CC picked up Rhonda just before ten and went to the airport. They had a twelve thirty flight that would get them to Grand Cayman just before four o'clock. Arriving in Grand Cayman, there was a driver waiting for them at the airport. They got their bags and gave them to the limo driver. When they got into the limo, there was a bottle of champagne, cheese, crackers and grapes waiting for them. The trip from the airport to the resort only took fifteen minutes. At the resort, they were greeted by the concierge at the front door and shown to the suite, where she handed CC two keys. "If you need anything at all, pick up the phone and press the number seven. The bellman will have your bags in the room in a few minutes." CC thought it might be nice to just stay in the room for the night, and get to know Rhonda better, but decided not to come on too aggressively.

"Would you make us a reservation for dinner in the hotel restaurant? Eight o'clock would be perfect."

The concierge said to consider it done.

After the concierge left the room, there was a knock. The bellman delivered the bags. CC tipped him and he left. "Let's take a walk around the place," CC suggested. "I'd love to. It's good to find out what a place has before you have to leave" Rhonda replied. The two walked, hand in hand, for a couple of hours, stopping once in the lounge to have a drink, then headed back to the room.

Rhonda walked over to the french doors, opened them and stepped out onto the balcony. It had a fantastic view of the bay, which seemed to go on forever. Palm trees, white sand and teal blue water made it like a picture postcard. Their room was facing west and the sun was just starting to set in the western sky. CC asked Rhonda if she would like another glass of champagne and she said yes. He went inside and opened the bottle and poured two glasses. When he came out onto the balcony, Rhonda had shed her clothes and was naked in the hot tub. CC just stood and looked at her perfectly shaped body.

"Please join me."
"I'll be right with you."
He placed the glasses on the edge of the tub, went back inside and quickly shed his clothes. He came back out on the balcony in a robe. Then he took it off and joined her in the hot tub.

369

Rhonda picked up the glasses of champagne CC had set on the side of the hot tub and made a toast. "To a relaxing weekend in paradise."

"I'll drink to that."

She put her glass down and moved on top of Charles. She reached down under the water and took hold of him. He put his arms around her and kissed her. Their tongues met and he became excited. She felt him grow; "Now that's more like it."

CC cupped her breasts and noticed they were firm. He said, "very nice."

He started to stand to get out of the hot tub while she was on her knees. She leaned in to him and gently kissed him. Then she took him in completely. CC sighed. She moved in and out until he couldn't stand it anymore. Before loosing it, he took hold of her elbows and coaxed her to rise. As she did, they embraced and kissed. They got out of the hot tub and CC carried her to the bed where he quickly found his way. They moved as one enjoying the moment. After a few minutes, Rhonda's breathing became very heavy and she reached climax. Instantly, CC did the same. They continued in unison for a few more minutes until he went soft. They lay next to each other quietly.

"That was a wonderful way to kick off our vacation Charles."

"You're a beautiful, wealthy woman Mrs. Ronaldi. It would be an honor for me to please you as much as you can stand it this weekend."

"Your not a pauper yourself Mr. Chamberlin. That was a nice commission you made for yourself closing that deal. And I'm sure you've been successful with other clients as well."

"I've done ok for myself recently and I'm appreciative you feel the way you do about my efforts."

She reached down and took hold of him again and said, "I definitely appreciate your efforts. Do you want to try again?"

"I'm spent right now, but maybe again after dinner."

"I'll hold you to it," and she squeezed him.

Charles told her he was going to take a shower and get ready for dinner. He said they had a reservation for eight o'clock and that would give them about forty-five minutes to get ready. There were two full bathrooms in the suite, so they could get ready simultaneously and not get in each other's way. Both headed off, and forty minutes later she emerged looking stunning. The dress was an emerald green, cut deep in both the front and back. To CC, it looked like the back opening ended just at the top of her ass, and the front at her belly button. She was not wearing a bra and from behind, CC couldn't make out any panty lines. He wondered if she had any on. The dress was so suggestive he didn't know if he would be able to control himself during dinner or if he would have to fight other men off who would be coming on to her. CC had dressed in navy slacks and a pink short sleeved, button down dress shirt. Not nearly as sexy as her outfit, but he looked nice.

"You look great. I don't know if I can take you out in public. Everyone will be looking at you."

"Don't be silly. Anyone looking at me will think I'm your wife."

"Well that wouldn't be such a bad idea now would it."

"Are you proposing to me Mr. Chamberlin?"

"I'm just saying you would make any man happy just being with you."

"Well, I'm available if you're interested."

"We'll talk about it again after our weekend and see if you still feel the same."

"If you make the rest of the weekend as good as it has been so far, I'm sure my impression of the weekend will be most favorable."

"You're just saying that because you want more sex."

"No, I'm sure I'm going to have more sex this weekend. Unless you leave me right here and now, I feel confident you'll deliver."

"I like a confident woman."

"Confident and hungry."

"Yeah, that too."

371

"I didn't mean dinner, you know."

The two left the suite laughing and went to the restaurant. Every man they passed turned his head and looked at Rhonda. She was stunning.

The entire weekend was all CC had hoped it would be. He and Rhonda made love many times. They went shopping, to the beach, took a few excursions and ate at the best restaurants on the island. On the trip back home, Charles asked her if she wanted him to move in with her. She said it was too soon after her husband's death but she would like to keep seeing him. He thought she might be looking to slow things down. He thought about the other women that had recently been in his life and he could be happy with just Rhonda. He had no plans to take any money from her accounts. She had paid him nicely for representing her and he knew if he were patient, he had a good shot at a permanent relationship with Rhonda. He decided to take it at a pace that worked for her.

While CC was away, the fraud department of Vanguard contacted the Harwich and Dennis Police Departments. The Vanguard people indicated transfers had taken place from Katherine Sterns' and Sarah Jacobs' accounts to the same offshore account in the Cayman Islands. Vanguard had concluded the funds were taken without the permission of their clients and asked the police to pursue the matter as a grand theft case.

Each of the detectives that had been involved in the cases had been assigned the task of contacting the funeral homes in their jurisdiction to find out if there had been any other deaths recently that might match the profile of the victims already identified.

Detective Jenkins followed up with the Doane Beal & Ames Funeral Home in Dennis.
Detective Tomlinson followed up with the Hallett Funeral Home in Yarmouth.

Detective Munson followed up with the Doane Beal & Ames in Harwich.

Detective Arnold followed up with the Nickerson-Bourne Funeral home in Bourne.

At each funeral home, the Detective visiting explained the cases being pursued. There were a few possibilities that came out of the interviews but only one visit proved worthwhile. When Detective Jenkins visited Doane Beal & Ames Funeral Home, he met with Mr. Carl Pruit. Showing Mr. Pruit the photo of Charles Chamberlin, Mr. Pruit said he had met Mr. Chamberlin twice recently at wakes at his funeral home. On one occasion he said he had a detailed conversation with Mr. Chamberlin so he was sure Charles had been there on more than one occasion. When Detective Jenkins asked when was the last time he saw Mr. Chamberlin, he was told Mr. Chamberlin had recently attended the wake for a Joe Ronaldi. Detective Jenkins asked Pruit for information so he could contact the widow. Mr. Pruit opened a file cabinet and took out a file labeled Ronaldi. He took out a fact sheet and made a copy of it and handed the copy to Detective Jenkins. Mr. Pruit told the detective what he knew of Mrs. Ronaldi. He concluded the meeting with wishing Detective Jenkins luck in resolving the cases.

Detective Jenkins tried to call Rhonda Ronaldi. He only got her voice message system. He left a message he would appreciate it if she would call him when she got the message. He said he wanted to talk to her about a case he was investigating.

The detectives all got together again on Saturday morning. Jenkins updated the group about his visit to Doane Beal & Ames Funeral and that Mrs. Ronaldi might be another target being pursued by Mr. Chamberlin. The other detectives reviewed their visits to the funeral homes as well. There were a few leads but Mrs. Ronaldi was the most promising. The group decided they should pursue her first and then if that didn't pan out, they would look at some of the other possibilities.

Detective Tomlinson talked about the setup he and Jenkins had orchestrated with Sterns and Dunn and Katherine Sterns. They mentioned Mr. Dunn of Sterns and Dunn had reported back the day after the information was provided to Mr. Chamberlin that someone had tried to access the 401k account belonging to Mrs. Sterns. The group agreed the perpetrator was still active and they were getting close to catching him.

Detective Arnold said, "Up to now, we only have circumstantial evidence on Mr. Chamberlin. We have to catch him in the act to make any of this stick. I suggest we check out his office and his home to determine what the best course will be to set a trap."

"I concur," said Rogers. "Since his office is in my jurisdiction, I'll have it checked out. Does anyone know where Mr. Chamberlin resides?"

"I think he lives in Dennis or Yarmouth," added Jenkins.

"Then we should follow up on his home," said Tomlinson.

Detective Munson said, "Can we meet back here on Monday to see what has been uncovered?"

They all agreed.

Chapter 43

Detectives Tomlinson and Jenkins had the task of locating the residence of Mr. Charles Chamberlin or perhaps, Mr. Charles Connors. Jenkins checked the phone directory, the DMV files and even did a Google search trying to find his address. When nothing showed up, Detective Jenkins went to Detective Tomlinson, "This guy just doesn't exist. I've tried all the places I know of and I can't find a home address."

Tomlinson thought for a minute. "The only victim that's different from the others is Mrs. Kelly. She was involved in an automobile accident with Chamberlin when he was known as Charles Connors. Mrs. Kelly told us her insurance company settled a suit with Connors. Let's find out where they thought he lived. And see if you can find the accident report. I'm sure a police report exists somewhere and will have Connors home address in it."

"That's a good idea. I'm on it." Jenkins went back to his desk and called Mrs. Kelly. He asked her where the accident with Mr. Connors had occurred and she said on Route 28 in Yarmouth. Then he asked her if she knew where Mr. Connors lived. She said she didn't know, but her insurance company probably did because they sent him a check once the suit was settled. She gave Jenkins the telephone number for the insurance company.

Detective Jenkins called Mrs. Kelly's insurance company and spoke with a supervisor of claims. Jenkins explained the situation and the supervisor looked up the accident. The company records indicated Charles Connors listed his residence address as 297 Old Wharf Road in Dennisport and that was where the settlement check was sent. Jenkins thanked him for the information.

Detective Jenkins went to talk with Detective Tomlinson. He told Tomlinson about speaking with Mrs. Kelly and with her insurance company representative. He gave Tomlinson the address the claims representative had provided. "Jenkins, you go over to Yarmouth PD and see if you can get a copy of the accident report. I'm going to take a drive down to Old Wharf Road and snoop around Mr. Connor's residence."

"Do you want me to meet you there after I pick up the report?"

"No, too many police in the area might spook Chamberlin. Meet me back here in an hour."

"Will do."

Detective Jenkins left and went to the Yarmouth Police Department to get the copy of the accident report. Tomlinson went to Old Wharf Road to look around. Driving down Old Wharf Road, Detective Tomlinson noticed many of the residences were small seasonal cottages. The summer visitors hadn't arrived in full force yet, so most of the streets were quiet. He stopped his car a few houses down from number 297 and got out. There was a mailbox outside number 297 and it had the name Connors stenciled on it. When he looked in the driveway, it was empty. It looked like no one was home. The mailbox held at least three days worth of newspapers. He decided to look around.

Tomlinson walked around the house and looked in the windows. The house looked rather simple. One window he looked in revealed a computer on a desk, and it had been left turned on. Detective Tomlinson thought he now had the inside track on Chamberlin or was it Connors. He decided to come back with Jenkins and have Jenkins install PCTrackR on Chamberlin's computer and see what he was up to.

When Detective Tomlinson returned to the station, Jenkins was waiting for him. Detective Jenkins had obtained a copy of the Yarmouth police report detailing the accident and Connors had listed the Old Wharf address as his residence. The pieces were coming together.

Tomlinson said, "Jenkins, do you still have that software you showed us the other day?"

"You mean PCTrackR?"

"Yeah, that's the one."

"Yes. It's on my desk."

"Go get it. I want you to install it on Chamberlin's computer."

"How am I going to do that?"

"When I cased Chamberlin's place, it didn't look like anyone was home, but one window I looked through revealed his computer and it was left turned on."

"So you want me to break in and install the software on his computer?"

"That's right. Let's see if we can catch him at his own game."

"Do you have a warrant or something authorizing me to do that?"

"No, if this is our guy, he would have the software already and we can say he had installed it himself."

"I don't know. It seems to me we might have a problem with evidence down the road if we end up in court with this guy."

"Don't worry about it. I'll take the heat if it comes to that."

"Ok. But for the record, I don't like it."

Detectives Tomlinson and Jenkins went back to 297 Old Wharf Road. It was getting late in the afternoon and Tomlinson wanted to make it quick as he feared Chamberlin might return home at any time. Jenkins quickly jimmied the door. Tomlinson showed him where the computer was located and Jenkins installed PCTrackR on it in the same manner as he had done at the station. He instructed PCTrackR to send the captured data file nightly to his e-mail address at the station. When the package was installed, he said, "Ken, I'm done. The

377

software is installed and it will send me a file of anything entered into this computer ever night. If this is our guy, we should know something soon."

"Ok, lets get out of here. Make sure you don't disturb anything. I don't want to tip this guy off."

"Everything is as it was when we came in."

The two left the way they had come in. On their way out the door, a neighbor who lived behind the house across the street from 297 just happened to be looking out her window and saw the two coming out of the house. Being on the next street over, the detectives didn't notice her looking out her back window. The detectives got in their car and left, unaware they had been seen.

Upon returning from their long weekend in Grand Cayman, Charles dropped Rhonda off at her home. He assisted her with her luggage. When they went inside her house, she closed the door behind them and put her arms around him and kissed him.

"Charles, can I get you a drink?"

"Sure."

"What'll you have?"

"Do you have any champagne?"

"Yes, it's in the frige."

"I'll get it."

"Glasses are in the hutch."

Charles went to the hutch and took out two flutes. He went into the kitchen and got the champagne out of the refrigerator. He popped the cork, and while pouring, he heard Rhonda retrieving her voice messages from the answering machine in her study.

"Mrs. Ronaldi, this is Detective Jenkins of the Dennis Police Department. I'm investigating a case involving a recent widow and you might have information that's pertinent to my investigation. A Mr. Carl Pruit of Doane Beal & Ames Funeral gave me your name indicating your husband died recently as well. I'd like to talk to you as soon as possible. Can you call me at the Dennis Police Station? My number is…" Rhonda wrote down "Jenkins", "Pruit" and the telephone number on a post it sitting by the phone.

When Rhonda came into the kitchen, she told Charles about the call. "I overheard the message. I wonder what the police want?"

"I don't know. The Detective asked me to call as soon as possible. I'll call him later."

Then she took a flute from Charles, "To a wonderfully long weekend that wasn't long enough. I really had a good time."

"Me too. You know we could make every day like that if we wanted?"

"Wouldn't that be wonderful?"

"It sure would."

"Isn't it nice to dream?"

"It doesn't have to be a dream."

"You aren't serious are you?"

"I might be. You think about it."

Charles finished his drink and started to head for the door. "Are you leaving?"

"Yes, I have a few things I left hanging when I left last week. I'm sure I have clients, or ex-clients, who are waiting to hear from me."

"See, you wouldn't be able to give up your interests. You are too dedicated."

"Maybe. You just think about what I said."

He kissed her mouth, slowly and gently, closed the door behind him and left.

Leaving Rhonda's, Charles went to his office in Hyannis. When he arrived there, it was just after dark. As he unlocked the door to his office, Mr. Pearl who ran a Real Estate office out of the adjoining office to Chamberlin Financial Consulting was just leaving for the day. He recognized Charles and said, "Charles, how are you doing?"

"Just fine Hank, how about you?"

"Business is just starting to pick up for the season so I'm optimistic."

"Hopefully it will be a good year for you."

"Charles, I had a visitor today from the Hyannis Police Department. A Detective Rogers stopped in and was asking questions about you and your business. Are you in some trouble?"

"Not that I know of. What kind of questions was he asking?"

"Oh, he wanted to know if I knew how your business was doing, who your clients were and if I ever saw you with any women."

"I wonder what that could be all about."

"I don't think I helped him out very much. I told him I only know you well enough to say hello."

"Well thanks for letting me know Hank. I'll have to find out what that was all about."

"Have a good night."

Charles went into his office and closed and locked the door. The police were on to him, he knew it now. He went through his files and cleared out everything and anything that might shed any light on his targets and his now executed plan. Much of it had already been cleaned out, but this time he even grabbed the Ronaldi file. A half hour later, he left the office for the last time.

Arriving home, he flicked the lights on as he entered the house. He made a few trips from the car to the house bringing in the things he had taken from his office. He set the two boxes of information down in his living room next to the fireplace and then started a fire. Methodically, he took the materials out of the two boxes and fed them into the fireplace. When he was just about finished, there was a knock on his door. He had left the outside light on when he brought in the boxes from his car so when he looked outside, he saw Mrs. Osborne standing at his door swatting at bugs that were circling the light and now her face. He opened the door.

"Mrs. Osborne, what are you doing here?"

"I saw your lights on and I had to come over here and talk with you."

"You shouldn't be out walking the neighborhood at night."

"I'm not. But I had to come over here and warn you."

"Warn me about what?"

"Earlier this evening, I saw two men coming out of your house."

"My house? Do you know who they were?"

"No, but they were in here for about fifteen minutes and then they left."

"Are you sure?"

"Yes." She turned and pointed past the house across the street and said, "You see right there. That's the back window in my house. I had a clear view of your house, and it was just after sunset I saw two people coming out of your house, your back door. I just had to come over and tell you about it. They were dressed nice though, no thugs or anything."

"Well thank you Mrs. Osborne. I'll have to find out who they were."

"Do you plan on calling the police?"

"I might. I'll look around and see if I'm missing anything. Now, let me walk you back to your house."

"Thank you. But I think I can do it by myself if you'll just leave your light on for a few more minutes."

"I can do that."

Charles watched her cross the street and cut through the yard of the house opposite his. He could see her round the corner of her house and a few seconds later she flicked her kitchen light off and on. He went back inside his house and closed the door. He went to the fireplace and put the last of the materials he had taken from his office into the fireplace. Now all of the evidence was gone.

Thinking about what Mrs. Osborne had said, CC looked around his place. Everything seemed to be in order. What could they be doing in his house, and who was it? Putting two and two together, a visit at his office from a Detective, Rhonda's call from the police and someone breaking into his house, CC assumed the police were hot on his trail. He went to his computer. He had left it running and when he moved the mouse, it came to life. He went to the Orbitz website and looked something up. Later that night, PCTrackR sent an e-mail to the address Detective Jenkins had specified, and a file detailing everything CC had done was attached. The cat was getting dangerously close to the rat.

Chapter 44

When Detective Jenkins got to work the next morning, the first thing he did was log into his e-mail account. He had an e-mail from Mr. Chamberlin's computer. He selected the attachment and opened the file. It showed someone going to the Orbitz website. A few keystrokes followed but Jenkins didn't know what they represented. It looked like Chamberlin was looking something up. The next thing in the file showed Chamberlin going to the Google website. After the website address, Jenkins could make out the name Frank Rosen. There were a few keystrokes that followed but again Jenkins couldn't tell what Chamberlin was doing. That being the end of the captured data, Detective Jenkins saved the e-mail, printed it and logged out.

Meeting with Detective Tomlinson, Detective Jenkins told him about the information he had received. Tomlinson said, "Maybe our guy has identified another target. Take a look at the obituaries in the Times for the past few days and see if that name shows up. You should be able to see that information on their web site."

"I'll get right on it."

Detective Jenkins went back to his computer, and found the Cape Cod Times web site. There was a link to Obituaries, and he clicked on it. Starting with today's date, he searched on the Last Name 'Rosen'. There was nothing in today's or yesterday's listings, but two days ago, a Mr. Frank Rosen had a listing. Reading the obituary, Jenkins saw the wake for Rosen was that night from seven to nine at the Doane Beal & Ames Funeral Home. He reported back to Tomlinson.

"We have a hit. Frank Rosen died a few days ago. His wake is tonight at Doane Beal. What do you think?"

"I think we need to get the other detectives here as soon as possible for a meeting."

"I'll get right on it."

"See if they can be here for one o'clock."

"Will do."

Detective Jenkins called all of the other detectives. Everyone except Detective Akron would be there by one and Akron would be there around one thirty. Jenkins told Tomlinson the meeting was all set for one. He called Mike Delano too, because the guy had put a lot of time in on behalf of his client, and he should probably be kept updated in case his client lost more money.

At one o'clock, the participants gathered at the Dennis Police Department. Tomlinson took them through what he and Detective Jenkins had discovered. Detective Munson asked, "How did you find out Chamberlin was targeting another victim?"

Jenkins said, "We installed the spy software on his home computer. It worked as advertised and this morning I got an e-mail from his computer showing his inquiries."

"How did you get to install the software on Chamberlin's computer?" asked Rogers.

Tomlinson spoke up "We had an opportunity to visit Mr. Chamberlin's residence and while there Jenkins installed the software."

"And he let you do it?" remarked Munson.

"He wasn't home," said Jenkins.

"I don't think anything we find out via this route would be admissible in court if it comes to that, do you?" said Rogers questioning Tomlinson.

"We'll cross that bridge when we come to it" said Tomlinson.

"I hope you know what you're doing," said Rogers, shaking his head and tapping his pencil on his pad.

Tomlinson refocused the meeting and told about Chamberlin's interest in Frank Rosen. He said the wake for Rosen would be that night at Doane Beal and he and Jenkins would be going there to see if Chamberlin shows up."

"Do you think that's wise?" asked Rogers. This guy was getting to be a downer and Tomlinson was getting a little annoyed.

"We aren't going to do anything, we just want to see if we can figure out how he's getting away with these crimes. Remember, we know what he looks like, he doesn't know us. Relax Rogers, we'll leave our guns at home."

"We still don't have any hard evidence on Chamberlin. All we know is he had some kind of contact with the victims. We don't know if he's the owner of the account where the funds were being transferred nor do we know where the money is right now" said Rogers.

Detective Arnold added, "I want to make sure anything that gets done does not compromise our ability to get this guy. Can you assure us of that Tomlinson?"

"I can't assure you of anything. I just know this guy is smart. He has figured out how to steal millions from the victims we have already identified and it looks like he's going to do it again. We aim to find out how he's doing it and then to figure out a way to charge him and make it stick. If we're really lucky, the victims will get restitution."

"I hope you're right," said Rogers. "What do you want us to do?"

Tomlinson went on to explain exactly what he and Jenkins would be doing. He asked the other detectives to stay clear of Chamberlin's residence and business. He didn't want to tip Chamberlin off. He concluded if all went well, they should know in a few days how Chamberlin was committing these crimes.

CC had done his homework on Frank Rosen. Mr. Rosen had been a successful businessman in the area having founded a chain of convenience stores mostly in the western end of Cape Cod. An article in the Times said the chain Mr.

Rosen had founded had grown to eighteen stores and it employed over one hundred people. Mr. Rosen was a resident of Arlington, Virginia and Dennis, Massachusetts. Both very expensive areas to live. Mr. Rosen had grown up on Cape Cod and he had lived there most of his life only recently taking up a residence in Virginia. The article suggested Mr. Rosen bought a place in Virginia because he had political ambitions in representing the region as a Congressman if he could get elected. CC thought, "Why not?" Sure, he had plenty of money already, but in one or two days, he could have a lot more. He would see what he could get from this guy's widow. He had a routine down. He made plans to go to the Funeral Home that night. But this would be the last. Then he would take a life long vacation.

At seven that night, CC arrived at the Doane Beal & Ames Funeral Home. Wearing his typical wake attire, business casual, Carl Pruit saw him. Carl went into his office and called the Dennis Police Department. He asked for Detective Tomlinson.

"This is Detective Tomlinson, how can I help you?"

"Detective, this is Carl Pruit at Doane Beal & Ames Funeral Home."

"Hello Mr. Pruit, Detective Jenkins and I are just getting ready to come over to your place. We think Mr. Chamberlin might be targeting Frank Rosen's widow. You're holding his wake there tonight, right?

"We are and he's already here."

"Who?"

"Chamberlin. I just saw him come in."

"Well, don't scare him away. We're on our way. We should be there in a few minutes."

"I'll try to keep an eye on him."

Detective Tomlinson hung up and hollered down the hall "Lets go Jenkins. Chamberlin is already at the wake."

Riding over, they agreed they would just act as mourners, nothing out of the ordinary. Frank was just a guy who owned stores that the officers came to depend on late at night for a cup of joe. They respected hard work, and would show respect.

During the next ten minutes, Carl Pruit kept sticking his head into the room where the wake was being held. He saw Charles standing in the back of the room and when Charles looked at him, he ducked back out into the hall. After doing this same thing a few times over the next few minutes, CC got nervous. He hadn't talked to anyone there yet and decided to leave. As he was leaving, Pruit tried to engage him in a conversation. Pruit kept looking out the door as if he were waiting for someone to arrive and CC finally said he had to go. Maybe he had gotten greedy. Maybe he didn't really need one more target.

Pulling out of the parking lot, CC passed an unmarked police car. He stepped on the gas, cutting a car off, but got away. Pruit came running out of the building when he saw the detectives. "He just left. You must have passed him on the way in."

"What was he driving?"

"I didn't pay attention to his car. I thought you would get here before he left. I kept looking into the wake to make sure he was still there."

"I'll bet you did, and scared him away you dweeb" Tomlinson thought to himself. "Well, thanks for calling Mr. Pruit. We'll take it from here."

The two returned to the Dennis Police Station. When they got back, Tomlinson told Jenkins to call the other detectives and leave a message for them to meet at eleven o'clock tomorrow at the Dennis Police Station. Jenkins called each one and left the message.

CC went home and got all of his things together. He had to get out and now. He got on to his computer and brought up the Orbitz website again. He was looking for a flight to Florida for first thing in the morning. When he found what he was looking for, he made a reservation. His flight would leave at ten in the morning. He probably wouldn't stay there permanently. He didn't like Florida; too many old ladies. But he could disappear for a little bit, then hop down to South America somewhere, or the Caribbean.

He called Rhonda Ronaldi and told her he had to go out of town on business for a few days and he would like to stop by and see her for a little while. She asked him where he was going and he said he was going to Washington, D.C. She asked if he wanted company and he said he would be tied up in meetings and there wouldn't be any time for them to be together. He said he would make it up to her when he got back. "Ok. When should I expect you?"

"I'll be there within a half hour."

"See you soon."

When she hung up the phone, Rhonda called the Dennis Police Department as she was instructed to do. She asked for Detective Jenkins.

"Detective Jenkins, how can I help you?"

"Detective, this is Rhonda Ronaldi. You had told me to call you when I next spoke with Mr. Chamberlin."

"Thank you for calling Mrs. Ronaldi. What did he say?"

"He's taking a business trip tomorrow for a day or two to Washington, D.C. He told me he expected to be back in town in a few days and we would get together when he gets back."

"Did he say who he was meeting with in Washington?"

"Something about meeting with investors in a convenience store chain."

"Thank you for calling Mrs. Ronaldi."

"You're welcome." She didn't mention anything about Charles coming over to her house in thirty minutes.

Jenkins thought Charles was going to Washington to meet with Frank Rosen's representatives. That might be how he'll get access to the widow's weath. He thanked Rhonda for calling and went to see Detective Tomlinson.

"Are you sure he's going to Washington?" asked Tomlinson.

"That's what Mrs. Ronaldi said."

"Well, that would mean he's pursuing another victim, and Mrs. Rosen will be going back to Virginia after the funeral tomorrow. Washington is right next door."

"That's what it looks like to me, too" said Jenkins.

"Get what info you can from the e-mails first thing tomorrow and bring it to the meeting at eleven. We're getting very close with this guy."

"Ok. I'm on it."

CC got into his car and went to Rhonda's place. As he was getting out of his car in front of her house, he noticed the neighbor across the street looking out her window from a break in the drapes. He followed her line of site and looked in that direction. Just around the corner, he could make out a police car parked on the side street, and someone was sitting in the car. CC got back into his car and executed a quick U-turn without turning on his lights and without having to step on the brakes. He hoped whomever was sitting in the police car didn't notice him. As he rode away, he kept looking in his rear view mirror. The police car didn't follow.

Chapter 45

When CC got back to his house, he went through everything he had there and selected those things he wanted to keep. He took two suitcases out of the hall closet and packed those things. After packing clothing and personal belongings, he went to his home desk. He selected the things he wanted and put those in his briefcase. When done, he straightened up the house and made sure everything was in order. He put the suitcases and briefcase next to the front door.

CC got on to his computer. Response time was slow. He pressed control, alt and delete and noticed that PCTrackR was running. He shut it down. Then he went to the Orbitz website. There, he selected the Flights tab, then entered RSW as the destination. His reservation popped up, and he clicked on the 'Print Boarding Pass' link. Once printed, he shut his printer off.

When done, he looked around his place to make sure he hadn't forgotten anything. Then he set the alarm for five a.m. and went to bed.

While sleeping, PCTrackR sent another e-mail to Detective Jenkins e-mail inbox. The attached file was once again full of valuable information about CC.

At five in the morning, the alarm went off, and CC popped right up, showered, shaved, brushed his teeth and got dressed. When traveling he liked to be comfortable, so he wore Levi's jeans, and a cotton tee shirt from a Key West bar.

He put a button down over the tee shirt for now, but would probably take it off as it warmed up. His deck shoes were by the door, and he added his toiletries bag to the pile. CC looked around the place for one last time, then slipped on his shoes, picked up his briefcase, suitcases and left.

When CC was loading his car, Mrs. Osborne was walking her little dog and said good morning to Charles.

"You're going out pretty early Mr. Chamberlin."

"Yes, I have a business meeting and I have to get to the airport for a nine o'clock flight."

"Well have a good trip. When do you expect to return? Can I collect your mail and papers for you?"

"I should be back in three or four days if all goes well. I've stopped the mail and papers so I'm all set."

"I'll keep an eye on things while you're gone in case anyone comes snooping around again."

"Thank you Mr. Osborne. I know I can count on you."

"Good bye and safe trip Mr. Chamberlin."

CC started up his car and drove off. He drove the hour to Logan Airport arriving there just before seven. He used the Kiosk to check in and then showed the attendant his driver's license to check his bags. The attendant printed out two checked baggage tags and put them on the bags. Then the bags were put on the conveyor belt and sent off to be loaded on the plane.

CC picked up his briefcase and went to the security checkpoint. There, he presented his license again and his boarding pass. It took about twenty minutes for him to get through the security checkpoint. Then he went to the gate to await boarding. For the hec of it he checked to see if any first class seats were open. Sometimes the airline would upgrade you if you asked. The gate agent took CC's ticket and keyed in information on her terminal. No, she was sorry, but no first class seats were open for him. At around eight thirty, the gate agent called for passengers in group A to begin boarding. CC had group B on his ticket so he had to wait a little longer. While waiting to board, two policemen came up to the agent at the gate and said something to her. The agent pointed in CC's direction and the two officers walked in his direction. As they approached, CC started to sweat but he remained seated in the waiting area. The officers walked right up to where he was seated, "Sir, you'll have to come with us."

CC was about to get up when the person next to him stood and went with the officers. CC overheard the man saying to the officers as they were walking away, "I must have left it at the checkpoint. Thank you for finding me."

A few minutes later, the man came back to the boarding area with a paper bag that looked like it had shopping items in it. The man sat back down next to CC, "I almost forgot the souvenirs I got for my kids. I must have left it at the security checkpoint. Thankfully my credit card receipt was in the bag with my name on it. It's a good thing these guys are on the job."

CC felt a sigh of relief. He thought the police had caught up with him but they were only helping someone else out. When group B was called to board, CC got in line and boarded the flight. It took about three hours and then the plane landed at Ft. Myers in Florida. CC went to baggage claim and picked up his two suitcases, and then he went to the rental car counter and rented a small compact car. He specified the drop off point for the car as the Atlanta airport. Making small talk with the agent, he said he had a number of business appointments between Ft. Myers and Atlanta and he would drop the car off there when he was done.

CC got the rental car and then drove north on Interstate 75 headed to Atlanta. It took him most of the day to get there. When he did, he returned the rental car and went to the departure terminal to get another flight. He booked a flight for the first thing the next day to Grand Cayman. Then he called LaQuinta Hotel on the airport property to see if they had a room for the night. They did so he went and stayed there. He paid cash for the room. The next morning, he would be taking the flight to Grand Cayman.

Detective Jenkins began his official duties of the day by opening his e-mail and going through the messages. Jenkins saw where CC had gone to the Orbitz website again.

CC had entered RSW. There were a few more characters in the data stream and it looked to Jenkins that CC had purchased an airline ticket.

After finishing with the information, Jenkins went to Tomlinson, "It looks like Mr. Chamberlin is taking a trip. The information indicates Mr. Chamberlin purchased a ticket for a flight."

"Did you get the flight destination, date and departure time?"

"No, the program only captures what the person at the keyboard enters. There were a few keystrokes that followed when he went to the site but I don't know what they were represented."

"Is there any way of finding out?"

"I could try to duplicate what he was doing. But the easiest way would be for us to get on his computer and see what it shows."

"Ok, you go over to his house and see if you can find out where he's going from his computer."

"I should be back in an hour or so."

"Good. We have a meeting with the other detectives at eleven. I'd like to have that information when we meet."

Detective Jenkins went to CC's residence. He jimmied the door again and went to CC's computer. He got on it and then looked at the trail of activity that had most recently occurred. He went to the Orbitz website to see what he might find out there. When he saw the login section on the screen he tried a few things as ID and password but they didn't work. He looked around the computer and discovered a pad of paper with notes: cconnors and CC4ME. It was worth a shot, so Jenkins entered those as the ID and password. It worked. The computer returned with the accountholder information. Jenkins looked at it and could see the personal information that would be used to make travel arrangements under the profile. He then looked at the tab for Recent Travel and discovered that CC had made travel plans to go to Fort Myers, Florida that morning and to return in three days. He wrote down the flight information and left the house.

Returning to the station, Jenkins told Tomlinson what he had found out. It was already ten in the morning. Mr. Chamberlin's flight was already in the air. Tomlinson said, "Contact the Fort Myers Police Department and see if they can get someone over to the airport to confirm Mr. Chamberlin's arrival."

"Why not just call the airline?"

"Because our Mr. Chamberlin may be on the run. And if he isn't and he sees someone looking for him he might try to run. And if he does, I want him arrested. And that would have to be done by the police."

Detective Jenkins got on the phone and called Fort Myers. It took some time to explain what the situation was all about and for the Fort Myers police to agree to help out. The Captain on duty radioed to a unit who was on duty at the airport and asked them to go to the Southwest Airlines counter and see if they could find Mr. Chamberlin. When the officer went to the airline counter, he was told the flight had already landed and the passengers already left the plane. When the officer asked for the agent to confirm Mr. Chamberlin had been a ticketed passenger on the flight, the agent looked up the passenger list and said no one by that name was on the flight. The officer called his Captain back and told him of the situation. The Captain called Detective Jenkins back and told him the same thing.

Detective Jenkins went to Detective Tomlinson and said, "They were too late. Chamberlin's plane already landed and the passengers all got off over an hour ago. Fort Myers PD said no one by the name Chamberlin was on the flight."

"Did they try to get him at baggage claim?"

"The Captain I talked to said there was no way they were going to catch up to him without a photo or some way of identifying Chamberlin. They didn't have enough time to be ready. An hour is plenty of time to get your bags and be long gone."

"Ok. When's he supposed to be coming back?"

"From what I could see on his computer, he is scheduled to come back in three days. Plus, while I was at his house, a neighbor, a Mrs. Osborne, asked me what I was doing there. I identified myself as a police officer and she said Mr. Chamberlin had left early that morning on a business trip. She told me he said he was coming back in three or four days."

"Then we're just going to have to wait him out."

At eleven, all of the involved detectives met at the Dennis Police Department. Detective Tomlinson went through what he and Jenkins had uncovered. They indicated they thought Chamberlin was either on a legitimate business trip or he was pursuing another victim. Tomlinson said Chamberlin was due to be back in the area in three days and they would resume the surveillance at that time. Although it was curious why Chamberlin was going to Florida, but told Rhonda he was going to Washington.

Detective Akron said, "While it's been helpful for us to share the information we have gathered about the suspect, my chief wants me to pursue our case against him right away. The victim in my case is out six million dollars and she has ties in the community. We expect to post a warrant for his arrest today. For what we know, I don't think a judge will have any problem issuing it. By the time the case comes to trial, you can have all the loose ends tied up."

Detective Munson said, "I'm getting pressure too. I think each of us need to start to take action."

"I know I'm going to have to do something soon as well. My department thinks I'm spending a lot of time and money on this case and not having much to show for it," said Rogers.

Arnold said, "I'm going to wait a few more days and see what Tomlinson and Jenkins here turn up."

Detective Tomlinson said, "Thanks Will. I know some of you are getting pressured for action. We are also. But I don't think we have enough evidence yet that will stick."

Detective Munson said, "and Ken, you still haven't told us how any of us are going to get around how you've been getting the information."

"I'm working on that. We hope Chamberlin will slip up on this next victim and we'll catch him in the act. Then I don't think we need to even mention how we went into his home and put that computer program on his computer."

"I hope you're right," said Munson.

"Look, Chamberlin is out of town for a few days. Lets all continue to work our cases and make sure we have our facts right. Try to hold off for a few more days if you can."

"I can't," said Akron. "My Captain wants something done and today."

"Ok. You have to do what you have to do. Keep us informed if you would," said Tomlinson.

"I will."

The meeting broke up. Tomlinson hoped he and Jenkins would be able to solidify their case over the next few days so they would be able to nail Chamberlin when he got back. If he gets back.

Chapter 46

The detectives involved in the cases got back together the day after Charles Chamberlin disappeared. Detective Tomlinson started the meeting off by recapping what the Dennis PD had tried to do to catch Chamberlin in the act of another crime. He described how they had installed PCTrackR on Chamberlin's computer just as Chamberlin had done to the victims. Then he told about getting the incoming e-mail identifying Chamberlin's next potential victim. Next, Jenkins told about trying to track Chamberlin during his travels and Chamberlin had somehow eluded the police. After an hour of describing the facts that had been assembled, the detective group felt they had a pretty good handle on just how Chamberlin went about the crimes.

Detective Tomlinson stood at the front of the room. He walked to the easel and wrote out all the victims and the amounts each victim had taken from them.

Sharon Kelly	$1,500,000
Carol Tindle	$2,000,000
Katherine Sterns	$2,000,000
Theresa Lee	$6,000,000
Ann Pierce	$2,500,000
Sarah Jacobs	$245,000
Total	$14,245,000

"Nice haul for a pretty simple crime," Rogers observed.

Will Arnold, late in the loop, but sharp, said, "What happened to that other widow we had talked about? What was her name? Ridondo or Ronaldo or something like that?"

"Ronaldi. Rhonda Ronaldi" Tomlinson sighed. "It doesn't look like Chamberlin stole anything from her. She said he represented her in a financial transaction and had earned a nice commission for his work. Maybe he plans on coming back and taking more from her sometime down the road."

"And as of right now," Rogers said, "this is all we have on our list of victims. There might be more."

Tomlinson said, "Well, if any of you hear of anyone else, please give me or Jenkins a call. We intend to keep working on this case until something breaks."

"I'm sure my department will want to know anything as well. The victim from my jurisdiction lost a bundle." Akron was a little frustrated because this investigation had not panned out as he expected and Tomlinson was a bit unconventional as far as Akron was concerned.

"The FBI is involved and it will be up to them to apprehend Chamberlin if and when he re-surfaces. I think it's time each of us go back to the victims in our jurisdiction and tell them what we know."

"Do the Feds think they have a chance of catching this guy before he blows the loot?"

"They're being tight lipped right now but I think they have some ideas," but Tomlinson wasn't convincing anyone with his answers. They thought he had already tainted their cases by breaking into Chamberlin's house.

Akron said, "I wonder why the guy didn't take all of the money he could've from the widows?"

Jenkins responded, "It looks like Chamberlin wanted to make it look like the transactions were intentional. By not taking all of the funds, the transactions looked legitimate. By doing it the way he did, the institutions involved didn't have any real reason to question the movement of the funds."

"Real slick," said Munson. But why didn't he take anything from Ronaldi. I understand he made a nice commission and that widow has a bundle."

"Like Jenkins said, maybe he isn't done just yet" Tomlinson was hopeful.

Arnold asked, "Looking at what we have, I'd say this Chamberlin fellow is pretty much set for the rest of his life. Anyone disagree?"

Jenkins wasn't happy but said, "We know he's still considering a crime against Mrs. Rosen. We intend to watch very carefully and see if he shows up in Virginia or if he tries to contact her, we'll be ready."

"Sounds like a lot of ifs. What if this guy was just baiting us to buy himself time to disappear?"

Tomlinson said, "If he did that, he's craftier than we've given him credit."

Arnold added, "And he's given himself a significant jump on getting away."

"Maybe so. Each of you needs to go back to the victims and the institutions involved in the crimes and let them know where things stand. There's going to be a number of unhappy parties in all of this and it's time we brought them all up to date."

With that, the meeting broke up and the detectives went back to their offices.

Jenkins called Mrs. Sterns on her cell phone. She was at Sundancers in West Dennis.

"Mrs. Sterns. This is Detective Jenkins."

"Detective, what can I do for you?"

Jenkins could hear loud music in the background.

"Mrs. Sterns. I'd like to meet with you to discuss the case."

"Detective, why don't you come down to Sundancers? They have a band here today and it's such a nice day. We could mix business with pleasure."

"I don't think that would be the right place for us to meet. Can I call on you tomorrow?"

"Sure. What time did you have in mind?"

"I'm free in the morning. Are you available then?"

"I'm home all morning. Come by anytime and we can talk."

Jenkins could hear a guy in the background, "Kat, let's go."

"I'll come by in the morning."

"See you then."

Katherine had been at Sundancers for a few hours. She had come into the bar and took up a seat on the window side so as to have a good view of the band and overall bar. After having a few martinis, they made great pomegranate pink lemonade martinis, she struck up a conversation with one of the younger patrons. He looked to be in his late twenties. When the two got up to leave the bar, one of the bartenders was overheard saying, "Another cougar."

Arriving in Grand Cayman, CC picked up his bags at baggage claim and then left the airport. As he left the airport, the heat hit him like a furnace. He needed to change into more appropriate clothes, but he had business to take care of first. He headed over to the Grand Cayman Bank and closed his account, taking some in cash, and the rest in a cashier's check. Returning to the airport, he went to ticketing and purchased a ticket to Rio in South America. He waited a few hours at the airport for the flight departure time. An hour before the flight was to depart, he went through security again. He presented his passport and boarding pass to the security agent and proceeded through the checkpoint. As he was picking up his briefcase on the conveyor belt at the security checkpoint, the security agent handed him back his passport and boarding pass, "Have a nice trip, Mr. St. Lawrence."

"Thank you, I will," responded Roger St. Lawrence.

The next morning, at nine, the doorbell rang at the Sterns residence. Katherine answered the door in a bathrobe, barely. "Detective Jenkins, I didn't expect you so early."

"I was anxious to get to talk to you. Can I come in?"

"Sure. I'm just putting on coffee. Join me?"

"Sure. I can always use another cup."

400

Just then, a young man came down the stairs putting on his shirt over a pair of jeans. "Donnie, this is Detective Jenkins."

Donnie just headed to the door and said he had to get to work.

"Didn't seem like he wanted to meet me," said Jenkins.

"I guess not. Maybe he's had some run-in's with the law."

"I'm not here to talk with him."

"And he got what he wanted and now he's on his way."

"You do this often?"

"I asked you to come over when we talked yesterday. That could've been you coming down those stairs today."

"I'll keep that in mind for future reference."

Katherine poured two cups of coffee and said, "How do you take it?"

"Cream, no sugar."

"That's the way I like it, too"

She handed him a cup and the two went to the living room to talk.

"After having a conversation with the other detectives at the station, we think there might have been more to your husband's death than what was in the report. But, the fact the possible crime scene doesn't exist anymore and the coroner couldn't be any more conclusive than what was reported has left us with nowhere to go."

"Can't you question Tom Bowman?"

"We could. But I'm not sure where that would get us."

"What do you mean?"

"Since you've cut off your relationship with him and he has returned to Virginia, we don't think he would be cooperative."

"So he might have murdered Sam and gotten away with it?"

"That's what it looks like."

"Maybe I could get involved with him again and get him to tell me all about it."

"I'm not sure that's such a good idea."

"Why not?"

"Well, let's just say he did it. You subsequently spurn his attempts to get close to you and in fact told him it was all over. You didn't leave him with anywhere to go. Our experience has told us people boxed into a corner can be very unpredictable. You might even be jeopardizing your own safety."

"So what do you think I should do?"

"Nothing. Leave it to us for now. The investigation is still open and if we think there is a way to pursue it further, we'll initiate action and you'll be notified."

"Ok. Was there anything else you wanted to speak to me about?"

"Yes. It looks like your Mr. Chamberlin has skipped the country."

"Skipped the country? Like he ran away?"

"We tracked him to Florida and then he rented a car. From there we lost the trail. An all points bulletin has been put out on him but nothing has surfaced. Since he's gone interstate, the FBI is now involved."

"The FBI?"

"Yes, as it turns out, you're not the only person he stole money from."

"There were others? And I thought I was special."

"Yes. Mr. Chamberlin took funds from as many as five other widows and there may be more."

"You know I saw him with other woman from time to time and he told me they were all clients of his."

"It looks to us he did do legitimate work for a number of people, some of whom he also robbed."

"Let me think. I know I saw him with Rhonda Ronaldi and I saw him another time with someone else at Alberto's."

"That's good information. I have the names of the other victims we know about and I'll bring them with me the next time we get together."

"Oh, so there will be a next time?"

"If you like."

"Why don't you come over tomorrow for dinner and you can bring your information with you."

"I think I can work that into my schedule."

"Great. Plan on spending the night."

On the flight to Rio, CC thought about what had happened over the past few months. He recalled the accident and the lawsuit; the women he had met. He smiled thinking about Katherine, Carol and Rhonda. Rhonda kept coming back to his thoughts. He went through his targets one by one and with each one he smiled. His plan had succeeded. He had taken one and a half million from Sharon Kelly, two million from Carol Tindle, two million from Katherine Sterns, six million from Theresa Lee, two million five hundred thousand from Ann Pierce and two hundred forty-five thousand from Sarah Jacobs. And on top of all of this, representing Rhonda Ronaldi. What a run.

Arriving in Rio, CC or rather Roger St. Lawrence picked up his luggage at baggage claim and got in the first available cab outside the terminal. "Take me to the best hotel in town." As the cab pulled up to the Registration entrance of the sprawling facility, CC peered overhead at the marquis. He was staying at St. Katherine's Resort. "Karma. I hope it's a good thing." Charles walked to the desk confidently, "Reservation for Donleavy."

Coming Attractions:

Look for the next book in the series of Cape Cod Mystery/Thrillers by F. Edward Jersey, *"Cougar Attack."*

Made in the USA